INTERNATIONAL ACCLAIM FOR

Such a Long Journey

"Mistry is a writer of considerable achievement.... Patiently and with loving humour, [he] develops a portrait and draws his people with such care and understanding that their trials become our tragedies."

— *Time*

"A seamless, gracefully written trek through a rocky period in one man's life.... A rewarding literary excursion." — *Maclean's*

"This fine first novel demonstrates the bright-hard reality of India's middle class.... Mistry is a singular pleasure to read, and his description of India is a lucid, living account."

— *San Francisco Chronicle*

"A passionate embracing of life in all its manifestations."

— *Books in Canada*

"A rich, humane work, undoubtedly one of the best novels about India in recent years." — *The Spectator* (U.K.)

"The world of *Such a Long Journey* is vivid, lively, and comic – a rich and richly recreated setting." — *Winnipeg Free Press*

"Fascinating . . . Mistry manages to convey a vivid picture of India through sharp affectionate sketches of Indian family life and a gift for erotic satire." — *New York Times Book Review*

"A highly poised and accomplished work."

— *The Observer* (U.K.)

BOOKS BY ROHINTON MISTRY

ROHINTON MISTRY

SUCH

A

LONG

JOURNEY

EMBLEM EDITIONS
Published by McClelland & Stewart Ltd.

Published in trade paperback with flaps by McClelland & Stewart 1991
Trade paperback edition first published 1997

National Library of Canada Cataloguing in Publication Data

Mistry, Rohinton, 1952–
Such a long journey

ISBN 0-7710-6057-2

I. Title.

PS8576.I853S79 2001   C813'.54   C2001-901849-5
PR9199.3.M48S79 2001

We acknowledge the financial support of the Government of Canada through the Book Publishing Industry Development Program for our publishing activities. We further acknowledge the support of the Canada Council for the Arts and the Ontario Arts Council for our publishing program.

SERIES EDITOR: ELLEN SELIGMAN

Cover design: Sari Ginsberg
Cover photograph: Geuorgui Pinkhassov/Magnum Photos, Inc.
Series logo design: Brian Bean

Printed and bound in Canada

EMBLEM EDITIONS
McClelland & Stewart Ltd.
The Canadian Publishers
481 University Avenue
Toronto, Ontario
M5G 2E9
www.mcclelland.com/emblem

7 8 9 10 11   06 05 04 03 02

For Freny

He assembled the aged priests and put questions to them concerning the kings who had once possessed the world. 'How did they,' he inquired, 'hold the world in the beginning, and why is it that it has been left to us in such a sorry state? And how was it that they were able to live free of care during the days of their heroic labours?'

Firdausi, *Shah-Nama*

A cold coming we had of it,
Just the worst time of the year
For a journey, and such a long journey . . .

T. S. Eliot, 'Journey of the Magi'

And when old words die out on the tongue, new melodies break forth from the heart; and where the old tracks are lost, new country is revealed with its wonders.

Rabindranath Tagore, *Gitanjali*

SUCH

A

LONG

JOURNEY

ONE

i

The first light of morning barely illumined the sky as Gustad Noble faced eastward to offer his orisons to Ahura Mazda. The hour was approaching six, and up in the compound's solitary tree the sparrows began to call. Gustad listened to their chirping every morning while reciting his *kusti* prayers. There was something reassuring about it. Always, the sparrows were first; the cawing of crows came later.

From a few flats away, the metallic clatter of pots and pans began nibbling at the edges of stillness. The *bhaiya* sat on his haunches beside the tall aluminium can and dispensed milk into the vessels of housewives. His little measure with its long, hooked handle dipped into the container and emerged, dipped and emerged, rapidly, with scarcely a drip. After each customer was served, he let the dipper hang in the milk can, adjusted his dhoti, and rubbed his bare knees while waiting to be paid. Flakes of dry dead skin fell from his fingers. The women blenched with disgust, but the tranquil hour and early light preserved the peace.

Gustad Noble eased his prayer cap slightly, away from the wide forehead with its numerous lines, until it settled comfortably on his grey-white hair. The black velvet of the cap contrasted starkly with his cinereous sideburns, but his thick, groomed moustache was just as black and velvety. Tall and broad-shouldered, Gustad was the envy and admiration of friends and relatives whenever health or sickness was being discussed. For a man swimming the tidewater of his fifth decade of life, they said, he looked so solid. Especially for one who had suffered a serious accident just a few years ago; and even that left him with nothing graver than a slight limp. His wife hated this kind of talk. Touch wood, Dilnavaz would say to herself, and look around for a suitable table or chair to make

1

surreptitious contact with her fingers. But Gustad did not mind telling about his accident, about the day he had risked his own life to save his eldest.

Over the busy clatter of the milk container, he heard a screech: '*Muà* thief! In the hands of the police only we should put you! When they break your arms we will see how you add water!' The voice was Miss Kutpitia's, and the peace of dawn reluctantly made way for a frenetic new day.

Miss Kutpitia's threats lacked any real conviction. She never bought the *bhaiya*'s milk herself but firmly believed that periodic berating kept him in line, and was in the interest of the others. Somebody had to let these crooks know that there were no fools living here, in Khodadad Building. She was a wizened woman of seventy, and seldom went out these days, she said, since her bones got stiffer day by day.

But there were not many in the building she could talk to about her bones, or anything else, for that matter, because of the reputation she had acquired over the years, of being mean and cranky and abusive. To children, Miss Kutpitia was the ubiquitous witch of their fairy stories come to life. They would flee past her door, screaming, 'Run from the *daaken*! Run from the *daaken*!' as much from fear as to provoke her to mutter and curse, and shake her fist. Stiff bones or not, she could be seen moving with astonishing alacrity when she wanted to, darting from window to balcony to stairs if there were events taking place in the outside world that she wished to observe.

The *bhaiya* was accustomed to hearing that faceless voice. He mumbled for the benefit of his customers: 'As if I make the milk. Cow does that. The *malik* says go, sell the milk, and that is all I do. What good comes from harassing a poor man like me?'

The women's resigned and weary faces, in the undecided early light, were transformed fleetingly into visages of gentle dignity. They were anxious to purchase the sickly, watered-down white fluid and return to their chores. Dilnavaz also waited, aluminium pan in one hand and money in the other. A slight woman, she had had her dark brown hair bobbed for their daughter Roshan's first birthday party, eight years ago, and still wore it that way. She was not sure if it suited her now, although Gustad said it certainly did. She never could trust his taste. When mini-skirts came into fashion,

2

just for a joke she had hiked up her dress and sashayed across the room, making little Roshan burst into laughter. But he thought she should seriously consider it – imagine, a woman of forty-four, mini-skirted. 'Fashions are for the young,' she had said, a little flustered. Then he began singing that Nat King Cole song, in his deep voice:

> You will never grow old,
> While there's love in your heart,
> Time may silver your dark brown hair,
> As you dream in an old rocking chair . . .

She loved it when Gustad changed the song's words from 'golden hair', always breaking into a big smile at the third line.

Traces of yesterday's milk lingered in the pan she was holding. The last drops had just been used by Gustad and herself in their tea, and she had not had time to wash it out. There would have been time enough, she felt, if she hadn't sat for so long, listening to Gustad read to her from the newspaper. And before that, talking about their eldest, and how he would soon be studying at the Indian Institute of Technology. 'Sohrab will make a name for himself, you see if he doesn't,' Gustad had said with a father's just pride. 'At last our sacrifices will prove worthwhile.' What had come over her this morning, she could not say, sitting and chatting away, wasting time like that. But then, it wasn't every day such good news arrived for their son.

Dilnavaz edged forward as some women left, her turn was approaching. Like the others, the Nobles were endlessly awaiting a milk ration card from the government office. In the meantime she had to patronize the *bhaiya*, whose thin, short tail of hair growing from the centre of his otherwise perfectly shaven head never ceased to amuse her. She knew it was a Hindu custom in some particular caste, she was not exactly sure, but couldn't help thinking that it resembled a grey rat's tail. On mornings when he oiled his scalp, the tail glistened.

She purchased his milk and remembered the days when ration cards were only for the poor or the servants, the days when she and Gustad could afford to buy the fine creamy product of Parsi Dairy Farm (for Miss Kutpitia it was still affordable), before the prices started to go up, up, up, and never came down. She wished Miss

3

Kutpitia would stop screaming at the *bhaiya*. It did no good, only made him resent them more. God knows what he might do to the milk – as it was, these poor people in slum shacks and *jhopadpattis* in and around Bombay looked at you sometimes as if they wanted to throw you out of your home and move in with their own families.

She knew Miss Kutpitia's intentions were good, despite the bizarre stories about the old woman that had circulated for years in the building. Gustad wanted to have as little as possible to do with Miss Kutpitia. He said her crazy rubbish could make even a sane brain somersault permanently. Dilnavaz was perhaps the only friend Miss Kutpitia had. Her childhood training to show unconditional respect for elders made it easy for her to accept Miss Kutpitia's idiosyncrasies. She found nothing repugnant or irritating about them – sometimes amusing, sometimes tiresome, yes. But never offensive. After all, for the most part Miss Kutpitia only wanted to offer help and advice on matters unexplainable by the laws of nature. She claimed to know about curses and spells: both to cast and remove; about magic: black and white; about omens and auguries; about dreams and their interpretation. Most important of all, according to Miss Kutpitia, was the ability to understand the hidden meaning of mundane events and chance occurrences; and her fanciful, fantastical imagination could be entertaining at times.

Dilnavaz made sure never to unduly encourage her. But she realized that at Miss Kutpitia's age, a patient ear was more important than anything else. Besides, was there a person anywhere who, at one time or another, had not found it difficult to disbelieve completely in things supernatural?

The clatter and chatter around the milkman seemed remote to Gustad Noble while he softly murmured his prayers under the neem tree, his handsome white-clad figure favoured by the morning light. He recited the appropriate sections and unknotted the *kusti* from around his waist. When he had unwound all nine feet of its slim, sacred, hand-woven length, he cracked it, whip-like: once, twice, thrice. And thus was Ahriman, the evil one, driven away – with that expert flip of the wrist, possessed only by those who performed their *kusti* regularly.

This part of the prayers Gustad enjoyed most, even as a child, when he used to imagine himself a mighty hunter plunging fearlessly into unexplored jungles, deep in uncharted lands, armed

4

with nothing except his powerfully holy *kusti*. Lashing that sacred cord through the air, he would slice off the heads of behemoths, disembowel sabre-toothed tigers, lay waste to savage cannibal armies. One day, while exploring the shelves in his father's bookstore, he found the story of England's beloved dragon-slayer. From then on, whenever he said his prayers, Gustad was a Parsi Saint George, cleaving dragons with his trusty *kusti* wherever he found them: under the dining-table, in the cupboard, below his bed, even hiding behind the clothes-horse. From everywhere there tumbled the gory, dissevered heads of fire-breathing monsters.

Doors opened and slammed shut, money jingled, a voice called out with special instructions for the *bhaiya*'s next delivery. Someone joked with the man: '*Arré bhaiya*, why not sell the milk and water separately? Better for the customer, easier for you also – no mixing to do.' This was followed by the *bhaiya*'s usual impassioned denial.

The early morning news on government-controlled All-India Radio emerged softly, cautiously, from an open window. The clear mellifluence of its Hindi vocables tested the morning air, and presently offered a confident counterpoint to the BBC World Service that brashly cut in from another flat, bristling with short-wave crackle and hiss.

Gustad's prayers were not disturbed by the banter nor distracted by the radio. Today the news was powerless to tempt him into irreverence, for he had already seen *The Times of India*. Unable to sleep, he had risen earlier than usual. When he turned on the tap to gargle and brush his teeth, the water burst through in a loud wet explosion. It caught him by surprise. He jumped back, snatching away his hand. Air, he told himself, being discharged from the pipes empty since seven a.m. yesterday, when the municipality had ended the daily water quota. He felt foolish. Scared by a noisy tap. He turned off the water, then rotated the handle slowly, just a little. It continued to gurgle threateningly.

For Dilnavaz, that familiar hissing, spitting, blustering was a summons to waken. She sensed the empty bed beside her and smiled to herself, for she had expected Gustad to be up first today. She stared sleepily at the clock till it yielded the time, then turned over on to her stomach and closed her eyes.

Long before the sun had risen that morning, before it was time to pray, Gustad had been waiting anxiously for *The Times of India*. It was pitch dark but he did not switch on the light, for the darkness made everything seem clear and well-ordered. He caressed the arms of the chair he sat in, thinking of the decades since his grandfather had lovingly crafted it in his furniture workshop. And this black desk. Gustad remembered the sign on the store, he could see it even now. Clearly, as though it is a photograph before my eyes: *Noble & Sons, Makers Of Fine Furniture*, and I also remember the first time I saw the sign – too young to read the words, but not to recognize the pictures that danced around the words. A glass-fronted cabinet with gleaming cherry-coloured wood; an enormous four-postered canopy bed; chairs with carved backs and splendidly proportioned cabrioles; a profoundly dignified black desk: all of it like the furniture in my childhood home.

Some of it now here, in my house. Saved from the clutches of bankruptcy – the word cold as a chisel. The sound cruel and sharp and relentless as the metal cleats on the bailiff's shoes. The cleats had sounded their malicious clatter on the stone tiles. Bastard bailiff – seized whatever he could get his filthy hands on. My poor father. Lost everything. Except the few pieces I rescued. With Malcolm's help, in the old van. Bailiff never found out. What a good friend was Malcolm Saldanha. Sad, he and I did not keep in touch. A true friend. Like Major Bilimoria used to be.

The last name made Gustad shake his head. That bloody Bilimoria. After the shameless way he behaved, he had a nerve, writing now to ask for a favour, as though nothing had happened. He could wait till his dying day for a reply. Gustad pushed the Major's audacious letter out of his mind, it threatened to disrupt the well-ordered darkness. Once again, the furniture from his childhood gathered comfortingly about him. The pieces stood like parentheses around his entire life, the sentinels of his sanity.

He heard the metal flap of the mail slot lift and, almost simultaneously, discerned the white outline of the newspaper as it slid into the room. Still he sat, unmoving: let the man pass, no need for him to know I am waiting. Why he did this, he could not say.

When the bicycle pedalled away, all was quiet again. Gustad switched on the light and put on his glasses. He ignored the grim headlines about Pakistan, barely glanced at the half-naked mother weeping with a dead child in her arms. The photo caption, which he did not stop to read because the picture looked the same as the others that had appeared regularly in the past few weeks, was about soldiers using Bengali babies for bayonet practice. He turned to the inside page, the one which listed the Indian Institute of Technology's entrance exam results. He laid the page flat on the dining-table. From the sideboard he fetched the little piece of paper with Sohrab's roll number, checked, and went to wake Dilnavaz.

'Come on, get up! He got admission!' He stroked her shoulder. There was affection and impatience. Also some guilt: that letter. He had hidden Major Bilimoria's letter from her.

Dilnavaz rolled over and smiled. 'I told you he would. Simply at all you kept worrying.' She went to the bathroom and connected the transparent plastic hose to fill the water drums, even though today there was time enough to brush her teeth first, and make tea. It was only five o'clock – two whole hours before the taps went dry. She turned the brass handle, and the head of water surged through the hose. A long tail of air bubbles followed close behind. Like the bubbles that used to gush in her younger son's little fish tank. How fond Darius had been of the tiny colourful creatures with the pretty names he proudly recited when showing them off: guppy, black molly, angelfish, neon tetra, kissing gourami – for a little while they had been the centre of his universe.

But the tank was empty now. And the birdcages. They lay covered in dust and cobwebs on the dark shelf in the *chawl* beside the WC, along with Sohrab's butterfly display case. And that silly book he won long ago on Prize Distribution Day. *Learning About Entomo* . . . something-or-other. There had been such an argument just because she said it was cruel to kill the colourful little things. But Gustad said that Sohrab should be encouraged – if he persevered and took it up in college, doing research and all that, he could make a world-famous name for himself.

The rusted mounting pins still held a few thoraxes in place, but little else. An assortment of wings, like fallen petals of exotic flowers, littered the bottom of the case, mingled with broken antennae and tiny heads which did not resemble heads after they separated from the thoraxes. They had once made Dilnavaz wonder, briefly, how whole black pepper had found its way inside, till she

7

realized with a shudder what the round things were.

The gush of water, the effervescent upstream rush, the quickening of the hose, always engaged her senses. Then the flow became regular, and it might have been an empty piece of tubing but for the slight throb felt in her palm where she held the hose to keep it from slipping out of the drum.

Gustad wanted to wake Sohrab. Dilnavaz stopped him. 'Let him sleep. His admission result is not going to change if he knows it one hour later.'

He agreed readily. All the same, he went to the back room. In the darkness he could see the slatted frame-door he had hinged to the side of the bed fifteen years ago for Sohrab, who had been a turbulent little sleeper, as though his mischievous daytime games were continuing into the night. The nightly barricade they used to form alongside the bed with dining chairs did not work, he always pushed the chairs away. So the slatted door it had to be. Sohrab promptly named it the bed-with-the-door, and found the addition a useful appendage when he constructed a bed-house out of all the bolsters and blankets and pillows he could gather.

The bed-with-the-door now belonged to Roshan. One of her skinny arms, having found its way out between the door slats, hung over the side. It would soon be her ninth birthday. Took after her mother, thought Gustad, gazing upon her fragile figure. He turned his eyes to where Sohrab slept, on the narrow *dholni* which was rolled away under Darius's bed during the day. Gustad had always wanted to get a proper third bed, but there was no place for it in the small room.

Looking upon his son, his eyes filled with joyful pride, and he was reassured: the face of nineteen years was still untroubled, as it used to be during the childhood nights in the bed-with-the-door. He wondered if time would put an end to it. For himself, the day had come, he knew, when his father's bookstore had been treacherously despoiled and ruined. The shock, the shame of it had made his mother ill. How swiftly moved the finger of poverty, soiling and contaminating. Soon afterwards, his mother had died. Sleep was no longer a happy thing for him then, but a time when all anxieties intensified, and anger grew – a strange, unfocused anger – and helplessness; and he would wake up exhausted to curse the day that was dawning.

8

And so, as he watched Sohrab sleep his innocent sleep, with the face that seemed on the verge of a smile; and Darius, at fifteen a younger, shorter reflection of his father's muscular frame; and little Roshan, who filled such a small part of the bed-with-the-door, her two plaits sidelong on the pillow: as Gustad observed them silently, in turn, he wished for all the nights in his sons' and daughter's lives to be filled with peace and tranquillity. Very, very softly, he hummed the wartime song he had adapted to sing them to sleep when they were little:

> Bless them all, bless them all,
> Bless my Sohrab and Darius and all,
> Bless my Sohrab and Darius
> And Roshan and . . .

Sohrab turned in his sleep, and Gustad stopped humming. The room was dark like the others in the flat, with blackout paper taped over the glass panes of the windows and ventilators. Gustad had put it up nine years ago, the year of the war with China. How much happened that year, he thought. Roshan's birth, and then my terrible accident. What luck. In bed for twelve weeks, with the broken hip between Madhiwalla Bonesetter's sandbags. And riots in the city – curfews and lathi charges and burning buses everywhere. What a dreadful year 1962 had been. And such a humiliating defeat, everywhere people talking of nothing but the way the Chinese had advanced, as though the Indian Army consisted of tin soldiers. To think that till the very end both sides had been proclaiming peace and brotherhood. Especially Jawaharlal Nehru, with his favourite slogan, 'Hindi-Chinee *bhai-bhai*', insisting that Chou En-lai was a brother, the two nations were great friends. And refusing to believe any talk of war, even though the Chinese had earlier invaded Tibet, positioning several divisions along the border. 'Hindi-Chinee *bhai-bhai*', all the time, as though repeating it often enough would verily make them brothers.

And when the Chinese came pouring over the mountains, everyone said it confirmed the treacherous nature of the yellow race. Chinese restaurants and Chinese hair salons lost their clientele, and the Chinaman quickly became the number one bogeyman. Dilnavaz used to caution Darius, 'The wicked Chino will carry you off if you don't finish your food.' But Darius would defy her, he

9

was not afraid. He had made his plans after discussions with his first-standard classmates about the yellow fellows who collected children to make a stew, along with rats, cats, and puppy dogs. He said he would get his Diwali cap pistol, put a roll of *toati* in it and bang-bang, kill the Chino if he ever dared come near their flat.

But much to Darius's disappointment, no Chinese soldiers approached Khodadad Building. Instead, teams of fund-raising politicians toured the neighbourhood. Depending on which party they belonged to, they made speeches praising the Congress government's heroic stance or denouncing its incompetency for sending brave Indian Jawans, with outdated weapons and summer clothing, to die in the Himalayas at Chinese hands. Every political party unleashed flag-emblazoned lorries to crisscross the city with banners that were paradigms of ingenuity: weaving together support for the party and support for the soldiers, while the fund-raisers shouted themselves hoarse through megaphones, exhorting people to be as selfless as the Jawans who were reddening the Himalayan snow with their precious blood to defend Bharat Mata.

And the people were moved to staunch the flow of yellow invaders. They threw blankets and sweaters and scarves out of their windows into the open lorries that passed below. In some wealthy localities, the collection drive turned into a competition, with neighbours trying to outdo one another in their attempts to simultaneously seem rich, patriotic and compassionate. Women removed gold bangles and earrings and finger rings from their persons and gave them away. Money – notes and loose change – was wrapped in handkerchiefs and tossed into the fund-raisers' grateful hands. Men tore shirts and jackets off their backs, yanked shoes off their feet, belts off their waists, and flung them into the lorries. What a time it was, and it brought tears of pride and joy into the eyes of everyone to see such solidarity, such generosity. Afterwards, it was said that some of the donated goods had turned up for sale in Chor Bazaar and Nul Bazaar, and in the stalls of roadside hawkers everywhere, though not much attention was paid to that nasty allegation; the glow of national unity was still warm and comforting.

But everyone knew that the war with China froze Jawaharlal Nehru's heart, then broke it. He never recovered from what he perceived to be Chou En-lai's betrayal. The country's beloved

Panditji, everyone's Chacha Nehru, the unflinching humanist, the great visionary, turned bitter and rancorous. From now on, he would brook no criticism, take no advice. With his appetite for philosophy and dreams lost for ever, he resigned himself to political intrigues and internal squabbles, although signs of his tyrannical ill temper and petulance had emerged even before the China war. His feud with his son-in-law, the thorn in his political side, was well known. Nehru never forgave Feroze Gandhi for exposing scandals in the government; he no longer had any use for defenders of the downtrodden and champions of the poor, roles he had himself once played with great gusto and tremendous success. His one overwhelming obsession now was, how to ensure that his darling daughter Indira, the only one, he claimed, who loved him truly, who had even abandoned her worthless husband in order to be with her father – how to ensure that she would become Prime Minister after him. This monomaniacal fixation occupied his days and nights, days and nights which the treachery of Chou En-lai had blighted for ever, darkened permanently, unlike the blacked-out cities, which returned to light after the conflict ended and people uncovered their doors and windows.

Gustad, however, left his blackout paper undisturbed. He said it helped the children to sleep better. Dilnavaz thought the idea was ridiculous, but she did not argue because his father had passed away recently in the nursing home. Perhaps, she thought, he found the darkness soothing after death's recent visitation.

'Remove the black paper whenever you are ready, baba. Far be it from me to force you,' she said, but registered pointed observations at regular intervals: the paper collected dust and was difficult to clean; it gave spiders ideal places to spin their webs; it provided perfect cover for cockroaches to lay their eggs; and it made the whole house dark and depressing.

Weeks went by, then months, with paper restricting the ingress of all forms of light, earthly and celestial. 'In this house, the morning never seems to come,' Dilnavaz continued to complain. By and by, she learned new ways to deal with dust, webs, and household pests. The family grew accustomed to living in less light, as if blackout paper had always covered the windows. Occasionally, though, when Dilnavaz was feeling particularly harassed by quotidian matters, the paper became the target of her frustration: 'Very

11

nice this is. Son collects butterflies and moths, father collects spiders and cockroaches. Soon Khodadad Building will become one big insect museum.'

But three years later, the Pakistanis attacked to try to get a piece of Kashmir as they had done right after Partition, and blackout was declared once again. Then Gustad triumphantly pointed out to her the wisdom of his decision.

iii

He left his sleeping children and returned to read the rest of the paper. It was not yet time for his prayers: light had not yet broken on the horizon. He followed Dilnavaz to the kitchen and read the headline for her benefit: 'Reign of Terror in East Pakistan'.

'Wait, I am filling the *matloo*,' she said, unable to hear over the gush of running water. The water pressure was low today, the drums took longer to fill. She wondered why, washing the square of lawn cloth to strain and store the day's drinking water. She tossed the soggy cloth flat over the open mouth of the earthen pot. It landed with a sharp, wet slap. She bore downwards expertly at its centre, with her fingers, to create a cloth funnel.

'It says that the Republic of Bangladesh has been proclaimed by the Awami League,' Gustad continued when the tap was turned off. 'In the canteen at lunch-time I told all the fellows this is exactly what would happen. They were saying that General Yahya would allow Sheikh Mujibur Rahman to form the government. My right hand I will cut off and give you, I said, if those fanatics and dictators respect the election results.'

'What will happen now?' He ignored her question and read silently, about Bengali refugees streaming over the border with tales of terror and bestiality, of torture and killings and mutilations; of women in ditches with their breasts sliced off, babies impaled on bayonets, charred bodies everywhere, whole villages razed.

The earthen pot was full to the brim. Dilnavaz measured six drops of the dark crimson solution. It never stopped nagging her that they did not boil the water. But Gustad said that straining and adding potassium permanganate was precaution enough. She tried to wring dry a soaked corner of her faded floral nightgown. The veins, prominently blue on her much-too-rapidly ageing

12

hands, swelled with the effort. The lid of the boiling kettle jiggled and rattled.

'I wonder what Major Bilimoria would have thought,' she said, scooping in three spoons of Brooke Bond. The kettle's noisy gurgles became soft murmurs. She hated making tea directly in the kettle, but the dark brown English teapot they had used for more than twenty years had cracked. The frayed tea cozy, spilling mildewy stuffing, also needed to be replaced.

'Major Bilimoria? Thought of what?' He wondered if she suspected anything about the hidden letter, and tried to sound indifferent.

'About this trouble in Pakistan, people saying there will be war. With his army background he would have inside information.'

Major Jimmy Bilimoria had lived in Khodadad Building for almost as long as the Nobles. Gustad always pointed him out to the children as a good example, urging them to walk erect, with chest out and stomach in, like Major Uncle. The retired major loved to regale Sohrab and Darius with tales from his glorious days of army and battle. For his young listeners, the stories quickly acquired the stature of legend, with their Major Uncle the legendary hero, as he told of the cowardly Pakistanis who turned tail and ran in 1948, when confronted by Indian soldiers in Kashmir, or about the fiasco of the dreaded tribesmen from the North-West Frontier, who had been the scourge of the mighty British Army in the days of Empire. To the wild and ferocious tribesmen, said Major Uncle, fighting and killing was no more than a favourite game. Turned loose by the Pakistanis, they got drunk and began to loot the first village they passed through, instead of pushing on to attack the capital. The hours went by as they hacked up their victims and went from house to house in search of money and jewels and women. All their fun and games, said Major Uncle, provided precious time for Indian reinforcements to arrive. Kashmir was safe, the battle was won. Then the children would heave a sigh of relief and applaud. His stories, as he described the various episodes – the crossing of Banihal Pass, the battle for Baramullah, the siege of Srinagar – were so fascinating that Gustad and Dilnavaz too would listen, enthralled.

Last year, Major Bilimoria vanished from Khodadad Building. He left without a word to anyone, and no one could guess as to his whereabouts. Shortly after, a lorry had arrived with a key to his flat and instructions to take away his belongings. Hand-painted on its rear fender was a message in letters heavily ornate with curlicues: *Trust In God – Horn Please To Pass.* When questioned by the neighbours, the driver and his helper would say nothing: *Humko kuch nahin maaloom*, we don't know anything, was all that could be got out of them.

The Major's abrupt departure had wounded Gustad Noble more than he allowed anyone to see. Only Dilnavaz could sense the depth of his pain. 'To leave like this, after being neighbours for so many years, is a shameful way of behaving. Bloody bad manners.' He said no more than that on the subject.

But although Gustad would not admit it, Jimmy Bilimoria had been more than just a neighbour. At the very least, he had been like a loving brother. Almost one of the family, a second father to the children. Gustad had even considered appointing him as their guardian in his will, should something untimely happen to himself and Dilnavaz. A year after the disappearance, he still could not think of Jimmy without the old hurt returning. He wished Dilnavaz had not brought up his name. Receiving that letter had been bad enough. And such a letter – makes my blood boil, every time I think of it.

Trying to maintain his posture of indifference, he overdid the sarcasm: 'How would I know what Jimmy would think about Pakistan? He didn't leave us his new address, did he? Or we could have written and asked for his expert opinion.'

'You are still upset,' said Dilnavaz. 'But I still believe that without a good reason he would not have left like that. One day we will find out why. He was a good man.' She nodded meditatively, stirring the tea in the aluminium kettle. The colour seemed right, and she poured two cups. From the icebox, she fetched the bit of milk left over from yesterday: the *bhaiya* had not yet arrived but this would do for now. Gustad filled his saucer and blew on it. By the time he finished the newspaper, it was almost prayer time, so he fetched his black velvet prayer cap and stepped outside. The sparrows were twittering reassuringly in the solitary tree in the compound.

And when he reached halfway into the *kusti* recitation and the radio started somewhere, first in Hindi, and then mingled with the BBC World Service, he was not distracted because he already knew all the news.

14

The Hindi broadcast ended, and the radio began a series of jingles and ads: Amul Butter ('. . . utterly, butterly delicious . . .'), Hamam Soap, Cherry Blossom Shoe Polish. The other set, tuned to the rasping, crackling BBC, was switched off.

Gustad finished retying the *kusti* round his waist and noted with satisfaction that the two ends, as usual, were of equal length. He raised and lowered his shoulders to let his *sudra* settle comfortably around him. The vest slid from under the *kusti* in response to the movement, providing the slack he liked to feel around his stomach. A draught crept across his lower back. It reminded him of the vertical tear. Most of his *sudras* had rents in them, and Dilnavaz kept fretting that a new batch was needed. Mending was useless – no sooner was one tear sewn up than another appeared because the mulmul itself was worn. He told her not to worry: 'A little air-conditioning does no harm,' laughing away, as usual, the signs of their straitened circumstances.

He turned his face to the sky, eyes closed, and began reciting the Sarosh Baaj, silently, forming the words with his lips, when the domestic sounds of the building were drowned by the roar of a diesel engine. A lorry? The engine idled for a few moments, and he resisted turning around to see. There was nothing he disliked more than to permit a break in his morning prayers. Bad manners, that's what it was. He would not rudely interrupt when talking to another human being, so why do it with Dada Ormuzd? Especially today, when there was so much to be grateful for, with Sohrab's admission to IIT which, with one wonderful, blessed stroke redeemed all his efforts, all the hardships.

The thundering lorry pulled away, leaving a cloud of diesel fumes to linger at the gate. By and by, the morning air carried in the acrid smell. Gustad wrinkled his nostrils and continued with the Sarosh Baaj.

By the time he finished, the lorry was quite forgotten. He went to the two bushes growing in the small patch of dusty earth under his window, opposite the black stone wall, and performed his daily bit of gardening. There were scraps of paper tangled in the leaves. Every morning he tended both bushes, although the vinca was the only one he had planted – the mint had begun to sprout of its own accord one day. Assuming it was a weed, he had almost uprooted it. But Miss Kutpitia, watching from her balcony upstairs, had deftly elucidated the medicinal uses of this particular variety. 'That is a very rare *subjo*, very rare!' she shouted down. 'The fragrance controls high blood-pressure!' And the tiny two-lipped white flowers, growing in spikes, contained seeds which, soaked in water and ingested, cured numerous maladies of the stomach. So Dilnavaz insisted that he let the plant stay, to please the old woman if for nothing else. Word of the newly discovered medicine had spread quickly, however, and people stopped by to ask for its leaves or the magic seeds. The daily demand for *subjo* kept in check its vigorous growth, which threatened to overwhelm the vinca and its five-petalled pink blooms that gave Gustad such joy.

He cleared away the paper scraps, cellophane sweet-wrappers, a Kwality ice-cream stick, and attended next to his rose plant. He had secured its pot by thick picture-hanging wire to a post within the entrance-way, with several complicated loops and knots, so that anyone with mischief in mind would have to spend hours undoing the intricacies. He picked up the petals of a faded rose. Then the smell of diesel fumes came again, and drew him to the gate.

A notice was pasted to the pillar, while a shining black oil puddle marked the spot where the lorry had stopped. The official document from the municipality bulged in places with glue and air bubbles. He did some quick calculations after reading it. The bloody bastards were out of their minds. What was the need to widen the road? He measured the ground with hurried strides. The compound would shrink to less than half its present width, and the black stone wall would loom like a mountain before the ground-floor tenants. More a prison camp than a building, all cooped up like sheep or chickens. With the road noise and nuisance so much closer. The flies, the mosquitoes, the horrible stink, with bloody shameless people pissing, squatting alongside the wall. Late at night it became like a wholesale public latrine.

But it was just a proposal, nothing would come of it. Surely the landlord would not give away half his compound for the 'fair market value' that the municipality offered. It was hard to find anything these days more unfair than the government's fair market value. The landlord would certainly go to court.

The diesel smell persisted, following him through the compound as he returned home. It reminded him of the day of his accident, nine years ago, when such a smell had been present, also strong and undiminishing, while he lay in the road with his shattered hip, in the path of oncoming cars. He wrinkled his nose and wished the wind would change. His hip, the one which made him limp, began to hurt a little as he entered the flat.

i

Dilnavaz decided to be of no help to Gustad, not while he was embarked on his mad and wholly impractical scheme. A live chicken in the house! Whatever next? Never had he meddled like this in her kitchen. It was true he came sometimes and sniffed in her pots or, especially on Sundays, cajoled her to make a *kutchoomber* of onions, coriander and hot green chillies to go with the *dhansak* simmering on the stove. But in twenty-one years this was the first time he was interfering in kitchen-and-cookery in a very fundamental manner, and she was not sure what it meant or where it was leading.

'Where did we get this basket from anyway?' asked Gustad, covering the chicken with the wide wicker basket that had hung for ages on a nail near the kitchen ceiling. He did not really care to know, just wanting words to flow again between them, get rid of the chill she had been exuding since he got back from Crawford Market with the throbbing, unquiet bulge in his shopping bag.

'I don't know where the basket came from.' Curt and frigid was her reply.

He suspected that Miss Kutpitia may have been advising her about omens, but prudence made him return to his peace-making voice. 'At last we have a use for this basket. Good thing we did not throw it away. Where did it come from, I wonder.'

'I told you once, I don't know.'

'Yes, yes, you did, Dilnoo-darling,' he said soothingly. 'Now, for two days it will be a roof over the chicken's head. They relax and sleep quietly, put on more weight, if they are covered with a basket.'

'How would I know? In my family a chicken was always brought home slaughtered.'

'You will taste the difference, trust me, when it is swimming in your brown sauce in two days. With onions and potatoes. Ah ha ha, that brown sauce! So perfect you make it, Dilnoo.' He smacked his lips.

The entire plan had come to Gustad yesterday. He had dreamt of his childhood the previous night, and remembered the dream in detail on waking: it was a day of great gaiety and celebration, of laughter ringing through the house, flowers filling up the rooms – in vases, in strands of *tohrun* over doorways – and music, music all day long: 'Tales From the Vienna Woods', 'Gold and Silver Waltz', 'Skater's Waltz', 'Voices of Spring', the overture to *Die Fledermaus*, and much, much more, playing non-stop on the gramophone, playing in his dream, while his grandmother sent the servants out repeatedly to buy special herbs and *masala* for the feast cooking under her supervision.

There was such excitement and happiness filling his beloved childhood home, the sadness in his heart was acute when he awoke. He could not remember the exact occasion being celebrated in the dream – probably some birthday or anniversary. But live chickens had been brought home from the market by his father, and fattened for two days before the feast. And what a feast it had been.

When Gustad was a little boy, live chickens were standard procedure in his father's house. Grandma would have it no other way. Not for her the scraggy fowl brought home slaughtered and plucked and gutted. Gustad remembered them arriving in a covered basket balanced on the head of the servant who walked behind his father, sometimes two, sometimes four, or eight, depending on how many guests were invited. Grandma would inspect the birds, invariably applauding her son's choice selections as they clucked away, then check off the packets of spices and ingredients against her list.

But spices, ingredients, were only half the secret. 'Chicken if you buy,' she would say when praised for her delicious cooking, 'then you must buy alive and squawking, *jeevti-jaagti*, or don't buy at all. First feed it for two days, less will not do. And always feed best grain, the very best. Always remember: what goes in chicken-stomach, at the end comes back to our stomach. After two days prepare the pot, light the stove, get *masala* ready. Then slaughter, clean, and cook. Quick-quick-quick, no wasting time.' And what a difference that made to the taste of the meat, she would claim, juicy and fresh and sweet, and so much more than the stringy scraps which clad the bones of the scrawny, market-fed birds two days ago.

Gustad's dream about those blissful, long-ago times stayed with him all through the day. For once, he was determined, just once – for one day at least, this humble flat would fill with the happiness and merriment that used to reside in his childhood home. And that day, he decided, would be Saturday. Invite one or two people from the bank for dinner – my old friend Dinshawji for sure – just a small party. With chicken, never mind the extra expense. To celebrate Roshan's birthday and Sohrab's admission to IIT.

As the basket descended over the bird, it peered curiously through the narrow slits in the wickerwork. Safe under the protective dome, it began to cluck intermittently. 'A little rice now,' said Gustad.

'I'm not going to touch the chicken,' snapped Dilnavaz. If he thought she could be tricked into looking after the creature, he was sadly mistaken.

'Boarding and lodging is my department,' he had joked earlier, to win her over. But there was an edge in his voice now. 'Who is asking you to touch? Just put a little rice in a small pan and give me.' His peace-making voice was flagging in its efforts. He had gone straight from work to Crawford Market, and was still in his office clothes: tie, white shirt, white trousers. White except for where the chicken soiled it while he was tying it to the kitchen table-leg with a yard of bristly coir twist. It had been a long day, and he was tired.

Besides, Crawford Market was a place he despised at the best of times. Unlike his father before him, who used to relish the trip and looked on it as a challenge: to venture boldly into the den of scoundrels, as he called it; then to badger and bargain with the shopkeepers, tease and mock them, their produce, their habits, but always preserving the correct tone that trod the narrow line between badinage and belligerence; and finally, to emerge unscathed and triumphant, banner held high, having got the better of the rogues. Unlike his father, who enjoyed this game, Gustad felt intimidated by Crawford Market.

Perhaps it was due to their different circumstances: his father always accompanied by at least one servant, arriving and leaving by taxi; Gustad alone, with his meagre wallet and worn basket lined with newspaper to soak up meat juices that could start dripping in the bus, causing embarrassment or, worse still, angry protests from vegetarian passengers. Throughout the trip he felt anxious and guilty – felt that in his basket was something deadlier than a bomb. For was he not carrying the potential source of Hindu-Muslim riots? Riots which often started due to offences of the flesh, usually of porcine or bovine origins?

For Gustad, Crawford Market held no charms. It was a dirty, smelly, overcrowded place where the floors were slippery with animal ooze and vegetable waste, where the cavernous hall of meat was dark and forbidding, with huge, wicked-looking meat hooks hanging from the ceiling (some empty, some with sides of beef – the empty ones more threatening) and the butchers trying various tacks to snare a customer – now importuning or wheedling, then boasting of the excellence of their meat while issuing dire warnings about the taintedness of their rivals', and always at the top of their voices. In the dim light and smelly air abuzz with bold and bellicose flies, everything acquired a menacing edge: the butchers' voices, hoarse from their incessant bellowings; the runnels of sweat streaming down their faces and bare arms on to their sticky, crimson-stained vests and loongis; the sight and smell of blood (sometimes trickling, sometimes coagulated) and bone (gory, or stripped to whiteness); and the constant, sinister flash of a meat cleaver or butcher's knife which, more often than not, was brandished in the vendor's wild hand as he bargained and gesticulated.

Gustad knew his fear of Crawford Market had its origins in his grandmother's warnings about butchers. 'Never argue with a *goaswalla*,' she would caution. 'If he loses his temper, then bhup! he will stick you with his knife. Won't stop to even think about it.' Then, in milder tones, less terror-striking but more pedagogic, she revealed the underpinnings from whence this wise dictum rose. 'Remember, the *goaswalla*'s whole life, his training, his occupation, is about butchering. Second nature. *Bismillah*, he says, that is all, and the knife descends.'

If she was teased about it, Grandma would staunchly claim to have witnessed a situation where a *goaswalla* had gone bhup! with his knife into flesh of the human sort. Gustad had relished the gruesome tale in those days, and when he began shopping at Crawford Market, he would remember her words with a nervous amusement. He never could feel quite at ease in that place.

He tried to select a chicken for Roshan's birthday. It was hard for him to tell under all those feathers, as the shopkeeper held up bird after bird for inspection. 'Look at this one, *seth*, good one, this. See under wing. Spread it, spread it, does not hurt the *murgi*, not to worry. See, poke here. How thick, how much meat.' He did this with one chicken after another, holding its legs and dangling it upside-down, hefting it to emphasize the weight.

Gustad watched, thoroughly confused, squeezing and prodding to pretend he knew what he was doing. But each chicken was very much like the next. When he finally approved one, it was the vocal protestations of the bird, seemingly louder than the others, that made him decide. He would have been the first to admit his inexperience with poultry. The number of times he had been able to afford chicken for his family in the last twenty years, he could count on the fingertips of one hand without using up the digits. Chicken was definitely not his area of expertise.

But beef was a different matter. Beef was Gustad's speciality. Years ago, his college friend, Malcolm Saldanha, had taught him all about cows and buffaloes. It was around the same time that Malcolm had helped him hide the furniture from the clutches of the vulturous bankruptcy bailiff.

The loss of the bookstore had turned Gustad's father into a broken and dispirited man, no longer interested in those weekly expeditions to Crawford Market. When his beloved books and his business disappeared, his appetite was also misplaced, somewhere in the labyrinth of legal proceedings. Gustad worried deeply as his father visibly shrank. He did the best he could now as breadwinner, with his meagre income from private tuitions to schoolchildren. But under Malcolm's advice and guidance, the rupees were stretched further than he had imagined possible.

Malcolm was tall and exceedingly fair-skinned for a Goan. He was fond of explaining his colour by telling about the blood of Portuguese colonizers that had mingled with the local stuff. He had thick red lips and slick, gleaming black hair, always parted on the left, brushed back. Malcolm's father, whom Malcolm closely resembled in looks and talents, taught piano and violin, and prepared his students for the examinations periodically held in Bombay by the Royal School of Music and Trinity College. Malcolm's mother played first violin with the Bombay Chamber Orchestra, and his elder brother, the oboe. Malcolm played the piano for the college choir's practices and performances. He was going to be a professional musician, he said, but his father insisted on the BA to round out his education.

Gustad admired Malcolm, even slightly envied him, wishing he, too, could play some instrument. For all the music that had filled his home in happier times – his father's huge radiogram in its dark cabinet of polished *seesum*, the records lining row upon row of shelves – there was not a single musical instrument in the house. The closest Gustad came to one was in a photograph of his mother as a child, posing with her mandolin. The photograph intrigued him, and sometimes, her eyes far away, she would describe the mandolin for Gustad, telling him about the songs she used to play, in her gentle, accepting voice which lacked the necessary force to influence things in the Noble household.

Though he was the odd one out, Gustad was always welcomed at Malcolm's home. Sometimes, Mr Saldanha performed a piece for solo violin, or Malcolm accompanied his father, and Gustad forgot his troubles for a while. In those extremely lean days, when every anna, every paisa counted, Malcolm the musician taught him to eat beef and mitigate the strain on his pocket-book. 'Lucky for us,' Malcolm always said, 'that we are minorities in a nation of Hindus. Let them eat pulses and grams and beans, spiced with their stinky asafoetida – what they call *hing*. Let them fart their lives away. The modernized Hindus eat mutton. Or chicken, if they want to be more fashionable. But we will get our protein from their sacred cow.' At other times he would say, mimicking their economics professor, 'Law of supply and demand, always remember. That's the key. Keeps down the price of beef. And it is healthier because it is holier.'

On Sunday mornings, Gustad would set off with Malcolm for Crawford Market, but their first stop was always the church where Malcolm attended Mass. Gustad went in with him, dipping his fingers in the font of holy water and crossing himself, imitating his friend closely, to fit in and not give offence to anyone.

The first time, Gustad was quite intrigued by the church and its rituals, so different from what went on in the fire-temple. But he was on his guard, conditioned as he had been from childhood to resist the call of other faiths. All religions were equal, he was taught; nevertheless, one had to remain true to one's own because religions were not like garment styles that could be changed at whim or to follow fashion. His parents had been painstaking on this point, conversion and apostasy being as rife as it was, and rooted in the very history of the land.

So Gustad quickly decided that while the music was good and the glittering icons and sumptuous vestments were highly impressive, he preferred the sense of peaceful mystery and individual serenity that prevailed in the fire-temple. Sometimes it made him wonder, though, if Malcolm was not making an amateurish, half-hearted attempt at proselytism.

Whatever Malcolm the musician's intentions, over the course of several Sunday mornings he presented a prelude on Catholicism before launching into the theme of beef and variations thereon. Christianity came to India over nineteen hundred years ago, when Apostle Thomas landed on the Malabar coast amongst fishermen, said Malcolm. 'Long before you Parsis came in the seventh century from Persia,' he teased, 'running away from the Muslims.'

'That may be,' rejoined Gustad, 'but our prophet Zarathustra lived more than fifteen hundred years before your Son of God was even born; a thousand years before the Buddha; two hundred years before Moses. And do you know how much Zoroastrianism influenced Judaism, Christianity, and Islam?'

'OK man, OK!' Malcolm laughed. 'I give up.' Since Crawford Market was only a short walk from the church, they were soon in the great hall of meat. There, Gustad received an overview about beef: its nutritional value, the best ways to cook it, the choicest parts, and, most importantly, the butchers in Crawford Market who sold the choicest parts.

The following Sunday, Malcolm continued the story of Christianity. Saint Thomas was approached courteously by Hindu holy men, by brahmins, sadhus and acharyas, who wanted to know who he was and why he was loitering around these parts. The meeting took place at the sea-shore. Saint Thomas revealed his name, then said, Do me a favour, cup your palms, immerse them under water, and fling water to the sky. They did so, and the water splashed upwards and fell back into the sea. Saint Thomas asked, Can your God keep the water from falling back? What nonsense, Mister Thomas, said the Hindu holy men, it is the law of gravity, the law of Brahma, Vishnu and Shiva, so it must fall back.

Then Malcolm the meat maestro pointed out a most critical point about beef-buying: if the fat had a yellowish tint, it came from a cow, not as desirable as buffalo, whose fat was white. And it was not easy, he said, to distinguish between the two – there was such a variety of gradations, and the light in that huge hall of meat could play tricks, so that very often yellow seemed white. After the first few times, he let Gustad lead the way, to give him practice, he said, practice and more practice, the secret weapon of all virtuosi.

Then Saint Thomas turned to the fishermen and asked, If my God can do it – if He can keep the water from falling back – will you worship Him and forsake your multitude of pagan gods and goddesses, your shoals of idols and deities? And the Hindu holy men whispered amongst themselves, Let us have a little bit of fun, let us humour this Thomasbhai, this crazy foreigner. They said to him, Yes, yes, we will, Thomasji, most definitely.

So Saint Thomas briskly waded out a few feet, cupped his hands, and flung sea-water to the sky. And, lo and behold, it stayed suspended in the air: all of it: the tiny droplets, the big drops, the elongated ones and the round ones, all stood suspended, and refracted the sunlight and sparkled most wondrously, with the perfect glory of the Lord God who created all things. And the crowds gathered on the beach: the fisherfolk, foreign tourists, pilgrims, diplomats, committee chairmen, bankers, mendicants, scallywags, lazy idle loafers, vagabonds, along with the Hindu holy men, all fell promptly to their knees and asked Saint Thomas to tell them more about his God so they too could worship Him.

The last step (after learning to distinguish between buffalo and cow) involved the ability to identify the choicest sections. Malcolm revealed that the neck portion, which the butchers called neckie, was the tenderest, with the least fat, and quickest to cook, thus saving on fuel bills. Neckie was also the sweetest-tasting, and Malcolm assured Gustad that once he learned to appreciate it, he would never return to mutton, not even if he could afford it some day.

Years later, when Gustad was shopping on his own, he was always willing to share Malcolm's wisdom with friends and neighbours. He wanted to train them in the art of beef-eating, so they too could give up the expensive mutton habit. No one, however, was as receptive to the idea as he had been with Malcolm. Eventually, Gustad had to abandon all hope of spreading the gospel of beef.

And a time also arrived when Gustad himself shopped no more at Crawford Market, settling instead for whatever stringy bits of goat, cow or buffalo that the door-to-door *goaswalla* of Khodadad Building brought. By this time, he had lost touch with Malcolm, and was spared embarrassing explanations about the tenuous, tangled connection between his desertion of Crawford Market and the sadhus' nationwide protest against cow slaughter. It was easier to remain the silent, unknown apostate of beef.

ii

Roshan peered through the cracks in the wickerwork and refused to feed the chicken. She had never seen a live chicken, or even a dead one that had not been cooked. 'Come on, don't be frightened,' said her father. 'Picture it on your birthday dinner-plate and you won't be afraid.' He lifted the basket. Roshan flung the grain and snatched away her hand.

The chicken was used to its new surroundings by now, and pecked busily at the grain, clucking contentedly. Roshan was fascinated by the bird and its movements. She imagined the chicken as her pet. It would be like a dog story in her *English Reader*. She could take it out in the compound for a walk, holding the bristly coir cord like a leash, or it could perch on her shoulder, like the picture in the *Reader* of a green parrot with a boy.

She was still dreaming in the kitchen when Darius and Sohrab came to inspect the chicken. Darius put rice on his palm. The chicken ate from his hand.

'Show-off,' said Sohrab, stroking its wings.

'Does the beak hurt?' asked Roshan.

'No, just tickles a little,' Darius answered. Now Roshan wanted to pet it too and reached out gingerly, but the chicken was suddenly nervous again. It flapped its wings, evacuated its bowel and retreated.

'It did chhee-chhee!' exclaimed Roshan.

Dilnavaz's sorely tried patience ran out. 'See that mess? Everywhere a mess! In the kitchen your silly chicken makes the mess! And in the front room all your books and newspapers, and blackout paper over the windows and ventilators! Dust and dirt and mess everywhere! I am fed up!'

'Yes, yes, Dilnoo-darling, I know,' said Gustad. 'Sohrab and I will make that bookcase one of these days, then all the books and papers will fit nicely. OK, Sohrab?'

'Sure,' said Sohrab.

She looked at them. 'Bookcase is all very fine. But if you think I am going to clean that chhee-chhee, you are making a mistake.'

'By the time Saturday morning comes, there will be a lot more,' said Gustad. 'Don't worry, I will clean.' He took it in his stride, but it was a definite miscalculation. In his childhood home there were servants to clean up after the flock.

Sohrab calmed the chicken, holding down its wings, and invited his sister to pet it. 'Come on, it won't hurt you.'

'Look at that,' said Gustad, very pleased. 'You would think he has been handling chickens all his life. Look at the expert way he holds it. I'm telling you, our son will do wonderfully at IIT, he will be the best engineer ever to graduate from there.'

Sohrab released the bird. It dashed under the table, its movements making the roughly-braided coir twist come alive, writhe like a thin, fraying snake. 'Stop it,' he said to his father, clenching his teeth. 'How does a chicken have anything to do with engineering?'

Gustad was taken aback. 'Why are you getting so upset, with just a little joke?'

'It's not just a little joke,' said Sohrab, becoming louder. 'Ever since the exam results came, you are driving me crazy with your talk of IIT.'

'Don't raise your voice at Daddy,' said Dilnavaz. It was true, she realized, they had been discussing it endlessly, making plans and provisions. How he would live in the student hostel at Powai, and come home at the weekends, or they would visit him with a picnic lunch, the college was so close to the lake and the scene-scenery was so beautiful. And after he had finished IIT he would go to an engineering college in America, maybe MIT, and – . But when this point was reached Dilnavaz would say it was time to stop dreaming and tempting fate, because Sohrab had not even started at IIT as yet.

She understood how he felt. Even so, he could not be allowed to shout. 'We are feeling very happy about it, what else? Why do you think your father bought the chicken? After hard work all day he went to Crawford Market. With two grown boys in the house, it is a disgrace that he has to do the *bajaar*. When he was your age he paid his own college fees. And supported his parents.'

Sohrab left the kitchen. Gustad replaced the basket over the fowl. 'Come, leave it alone now, must not be disturbed all the time.'

*

Around midnight, Dilnavaz awoke to go to the WC and heard the chicken clucking softly. Must be hungry again, she thought, switching on the light. The faint beseeching sounds made her forget how firmly she had spoken against live chickens. She went to the rice jar and knocked over the copper measuring cup. It hit the floor with a clang that woke the flat. Everyone soon assembled in the kitchen.

'What happened?' asked Gustad.

'I was going to the back, and the chicken made a sound. I thought it was asking for more food,' she said, holding out her fistful of rice.

'Asking for more food! How much do you know about chickens that you understand what it is saying?' said Gustad.

Cluck-cluck-cluck-cluck came the muted response from the basket. 'Look, Daddy,' said Roshan, 'it's so happy to see us.'

'You think so?' The child's remark pleased him and erased his annoyance. He patted her hair. 'Since the chicken is awake, you can give it some food, then back to sleep.'

They repeated their goodnight-Godblessyou's to one another and returned to their beds.

iii

Roshan fed the chicken and played with it all next evening after school. 'Daddy, can we keep it for ever? I will look after it, promise.'

Gustad was amused, also a little touched. He winked at Darius and Sohrab. 'What do you think? Shall we save its life for Roshan?' He expected them to protest and lick their lips in anticipation of the feast tomorrow.

But Sohrab said, 'I don't mind, if Mummy can live with it in the kitchen.'

'Please Daddy, can we keep it, then? Even Sohrab wants it. No, Sohrab?'

'Enough silliness for one day,' said Gustad.

On Saturday morning, the butcher who made deliveries to Khodadad Building knocked at the door. Gustad took him to the kitchen and indicated the basket. The butcher held out his hand.

Gustad was annoyed. 'Years and years we have been your customers. Now for one small favour you want payment?'

'Don't get angry, *seth*, I don't want payment. Something must be put in my palm so I can use the knife without sinning.'

Gustad gave him a twenty-five paisa coin. 'I forgot about that.' He left the kitchen, not anxious to watch or hear the squawk of final desperation, and waited at the front door.

Moments later, the chicken whizzed by his legs and into the compound. The butcher came running after. '*Murgi, murgi!* Catch the *murgi!*'

'What happened?' yelled Gustad, joining the chase.

'O *seth*, I held the string, lifted the basket!' the butcher panted. 'Then string is in one hand, basket in the other, and chicken runs between my legs!'

'Impossible! Tied it myself!' Gustad's slight limp became an ugly hobble when he ran. The faster he ran, the worse it grew, and he did not like people to see. The butcher was ahead of him, gaining on the bird. Fortunately, it had turned right when it emerged in the compound, keeping close to the black stone wall, which led it to a dead end instead of the main road.

Lame Tehmul was there, pacing with his swaying, rolling gait. He dived for the chicken, and, to everyone's surprise, including his own, was successful. He held it up by the legs, waving it at Gustad with frantic glee as it screeched and flapped desperately.

Lame Tehmul could be found in the compound from morning till night, rain or shine. Whenever Gustad reflected on the miraculous cure that Madhiwalla Bonesetter had worked on his fractured hip, it was Tehmul who came to mind. For Tehmul-Lungraa, as everyone called him, was a supremely pathetic example of hip-fracture victims who had had the misfortune to be treated by conventional methods, condemned to years on crutches and walking-sticks, with

29

nothing to look forward to but a life of pain, their bodies swaying frighteningly from side to side while they strained and panted and heaved in their pitiful pursuit of ambulation.

Tehmul-Lungraa gave the compound's solitary tree a wide berth, as though it was going to reach out and deal him a blow with one of its branches. He had, as a little boy, fallen from its height in his attempt to rescue a tangled kite. The neem tree had not been kind to Tehmul, the way it had to others. For children in Khodadad Building, cuttings from its soothing branches had stroked the itchy rashes and papules of measles and chicken-pox. For Gustad, neem leaves (pulped into a dark green drink by Dilnavaz with her mortar and pestle) had kept his bowel from knotting up during his twelve helpless weeks. For servants, hawkers, beggars passing through, neem twigs served as toothbrush and toothpaste rolled into one. Year after year, the tree gave unstintingly of itself to whoever wanted.

But there had been no such benevolence for Tehmul. The fall from the neem had broken his hip. And although he had not landed on his head, something went wrong inside due to the jolt of the accident, perhaps in the same way that earthquakes will crack houses far from the epicentre.

After the fall, Tehmul was never the same. His parents kept him in school, hoping to salvage something. Whether it worked or not, he had been happy trudging there on his little crutches, and they paid his fees till the school refused to accept them any more, politely advising that it would be better for all concerned if Tehmul's scholastic career was terminated. His parents were long since dead, and his older brother looked after his needs. The latter was a sort of travelling salesman and usually away from home, but Tehmul did not mind. In his mid-thirties now, he still preferred the company of children to adults, with the exception of Gustad Noble. For some reason he adored Gustad.

Tehmul-Lungraa could often be seen directing traffic around the demon tree, warning children to keep away from it if they knew what was good for them, lest they suffer his fate. He no longer used crutches, but walked up and down indicating his rolling gait and twisted hip for their benefit.

And the children, by and large, treated him well; there were very few instances of vicious harassment, not counting the advantage

30

they took of a weakness Tehmul had. Things that travelled through the air enchanted him – things that soared, swooped or dived, things flying and fluttering in freedom. Whether it be bird or butterfly, a paper dart or a falling leaf, he never tired of trying to possess it. Aware of his fascination, sometimes the children would toss a ball or twig or pebble his way, but always slightly out of reach. Always, he would gamely persevere to catch it and fall over himself. Or they would throw a football away from him, then stand back and watch him stumble after it. Just when he thought he was catching up, his uncoordinated feet would kick the ball further, and his frustrating chase began over again.

But on the whole, Tehmul got along well with children. It was the grown-ups who ran out of patience with some of his annoying habits. He loved following people: from the compound gate to the building entrance, and up the stairs, always wearing a big grin, till they shut the door in his face. It bothered some of them so much, they would hide by the gate and peer into the compound to see if the coast was clear, or wait till his back was turned and then sneak through. Others dealt with it by yelling and shooing him off, wildly waving their arms till he understood he was not wanted, though utterly bewildered as to why this should be so.

If Tehmul's trailing habit did not irritate them, his scratching habit was certain to. He scratched perpetually, like one possessed, mainly his groin and armpits. He scratched with a circular movement, a churning, scrambling, stirring motion of his hand, and those who sought more subtlety in a nickname than Tehmul-Lungraa called him Scrambled Egg. Women claimed he did it deliberately to annoy them. They said that his hand regularly moved downward in their presence, and it was rubbing and caressing himself that he did, more than scratching. *Muà lutcha*, they said, knew perfectly well what all his parts were for, never mind if his head was not right – what with a big packet like that, and no underwear even to keep it all in place, it was shameful to have him wandering around dingle-dangle.

Lastly, the words of Tehmul-Lungraa's abbreviated vocabulary always emerged at breakneck speed, whizzing incomprehensibly past the listener's ear. It was as if some internal adjustment had been made to make up for the slowness of his legs with the velocity of his tongue. But the result was extreme frustration for both

Tehmul and the listener. Gustad was one of the few who could decipher his speech.

'GustadGustadchickenrace. GustadGustadchickenranfastfast. I-caughtIcaughtGustad.' Tehmul proudly displayed the bird by its legs.

'Very good, Tehmul. Well done!' said Gustad, his practised ear sorting out the spate of words. Tehmul's cascading utterances were always bereft of commas, exclamation marks, semicolons, question marks: all swept away without the slightest chance of survival. The verbal velocity only allowed for the use of the full stop. And it was not really a full stop the way Tehmul used it; rather, a minimal halt anywhere he chose to re-oxygenate his lungs.

'GustadGustadrunningrace. Fastfastchickenfirst.' He grinned and pulled its tail.

'No, no, Tehmul. Race is over now.' He took the chicken and handed it to the butcher waiting, knife in hand. Tehmul clutched his own throat, performed a slitting gesture and emitted a terrified squawk. Gustad could not help laughing. Encouraged, Tehmul squawked again.

Miss Kutpitia had watched the chase from her window upstairs. She stuck her head out and applauded: '*Sabaash*, Tehmul, *sabaash*! Now we will get you a job as the chicken-catcher of Khodadad Building. Now you are not only the rat-catcher, you are rat- and chicken-catcher.' Shaking with what might have been silent mirth, she withdrew her head and shut the window.

Tehmul did not actually catch the rats, he merely got rid of the ones caught by the tenants of Khodadad Building. The Pest Control Department of the municipal ward office offered twenty-five paise for every rat presented to it, dead or alive, as part of its campaign to encourage all-out war against the rodent menace. So Tehmul earned a little money this way, collecting and delivering rats trapped in his neighbours' wood-and-wire cages. Those who were squeamish gave the cages to Tehmul with the rats still alive, the job to be completed by the municipality. Death by drowning was the official policy. The cages were immersed in a tank and withdrawn after a suitable interval. The corpses were thrown on a heap for disposal, the empty cages returned with the appropriate sum of money.

But when his brother was out of town, Tehmul did not convey

the live rats directly to the municipality. He first brought them home with a desire to entertain them in the municipal manner, to teach them to swim and dive. A bucket of water was filled and the rats ducked one by one. He pulled them out before the end, gasping and suffocating, and kept on till he was bored with the game, or a miscalculation drowned the rats.

Sometimes, for variety, he boiled a large kettle of water and poured it over the rats, emulating the neighbours who were brave enough to exterminate their own trappings. But unlike them, he poured the boiling water a little at a time. As the rats squealed and writhed in agony, he watched their reactions with great interest, particularly their tails, proud of the pretty colours he could bestow on them. He giggled to himself as they turned from grey to pink, and then red. If the scalding did not kill them before he ran out of boiling water, he dropped them in the bucket.

One day, Tehmul's secret was discovered. No one seriously censured him for it. The neighbours agreed, however, never again to hand over a live rat to Tehmul.

But perhaps he understood more than people assumed. When Miss Kutpitia mentioned rat-catcher his grin disappeared and his face clouded shamefully. 'Gustadbigbigfatrats. Municipalrats. GustadGustaddrowningswimmingratsdivingrats. Chickenranbigknife.'

'Yes,' said Gustad, 'OK.' He had never quite decided on the best way of conversing with Tehmul. He invariably found himself speaking faster and faster if he was not careful. It was safest to use nods and gestures, combined with monosyllabic responses.

Tehmul followed him to the flat. He grinned and waved goodbye. Dilnavaz, Roshan and the boys were waiting by the door. 'The string was untied from the chicken's leg,' said Gustad. 'How that happened is what I am wondering.' He looked meaningfully at them. The butcher returned to the kitchen, the bird firmly in his grasp this time, and Roshan's eyes started to fill. 'Yes,' said Gustad sternly, 'I would like to know very much how. Expensive chicken I buy, to celebrate birthday and IIT, then the string is untied. What kind of thanks is that?'

From the kitchen came the tell-tale screech. The butcher emerged, wiping his knife on a rag. 'Good chicken, *seth*, lots of meat.' He left with a salaam in Gustad's general direction.

Roshan burst into sobs, and Gustad abandoned his line of questioning. All four looked at him accusingly, then Dilnavaz went to the kitchen.

Two crows were peering curiously through the wire mesh of the window. The limp mass of feathers and flesh on the stone parapet beside the tap held their attention. When she entered, they cawed frantically and spread their wings, hesitating for a moment, then flew away.

i

Just hours before the dinner party, Miss Kutpitia excused herself from the invitation Dilnavaz had extended against Gustad's express orders. Miss Kutpitia explained that when she sat down to breakfast that morning, at the table's very centre was a lizard, motionless, staring insolently, flicking its tongue. If that wasn't bad enough, when she wrenched her leather *sapaat* from her left foot and thwacked the lizard dead, its tail broke off, and continued to wriggle and dance on the table top for at least five minutes. That, said Miss Kutpitia, was a definite omen. She was not going to step outside her home for the next twenty-four hours.

The news had Gustad laughing uproariously, till Dilnavaz threatened to turn off the stove and put her spoon down permanently. 'I will see where your laughter goes when your silly Dinshawji arrives and the chicken is still uncooked.'

'Sorry, sorry,' he said, struggling to keep a straight face. 'I was just imagining the lizard sticking its tongue out at Kutpitia.' He tried to get busy and help in the evening's preparations. 'Where's the *sev-ganthia* and monkey nuts? To serve with drinks?'

'I am walking around with them on the top of my head!' She finished stirring something on the stove and dropped the spoon with a loud clatter. 'In the jars, where else?'

'Don't get upset, Dilnoo-darling. Dinshawji is a very nice fellow. Just resumed work after his sickness, and still looking *fikko-fuchuk*, white as a ghost. He needs our company, and some of your tasty cooking.' The fragrance of *basmati* rice filled the kitchen as she opened the pot and squeezed a grain between thumb and finger. She slammed shut the lid, no fonder of Gustad's friend.

Dinshawji had joined the bank six years before Gustad. That gave him thirty unbroken years of service, he often said, proudly or complainingly, whatever the situation called for. He was older than Gustad, but it did not preclude the fellowship that had grown between them. It was the sort of bond peculiar to such institutions, nurtured from strength to strength by the dryness and mustiness native to the business of banks.

Gustad found the two jars and emptied the snacks into small bowls before noticing that one was chipped, the other had a crack limned by light brown residues. Never mind, no fuss or formalities needed for good old Dinshawji. Now for the drinks.

There was a little rum in the dark brown bottle: Hercules XXX. Major Bilimoria's final gift, shortly before he disappeared. Gustad debated whether to bring out the bottle. He held it up again, tilted it, trying to estimate. Almost two pegs. Would do for Dinshawji – he could offer him a choice between it and Golden Eagle beer. There were three tall bottles in the icebox.

From the kitchen, Dilnavaz could see the sideboard and the Hercules rum. 'That is the man,' she said, pointing, 'who should be here tonight instead of your silly Dinshawji.'

'You mean Hercules?' He pretended to laugh. That bloody Bilimoria. Should have shown her the letter instead of hiding it. Then she would know what a shameless rascal he is.

'You always get rid of everything by joking. You know what I mean.' The doorbell rang, loud and confident. 'Here already,' she grumbled, rushing back to the stove.

'We said seven, and it is seven.' He went to the door. '*Aavo*, Dinshawji, welcome! A hundred years you will live, we were just talking about you.' They shook hands. 'But alone? Where's the wife?'

'Not well, *yaar*, not well.' Dinshawji looked extremely pleased about it.

'Nothing serious, I hope.'

'No, no, just a little woman-trouble.'

'We were thinking that finally today we will meet Alamai. This is very sad. We will miss her company.'

Dinshawji leaned forward and whispered, chuckling, 'Believe me, I won't. Good to leave the domestic vulture behind.'

Gustad had often wondered how much truth there was behind Dinshawji's habitual references to the tribulations of his marriage. He smiled, inhaling cautiously as Dinshawji's whisper brought him close, and was relieved that his friend's chronically carious mouth gave off only a faint smell today. The odour had a cycle of its own, periodically going from a gale-force stench to a harmless zephyr. Presently, it was passing through the abatement phase. Of course, there was no guarantee it would not issue full strength during the evening if his mood changed. There had been mornings at the bank when Dinshawji arrived with fresh breath that turned foul after an argument with a whining, complaining customer. And because of the incident, if Mr Madon the manager heaped animadversions upon Dinshawji, the stench quickly became unbearable.

Dinshawji's stubborn case of caries had resisted the medications of numerous doctors. But after Gustad became a believer in Madhiwalla Bonesetter's miraculous powers, he convinced Dinshawji to consult him too. Mouth problems and gums and teeth were bone-related matters, after all. Dinshawji resisted at first, trying to make light of it. 'Forget it, *yaar*. My biggest bone problem is not in the mouth. It's much lower, between my legs. With my domestic vulture, that bone gets no exercise. Withering away for years. Can your Bonesetter set that right?'

But he finally came around and paid a visit to Madhiwalla. The resinous secretion of a particular tree was prescribed, which Dinshawji had to chew on three times a day. Within a week, the results were plain to see. At the bank, for instance, customers no longer leaned backwards from the counter while waiting for their money. One day, however, Dinshawji sprained a jaw muscle while zealously masticating the resin. So severe was the pain, he had to restrict himself to a liquid diet for a fortnight, and after the jaw healed, he refused to go back to the resin. The thought of that agony was far more fearful than the carious mouth. So his friends and colleagues learned to live with the ebb and flow of the foul smell, as unpredictable as a roulette wheel.

Dinshawji's problem no longer embarrassed him, his concern was more for those around him and their discomfiture. 'And where is your missis, if I may ask?'

'Just finishing in the kitchen.'

'*Arré*, that means I came too early.'

'No, no,' Gustad assured him, 'you are exactly on time.'

Dinshawji made a gallant bow when Dilnavaz entered. Pinpoints of perspiration glistened on his bald pate as he lowered his head.

37

His hair restricted its growth patterns to the regions over the ears, and at the back over the nape. Prominent strands also flourished inside his ears, and in the dark, capacious recesses of his imposing nostrils, from whence they emerged unabashedly to be counted with the rest.

He held out his hand. 'It is such an honour for me to come to dinner.'

In return, Dilnavaz bestowed upon him the tiniest of her smiles. He turned again to Gustad. 'I think the last time I was here was seven or eight years ago. When you were in bed after the accident.'

'Nine years.'

'Gustad told me you were not well,' said Dilnavaz politely, diluting her haughtiness. 'How are you feeling now?'

'Absolutely first-class, everything tiptop. Just look at my red-red cheeks.' Dinshawji pinched both sides of his waxen face as one would a baby's. The sickly skin retained the imprints of his digits for a long time.

'*Chaalo*, time for drinks,' said Gustad. 'Speak, Dinshawji.'

'A glass of cold water for me, *bas*.'

'No, no, a proper drink. No arguments. There is Golden Eagle, also some rum.'

'OK, if you insist, Golden Eagle.'

Gustad poured the beer as Dilnavaz disappeared into the kitchen. They settled down with their drinks. 'Cheers!'

'Ahhh!' said Dinshawji, taking a large swallow and exhaling. 'This is nice. Much nicer than visiting you in bed with your fracture. Remember how I used to come every Sunday? To give you my personal bank bulletin, bring you up to date?'

'I always said you should have been a reporter instead of a bank teller.'

'What days those were, *yaar*. What fun we used to have.' Dinshawji touched the corners of his lips to wipe the foam. 'Parsis were the kings of banking in those days. Such respect we used to get. Now the whole atmosphere only has been spoiled. Ever since that Indira nationalized the banks.'

Gustad topped up Dinshawji's glass. 'Nowhere in the world has nationalization worked. What can you say to idiots?'

'Believe me,' said Dinshawji, 'she is a shrewd woman, these are vote-getting tactics. Showing the poor she is on their side. *Saali* always up to some mischief. Remember when her pappy was Prime Minister and he made her president of Congress Party? At once she began encouraging the demands for a separate Maharashtra. How much bloodshed, how much rioting she caused. And today we have that bloody Shiv Sena, wanting to make the rest of us into second-class citizens. Don't forget, she started it all by supporting the racist buggers.'

Dinshawji mopped his head and left the handkerchief draped over one knee. Gustad rose to switch on the ceiling fan. 'That rioting was the time when Madhiwalla's sandbags were around my legs.'

'That's right, you never got to see the big processions at Flora Fountain. Every day fighting and some *morcha* or other.' He took a quick swallow of beer. 'In the bank we thought our innings were over when those *goondas* broke the windows, even the thick glass of the main entrance. There goes our bonus, I thought. They were shouting "Parsi crow-eaters, we'll show you who is the boss." And you know what Goover-Ni-Gaan from Ledgers Department did?' Gustad shook his head.

Goover-Ni-Gaan was a morose and lugubrious elderly employee named Ratansa. But the nickname had stuck ever since the day a young fellow, part-time and temporary with nothing to lose, insolently asked him why he went around with a face like an owl's arse. Now, in private, people always referred to Ratansa as Goover-Ni-Gaan, or Ratansa Goover if they were being polite.

'Take a guess, *yaar*,' said Dinshawji. 'What do you think he did?'

'Give up.'

'First Goover-Ni-Gaan told people not to panic, it was just a few *goondas*. But as things got hotter, he covered his head with his white hanky and began doing his *kusti*. Loudly, like a *dustoorji* in the fire-temple. Afterwards, some of the chaps were teasing him non-stop, to take it up as a full-time job, that he would earn much more.' Dinshawji dabbed his forehead again and fanned himself with the kerchief while Gustad laughed. He wiped round the neck, under his collar. 'But really, *yaar*, we all thought our number was up. Thank God for those two Pathans doing *chowki* at the entrance. I used to think they were nothing but decorations with their uniforms and turbans and shiny rifles.'

'Solid fellows,' said Gustad. 'What a smart salute they give when the big shots pass by.'

'Yes, but because of the Pathans and their guns, all those Sakarams and Dattarams and Tukarams only stood outside, screaming like fishwives. If they came close, one of the Pathans stamped his foot and at once they went in reverse gear.' Dinshawji demonstrated with his size twelve Naughty Boys from Bata, making the beer bottles vibrate on the teapoy. He had enormous feet for a man on the short side. 'Bhum! That's all, and the Maratha brigade ran like cockroaches.' He took a long draught and set down the glass. 'Lucky for us that just as the bloody cockroaches were getting braver, the police came. What a day it was, *yaar*.'

Dinshawji wiped his forehead once more, then neatly folded the handkerchief and put it away, content with the ceiling fan. 'One question may I ask?'

'Sure, speak.'

'Why is this black paper covering all the windows?'

'You remember the war with China,' said Gustad, but was spared from explaining further because the two boys and Roshan entered the room and said 'Sahibji' to Dinshawji.

'Hallo, hallo, hallo!' he said, delighted to see them. 'My God, how tall they've grown. *Arré* Roshan, you were this big – only one *billus* – when I last saw you,' and he extended a hand with the thumb and little finger outstretched. 'Hard to believe, no? Happy birthday to the birthday girl! And congratulations for Sohrab. The IIT genius!'

Sohrab ignored him and glared at his father. 'Have you told the whole world about it already?'

'Behave yourself,' said Gustad under his breath, facing the sideboard where he was opening a beer bottle. His voice could be heard plainly, but turning away provided the opportunity to pretend otherwise.

Sohrab persisted. 'You keep boasting to everyone about IIT. As if you were going there yourself. I'm not interested in it, I've already told you.'

'Don't give me any idiotic-lunatic talk. God knows what has happened to you in the last few days.'

Dinshawji, sensing the necessity, tried a diversion. 'Gustad, I

40

think your Darius wants to make an *oollu* out of me. Says he can do fifty push-ups and fifty squats.'

Roshan also did her bit. 'Daddy, sing the song about the donkey! For my birthday, please, please, please!'

Sohrab interrupted: 'I'm going to drink the rum if no one wants it.'

Gustad paused. 'Are you sure? You never liked it before.'

'So what?'

Gustad swallowed and made a dismissive gesture with his hands, a gesture of acquiescence, resignation and rejection rolled into one. He turned to Dinshawji and Darius. 'It's true, fifty push-ups and fifty squats, every morning. And he will keep increasing till he reaches hundred, like me.'

'Hundred?' Dinshawji dramatically fell back in his chair.

'Daddy, the donkey song,' reminded Roshan.

'Later, later,' said Gustad. 'Yes, absolutely, one hundred push-ups and one hundred squats. Every morning till my accident, just like my grandfather taught me when I was a little boy.'

Gustad's grandfather, the furniture-maker, had been a powerful man, standing well over six feet, with tremendous strength in his arms and shoulders. Some of that strength had passed on to his grandson. Grandpa often said to his son, discussing Gustad's upbringing and welfare: 'With your bookstore and your books, you develop his mind. I won't interfere. But I will take care of the body.' On mornings when the little Gustad was still rubbing his sleepy eyes, reluctant to perform his exercises, Grandpa would fire him up with the exploits of wrestlers and strong men who did a thousand push-ups every morning: Rustom Pahelwan, who could lie flat and allow a truck to pass over him; or Joraaver Jal, supporting on his back a large platform with a symphony orchestra for the duration of Beethoven's Fifth. From time to time Grandpa took him to wrestling matches so he could see, in person, titans like Dara Singh, the Terrible Turk, King Kong, Son of Kong, and the Masked Marauder.

Gustad's grandmother, also an ardent wrestling fan, attended the matches with them. Besides being an expert on chickens and butchers, she was very knowledgeable about the sweaty sport. Able to identify the ring personalities as readily as the spices in her kitchen, she had no trouble following the various holds that the wrestlers knotted each other's bodies into, or the drop-kicks, flying mares, body scissors and airplane spins that whizzed around the arena. She could anticipate falls, escapes, take-downs and reversals better than Gustad or Grandpa, and very often outdid them in predicting the winner.

And if Grandpa was a strong man, Grandma, in her own way, was a powerful woman. Had it not been for her knowledge of wrestling, she used to tell Gustad laughingly, there would have been no Noble family as he knew it. For Grandpa, timid and shy and indecisive, as men of his size and strength often are in such matters, kept putting off asking the crucial question. Till one day, when he was tying himself in knots as usual, hemming and hawing, she decided to take the initiative with a lightning-quick half-nelson to force him to his knees so he could propose.

Grandpa denied the entire story, but, she would laugh and say, what started out as discreet and circumspect matchmaking ended in an exciting wrestling match.

'Yes sir,' said Gustad, 'one hundred push-ups and squats every morning. Best possible exercise. I said to Darius, my right hand I will cut off and give you if your biceps don't increase by one inch in six months. And same guarantee I can give you, Dinshawji.'

'No, no, forget it. At my age, only one muscle needs to be strong.'

Darius laughed knowingly, and Dinshawji said, 'Naughty boy! I am talking about my brain!' He reached out and gingerly touched Darius's right arm. 'O my God! Solid, *yaar*! Come on, let's see it.'

Darius shook his head modestly and tugged his short sleeves, trying to stretch them towards the elbows. 'Go ahead, don't be so shy,' said Gustad. 'Look, I'll show mine first.' He rolled up his sleeve to flex in the classic fist-against-forehead pose.

Dinshawji clapped. 'Like a big mango *goteloo*! Bravo, bravo! Your turn now, Mr Body-builder. Come on, come on!'

Darius affected boredom with all this fuss about biceps, but was secretly quite pleased. Body-building was his latest hobby, and the only successful one. Before that, his fascination with living creatures used to take him to the pet shop at Crawford Market. He started with fish. But one evening, just a fortnight after they came home, his guppies, black mollies, kissing gouramis, and neon tetra died following a spell of leaping and thrashing against the glass, very much like the lizard's tail on Miss Kutpitia's breakfast table.

Over the next four years, the fish were succeeded by finches, sparrows, a squirrel, lovebirds, and a Nepali parrot, all of which succumbed to illnesses ranging from chest colds to mysterious growths in their craws that prevented eating and led to starvation. At each demise, Darius wept bitterly and buried his departed friends in the compound beside his father's vinca bush. He spent long hours meditating on the wisdom of loving living things which invariably ended up dead. There was something patently ungrateful about the transaction, a lack of good taste in whoever was responsible for such a pointless, wasteful finish: beautiful, colourful creatures, full of life and fun, hidden under the drab soil of the compound. What sense did it make?

Over and over, the external world had let him down. Now it would be foolish, he decided, to invest any more time or energy on such a world, and turned his attention to himself. His physique became his hobby. Soon after he commenced his exercises, however, a severe case of pneumonia confined him to bed. Miss Kutpitia told Dilnavaz she was not surprised. The innocent little fish and birds in his custody had no doubt cursed him with their dying breaths, and here, for all to see, was the result of their curses.

She taught Dilnavaz how to appease the little creatures and put their spirits at rest. Dilnavaz listened good-naturedly, in one ear and out the other, till one day Miss Kutpitia arrived suddenly with the necessary ingredients to conduct the appeasement procedure. Certain herbs were burnt on hot coals while the patient inhaled the rising vapours.

Whether the birds and fish decided to forgive Darius, or whether Dr Paymaster's medicine overcame the illness was uncertain. But Darius resumed his exercise programme and was amply rewarded in muscles, to his father's delight, and his own relief that finally he had succeeded at something.

'Come on, come on! Show them!' said Dinshawji.

'Be a sport,' said Gustad, and Darius displayed his biceps.

Dinshawji feigned fear and fell back in awe, hands folded over his chest: 'Ohoho! Look at the size of that. Keep far away, baba. In mistake if you land one on me, I will be completely flattened and battened.'

'Daddy, please!' said Roshan. 'The donkey song!'

43

This time, Dinshawji seconded the proposal. He was familiar with Gustad's fine baritone. Sometimes, they had song sessions with friends in the bank canteen during lunch hour. 'OK, Gustad,' he said. 'Time for "Donkey Serenade". Let's have it.'

Gustad cleared his throat, took a deep breath, and began:

> There's a song in the air,
> But the fair señorita doesn't seem to care
> For the song in the air.
> So I'll sing to the mule,
> If you're sure she won't think that I am just a fool
> Serenading a mule . . .

When he came to the section that started with 'Amigo mio, does she not have a dainty bray', everyone tried to join in. They stayed with him till he reached 'hee hee haw', where the last note had to be held for so long that they all ran out of breath, while Roshan burst out laughing with the effort, and Gustad finished the song alone: 'You're the one for me! Olé!'

'Encore! Encore!' said Dinshawji. Everyone clapped, including Dilnavaz, who had appeared silently by the sideboard to listen. She loved to hear Gustad sing. She smiled at him and went back to the kitchen.

Dinshawji turned to Roshan. 'Now it's time for muscles again. How are your muscles today? Let us see, let us see!' She raised her arm, imitating her father and Darius, then aimed a playful blow at Dinshawji's shoulder.

'Careful, careful!' he moaned, 'or it will be twelve o'clock for me.' Reaching out with his bony, gangly fingers as though to test her muscle, he began tickling her. 'Ohohoho! What muscles! *Gilly gilly gilly*! Here's another muscle. And another one. *Gilly gilly gilly!*' Roshan was out of breath, laughing wildly and rolling over the sofa.

Dilnavaz emerged from the kitchen and looked disapprovingly at Dinshawji. She said dinner was on the table.

11

The chicken had been successfully divided into nine pieces. The absence of Miss Kutpitia and Dinshawji's wife, thought Dilnavaz, was fortunate. Even if Dinshawji started by taking two pieces, it

44

would leave something in the dish at the end. She made a polite gesture to the guest to begin.

'Ladies first, ladies first!' said Dinshawji, and Darius echoed him. 'Naughty boy!' Dinshawji pretended to chide him, winking broadly. 'Slow with that beer, it can climb quickly to the head!' The two had struck a rapport, and Gustad was pleased. He looked at Sohrab. Such a moody boy – if only he could be more friendly, like Darius.

The brown sauce, in which the chicken swam, was perfect, as Gustad had predicted. The aroma, said Dinshawji, could make even a corpse at the Tower of Silence sit up with an appetite, it was that wonderful. Whereupon Dilnavaz eyed him distastefully. Did the man have no sense of decency, mentioning such things at the dinner-table, on a birthday?

Besides chicken, there was a vegetable stew made of carrots, peas, potatoes and yam, liberally spiced with coriander, cumin, ginger, garlic, turmeric and whole green chillies. And there was rice, studded with cloves and cinnamon sticks: fragrant *basmati* rice that Dilnavaz had obtained from the black-market fellow for this special day, trading one week's quota of fat, tasteless ration-shop rice for four cups of the slender, delicious grain.

They helped themselves to the stew first. There was a tacit understanding that the chicken would provide the climax. Said Gustad to Dinshawji, 'You see this chicken waiting patiently for us? This morning it was anything but patient. What excitement! It escaped from the kitchen into the compound, and the *goaswalla* – '

'You mean you brought it home alive from the market?'

'Of course. Makes all the difference in the taste, you know, slaughtering fresh and cooking – '

'Can you please explain to Dinshawji later? After we eat?' said Dilnavaz sharply. The two men looked up, surprised, and glanced around the table. Her sentiments echoed silently from the other three faces.

'Sorry, sorry,' said Gustad. He and Dinshawji resumed attacking the stew with gusto, but the others pushed their food back and forth on the plate. Roshan's countenance had acquired the slightest tinge of green. Gustad realized how seriously he had erred: something had to be done to restore the good appetite. 'Wait, everybody, wait,' he announced. 'We haven't yet sung "Happy Birthday" for Roshan.'

'*Arré*, not allowed to delay "Happy Birthday". *Chaalo, chaalo*! Right now!' Dinshawji clapped his hands, having taken the cue.

'But food will get cold,' said Dilnavaz.

'How long does "Happy Birthday" take?' said Gustad. 'Ready: one, two, three,' and with a wave of his hand he led the singing. Once he had started, everyone joined in enthusiastically, and as they came to 'Happy Birthday, dear Roshan', and Roshan smiled with pleasure at the mention of her name, Dinshawji reached over to tickle her again, *Gilly gilly gilly!'* catching her completely by surprise. She almost fell off her chair with laughing.

Then Gustad raised his beer glass: 'God bless you, Roshan. May you live to be an old, old woman in good health – learn a lot, live a lot, see a lot.'

'Hear, hear!' said Dinshawji, and everyone sipped from their glasses. Roshan had Raspberry in hers. Dilnavaz had only water, but she swallowed a little beer from Darius's glass. 'For good luck,' she said, shutting tight her eyes as it went down bitterly, then opened them and beamed at everyone, looking slightly surprised.

'Wait, wait,' said Dinshawji, and Darius at once said, 'Hundred and twenty pounds.' 'Naughty boy!' parried Dinshawji, then continued, 'Hold on to your glasses, everybody.' He cleared his throat and placed his right hand over his heart. Unmindful of his tongue's perpetual difficulties with the 'sh' sound, he began reciting to Roshan:

> I wiss you health, I wiss you wealth,
> I wiss you gold in store;
> I wiss you heaven on earth,
> What can I wiss you more?

There was more clapping, and sips were taken from glasses round the table. 'Bravo!' said Darius, 'bravo!' and then the flat was plunged into darkness.

For a moment there was that surprised silence touched with fear which clutches the heart on such occasions. Almost immediately, however, the sound of breathing and other normal noises resumed. 'Everybody stay seated,' said Gustad. 'First, I will get my torch from the black desk. Check what's wrong.' He groped his way slowly. 'Probably a fuse or something.' He switched on the torch but the light was dim. The beam gathered strength after he thumped the bottom.

'Take me to the kitchen,' said Dilnavaz. 'Candles and the kerosene lamp will at least let us finish eating.'

While she busied herself, Gustad went to the window. He spied a figure in the compound whose walk was unmistakable. 'Tehmul! Tehmul! Over here, ground floor.'

'GustadGustadGustadalldarkandblack.'

'Yes, Tehmul. The whole building is dark?'

'Yesyeswholebuildingdarkeverythingdark. Blackroadlights. DarkeverythingdarkGustad. Darkdarkdarkdark.'

Dinshawji came to the window, trying to follow the exchange. 'OK, Tehmul,' said Gustad. 'Be careful, don't fall.'

Dilnavaz lit the kerosene lamp, which was not enough to brighten the entire room. But the table looked very warm and inviting. 'With the black paper everywhere, even starlight and moonlight is blocked out,' she said, to no one in particular.

'Was that a mouth or the Deccan Express?' asked Dinshawji. 'You understood anything?'

Gustad laughed. 'That's our one and only Tehmul-Lungraa. Takes a little practice to understand. Anyway, we don't have to check the fuse. Whole neighbourhood is blacked out, nothing to do but wait.'

'Do not wait,' said Dinshawji. 'Or you'll be late, just fill your plate.'

'One poem after another! You are in good form tonight, Dinshawji,' said Gustad. 'We will have to call you Poet Laureate from now on.'

'Laureate-baureate nothing, I am a son of Mother India. Call me Kavi Kamaal, the Indian Tennyson!' He grabbed the torch from Gustad and held it under his chin. The light cast an eerie glow over his sallow complexion. He hunched up his shoulders and began to prowl like a spectre around the table, reciting in an unearthly voice that emerged from a death mask:

> Gho-o-osts to right of them,
> Gho-o-osts to left of them,
> Gho-o-osts in front of them,
> Hungry and thirsty!

Everyone cheered and clapped except Dilnavaz who was now frantic about the food getting cold. Dinshawji took a bow and handed the torch back to Gustad. Flushed with success and inspiration, he declaimed, 'Though dark is the night, please take no fright, we shall eat by candlelight. Or kerosene light.'

'Absolutely,' said Gustad. 'But light or no light, I have one more wish to make. For Sohrab, my son, my eldest: to you, good luck, good health, and may you do brilliantly at IIT. Make us all very proud of you.'

'Hear, hear!' cried Dinshawji. 'For he's a jolly good fellow! For he's a jolly good fellow!' Everyone joined in, and the singing got louder and louder. They did not hear Sohrab saying 'Stop it' till he repeated with a shout, over the singing, 'STOP IT!'

The voices ceased abruptly, in mid-melody. Their features frozen, everyone looked at Sohrab. He sat staring angrily at his plate. The candles cast nervous shadows that shivered or yawed wildly when the flames were disturbed by breathing.

'Food is getting really cold,' said Dilnavaz, although it was the last thing she cared about now.

'Yes, we will eat,' said Gustad, 'but,' to Sohrab, 'what is the matter suddenly?'

'It's not suddenly. I'm sick and tired of IIT, IIT, IIT all the time. I'm not interested in it, I'm not a jolly good fellow about it, and I'm not going there.'

Gustad sighed. 'I told you not to drink the rum. It has upset you.'

Sohrab looked up scornfully. 'Fool yourself if you want to. I'm not going to IIT anyway.'

'Such brainless talk from such a brainy boy. How is it possible, I ask you,' he said, turning to Dinshawji. 'And why, after studying so hard for it?' Dilnavaz moved the dishes around, picked up serving spoons and set them down again. But the comforting clatter of crockery and cutlery was powerless to restore normalcy. Gustad silenced her with a wave of his hand. 'Say why. Becoming mute helps nothing.' He paused, more bewildered than angry. 'OK, I understand your silence. This is a birthday dinner, not the right time for discussion. Tomorrow we will talk.'

'Why can't you just accept it? IIT does not interest me. It was never my idea, you made all the plans. I told you I am going to change to the arts programme, I like my college, and all my friends here.'

Gustad could contain himself no longer. 'Friends? Friends? Don't talk to me of friends! If you have good reasons, I will listen. But don't say friends! You must be blind if you cannot see my own example and learn from it.' He stopped and stroked Roshan's hair as though to reassure her about something. 'What happened to the great friend Jimmy Bilimoria? Our Major Uncle? Where is he now, who used to come here all the time? Who used to eat with us and drink with us? Who I treated like my brother? Gone! Disappeared! Without saying a word to us. That's friendship. Worthless and meaningless!'

Dinshawji squirmed uncomfortably, and Gustad added gruffly, 'Present company excepted, of course. *Chaalo*, the stew was very tasty. Chicken is next. Come on, Dinshawji. Come on, Roshan.'

'Gentlemen first! This time gentlemen first!' said Dinshawji, doing his best to dispel the gloom. 'Let's play fair, fair ladies.' But no one laughed, not even Darius. Silence, for the most part, governed the remainder of the meal.

Dinshawji found the wishbone and offered to break it with someone, but there were no volunteers. Embarrassed, Gustad took hold of one end. They pulled and wrenched and fumbled with the greasy bone till it snapped. Gustad's was the shorter piece.

FOUR

i

The solitary guest departed, and Gustad locked the door for the night. Of the nine chicken portions, six remained in the dish. 'Now you are satisfied,' he said, 'ruining your sister's birthday. No one even felt like eating anything.'

'You brought the live chicken home and killed it and made us feel sick at the table,' said Sohrab. 'Don't blame me for your stupidity.'

'Stupidity? *Bay-sharam*! You are speaking to your father!'

'No quarrels on a birthday,' said Dilnavaz, half-cajoling, half-warning. 'That's a strict rule in our house.'

'I know I am speaking to my father. But my father does not want to know the truth when he hears it.'

'Truth? First suffer like your parents have, then talk about truth! I never had my college fees paid for me, I had to earn them. And study late at night with an oil lamp like that one, with the wick very low, to save –'

'You've told us that story a hundred times,' said Sohrab.

'Roshan!' Gustad's hands were shaking. 'Bring my belt! The thick brown leather one! I will teach this brother of yours a lesson in respect! He thinks he is all grown up now! His *chaamray-chaamra* I will peel off! Till not one inch of skin is left on him!'

Roshan stood still, her eyes wide with fear. Dilnavaz motioned to her to stay where she was. When the boys were little, she was often afraid that Gustad, with his immense strength, might do them grave injury while meting out the punishment that a father was supposed to, though afterwards it only made him feel wretchedly remorseful. She hoped Sohrab would remain quiet so that the threat could fade away.

But he would not back down. 'Go, bring the belt. I'm not scared of him or anything.'

50

Seeing that Roshan would not move, Gustad went himself. He returned with his instrument of retribution hanging over his shoulder, whose mention alone used to fill the boys with fear when they were little. He was panting with rage. 'Say, now, whatever you want to say! Let us hear your *chenchi* if you still have the courage!'

'I've already said everything. If you didn't hear, I can repeat it.'

Gustad swung, and the leather whistled as it cut through the air. Dilnavaz ran between the two, the way she used to when the boys were little. The cowhide lashed her calves and she screamed. Two red weals started to emerge.

'Move aside!' shouted Gustad. 'I am warning you! Tonight I don't care what happens! I will cut your son to pieces, I will –'

Roshan started sobbing and screaming. 'Mummy! Daddy! Stop it!' Gustad tried over and over to reach his target, but Dilnavaz's manoeuvres foiled him.

Through her sobs Roshan screamed once more. 'Please! For the sake of my birthday, stop it!'

The belt continued to swing, though nowhere as effectively as that first perfect stroke. The misplaced blow had taken away much of the vigour and keenness from Gustad's arm. 'You coward! Stop hiding behind your mother!'

Before either Sohrab or Dilnavaz could respond, a shrill cry rang out. 'Enough is enough! This is sleeping-time, not fighting-time! Save the rest for morning!'

The voice was Miss Kutpitia's. It had the same pitch and cadences that were evident on mornings when she decided to shriek at the milk *bhaiya*. Gustad was furious. He rushed to the window. 'Come to my door and speak if you have something to say! I am not living free here, I also pay rent!' He turned to Dilnavaz, livid. 'See? That's how your friend behaves. *Saali* witch!'

'But she is right,' said Dilnavaz resolutely. 'All this shouting and yelling in the middle of the night.'

'Very nice! Take her side against your husband. Always against me only.' Bitter to the marrow, he fell quiet. Outside, all was silent again. But he waited defiantly by the window in case a retort from Miss Kutpitia was forthcoming.

Dilnavaz took the opportunity to hustle Sohrab, Darius and Roshan out of the room and into bed. Left alone, Gustad's anger started to ebb. He saw the belt clenched tightly in his hand, and threw it in a corner, then blew out the candles on the dining-table. The room was still too bright for him. He adjusted the wick of the kerosene lamp and returned to stand by the window. The black stone wall could barely be discerned; it had melted into the inky night.

Dilnavaz returned. 'They are all in bed. Waiting for you to say goodnight-Godblessyou.' He did not answer. She tried again. 'I went to Sohrab. See.' She held out her sleeve where it was damp. 'His tears. Go to him.'

Gustad shook his head. 'He will have to come to me. When he learns respect. Till then, he is not my son. My son is dead.'

'Don't say such things!'

'I am saying what must be said. Now he is nothing to me.'

'No! Stop it!' She caressed the welts on her calves, and he saw her do it.

'Seventeen times I have told you not to come in the middle when I am dealing with the children.'

'Nineteen years old now, he is no longer a child.'

'Nineteen or twenty-nine, he cannot speak to me like that. And for what reason? What did I do except be proud of him?'

The bewilderment behind his anger was touching, and she wanted to comfort him, help him understand. But she did not understand herself. She touched his shoulder gently. 'We must be patient.'

'What have we been all these years if not patient? Is this how it will end? Sorrow, nothing but sorrow. Throwing away his future without reason. What have I not done for him, tell me? I even threw myself in front of a car. Kicked him aside, saved his life, and got this to suffer all my life.' He slapped his hip. 'But that's what a father is for. And if he cannot show respect at least, I can kick him again. Out of my house, out of my life!'

She touched his shoulder once more, and went to the table. 'I'll put away everything in the kitchen. Then we can go to sleep.' She began piling up the dirty plates and glasses

ii

Long after Dilnavaz had cleared the table, wiped off the crumbs with a moist rag and gone to bed, Gustad sat beside the soft glow of

52

the kerosene lamp. He was grateful for the lamp. He knew that if the electric light was on, he would still be angry.

Feeling reckless, he mixed together whatever remained in the bottles: Bilimoria's XXX rum, lemon, Golden Eagle, soda water. He tasted it and made a wry face. Nevertheless, he drank half the glass, then went to his grandfather's black desk. It had two side-by-side drawers. The one on the right was smaller, and under it, a cabinet formed the supporting pedestal. He tried to open the cabinet door quietly; it had always been tight. His hands were a little unsteady. It swung open with a soft moan of wood against wood.

The smell of old books and bindings, learning and wisdom floated out. On the top shelf, at the rear, were E. Cobham Brewer's *Dictionary of Phrase and Fable* and the two volumes of Barrère and Leland's *Dictionary of Slang, Jargon & Cant*, the 1897 edition. Like the furniture, Gustad had rescued these from his father's bankrupt bookstore. Reaching in, he pulled out Brewer's Dictionary and opened it at random. He held it up to his nose and closed his eyes. The rich, timeless fragrance rose from the precious pages, soothing his uneasy, confused spirit. He shut the book, tenderly stroking its spine with the back of his fingers, and replaced it on the shelf.

Some works by Bertrand Russell, a book titled *Mathematics for the Millions*, and Adam Smith's *An Inquiry into the Nature and Causes of the Wealth of Nations* also stood on this shelf. They belonged to his college days, the only books he had managed to keep. He used to joke with Malcolm the musician that he was going through college on the Buy-This-Year, Sell-Next-Year textbook plan. How nicely all these would have stood in the bookcase Sohrab and he were planning to make. Not now. The boy is nothing to me now.

Occupying the front of the shelf, flat on their covers, lay an abridged Webster and a pocket edition of Roget blanketed by a higgledy-piggledy miscellanea: dog-eared envelopes, plastic boxes containing paper clips and rubber bands, two rolls (half- and three-quarters-used respectively) of sellotape, a bottle of Camel Royal Blue Ink, an unlabelled bottle of red ink (used exclusively for inscribing greeting cards or white wedding-gift envelopes: salutations, blessings for a long, happy life and, in the bottom left-hand corner, the amount enclosed). Other odds and ends on the shelf were not readily identifiable. Parts of dismembered pens, a glue bottle's rubber cap-cum-nipple, a bladeless penknife, a metal clamp assembly divorced from its file, lay tangled in string and rubber bands.

The bottom shelf was devoted entirely to files, folders and old magazines. He carefully lifted a stack overflowing with variegated rectangles of yellowed newsprint, and groped for the letter. His fingers closed on it. He let the stack settle back. A box of ancient rusting nibs, from the days before ballpoint pens, lost its perch. The nibs inside collided, metal to metal, and metal to cardboard. The sound came and went, like a maraca played and silenced instantaneously.

He took the letter to the lamplight. He had read it several times, secretly, since its arrival. The envelope was typewritten. The return address was a post office box in New Delhi, and the sender's name was absent. It had elicited a mixture of nervousness and curiosity the first time: he did not know anyone in New Delhi. Inside was a single sheet of paper, of excellent quality, thick and fibred. He read it again.

My dear Gustad,

This letter must come as a big surprise to you. After all this time, you must have given up on me, especially because of the way I left Khodadad Building.

You are very angry with me for that, I know. I am not good at letter-writing, but please accept my sincere apologies, and believe me when I say I had no choice. If I make up some excuse, I would be lying, and I do not want to do that. I am still not at liberty to tell you details, except it is a matter of national security. You know I was doing work for the government after leaving the army.

Something relating to my assignment needs to be done in Bombay. I immediately thought of you, since there is no one I trust more. Your friendship means a lot to me, and your dear wife Dilnavaz, and your two wonderful sons and sweet little Roshan. I don't have to tell you that all of you were, and still are, like my own family.

What I need is quite simple. It just involves a parcel which I would like you to receive on my behalf. If you cannot do this favour, I understand. But I will have to turn to less reliable people. Please let me know. And please do not be offended by the post office box number, my address remains confidential because of regulations.

Once again, I beg your forgiveness. Some day, I will tell you the whole story, when our family (if you do not mind my calling us that) is together again.

Your loving friend,
Jimmy

Gustad felt the paper between thumb and finger. How rich, he thought, comparing it to the thin sheets in his own desk. Jimmy was always well-off, but so generous. Constantly buying gifts for the children. The badminton racquets, cricket bat and stumps, table-tennis set, dumb-bells. And he would never give them to the children himself. Always gave them to me, said they were my children, so I had first right to their gratitude and joy. But whenever Jimmy arrived, Roshan, Darius and Sohrab would at once leave what they were doing to sit with him. He was their hero, even Sohrab's, who was always so selective. Look at him now, turning up his nose at Dinshawji.

Gustad lowered the wick of the kerosene lamp and leaned back in the armchair. The light, very soft now, made the room dreamlike in its glow. O Dada Ormuzd, what kind of joke is this? In me, when I was young, You put the desire to study, get ahead, be a success. Then You took away my father's money, left me rotting in the bank. And for my son? You let me arrange everything, put it within reach, but You take away his appetite for IIT. What are You telling me? Have I become too deaf to hear You?

He took up his glass again. The rum-beer was tasting better now, he decided, and swallowed more. How many years have I watched over Sohrab and waited. And now I wish I was back at the beginning, without knowledge of the end. At the beginning, at least there was hope. Now there is nothing. Nothing but sorrow.

What kind of life was Sohrab going to look forward to? No future for minorities, with all these fascist Shiv Sena politics and Marathi language nonsense. It was going to be like the black people in America – twice as good as the white man to get half as much. How could he make Sohrab understand this? How to make him realize what he was doing to his father, who had made the success of his son's life the purpose of his own? Sohrab had snatched away that purpose, like a crutch from a cripple.

The rum-beer was delicious. He drained the glass. The tension was slowly going out of him. Kicked him nine years ago to save his life . . . I can kick him again. Out of my house, out of my life. To learn respect . . . how much he means to me . . . meant to me . . . that day . . .

That day, it had been a morning of rain. No, a whole day of rain: rain mingled with the smell of diesel fumes. And he had got on the wrong bus with ten-year-old Sohrab while heading for lunch. Gustad had taken a special half-day's leave from Mr Madon the bank manager, to celebrate Sohrab's first day at St Xavier's High School. Gaining admission was not easy. The school's motto was *Duc In Altum*, adhered to with especial rigour when selecting new students. There was a tough entrance examination, followed by an interview, and Sohrab had done so well in both. Ten years old, and already his English was fluent. Not like that other interview for kindergarten when he was three, where the headmistress had asked, 'What soap do you use?' and Sohrab had answered, '*Sojjo* soap,' using the Gujarati word for good.

Gustad wanted to give him a real treat. The Parisian served the best fish curry and rice in the city. Each order came with crisp *paapud*, the fish was always fresh pomfret, and the waiter would, upon request, serve any portion of the fish's anatomy. This last was important, because Sohrab adored the tail triangle of the pomfret.

But somehow, what with the rain and the crowds and the confusion, Gustad misread the bus number. They found out only after it had pulled away from the stop and was in the midst of traffic. The conductor approached with a swagger down the aisle, his leather money pouch and ticket case slung in a devil-may-care style over his shoulder.

Gustad held out his change and said, 'One full, one half, Churchgate.' After lunch at the Parisian, he was going to surprise Sohrab by walking him to K. Rustom & Co for a slab of their famous pistachio ice-cream, served between two biscuits that remained crisp till the end. The ice-cream was Dilnavaz's idea. It was expensive, Sohrab had had it just once before: to celebrate his *navjote*, after the ceremony at the fire-temple.

The conductor ignored the outstretched hand, and muttered disinterestedly, 'Not going to Churchgate.' He snapped vigorously with his empty ticket punch: tidick-tick, tidick-tick. The sharp noise made his speech seem hostile. He glared out into the rain and traffic, past Gustad's face.

Rain had started in the early morning: great sheets of water pouring out of dark skies. Gustad remembered Dilnavaz saying, as he left with Sohrab for the new school, 'It's good luck if it rains when something new is beginning.' Sohrab was also pleased: it meant he could wear his new Duckback raincoat and gumboots. He hoped there would be floods to wade through.

Before leaving, he had been adorned with a vermilion dot on the forehead, and a garland of roses and lilies. Dilnavaz did the *overnaa* and sprinkled rice, presenting him with a coconut, betel leaves, a dry date, one areca nut, and seven rupees, all for good luck. She popped a lump of sugar in his mouth, then they hugged him and murmured blessings in his ear. They said more or less the same things as on a birthday, but the emphasis was on school and studies.

Waiting first in line, Gustad had wished it would let up for a while. The rain crashed deafeningly on the bus shelter's corrugated metal roof. The air was heavy and disagreeable. Traffic lay like a soporous monster on the shiny wet surface of the road, throbbing and spewing out its effluvium, rousing itself now and again to move a little, sluggishly. The petrol and diesel fumes were strong and noisome; they seemed to have dissolved in the very moisture; and the moisture blanketed everything.

'Not going to Churchgate,' repeated the conductor, clicking away absently with his ticket punch: tidick-tick, tidick-tick, tidick-tick. His left hand played with the sea of coins in his leather pouch, running his fingers through them or lifting a handful and letting them cascade like a metallic waterfall back into the pouch, where they landed with tinny splashes. Part of the leather had been polished to a satiny smoothness by the conductor's constant caresses. It glowed warm and lustrous. And this picture of the conductor was what Gustad saw most clearly as he lay on the road in the pouring rain, in the path of oncoming traffic, unable to rise. Something had broken; the first great bolts of pain were thundering through his body.

But first, there was the argument with the surly conductor. 'Not going to Churchgate,' he said. Rain and slow traffic had affected everyone's temper. 'Buying a ticket or what?'

'If this bus is not going to Churchgate we will get off.'

'Then get off.' Tidick-tick, tidick-tick, tidick-tick. 'Or buy. No free ride.'

'But pull the bell at least.' Gustad's speech was yanked undignifiedly from him, as the bus lurched in the middle of the sentence and his words tumbled wildly.

'The bell will be pulled for the next stop only. If you stay, buy a ticket. Or –' he pointed to the exit.

Gustad eyed the bell rope: what if he made a grab for it? The conductor would try to stop him, and a physical confrontation would result. He knew he would acquit himself admirably in a fair fight, but it would be unsuitable in front of Sohrab. And there had been instances when conductors had smashed their metal ticket boxes over a passenger's head if things were not going their way in a brawl. He tried one more time to reason. 'You want us to get down in the middle of the road and kill ourselves or what?'

'Nobody is going to die,' said the conductor scornfully. 'Everything is completely stopped, look.'

The bus was at a standstill in the middle lane, and cars everywhere had come to a halt. 'Come on, Daddy,' said Sohrab. He had been embarrassed by the exchange. 'It's easy to go now.' The other passengers, bored in the frozen traffic, had been following the exchange interestedly. They watched with disappointment as the two made their way down the aisle.

The bus jerked forward at the very moment that Sohrab stepped off. He lost his balance on the asphalt, slick and treacherous with rain, and fell. Gustad yelled, 'Stop!' and leapt from the moving bus.

In that split second between witnessing and leaping, he realized he could either land on his feet or save his son. He aimed for Sohrab with his feet and kicked him out of the path of an oncoming taxi. His left hip took the brunt of the fall. He heard the sickening crunch. The smell of diesel fumes was strong in his nostrils as he blacked out.

The taxi-driver slammed on his brakes inches from Gustad. People from the footpath ran to where he lay. A small crowd gathered.

'Lay him out comfortably,' said one.

'Needs water, he has fainted,' said another. Gustad could hear their voices, and felt as if someone was pushing him back, keeping him from rising.

The taxi-driver asked his passengers to leave. They protested, then departed hurriedly when they realized they would not have to pay what was on the meter. Someone called for the water-seller across the road. The peculiar street sound carried well over other noises, a mixture of hissing, aspirating and susurrating. 'Hss-sst-sst-sst! Paaniwalla!' The man crossed the road at a trot with his bucket and glasses. Gustad's forehead was bathed, although his entire face was already wet with rain. Perhaps they felt that water colder than rain was required to revive the fallen man.

He opened his eyes. A second glass was filled and held to his lips, but he would not drink. The water-seller emptied it on the road and said, to no one in particular, 'Two glasses, twenty naye paise.'

'What?' said the taxi-driver, 'You have no shame? You can't see the man has had a serious accident, he is in pain, fainting?'

'I am a poor man,' said the water-seller, 'I have children to feed.' He had a large purple mark on one side of his face, and a high-pitched voice with an irritating whine.

The crowd took sides in the argument. Some said the heartless scoundrel should be driven away with a kick, while others saw his point. Determined not to be done out of his only sale all day, he spoke up again. 'The man has had an accident. So? He will pay the ambulance and the doctor and the hospital, to get mended. Why should I be the only one left out? What is my sin that I don't get my twenty naye paise?'

'Theek hai! Theek hai!' agreed the crowd. More were swayed to his side. Then Sohrab pulled a rupee out of the seven he had received that morning. Gustad wanted to say something to him about counting the change carefully, but could not produce the words. The paaniwalla left with his bucket and glasses, grumbling under his breath. In the rain, his high-pitched whining voice took up the futile cry. 'Ice-cold paani, sweet-sweet paani!'

Attention focused again upon Gustad. The taxi-driver offered to take him to a doctor or to hospital. But Gustad was able to whisper, 'Khodadad Building,' before almost passing out again. He remembered vividly what a kind man the taxi-driver turned out to be. He took charge of things calmly, cheering up Sohrab who was frightened and on the verge of tears now. 'We'll soon be there, don't worry, traffic cannot stand here for ever.' He asked him about his school, his studies, what standard he was in, and kept up a steady conversation till they reached Khodadad Building.

Major Bilimoria was at home, and he came immediately on hearing the news. He told Dilnavaz about Madhiwalla Bonesetter. 'Take him to a regular hospital like Parsi General, and all you will get is regular treatment. Or regular ill-treatment, depending on Gustad's luck.' He chuckled.

Dilnavaz imagined the Major had seen many gory injuries in the army, it was natural for him not to be worried. He continued, 'They love to use their chisels and saws and hammers and nails in the hospitals. And after their carpentry is done, they give you a big fat bill because their tools are so expensive.' Gustad heard him through his pain, and found the risible descriptions very reassuring. He knew it would be all right now, Jimmy would look after everything. 'With Madhiwalla Bonesetter there is no operation, no pins, no cast, nothing. No bill even, except whatever donation you want to give. And the Bonesetter's methods are amazing, I am a living witness. Sometimes, the army surgeons called him to help with difficult cases. The things he did were just like magic.'

It was decided. Using the same taxi, they proceeded to the large hall where Madhiwalla Bonesetter was in attendance that day. The taxi-driver refused his fare. 'I don't want profit from your pain,' he said.

Then Jimmy picked Gustad up in his arms like a baby and carried him inside. Jimmy was one of the few who was his equal in strength, as they had found out over the years during their bouts of arm-wrestling.

Jimmy waited by his side till Madhiwalla Bonesetter attended to him. Later, he brought the two long, heavy sandbags that the Bonesetter had insisted on for Gustad, to immobilize the leg while the fracture healed.

What would I have done that day without Jimmy, he wondered. But then, that was the amazing thing about him, he was always there when needed – call it coincidence, call it friendship, that was Jimmy's way.

iii

Gustad rubbed his eyes and opened them. His mouth was dry. He reached for the glass of rum-beer, then remembered it had been emptied earlier. He rose, raised high the wick of the kerosene lamp, and carried the light to his desk. For the thousandth time, his heart filled with gratitude for Jimmy Bilimoria. If it hadn't been for Jimmy's taking him to Madhiwalla Bonesetter, he would be a complete cripple today. Instead, here he was, without crutches or stick, or the terrible heaving-swaying walk of Tehmul-Lungraa.

He opened the wider of the two drawers to rummage for writing-paper. His limp was more pronounced than usual. Despite the years since the accident, Gustad had not fully accepted that it was his strength of spirit as much as Madhiwalla Bonesetter's miracle cure that had tamed his limp – suppressed it, kept it at an ignorable minimum.

He found an uncrumpled sheet, and tried a ballpoint on his palm: he disliked the difference in ink colour if a pen reneged in mid-letter. Then he changed his mind and opened the desk cabinet.

The ancient learned smell of books and bindings came again. He breathed it in deeply. The box of nibs lay on its side where it had tumbled earlier. He opened it and selected one after scratching the points of several against his left thumbnail. He found a holder, fitted the nib, and uncapped the bottle of Camel Royal Blue.

The holder-steel felt good in his writing hand, so much more substantial than a plastic ballpoint pen. Such a long, long while since I used one. No one wrote with them any more, not even in schools. But at one time that was how children made the transition from pencil to ink. This was the bloody problem with modern education. In the name of progress they discarded seemingly unimportant things, without knowing that what they were chucking out the window of modernity was tradition. And if tradition was lost, then the loss of respect for those who respected and loved tradition always followed.

It was almost two a.m. but Gustad was not sleepy. Mixing memory and sorrow, he thought fondly of the old days. At last, he dipped the nib in the ink bottle and began. The shadow of his writing hand fell on the paper. He moved the lamp to the left, completed the address, and dated the letter. As he wrote the salutation the power returned. The bulb blazed over the dining-table. After hours of darkness, the harsh electric light flooded the room insolently from corner to corner. He switched it off and resumed writing by the kerosene lamp.

i

At water-tap time Dilnavaz awoke automatically, and her first thoughts were about Gustad and Sohrab. The terrible, terrible things they had said to each other. Exhausted, she stumbled sleepily to the bathroom. Water, water. Drums to fill. Hurry. Kitchen tank to fill. That big bucket. And milk to buy . . .

While she waited outside for the *bhaiya*, Miss Kutpitia beckoned her upstairs. 'Please don't take it to mind,' Dilnavaz blurted out on reaching the landing. 'He was very upset.' It too had bothered her all night, Gustad's lack of restraint, shouting back at a lonely old woman.

'That's not why I called you. I am worried about your son.'

'Sohrab?'

'Your eldest,' said Miss Kutpitia. 'He reminds me so much of my Farad.' A flicker of tenderness played upon her face, then expired like a candle in the wind. Once, all of Miss Kutpitia's thoughts and dreams were reserved for her nephew, Farad. A long time ago, on a day that mixed great joy with profound sorrow, her brother's wife had died while giving birth to Farad. And on that day Miss Kutpitia took a vow: never to marry, for ever to dedicate her life to the widower and his child. So she became mother and teacher, friend and slave, and whatever else she could think of, to little Farad. Her devotion was returned by the child, who sensed very early on, without ever exploiting the fact, that he was her reason for living. It had been a golden time in Miss Kutpitia's life.

When Farad was fifteen, he and his father went for their usual week's holiday to Khandala. On the return journey, there was an accident on the Ghats. A lorry driver lost control, colliding first with a busload of vacationers, then the car in which Farad and his father were riding, and all three vehicles went off the mountain road. The lorry driver was the lone survivor. On that fateful day thirty-five years ago, Miss Kutpitia locked up her heart, her mind, her memories. From then on, no one was allowed into the flat beyond the front hallway.

'Your Sohrab reminds me in every way of my Farad,' she said. 'In looks, in brains, his way of walking, talking.' Dilnavaz knew nothing about Farad. It had happened long before she had married and come to Khodadad Building. She looked puzzled, and Miss Kutpitia continued. 'Brilliant boy. Would have taken over his father's law practice if he had lived.' That was all she said, grief no longer being something that needed unburdening. Over time, her carapace of spinsterhood had accreted in isolation. And there was no way for a person to tell if, under that hard shell, fate's cruelly inflicted gashes were still raw or had scarred over.

'Oh, I am so sorry,' started Dilnavaz.

'No need. Tears have all been cried long ago. Not one drop remains.' She placed two fingers on the bags under her eyes and tugged downwards. 'See? Fully dry.' Dilnavaz nodded sympathetically. 'But I called you because I heard everything last night. Do you know why Sohrab is behaving like this?'

Dilnavaz was grateful for the concern after her night of lonely anguish. 'My mind refuses to work when I try to understand. Makes no sense at all.'

'You are saying that suddenly he does not want to study at this IIT place?' Miss Kutpitia narrowed her eyes as Dilnavaz nodded. 'And up to now he wanted to go, no one forced him?'

'No one. I am trying to remember, but I think it was his own idea, when he was just a young boy in school.'

Miss Kutpitia's eyes became thin slits. 'In that case, only one thing is possible. Somebody has fed him something bad. In his food, or in a drink. Definitely *jaadu-mantar.*'

Dilnavaz politely masked her scepticism; and yet, she thought, how tempting, to believe in magic – how quickly it simplifies and explains.

Miss Kutpitia looked grim. 'Do you know someone who would profit by Sohrab's failure? Who would like to steal his brains for their own son, maybe?'

'I cannot think of anyone.' Dilnavaz shivered suddenly in spite of herself.

'It could even be an evil mixture he stepped on in the street. Many ways exist to do such black things.' Her eyes blazed wide with warning now. Big as meatballs, thought Dilnavaz. 'But don't worry, there are also ways to fight it. You can start with a lime.' She explained the process, and the precise gestures required. 'Do it for a few days. Before the sun sets. Then come to me again.' Turning to go inside, she said, 'By the way, you saw how right my lizard's tail was.'

'How?'

'Your dinner. All spoilt by quarrelling. And the power also went off. Chicken slaughtered in your house was very unlucky. The curse of the death-scream stayed under your roof.'

'It was Gustad's idea,' said Dilnavaz. On her way home, there floated in her sleepy mind a droll parallel between the chicken and Darius's revenant, pneumonia-inflicting fishes and birds. Poor Miss Kutpitia, such a sad life.

In her eagerness to get back to bed, the letters on Gustad's desk went unnoticed.

ii

She was still asleep when Sohrab awoke and found his father's writing implements abandoned after the long night of rumination and reverie. The vigil for dead days and dying hopes had ended when the early, bleary hours of morning crept upon Gustad, the rum-beer exacting its toll.

Sohrab picked up the holder-steel, wondering why his father had been using that fossil. He, too, had lain awake, agonizing over the hurt, the confusion, the harsh words – was he to blame for all of it? The answers were not easy to come by, they lay in the garden of the past, which memory had dug up and replanted in plots of its own choosing. The seed of Sohrab's troubles had germinated long ago, long before last night, when his parents discovered how easily things came to their first-born, at home, in school, at work or play. There seemed to be nothing Sohrab could not do, and do well. Whether it was arithmetic, or arts and crafts, or moral science, he bagged several prizes each year on Prize Distribution Day. Regularly, there were awards for elocution and debating. In the inter-school drama competition, the play he acted in walked away with the trophy. His exhibits in the school science fair finished first. And before long, Gustad and Dilnavaz were convinced their son was very special.

Thus, it was inevitable that when Sohrab showed an interest in model airplanes, Gustad was sure he would grow up to be an aeronautical engineer. Replicas of famous buildings, made to scale, brought forth predictions of brilliant architecture. And tinkering with mechanical things like can-openers could only mean one thing: a budding inventor. Of course, Sohrab's lot could have been much worse, for the love and adulation of parents for their firstling have been guilty of far more terrible things.

Sohrab's only perceptible failure during his school years befell his flirtation with insects. In the eighth standard he was awarded a prize for general proficiency, a book called *Learning About Entomology*. He read it, pondered the contents over a few days, then started catching butterflies and moths with a home-made net. He killed them in a tin containing wads of petrol-soaked cotton. When the fluttering ceased, he opened the tin and unfolded the wings gently. The wings were always clenched tight over the legs and proboscis, folded in the reverse of their natural direction, as if, *in extremis*, the butterfly had tried to fend off the noxious fumes by covering its head. In a race with rigor mortis, he stretched the four membranous wings symmetrically on a spreading board (also home-made). A few days later, dry and light as tissue paper, the butterfly would be ready for mounting.

Everyone praised his beautiful work. They admired the lovely colours and patterns on the wings as if he had had a personal hand in designing them. The specimens were pinned through their thoraxes and neatly mounted in the display case which he made from plywood with his great-grandfather's tools. This was Gustad's greatest source of joy: to see Sohrab use those tools. He repeated what he said so often, that it must be in the blood, this love of carpentry.

Then the moths and butterflies began to fall apart. Soon, maggots were crawling inside the case, and it was a nauseating sight. Day after day, Sohrab could do nothing but watch, paralysed. When the maggots finished their work, they disappeared as suddenly as they had arrived, and Sohrab threw the butterfly case on the dark shelf in the WC *chawl*.

But this failure, instead of scotching rumours of his genius, was not allowed to be his failure. Gustad was only too glad to shoulder the blame. 'It was my fault,' he said, 'for getting petrol instead of carbon tetrachloride, and for not obtaining the proper drying agent Sohrab wanted.'

Sohrab chased no more after butterflies. To be the world's premier insect scientist was deleted from Gustad's catalogue of careers for his son. Afterwards, Sohrab focused only on mechanical things and things of the imagination. He dismantled and reassembled the alarm clock, repaired his mother's mincer, and fashioned a still-projector with a magnifying glass found in Gustad's desk. He projected on the front-room wall the frames from comics that came with the Sunday paper: Dagwood Bumstead's family, or a life-size Phantom. Major Bilimoria was always there for the show, rising often to pose beside the image – imitating the Phantom by swinging a fist and uttering sounds like thud! pow! or wham! Then it would be time for the Sunday *dhansak* lunch.

Gustad's and Dilnavaz's proudest moment in Khodadad Building came when Sohrab put on a home-made production of *King Lear*, pressing Darius into service, plus a host of school and Building friends. The performance was held at the far end of the compound, and the audience brought their own chairs. Sohrab, of course, was Lear, producer, director, costume designer and set designer. He also wrote an abridged version of the play, wisely accepting that even an audience of doting parents could become catatonic if confronted by more than an hour's worth of ultra-amateurish Shakespeare. But it was not till Sohrab was in college that it struck him curiously: Daddy never made pronouncements or dreamed dreams of an artist-son. It was never: my son will paint, my son will act, he will write poetry. No, it was always: my son will be a doctor, he will be an engineer, he will be a research scientist.

Now, as he wiped the nib and screwed on the bottle cap, he remembered that Daddy had showed him the holder-steel once, when the age of pencils was ending. With the age of ink came plans for the future. The dream of IIT took shape, then took hold of their imaginations. And the Indian Institute of Technology became the promised land. It was El Dorado and Shangri-La, it was Atlantis and Camelot, it was Xanadu and Oz. It was the home of the Holy Grail. And all things would be given and all things would be possible and all things would come to pass for he who journeyed there and emerged with the sacred chalice.

To try and separate the strands of enthusiasm which went into that noble fabrication was futile. To determine whose idea it was, and who was to blame, was as difficult as identifying the monsoon's first raindrop to touch the earth.

Sohrab saw the two letters on the desk. He read the Major's quickly, then his father's elegantly penned nib-and-ink response, while Dilnavaz rose for the second time. It was her duty, she felt, to say something about last night. But he spoke first: 'Did you read Major Uncle's letter?'

'What letter?' He held it up. 'Must be an old one,' she said. 'You know how Daddy likes to collect things.'

'No, this came just four weeks ago. See the postmark.'

Gustad stumbled past to the bathroom, rings around his eyes. She waited for the stopper's tell-tale metallic rattle. 'He slept so late last night.' Her voice was gently accusing.

Later, when Gustad was having his tea she said, 'We saw the letter.'

'I don't know who is "we". For me you are the only one present here.'

She ignored that. 'You have started hiding mail. I wonder what else you are hiding.'

'Nothing! I wanted to think about Jimmy's letter without getting a thousand suggestions from all the geniuses in this house. That's all.'

'A thousand suggestions, is it?' Dilnavaz was stung. 'For twenty-one years we discuss everything together. Now I am a nuisance? And Jimmy doesn't even tell the details. How do you know you are doing the right thing?'

Gustad said the details did not matter, it was the principle, of helping a friend. 'All this time, it has been Major this and Major that. I said forget him, he is vanished like a thief. But no. Now he writes for help, I say yes, and you are still not pleased.'

'And what if it is something dangerous?'

'Rubbish.' He pointed to Sohrab. 'Why is that one grinning like a donkey?'

'Don't get angry again, Daddy,' he said, 'I think you made the right choice, but –'

'Oh! He thinks Daddy made the right choice! Haven't you told him he is no longer my son?' Fiercely sarcastic, Gustad bowed his head mockingly. 'Thank you, thank you sir! Thank you for your approval. Go on. But what?'

'I was just thinking about Jimmy Uncle and your friends talking politics. He always used to say, "Only two choices: communism or military dictatorship, if you want to get rid of these Congress Party crooks. Forget democracy for a few years, not meant for a starving country."'

His imitation of the Major's clipped bass-baritone was very good, and Dilnavaz laughed. Gustad enjoyed it too but was careful to conceal his approval, as Sohrab continued: 'Imagine if Jimmy Uncle is planning a coup to get rid of our corrupt government.'

With the saucer of tea in one hand, Gustad supported his forehead in the other. 'Idiotic-lunatic talk is starting again. Imagine something useful, imagine yourself in IIT!' He kneaded his forehead. 'What Jimmy used to say is just a way of talking. Everybody does it when there are droughts and floods and shortages, and things go wrong.'

'I know, I know, I was only joking. But what about the leaders who do wrong? Like the car manufacturing licence going to Indira's son? He said Mummy, I want to make motorcars. And right away he got the licence. He has already made a fortune from it, without producing a single Maruti. Hidden in Swiss bank accounts.' Dilnavaz listened intently as Sohrab described how the prototype had crashed in a ditch during its trial, yet was approved because of orders from the very top. She was the self-appointed referee between father and son, her facial expressions registering the scores.

'Good to see your son reads the newspapers,' said Gustad, finishing the tea in his saucer. 'He may be a genius, but let me teach him something. Whatever you read in the paper, first divide by two – for the salt and pepper. From what's left, take off ten per cent. Ginger and garlic. And sometimes, depending on the journalist, another five per cent for chilli powder. Then, and only then, will you get to the truth free of *masala* and propaganda.' Dilnavaz was pleased with his impromptu lesson. Her scoreboard updated itself. Gustad leaned back and slid his cup towards the kettle.

'But I heard this from an eyewitness,' said Sohrab. 'One of my college friends. His father works at the testing centre.'

'College friend! Filling your head with rubbish and idiotic-lunatic talk. Be grateful this is a democracy. If that Russiawalla was here, he would pack you and your friends off to Siberia.' He rubbed his forehead. 'When he talks like this, the blood in my brain begins to boil! If I have a stroke, it will be your son's fault, I am warning you!'

She watched, distressed. The vestiges of what had resembled a keen debate (she had half-enjoyed it, hoped it would usher in normalcy) was rekindling last night's pyre. She signalled to Sohrab to say nothing.

'For the last time, take my advice,' said Gustad. 'Forget your friends, forget your college and its useless degree. Think of your future. Every bloody peon or two-paisa clerk is a BA these days.' He picked up his response to Major Bilimoria and went to the desk for an envelope.

Dilnavaz motioned to Sohrab to follow her. In the kitchen she selected a lime from her basket and bade him close his eyes. 'What's this?' he protested. 'What are you doing with the lime?'

'It's not going to hurt, just makes your brain healthy.'

'What nonsense. My brain does not need any help.'

She shushed and pleaded that he do it for her sake, it was bad to have too much pride. 'So many things science cannot explain. And a lime cannot harm you, can it?'

'Oh, OK!' He closed his eyes resignedly. 'First Daddy gets dramatic, then you get necromantic. You two drive me crazy.'

'Don't be rude. And don't use big-big words.' She held the lime in her right hand and described seven clockwise circles over his head. 'Now open your eyes, look hard at it.' She drew it away from him with a downward motion, towards his feet, and tucked it in a brown paper bag. Later, it would be tossed into the sea. This last step was crucial, Miss Kutpitia had explained; it was imperative not to discard the lime with the garbage.

Suddenly, everything Miss Kutpitia said seemed imbued with deep wisdom.

iii

After the awkwardness at the dinner party, Gustad was uncomfortable when he met Dinshawji on Monday, but the latter put things at ease. 'Don't worry about it. Argument is normal when a boy is growing up. You think I have become old without seeing such things?'

At lunch-time, Gustad did not go to the stairwell where the *dubbawalla* deposited the tiffin boxes. He would let his lunch return home uneaten, and without his pencilled note to Dilnavaz which, over twenty-one years, was the one constant in their lives, always written and always read, no matter how much they fought or quarrelled. Until today. The daily notes did not say much: 'My Dearest, Busy day today, meeting with manager. Will tell you later. Love & xxx.' Or: 'My Dearest, *Dhandar-paatyo* was delicious. Aroma made everyone's mouth water. Love & xxx.'

Dinshawji approached Gustad's desk with his packet of sandwiches. Unlike the others, he carried his lunch in his briefcase every morning, usually last night's leftovers slopped between two slices of bread. He often turned up with gems like cauliflower sandwiches, brinjal sandwiches, French bean sandwiches, pumpkin sandwiches, and ate them cheerfully, soggy bread and all. If he was teased about his epicurean delights, he would say, 'Whatever my dear domestic vulture gives, I eat without a word. Or she will eat me alive.'

Dinshawji's lucky days, like the one today, were those when nothing remained from the previous night. On such days, Alamai fried a spicy omelette in the morning to go between the bread slices. As he unwrapped the paper, the pent-up smell of onion, ginger and garlic issued like a squirt. 'Come on *yaar*,' he said to Gustad. 'Get your *dubba* and let's go to the canteen.' He wanted to be on time for the daily feature.

Every day in the canteen, over lunch, their regular group told jokes. They told the perennially popular Sikh jokes (What did the Sardarji runner say, after finishing first in the Asian Games, when asked: 'Are you relaxing now?' He said: 'No, no, I am still Arjun Singh'); they told Madrasi jokes, mimicking the rolled-tongue sounds of South Indian languages (How does a Madrasi spell minimum? Yum-i-yen-i-yum-u-yum); they told Guju jokes, capitalizing on the askew English pronunciations of Gujaratis and their difficulties with vowels, 'o' in particular (Why did the Guju go to the Vatican? He wanted to hear pope music. Why did the Guju bite John Paul's big toe? He wanted to eat popecorn); they told Pathani jokes, about the Pathan's supposed penchant for rear-entry (A

Pathan went to his doctor: 'Doctor Sahab, in my stomach is a lot of pain.' So the doctor gave him an enema. The Pathan left in ecstasy, told his friends: '*Arré*, how pleasureful modern science is – belly in pain, but medicine beautifully arse-way rammed.' The next day, his friends lined up at the doctor's clinic for enemas).

The group in the canteen did not spare themselves either, joking about the vast reputation of the Parsi proboscis (What happens when a *bawaji* with an erection walks into a wall? He hurts his nose). No linguistic or ethnic group was spared; perfect equality prevailed in the canteen when it came to jokes.

Lunch-time was the highlight of the drab working day. Invariably, Dinshawji was the star performer, the group hanging on to his every word. There were contributions from others too, but these seemed to pale in comparison. Dinshawji stored away every-thing he ever heard; weeks, even months later, he would bring it forth, refurbished and improved, a brand-new story. It was a neces-sary bit of plagiarism that no one minded.

Sometimes, instead of jokes, they had a song-session. If Dinshawji was the star of the comic hour, it was Gustad who shone during the singing. Especially in demand were his renditions of Sir Harry Lauder's favourites like 'Roamin' in the Gloamin'' and 'I Love a Lassie' which Gustad delivered with a marvellous Scottish brogue. Although the custom was to sing together, everyone fell silent when he sang:

> By yon bonnie banks and by yon bonnie braes,
> Where the sun shines bright on Loch Lomond,
> Where me and my true love will ne'er meet again,
> On the bonnie, bonnie banks of Loch Lomond.

But they always found the refrain irresistible, and joined in with Gustad, drowning his efforts:

> So ye take the high road and I'll take the low road,
> And I'll be in Scotland afore ye,
> But me and my true love will ne'er meet again,
> On the bonnie, bonnie banks of Loch Lomond.

It was not all jokes and singing in the canteen, though. Sometimes the hour went in passionate argument about matters that con-cerned the community, such as the Tower of Silence controversy.

When the bank clerks and tellers debated the reformers' proposal to introduce cremation, tempers flared and there were bitter personal attacks. But Dinshawji would manage to end matters on a light note, saying things like: 'Better that my dear domestic vulture eats me up than the feathered ones. With her I have a guarantee – she at least won't scatter pieces of my meat all over Bombay.'

Biting into his omelette sandwich, he reminded Gustad about lunch. 'Forget it,' said Gustad. 'I'm not eating today.'

Much as Dinshawji enjoyed the canteen, he decided to stick by his friend. 'Sandwich? Half?' He held out his packet.

Gustad said no with his hand. 'Going for a walk.'

'I'll also come. I can eat walking-walking. Good for stomach and digestion.'

On the way out they passed the new typist, Laurie Coutino, daintily raising spoonfuls of gravy-covered rice to her mouth. Laurie Coutino's person was as impeccably ordered as her desk, with everything in its proper place. She did not like the canteen, and for lunch, her stationery was moved neatly to one side, making room for her napkin and tiffin. Her tongue snaked out and retrieved an errant grain of rice as the two went by.

'What a sweetie,' whispered Dinshawji. Her legs were crossed, and the short skirt had hiked up a fair but controlled distance. 'Oooh!' he moaned softly. 'Cannot bear this pain! Just cannot bear it! Have to get an intro with her soon.' He put his hand in his pocket and bunched it towards the groin, all part of the role he liked to play, ever the active candidate or, as the chaps called him, much to his delight, the Casanova of Flora Fountain.

They emerged under the hot sun, stepping out of the path of a tardy *dubbawalla* weaving through the crowds at a jog, his crate of lunch-boxes balanced on his head. A gust of wind picked up the sweat streaming down his face and sent it in their direction. Dinshawji instinctively shielded his packet of sandwiches. Exchanging looks of disgust, they wiped the salt spray from their cheeks with white handkerchiefs.

'This is nothing,' said Dinshawji. 'One day I had to take the train around eleven o'clock. You ever did that?'

'You know I never take the train.'

'It's the time of *dubbawallas*. They are supposed to use only the luggage van, but some got in the passenger compartments.

72

Jam-packed, and what a smell of sweat. *Toba, toba!* I began to feel something wet on my shirt. And guess what it was. A *dubbawalla.* Standing over me, holding the railing. It was falling from his naked armpit: tapuck-tapuck-tapuck, his sweat. I said nicely, "Please move a little, my shirt is wetting, *meherbani.*" But no *kothaa,* as if I was not there. Then my brain really went. I shouted, "You! Are you animal or human, look what you are doing!" I got up to show him the wet. And guess what he did. Just take a guess.'

'What?'

'He turned and slipped into my seat! Insult to injury! What to do with such low-class people? No manners, no sense, nothing. And you know who is responsible for this attitude – that bastard Shiv Sena leader who worships Hitler and Mussolini. He and his "Maharashtra for Maharashtrians" nonsense. They won't stop till they have complete Maratha Raj.'

Dinshawji's narration had brought them to the main intersection of Flora Fountain, where the great traffic circle radiated five roads like giant pulsating tentacles. Cars were pulling out from inside the traffic island and recklessly leaping into the flow. The BEST buses, red and double-deckered, careened dangerously around the circle on their way to Colaba. Intrepid handcarts, fueled by muscle and bone, competed temerariously against the best that steel, petrol and vulcanized rubber threw in their paths. With the dead fountain at its still centre, the traffic circle lay like a great motionless wheel, while around it whirled the business of the city on its buzzing, humming, honking, complaining, screeching, rattling, banging, screaming, throbbing, rumbling, grumbling, sighing, never-ending journey through the metropolis.

Dinshawji and Gustad decided to walk down Vir Nariman Road. At the corner a pavement artist sat cross-legged beside his crayon drawings of gods and goddesses. He got up now and then to collect the coins left by devotees. Gustad pointed to the dry fountain. 'For the last twenty-four years, you can count on your fingers the number of days there was water.'

'Wait till the Marathas take over, then we will have real Gandoo Raj,' said Dinshawji. 'All they know is to have rallies at Shivaji Park, shout slogans, make threats, and change road names.' He suddenly worked himself into a real rage; there was genuine grief in his soul. 'Why change the names? *Saala* sisterfuckers! Hutatma

Chowk!' He spat out the words disgustedly. 'What is wrong with Flora Fountain?'

'Why worry about it? I say, if it keeps the Marathas happy, give them a few roads to rename. Keep them occupied. What's in a name?'

'No, Gustad.' Dinshawji was very serious. 'You are wrong. Names are so important. I grew up on Lamington Road. But it has disappeared, in its place is Dadasaheb Bhadkhamkar Marg. My school was on Carnac Road. Now suddenly it's on Lokmanya Tilak Marg. I live at Sleater Road. Soon that will also disappear. My whole life I have come to work at Flora Fountain. And one fine day the name changes. So what happens to the life I have lived? Was I living the wrong life, with all the wrong names? Will I get a second chance to live it all again, with these new names? Tell me what happens to my life. Rubbed out, just like that? Tell me!'

It occurred to Gustad he had been doing his friend a grave injustice all these years, regarding him merely as a joker. A friend too, yes, but a clown and joker none the less. 'You shouldn't let it bother you so much, Dinshu,' he said. Never having had to deal with a Dinshawji who spoke of metaphysical matters, the affectionate diminutive was the best he could do, and he wondered what else to say. But the next moment, a man on a Lambretta, travelling down Vir Nariman Road, was hit by a car going in the opposite direction, and the subject of names was forgotten.

'O my God!' said Dinshawji, as the man flew over the handlebars and landed beside the pavement, not too far from them. A trickle of blood oozed from his mouth. Pedestrians and shopkeepers rushed to his assistance. Dinshawji wanted to go, too, but Gustad could not budge. Overcome by nausea and dizziness, he held on to Dinshawji's arm.

Meanwhile, the car had driven away. People were asking if anyone saw the licence plate. The policeman from the traffic circle came to take charge. 'Six inches closer,' said Dinshawji, 'and his skull would have cracked like a coconut. Lucky he landed in the gutter. What is it, Gustad? Why so pale?'

Gustad swayed, and put his hand to his mouth as his insides heaved. Dinshawji quickly diagnosed the condition. 'Tut-tut. No lunch is the problem,' he chided. 'An empty stomach is not good to see blood. That's why soldiers are always fed well before a battle.'

He marched him off to the restaurant at the corner.

It was cooler inside. They selected a table under a fan, and Gustad wiped the cold sweat from his brow. 'Better?' asked Dinshawji. Gustad nodded. The tables were covered with glass under which a one-page menu lay open to scrutiny. The glass was smeared and blotchy, but it magnified the menu. Gustad rested his bare forearms on the table, enjoying the cool surface. The thuuck-thuck, thuuck-thuck, thuuck-thuck of the slow-turning ceiling fan was soothing. Pungent odours wafted streetwards from the kitchen. On the wall behind the cashier was a handwritten sign: *Spitting or Playing Satta Prohibited.* Another sign, also handwritten, said: *Trust in God – Rice Plate Always Ready.*

'What fun it would be to take Laurie Coutino to the upper level,' said Dinshawji, pointing to the air-conditioned mezzanine with private rooms. 'Money well spent.' The waiter came with a wet rag in one hand and two water glasses in the other. He held them by the rims, his fingers immersed. They lifted their arms off the table while he rubbed briskly. Now a disagreeable odour, sour and fusty, lingered over the table. Dinshawji ordered. 'One plate mutton samosas. With chutney. And two Nescafé.' He raised the glass to his lips. Then the waiter's fingerprints along the rim reminded him of the way it had been carried, and he lowered it without drinking. 'Well, Gustad. All these years I knew you, I did not know blood could make you sick.'

'Don't be silly, blood does not bother me.' Something in his voice warned that jokes would not be tolerated. 'It was a great shock. I know that man on the Lambretta. He helped me when I fell from the bus. You remember my accident?'

'Of course. But I thought it was that Major who –'

'Yes, yes, that was later. This man was the taxi-driver, who took care of me and Sohrab, brought us home. Did not even charge for it.' He looked up at the fan. 'For nine years I have waited to thank him. Then I see him flying through the air and smashing his head.' The coffees arrived, and the platter of samosas. 'Just the other night I was thinking about him. Coincidence? Or what? Today it was my turn to help him and I failed. It was like a test set by God, and I failed the test.'

'*Arré*, nonsense. It was not your fault that you became sick.' Dinshawji added three spoons of sugar to his coffee and bit into a samosa. 'Come on, eat, you will feel better.' He pulled Gustad's coffee over, added two spoons of sugar, stirred, and slid it back towards him. 'So what about the Major? You found out where he disappeared?' The samosa was crisp; he ate it noisily. A layer of oily crust unfurled from its apex and dropped into his saucer.

'No.'

'Maybe he ran away to rejoin the army,' joked Dinshawji, conveying the crusty segments to his mouth. 'You think there will be war with Pakistan?'

Gustad shrugged.

'Have you seen all the pictures in the newspaper? Bloody butchers, slaughtering left and right. And look at the whole world, completely relaxed, doing nothing. Where is *maader chod* America now? Not saying one word. Otherwise, if Russia even belches, America protests at the UN. Let Kosygin fart, and America moves a motion in the Security Council.'

Gustad laughed feebly.

'No one cares because these are poor Bengalis. And that *chootia* Nixon, licking his way up into Pakistan's arsehole.'

'That's true,' said Gustad. 'Pakistan is very important to America, because of Russia.'

'But why?'

Gustad illustrated the geopolitical reality. 'Look, this samosa plate is Russia. And next to it, my cup – Afghanistan. Very friendly with Russia, right? Now put your cup beside it, that's Pakistan. But what is south of Pakistan?'

'Nothing,' said Dinshawji. 'You need another cup?'

'No, nothing south of Pakistan, only the sea. And that's why America is so afraid. If Pakistan ever becomes Russia's friend, then Russia's road to the Indian Ocean is clear.'

'Ah,' said Dinshawji. 'And then America's two little *golaas* are in Russian hands.' He liked the all-clarifying testicular metaphor. 'To protect their soft *golaas*, they don't care even if six million Bengalis are murdered, long as Pakistan is kept happy.' The waiter left the bill on the table. 'My treat, my treat,' insisted Dinshawji, keeping the little scribbled chit in his outstretched arm to dodge Gustad's reach as they made their way to the cashier.

Outside, the sunlight was harsh, and the two quickened their steps. The lunch-hour had almost ended when they entered the bank building; Laurie Coutino was preparing to resume work. 'Cannot bear this agony, *yaar*,' whispered Dinshawji. 'What a body! Ahahaha! Sugar and cream! What fun it would be to give her a mutton injection.'

Mention of sweet cream made Gustad's hungry stomach rumble, reminding him of the saucer he used to have every morning, with crusty *broon* bread, as a boy. Mamma would skim it off the top of the milk, after it was boiled and cooled. Nowadays, the *bhaiya's* milk was of such poor quality that no amount of boiling and cooling could produce anything worthy of the name of cream.

iv

The stench was strong along the black wall as Gustad returned home from work. Ignorant people will never understand the wall is not a public latrine, he thought. He flung his hands about his head to ward off the flies and mosquitoes. And it wasn't even the mosquito season yet.

He opened the door with his latchkey and confronted Dilnavaz's stern look. 'One after the other, your sons make trouble,' she said.

'Now what?'

'Mr Rabadi was here. Complaining that Darius is after his daughter, that it looks very bad in the building.'

'My son after that idiot's ugly little fatty? Rubbish.'

The feud between Gustad and Mr Rabadi went back several years. Mr Rabadi once owned what he liked to consider a great slavering brute of a dog: Tiger, a cross between Alsatian and Labrador. Tiger was very friendly, and quite harmless, but Mr Rabadi had created a menacing aura around him. He dressed him in collars that sprouted threatening studs and spikes, took him for walks on the end of a massive chain instead of a regular leash, and armed himself with a stout stick, purportedly to discipline the brute should he get unruly. While the master brandished his daunting paraphernalia, the portly Tiger plodded placidly beside him, gentle and at peace with the world.

Early in the morning and late at night, Mr Rabadi used to walk Tiger in the compound. Tiger would scratch and sniff in search of a suitable spot, usually selecting Gustad's vinca and *subjo* bushes, of which he had grown quite fond. Being a large dog, his deposits were copious and rather malodorous, and sat in the bushes till the *kuchravwalli* came next morning to sweep the compound. Gustad repeatedly requested Mr Rabadi not to let the dog go in the bushes, but the latter countered that it was not possible to control a big, powerful animal like Tiger. And in any case, asked Mr Rabadi, how would Gustad feel if someone dragged him out of the WC when he wanted to go?

So the quarrels and retaliations continued. Once, at night, when Gustad saw the two outside in the bushes, he opened the window and emptied a bucket of cold water, drenching them both. 'Oh! So sorry,' he said with a straight face. 'I was just watering my plants.' Tiger seemed to enjoy the ducking. He barked and wagged his tail, but Mr Rabadi stormed off shouting threats into the night, while the sound of laughter floated earthwards from various windows in the building.

By the time he was seven, Tiger had grown obese and inactive. The short walk in the compound was enough to drain him, and it took much encouragement to get him huffing and puffing back up the stairs. One morning, however, something got into his head and he bolted. Despite his corpulence, he did seven tearing laps round the compound, one for each year of his short life, before Mr Rabadi was able to stop him. But the strain must have been excessive for Tiger's unaccustomed heart. He expired that day with the setting sun, and Mr Rabadi promptly made an appointment with Dustoorji Baria, to seek an explanation for the strange death of Tiger the dog.

Dustoorji Baria prayed all day at the fire-temple except for the two hours spent each morning dispensing advice to people like Mr Rabadi. Unburdened of his normal priestly duties because he was getting on in years, he used the spare time to cement his relationship with his contact Up There who, he claimed, was the source of his divinations.

Dustoorji Baria gave advice freely and unstintingly; no situation was out of his realm. In a matter of moments he revealed why Tiger's death had to come the way it did. But more importantly, he gave precise instructions to Mr Rabadi regarding his next dog: it must be white in colour, he said, and female, weighing no more than thirty pounds, standing no taller than two feet; and Mr Rabadi could give it any name so long as it began with the fourth letter of the alphabet. He also prescribed a *tandarosti* prayer for the dog's health, to be recited on certain days of the month.

Armed with Dustoorji Baria's specifications, Mr Rabadi went shopping. It was a great relief for everyone in Khodadad Building when Tiger's successor turned out to be a little white Pomeranian called Dimple. Gustad's bushes held no special charm for Dimple because, by this time, all of Darius's departed fishes and birds had thoroughly decomposed. But the resentment between the two men did not decrease or disappear.

'The dogwalla idiot will say anything,' said Gustad. 'Where is Darius now?'

'Still playing outside, I think.' Dilnavaz swatted with a newspaper. 'What a nuisance, so many flies.'

'That disgusting wall,' said Gustad. 'And after it's dark the mosquitoes will come. I saw flocks of them today.'

When Darius arrived at dinner-time, Gustad demanded to know exactly what had happened. 'Nothing!' said Darius indignantly. 'Sometimes I talk to Jasmine if she is there with my friends. I talk to everyone.'

'Listen. Her father is a crackpot. So just stay away. If she is with your friends, you don't join them.'

'That's not fair,' protested Darius. But the truth was, Jasmine was the only reason he saw his friends so often of late. The melting effect that her soft brown eyes had on him was delicious, a feeling he had never known.

'Fair or not fair, I don't care. I don't want the dogwalla idiot complaining again. Discussion over. Let's have dinner.'

But dinner was quite a challenge, with flies buzzing and hovering over the food, and mosquitoes dive-bombing everywhere. Roshan shrieked each time one landed in her plate, while Darius tested his reflexes by trying to catch them on the wing. 'Shut all the windows tight,' said Gustad, 'and we'll kill the ones inside.' Everyone was sweating in the heat before long, however, and the windows had to be opened.

Somehow they got through dinner. 'People keep pissing on the wall as if it was their father's lavatory,' said Gustad, slapping his neck and prying off a dead mosquito. In the medicine section of the sideboard he found a small half-used tube of Odomos. 'Have to buy another one tomorrow. The mosquitoes will make the Odomos manufacturers fat, that's all.' They shared what was left in the tube in order to get through the night.

i

Gustad inquired hopefully, every day, when he came home from work, if Jimmy had written. But a fortnight later, there was still no word from the Major about the favour he wanted. One evening, Roshan rushed to the door as she heard his key rattle. 'Daddy, can I have a rupee for school? Mother Claudiana said during assembly that tomorrow is the last day to join the raffle and the prize is a beautiful imported doll from Italy which is as tall as me with a long white wedding dress and she also has blue eyes.' She stopped to inhale.

He drew her to his side and hugged her. 'My sweet little *bakulyoo*! So much excitement? You will become like Tehmul-Lungraa, talking fastfastfast.'

'But can I have one rupee?'

'This is the problem with convent schools. Money, all the time, money for Mother Superior with her big wide posterior.'

'Tch-tch,' said Dilnavaz, 'not in front of her,' as Roshan giggled.

'Tell me, did Mother Claudiana say what she would do with the raffle money?'

'Yes,' said Roshan. 'She said half will go for the new school building. And half will help the refugees.'

'And do you know what "refugee" means?'

'Mother Claudiana told us. They are people who ran away from East Pakistan and came to India because the people from West Pakistan are killing them and burning all their homes.'

'OK. One rupee for you.' He opened his wallet. 'But remember, it does not mean you get the doll. It's a raffle.'

'Yes, yes, Daddy, Mother Claudiana explained. We will all have a number, and the girl whose number is picked will get the doll.' She folded the rupee, took the pencil-box from her school-bag, and tucked the rupee under the ruler. 'Daddy, why is West Pakistan killing the people in East Pakistan?'

Gustad undid his tie and smoothed it where the knot had been. 'Because it is wicked and selfish. East Pakistan is poor, they said to West, we are always hungry, please give us a fair share. But West said no. Then East said, in that case we don't want to work with you. So, as punishment, West Pakistan is killing and burning East Pakistan.'

'That is so mean,' said Roshan, 'and so sad for East.'

'Lot of meanness and sadness in this world.' He hung up his tie and unbuttoned his cuffs, then asked Dilnavaz for the mail. Nothing from Jimmy, but there was an envelope from an education trust fund. He added the application form to the ones that had collected over the last few weeks. 'Look at that,' he said bitterly, hitting them with the back of his hand. 'All the places I went to for the ungrateful boy.' He held up the forms one by one. 'Parsi Punchayet Education Fund. R. D. Sethna Trust. Tata Scholarships. Wadia Charities For Higher Studies. All of them I went to, touched my forehead, joined my hands, and said sir and madam and please and thank you a hundred times to make them promise scholarships. Now your Lord Lavender says he is not interested in IIT.'

Dilnavaz put the forms neatly together. 'Don't get upset, it will be all right. God is great.'

Every day after sunset she had described the seven clockwise circles over Sohrab's head. And still nothing. I must have been crazy to think there was even a chance. On the other hand, Sohrab and Gustad did not shout or argue like they used to, touch wood. Could that not be because – ?

'What he will do if he does not go to IIT, God knows.'

She shuffled the forms. 'He told you he wants to continue at his college.'

'And that is called doing something? A useless BA?'

So the days went by with Gustad sad and angered by his son's betrayal, anxious about Jimmy Bilimoria's letter that would not come, and maddened by the clouds of mosquitoes that came, without fail, after sunset. 'Ignorant swine pissing on the road should be shot on the spot!' he would say. Or, 'Blow up the bloody wall with dynamite, then where will they shit?' This last showed the extent of his frustration, for the wall was dear to him.

Years ago, when Major Bilimoria had first moved to Khodadad Building, when the water supply was generous and the milk from Parsi Dairy Farm was both creamy and affordable, there had been a surge of construction activity everywhere in the city. The neighbourhood of Khodadad Building was not spared either, and tall structures began going up around it. The first to be blotted out was the setting sun – an office building was erected on the west side. Although it was only six stories, that was enough, for Khodadad Building was but three, being short and wide: ten flats in a row, stacked three high, with five entrances and stairways for each adjacent set of flats.

Shortly afterwards, construction started to the east as well. It was clear to all thirty tenants that an era had ended. Fortunately, the work dragged on for over ten years because of cement shortages, labour problems, lack of equipment and, once, the collapse of an entire wing due to adulterated cement, resulting in the deaths of seven workers. Youngsters from Khodadad Building went to the construction site to gaze in awe at some dark blotch on the ground, and wondered if that was the spot where the seven had perished, where their lifeblood had oozed out. The delays provided respite for Khodadad Building, and in time there grew a gradual acceptance of the altered landscape.

With the increase in traffic and population, the black stone wall became more important than ever. It was the sole provider of privacy, especially for Jimmy and Gustad when they did their *kustis* at dawn. Over six feet high, the wall ran the length of the compound, sheltering them from non-Parsi eyes while they prayed with the glow spreading in the east.

But to hell with privacy, to hell with the wall, to hell with the stink, said Gustad. Tubes of Odomos were purchased, and the ointment rubbed on all exposed parts, though the mosquitoes continued to buzz and sting and madden. For some reason, the ointment worked least efficaciously for him. Half the night he spent scratching and swatting and cursing.

To take his mind off it, Dilnavaz told him about a childhood neighbour who was immune to mosquitoes. 'It's a true story,' she said. 'When he was a little boy, this man ate lots of mosquitoes. Purposely or by mistake, it is not sure. You know how children put everything in their mouths.' But from then on, mosquitoes stopped biting this boy. He grew up into a mosquito-proof man. The insects would sit on his skin, walk in his hair, crawl down his back, but never sting. Perhaps the ones he ate changed his blood and his odour, making him one of their own. Their buzzing and hovering no longer annoyed him either; he said it was like a serenade sung lovingly in his ears.

'So what are you suggesting?' said Gustad, slapping his face, shoulder and chest in quick succession. 'That we should stop using Odomos and start munching mosquitoes?'

Then the price of Odomos went up, along with the price of every necessity and luxury, from matchsticks to sanitary napkins. 'This refugee relief tax,' he said, 'is going to make all of us into refugees.'

As if these problems were not enough, Roshan and Darius began demanding old newspapers. They were needed at school, on account of the refugees. Teachers arranged fund-raising contests, and the newspapers were weighed every morning. The results were announced during assembly. The English-language papers were kept separate because they used a newsprint quality superior to the regional ones, and fetched more by the kilo.

Dilnavaz tried to explain the household budget to Roshan and Darius: the only way they could pay the paper bill every month was by selling the old papers to the *jaripuranawalla*. When they pleaded their teachers would be angry if they went empty-handed, Gustad agreed to let them have five *Jam-E-Jamshed*'s each.

Darius said he would prefer five *Times of India*'s because his friends would make fun of the Parsi *bawaji* newspapers. Gustad would have none of that. 'You should be proud of your heritage. Take the *Jam-E-Jamshed* or nothing at all.'

So Darius decided to go to the neighbours for newspaper donations. His father scoffed, 'No one will give you a scrap.' Since Darius insisted on trying, he set two conditions: 'Stay away from Miss Kutpitia and the dogwalla idiot. And if you get any papers, you must share them with your sister.'

ii

A week later, when Gustad came home and sat to remove his shoes, Dilnavaz beamingly held out a letter. He was tired after standing all the way on the bus, but his fatigue vanished. At last!

One shoe off and the other shoe on, he took the envelope. It was blank on the outside. Strange, he thought, opening it:

Dear Mr and Mrs Noble,

    It is my pleasure to inform you, on behalf of Mother Claudiana, that your daughter has won first prize in our Annual School Raffle.

    May I trouble you to make arrangements for taking delivery of the prize? The doll is quite big, and I fear little Roshan will be unable to manage on the school bus. It would be a pity if it was damaged. The doll is in my office (off the main parlour) and I would appreciate it if you could arrange transportation as soon as possible.

    Please accept our sincere thanks for participating in the raffle and making our fund-raising drive a success. When our new school building goes up, it will be due to the generous co-operation of parents like yourselves.

Yours truly,
Sister Constance
(Raffle Committee)

Gustad was unable to hide his disgust. 'I thought it was Jimmy's letter. You couldn't say something before giving it to me?'

'Why do you have to look so unhappy? Major wants to write, he will write. But for Roshan's sake change your face, she is so excited, you know she has never had a doll in her life.'

He heeded her advice as Roshan came running in from the compound. 'Daddy! Daddy! I won the doll!'

He swept her up in his arms. 'My doll has won a doll. But you are the prettier of the two, I am sure.'

'No! That doll is much prettier, she has blue eyes, and fair skin, so pink, and a lovely white dress!'

'Blue eyes and pink skin? Chhee! Who wants that?'

'Daddy! Don't say chhee to my doll. Can we go and bring her now? Sister Constance said you must come and –'

'Yes, I read the note. But it's late now, maybe tomorrow, I have half-day.'

'But school is closed on Saturday.'

'That's OK, Sister Constance will be there,' said Gustad, and Dilnavaz agreed. She suggested that he telephone Sister, though, just in case she was planning to go to the market or the cinema. After all, it was no longer like the old days when the nuns stayed inside all the time, cleaning and sewing and praying.

'Take thirty paise and go to Miss Kutpitia,' she said, for Miss Kutpitia was the sole tenant of Khodadad Building with the luxury of a telephone. The luxury was often a nuisance, however, because neighbours (including the ones who thought her mean and crazy) would request its use or ('please, with your permission Miss Kutpitia') give the number to relatives and friends to receive emergency messages.

Those who went to telephone were never allowed more than two steps inside: the coveted black instrument squatted on a little table beside the front door. None the less, everyone had strange tales to report. Long conversations could be heard from the landing outside, they said, and when the door opened, there was only Miss Kutpitia inside. She lived like a miser, a typical loose-screw eccentric, with dust and cobwebs everywhere, stacks of old newspapers piled to the ceiling, empty milk bottles in corners, curtains tattered, sofa cushions spilling their insides, and cracked light shades hanging from the ceiling like broken birds and bats. There was no shortage of money, they said, that much was certain. How else could she afford Parsi Dairy Farm milk and custom-catered meals from the Ratan Tata Institute?

The reason, they said, that no one was allowed inside – not ayah or *gunga* or friend or relative – was because she had a dire secret: the bodies of two deceased relatives she had had embalmed and preserved, years ago, instead of handing them over for proper disposal at the Tower of Silence. Others claimed this was rubbish; there were no preserved bodies, only the dry bones. Miss Kutpitia had gone to the funeral, and after the vultures had picked the bones clean inside the Tower, she had bribed some *nassasalers* to retrieve them before disintegration within the central well in lime and phosphorus. Miss Kutpitia naturally shielded those bones from the eyes of the world, they said, and were the reason for her secrecy and strange ways.

'OK,' said Gustad. 'I'll go. But first let Roshan ask if it is all right. Say to her, Auntie, can Daddy please come and use your phone?'

'I'm scared to go there,' said Roshan.

'Don't be silly,' said Dilnavaz. 'You want your prize or not?' The waiting doll easily conquered Roshan's fears.

Gustad got the pruning shears and cut a rose from his precious plant. 'Say to her, Daddy sent this for you.'

'Now what new *farus* is this?' said Dilnavaz. He ignored her with a wave of his hand which said he knew how to take care of these things.

Roshan returned with Miss Kutpitia's consent, then accompanied him to the telephone. Night was falling, but Tehmul-Lungraa was in the compound. He spied them from the other end. 'GustadGustadGustad.' He had a sheaf of pages under one arm, and clutched a ballpoint pen. 'GustadGustadwaitwaitwait.' He came as fast as his swaying-rolling walk would permit, waving a page. 'ImportantGustadveryveryimportant.'

'Not now, Tehmul,' said Gustad. 'I'm busy.' Probably some rubbish that had been foisted on the poor fellow, he assumed, remembering the time the Shiv Sena had recruited him to distribute racist pamphlets aimed against minorities in Bombay. They had promised him a Kwality Choc-O-Bar if he did a good job. Gustad, returning from the bank, saw him, on the verge of being beaten up by a group of outraged South Indians who worked in the office building down the road. Gustad tried to explain, but they perceived him as the enemy too, for defending a Shiv Sena agent. Fortunately, Inspector Bamji was driving home to Khodadad Building from the police station. He stopped his Landmaster when he saw Gustad and Tehmul surrounded, and blew his horn. The crowd glimpsed the uniform and started to disperse before Inspector Bamji stepped out. Afterwards, Gustad had cautioned Tehmul not to accept things from strangers.

He spoke patiently, gently, to allay Tehmul's perpetual agitation. 'Come back in half an hour. Then we will read what you have.' Somebody had to look after God's unfortunate ones.

'PleaseGustadplease. Readpetitionpleaseplease.' He followed them to Miss Kutpitia's stairway entrance. At the foot of the stairs he stopped, gazing forlornly after them.

On the second floor, the cover of the peephole slid up and an eye stared out unblinkingly. 'Gustad Noble, for telephone.' He spoke loudly to the eye, making dialling gestures with the right hand and holding the other like a receiver to his ear. The eye disappeared, and the sound of turning latches and withdrawing bolts echoed sharply in the corridor as the door opened.

Without much subtlety, he tried to peer off the hallway but the rooms were locked or in darkness. She reprimanded him sharply. 'The telephone is right over here.' From the bunch that hung around her neck, she selected a key and unlocked the clasp immobilizing the receiver. He dialled the convent's number off Sister Constance's note. On top of the telephone directory lay his rose. Miss Kutpitia waited while he made arrangements, and said, 'Thirty paise,' when he hung up.

'Of course, of course.' He dug placatingly in his pocket.

'And take your rose with you when you leave.'

'That's for –'

'All this pretence with a rose no one needs.' She narrowed her eyes. 'Just remember one thing.' A trembling finger, skinny and fragile, pointed. The sight of it made him remorseful. 'Old age and sorrow comes to everyone some day,' she said. Her words made the passing of time into a terrible curse.

He penitently held out the thirty paise. 'Thank you for letting me phone.' His face felt hot as he heard, ringing in his ears, his voice shouting at her on the night of the dinner party.

When Miss Kutpitia spoke again, the sharpness was absent. 'Wait, Roshan.' She hefted up a large pile of newspapers. 'I heard you want these for school.'

'Thank you,' said Roshan, staggering under the weight.

'And you will show me your dolly, when she comes home?' Roshan nodded. 'Bye-bye,' said Miss Kutpitia.

'Bye-bye,' said Roshan.

Gustad relieved her of the stack as they descended. Outside, Tehmul had disappeared, but the quiet of the compound was suddenly broken. They looked up and saw Cavasji at his second-floor window. 'To the Tatas You give so much! And nothing for me? To the Wadias You give, You keep on giving! You cannot hear my prayers? The pockets of the Camas only You will fill! We others don't need it, You think?'

Cavasji was in his late eighties. He had the habit of leaning his ancient white-maned head out the window to reprimand the sky and register his displeasure with the Almighty's grossly inequitable way of running the universe. Demand for Gustad's medicinal *subjo* from Cavasji's household was constant, for Cavasji suffered from hypertension. Every day, his daughter-in-law fastened a fresh sprig of the mint on a string around his neck. As long as it dangled green and protective, his blood-pressure would not explode like his rage.

The window slammed shut, cutting short the skyward progress of Cavasji's cosmic criticisms, and Gustad lowered his gaze. He glanced at the topmost page in Miss Kutpitia's yellowed, dusty stack of newspapers. A photograph under the headlines was fleetingly illumined by light from a neighbour's window. He saw the huge cloud of an explosion, and then the dateline. My God – 1945. Saving papers for this long?

iii

The next day, Tehmul-Lungraa shuffled up as Gustad stepped out to pay the taxi-driver. 'GustadGustadwaitpleasewait.' The sheaf of pages was again under his arm.

Gustad decided to use the stern approach; it was good for Tehmul once in a while. 'What is this nonsense? All the time in the compound? Do something useful. Sweep the floor, wash the dishes, help your brother.'

'GustadGustadnotwasting. Timeveryimportantpetitionplease. PleasereadGustadplease.'

'You were going to bring it last night. What happened?'

'ForgotforgotGustadforgot. Veryverysorryforgot.'

The taxi-driver got impatient. 'First remove your memsahib, then talk all day if you like.' Gustad reached into the rear. He cradled the doll in full bridal array, and it responded with a mama-ing bleat. The blue eyes rolled open and shut.

'Ohhhhh,' said Tehmul. 'Ohhhhh. Gustadpleasepleaseplease. CanItouchcanItouchpleasepleaseplease.'

'Fingers far away,' said Gustad sternly. 'Just looking is allowed. Or you will dirty the white-as-milk dress.'

Tehmul rubbed his palms briskly on his shirt front, then held them out. 'SeeGustadseeclean. Cleanverycleanhands. PleaseGustadpleasepleasepleaseletmetouch.' Gustad examined the hands. No harm in satisfying the poor fellow's urge.

'OK. But once only.' Tehmul was thrilled. He stepped closer and stood on tiptoe. His eyes shining, he gazed upon the doll's face and gently stroked the little fingers. 'Enough.'

'PleasepleaseGustadpleaseonemoretime.' This time he petted the cheek, very lightly, and paused. 'GustadGustad,' he said, and

88

petted it again. 'Ohhhhh.' His eyes filled with tears. He looked from the doll's sleeping face to Gustad's, and back, then burst into sobs and hobbled away. Gustad went inside, shaking his head sadly. He sat the doll in his armchair and adjusted the long wedding dress, straightened the tiara, smoothed the veil.

'Daddy!' Roshan came running from the back room and tried to lift the doll.

'What is this, no hug for me? Only for the doll?' She put her arms around him briefly, then ran back to the doll. 'Careful, it's too big for you to carry.'

'All these expensive white clothes,' said Dilnavaz fretfully. 'They will get dirty.'

'So silly, to make it that big,' said Gustad, as Roshan climbed on to the deep, commodious seat of her great-grandfather's chair and sat beside the doll. 'How can any child play with such a big doll?'

'Maybe when she grows a little bigger.'

'Bigger? Already she is past the age for dolls. And in the meantime what? It cannot stay here.'

Dilnavaz said that what was needed was some kind of showcase in which it could stand, for this doll was not a toy. 'For now,' she said, 'put it flat on the bottom shelf in my cupboard.' Roshan did not like the idea at all, even though they convinced her it was only temporary. The doll would not fit on the shelf, however, clad in its voluminous garments, especially the enormous hoop petticoat. It would have to be undressed. The doorbell rang while they debated. Dilnavaz looked through the peephole. 'It's that idiot. Send him away.'

Gustad opened the door, and saw that Tehmul's eyes were dry. 'GustadGustadpleaseimportantpetition.' He spied the doll on the chair. 'Ohhhh,' he said. 'Gustadpleasepleasetouchonceonly.'

'No!' snapped Roshan, to everyone's surprise.

'Roshan.' That was Gustad, warningly. Then to Tehmul, 'How much touching do you want? You touched it so much in the compound. And then you will start crying again.'

'Crying? Why crying?' asked Dilnavaz.

'PleaseGustadpleasenocrying. PromisepleasecanItouch.'

Gustad gave in, and Tehmul immediately slipped his hand under the veil. He looked into the doll's blue eyes, petted the cheek, stroked the red lipsticked lips and laughed gleefully.

'OK, Tehmul, that's enough. Let's read the petition.' Tehmul touched those smooth, cold cheeks of plaster one last time before Gustad led him firmly to the dining-table. The petition was the landlord's response to the municipality, detailing hardships that would be imposed on the tenants if the compound was narrowed. In a covering letter, the landlord urged the tenants to attest their signatures to the petition, thereby registering their objection to the scheme and joining forces to defeat the pernicious proposition.

Dilnavaz began undressing the doll. First she removed the veil and tiara, next the little bouquet tied cleverly to the hand to create the illusion that the doll's fingers were holding it. The pearl necklace, shoes, stockings, came off one by one, as Tehmul watched, fascinated. When she started to unbutton the dress, he became quite restless.

'OK Tehmul, pay attention,' said Gustad. 'You know what to do with this?' But Tehmul was engrossed in the undressing of the doll. Dilnavaz was down to the underclothing when a trickle of saliva started its descent from one corner of his mouth.

'Tehmul!' His dark red tongue, yellow where it was coated, arrested the drool.

'GustadGustadveryimportantpetitionIbrahimtoldme.'

'Ah, he was here collecting rents? And you understood what he told you?'

'Veryimportantpetitionveryimportantmustbesigned.'

Gustad counted the number of copies. Thirty. He made Tehmul sit with his back to the doll. 'Listen carefully,' he said, but was interrupted by the mail. He dropped the letters on the table; they fanned out in falling. The return address of one was a post office box in New Delhi. 'Listen very carefully.'

'ListeninglisteningGustadlisteningveryveryverycarefully.'

'Take this petition to all the flats, OK?'

He nodded vigorously. 'Allallallflatsallflats.'

'Give one copy to each. Tell them to read and sign. And speak slowly. Say one word. Then stop. Then say another word. Slowly. Slowly. OK?'

'YesyesyesGustadslowlyslowly. ThankyouthankyouGustad.' On the way out he hesitated. The doll was stripped, down to its anatomically vague pink plaster. 'Ohhhhh.' His nostrils flared; his mouth began to move in the manner of a ruminant's; a hand reached out.

'Tehmul!' He moved on. At the door he turned and looked yearningly once more before Gustad shut it after him. Dilnavaz shook her head and began folding the veil, the train, the dress, and collapsed the hoop petticoat.

'It's arrived,' said Gustad quietly.

Like him, she contained her excitement. 'You read it?'

'Let's finish this first.' He fetched the empty suitcase from the top of the cupboard. She dusted it and packed the clothes inside. Roshan watched forlornly as the doll was swaddled in an old sheet and shut away on the lowest shelf of her mother's cupboard.

iv

Gustad opened the envelope with the ivory paper-knife that had belonged to his grandmother. The handle was sculpted into a finely detailed figure of an elephant, and delicate floral designs ornamented the blunt side of the blade, making the whole an exquisitely fragile instrument. He did not use it very often: heirlooms were special, he felt, to be cherished and handed down, not used up like a box of cocoa or a bottle of hair oil. But this was a special letter:

> My dear Gustad,
>
> Thank you for your reply. Overjoyed to hear from you. It would be too much for me to bear if our friendship was lost. Could not write immediately because I was away, visiting the border zones. Not a pretty sight. Thought I had seen it all in my time. Especially in Kashmir, the handiwork of the North-West Frontier tribesmen. What I have seen now in my work with RAW is beyond words. (Did I mention in my last letter I am working for Research and Analysis Wing?) This new breed of Pakistani butchers is something else. I tell you, Gustad, everything in the papers these days about the atrocities is true.
>
> But let me get to the main point. All you have to do is go to Chor Bazaar between two and four in the afternoon, any one of the next three Fridays after receiving this letter. Look for a pavement bookstall. There are many in Chor Bazaar, so I have told my contact to display prominently a copy of the Complete Works of Shakespeare. And just to be absolutely certain if it is the right one, open the book to Othello, end of act I, scene iii, where Iago gives advice to Roderigo. The line: 'Put money in thy purse' will be underlined in red.
>
> My man will give you a parcel. Please take it home and follow the

instructions in the note inside. That's all. I am sure you will recognize the man, you met him once, many years ago. The Shakespeare thing is just in case he cannot be there and has to use his back-up.

Good luck, Gustad, and thank you again. If anything about all this seems strange to you, just trust me for now. One day, when I am back in Bombay, we will sit with a bottle of Hercules XXX and talk about it.

Your loving friend,
Jimmy

Gustad was smiling by the time he came to the end. Dilnavaz looked at him impatiently. 'What does he say? Is he coming back? He can stay with us for a few days, we can move the teapoy and put a mattress beside the sofa for him at night.'

'There goes your express train brain. No one is coming, he only wants me to pick up a parcel. In Chor Bazaar.'

'Why Chor Bazaar? That's not a nice place.'

'Don't be silly. Because the old name is still used doesn't mean it's full of thieves. Even foreign tourists go there nowadays.'

'But why not just mail the parcel here?'

'Take.' He held out the letter. 'Read for yourself.' He wondered who the contact was that he was supposed to have met.

'It all sounds very strange to me. This business of going to Chor Bazaar, and the Shakespeare book. And that, what was that name? Here it is – Research and Analysis Wing. I did not know Jimmy was also a scientist.'

He laughed. 'RAW is the Indian secret service. Jimmy is no scientist, he is a double-o-seven.'

Through the window, she saw Sohrab approach, and opened the door in anticipation. He's early today, she said to herself. Then to Gustad, 'So you are going to do it?'

'Yes, a friend cannot be let down, I am going to do it.'

'Going to do what?' asked Sohrab as he walked in.

Gustad ignored him, but she explained eagerly. 'Major Uncle's letter has come. Read, read, tell us what you think.'

'No one needs your son's advice,' said Gustad.

Sohrab glanced quickly down the page. 'I am surprised Major Uncle joined RAW.'

His words awakened his father's irritation and bitterness. 'Genius has spoken.'

Sohrab continued: 'Our wonderful Prime Minister uses RAW like a private police force, to do all her dirty work.'

'Don't talk rubbish again! Jimmy is involved in something top-secret about East Pakistan. Just like that, you say dirty work! God knows what newspaper you have been reading!' He switched on the light with vehemence. Dusk had a habit of descending swiftly on the paper-darkened room.

'But it's true. She sends men from RAW to spy on opposition parties, create trouble, start violence so the police can interfere. It's a well-known fact.'

'I read the papers and I know what goes on. Rumours and allegations all the time, and no proof!' Like a malarial fever his irritation started to rise.

'What about the chemical election? Only RAW could have done that. She made a real mockery of democracy.'

He snatched the letter from Sohrab's hand. 'Another rumour! What do you think, the election was a children's magic show? All this nonsense about chemically treated ballots, and crosses appearing and disappearing automatically! Mockery of democracy is that people are willing to believe rumours. Without proper evidence.'

'Lots of evidence was presented in court. Enough for the judges to send the case to trial. Why do you think she transferred them?' Sohrab appealed to his mother in frustration.

She listened helplessly as Gustad said that the blood in his brain was boiling again. Now the boy was pretending to be an expert on law and politics and RAW. The enemy was at the border, that Pakistani drunkard Yahya was cooking something in partnership with China, and fools like her son went around saying rubbish about the Prime Minister. He lifted a finger and pointed. 'Better that the genius shuts his mouth before I shut it for him. Before he falls off that high roof he has climbed.'

Sohrab rose in disgust to leave the room. 'Wait,' said Gustad, and asked Dilnavaz, 'Where are those application forms?'

She handed him the lot, grieving. How silly to have hope in green limes. Unless. Unless, as Miss Kutpitia said, something stronger is needed. If the evil, the darkness, is more powerful than she estimated.

Gustad gave the forms to Sohrab, and told him to count the

93

number of places he had been to for a worthless, ungrateful boy, the number of times he touched his forehead and folded his hands, and said 'sir' and 'madam' and 'please' and 'thank you very much'. 'Count the forms,' he said, 'then throw them away.'

'OK.' Sohrab took the forms and riffled them while walking down the narrow passage to the kitchen.

'Shameless dog.' Gritting his teeth, Gustad heard the rustle and soft slap of paper against the rusted rubbish-pail. Dilnavaz hurried to rescue the forms from the gloppy stuff at the bottom. She hid them in the arched recess, under the *choolavati*, where coal was stored in the old days before kerosene and gas. The green limes were also collecting there, waiting for a sea burial.

i

On Monday, after another torturous night of mosquitoes, Gustad left early for work. Morning was the best time to see the manager, who, according to the staff, was a very stiffly-starched fellow, and not merely because of the hard, unyielding collars he wore regardless of heat or humidity. But Mr Madon could stay cold and aloof, thought Gustad, and tie silly bows round his rigid neck, so long as he was impartial in matters regarding the bank. And if he wanted to keep his first name a secret, that, too, was Mr Madon's own pompous business.

Twenty-four years ago, when Gustad had just joined the bank, Mr Madon was an assistant manager. It was rumoured that the then manager had found Mr Madon's snuff habit quite abhorrent, and ordered him to stop, despite the fact that it was a twenty-two karat gold snuffbox into which Mr Madon dipped with the utmost style. One thing quickly led to another, and though no one knew exactly what happened, it was the manager who departed under a dark cloud. Mr Madon immediately ascended the coveted chair.

An old peon who now spent his time in an unhectic corner on a stool as rickety as his person, doing nothing more strenuous than drinking glasses of tea or fetching them for others, claimed to have once overheard the secret first name. The peon, Bhimsen, who never used his own surname (it was not certain if he even had one) would tell of the time when he had barged in accidentally while Mr Madon and the manager were locked in a pungent quarrel. Accidentally, for one of the two had slammed a ledger on the desk, triggering the bell that was Bhimsen's summons. But the moment of eavesdropping had occurred so many years ago that though Bhimsen remembered the event, he had forgotten the name.

Mr Madon's heart, however, was as kind as his habits were finicky. He was absurdly particular about the arrangement of things on his desk: the calendar, pen stand, paperweight, lamp, all had to be positioned just so. When old Bhimsen was low on funds, he would come to work early, unshaven, and displace things while dusting Mr Madon's office. Then the manager would arrive, notice the misalignment, and ring for Bhimsen. Invariably, the perfunctory scolding was followed by a gift of fifty paise for a shave at the downstairs barber, which Bhimsen pocketed before proceeding to the bathroom where his razor was hidden.

'Half-day off?' said Mr Madon to Gustad. 'This Friday?' He leaned forward and looked at the desk calendar through gold-rimmed glasses. 'Hmmm.' He raised his eyes over the gold rims and tapped the snuffbox. 'Why?' The snappiness might have seemed rude to someone not familiar with his mannerisms.

Gustad tore his thoughts away from the rich, warm lustre of Mr Madon's leather chair. He had envied the occupant while admiring the chair for twenty-four years, and for the first few, had even harboured an ambition to make it his own some day. Very soon, though, he realized there was no room for him in that seat, given the nepotic scheme of things everywhere and the ragged path his own life had taken. He had prepared his story for Mr Madon. 'Have to go to doctor. This leg, giving trouble again.'

Last night in bed, while trying out the various offerable excuses for shape, size and credibility, his first plan was to say that his little girl had to be taken to the doctor. But he quickly abandoned that pretext in mid-creation. Fear of the Almighty's wrath, or something like it, caused him to steer away from making imaginary illnesses befall his children. There was a heavenly host of angels, his grandmother had taught him long ago, who, from time to time, listened to the words and thoughts of mortals, and granted whatever was desired therein. Of course, this did not happen very often, she explained, because it was only a minor host, which was a blessing, considering how carelessly and unthinkingly most people used words. All the same, it was of the utmost necessity to keep one's thoughts good, lest, at the moment of a bad thought, an angel might listen and make it come to pass.

'What happened to your leg?' asked Mr Madon. The snuffbox was open now.

'Nothing new, sir, just my accident from nine years ago.' Rather me than my children. 'It is causing –'

'I remember your accident. You were on leave for fourteen weeks.' He looked at the calendar again. 'What time?'

'One o'clock, please.' Each time Mr Madon leaned forward, the collar cut deeply into his neck. How did he suffer that day after day? Starch was one thing, plywood another.

'And you will come back to the office after your appointment?' The snuffbox moved closer. His index finger and thumb, pinched together, hovered like an insect over the dark brown powder.

'Yes, sir, if it is before six o'clock, definitely, sir.'

'Fine,' snapped Mr Madon, and was echoed by the calendar snapping shut. The audience was over. Then, quicker than Gustad's eye could follow, a trace of snuff was lifted to the right nostril.

'Thank you very much, sir,' he said, and limped to the door. As he shut it behind him, the Officers' Enclave resounded with a series of explosive sneezes. He walked down the corridor, remembering to limp pronouncedly.

Till Friday afternoon he would have to continue the exaggeration. But it was easier than pretending a sore throat or fever. The latter was the riskiest, for Mr Madon had been known to reach out and feel foreheads with the back of a slyly solicitous hand. If he suspected a blatant fraud, he led the wretch to his sanctuary where, swift as quicksilver, he whipped out a clinical thermometer from his desk drawer and tucked the bulb under the patient's armpit. The seconds were counted off on his gold Rolex chronometer. Then he held the glistening glass stem for the anxious malingerer to peruse the glinting message. 'Congratulations,' Mr Madon would say, 'fever all gone,' and the patient, expressing his thanks to the mercurial miracle-worker, returned quite crushed to the teller's cage.

Wending his way to his department, Gustad saw Dinshawji clowning around Laurie Coutino's desk. In the last few weeks, Dinshawji had succeeded in getting acquainted with the new typist, and now visited her at least once a day. But it was not the Dinshawji of the canteen joke-sessions who performed before Laurie. Forsaking his natural flair for humour, he tried to be dashing and flamboyant, or swashbuckling and debonair. The result was a pitiful spectacle of cavorting and capering during which he looked so ludicrous that Gustad was embarrassed for his friend. He could not understand what had come over Dinshawji, making a *kutchoomber* of his self-respect. At times like these, he was glad that although the paths of their working day crisscrossed, Dinshawji did not officially come under the jurisdiction of the Savings Department. Or it would have fallen into Gustad's greasy, overflowing dishpan of duties to say something about the inappropriate behaviour.

Laurie's desk was underneath a framed public notice: *Entry of Firearms or Other Articles Capable of Being Used as Weapons of Offence Inside the Bank Is Strictly Prohibited.* Which made it worse, because Dinshawji's antics were in full view of the customers. With Laurie's stapler in his hand, he was prancing around, making swooping, coiling, writhing movements of his arm, darting at her with its metal jaws, then hissing and withdrawing. Gustad admired her patience and her svelte figure.

A fellow clerk pointed to the notice. 'Hey, Dinshu! Your snake is a deadly weapon! Not allowed in the bank!'

'Jealousy will get you nowhere!' replied Dinshawji, and everyone laughed. He noticed Gustad watching. 'Look, Gustad, look! Laurie is such a brave girl! Not scared of my big, naughty snake!'

She smiled politely. Beads of perspiration were visible on Dinshawji's bald pate as the snake grew adventurous, moving with abandon into regions of daring proximity. Finally she said, 'I have so much typing to do. This place is always very busy, no?'

Gustad took the opportunity to intervene. 'Come on, Dinshu. Let Laurie do her work. Or she won't get paid.' It was done good-humouredly, and Dinshawji was willing to relinquish the stapler and go with him.

He noticed Gustad limping more than usual. 'What happened to the leg?'

He welcomed the question. 'Same old thing. That hip giving trouble again. Just now I was with Madon, asking him for Friday half-day to see doctor.' When the castle was imaginary, a strong foundation was helpful. They were alone now. He said, 'Careful, Dinshu. You never know, she might complain.'

'Nonsense. She enjoys my jokes. Laugh and the world laughs with you.'

He tried a different tack. 'This is a head office operation, you know, not a small branch. Maybe Mr Madon does not want the world to laugh in the office.'

Dinshawji became indignant. 'Bodyline bowling? Watch it,

Gustad!' A foul whiff escaped his mouth, the familiar warning. Something was different this time, he was not just playing his usual Casanova role. Or perhaps he was playing it too well.

'Don't be silly,' said Gustad. 'You know I am not a management *chumcha*. Only telling you what I think. This snake thing might be too non-veg for a shy girl like Laurie.'

Dinshawji laughed scornfully. '*Arré*, Gustad, these Catholic girls are all hot-hot things. Listen, my school was in Dhobitalao area, almost hundred per cent *ma-ka-pao*. The things I would see, my eyeballs would fall out. Not like our Parsi girls with all their don't-touch-here and don't-feel-there fussiness. Everything they would open up. In every gully-gootchy, *yaar*, in the dark, or under the stairs, what-what went on.'

Gustad listened sceptically. 'Really?'

'But I am telling you, no,' said Dinshawji. 'Swear,' and he pinched the skin under his Adam's apple between thumb and finger. Then he winked, nudging him with his elbow. 'You clever bugger! I think I know the truth! Lining Laurie Coutino for yourself or what? Naughty boy!' Gustad smiled and accepted the attempt at reconciliation.

ii

He needed to get his bearings in the maze of narrow lanes and byways that was Chor Bazaar. Where to begin? And so many people everywhere – locals, tourists, foreigners, treasure hunters, antique collectors, junk dealers, browsers. Away from the crowds' swirls and eddies, he stopped by a little stall selling a variety of used sockets and rusty wrenches. There were other tools as well: pliers, hammers with rough wooden handles, screwdrivers, a planer, worn-out files. 'Very cheap. Best quality,' said the shopkeeper, picking up a hammer and swinging it demonstratively before offering it to Gustad who declined. The man gathered up a bunch of screwdrivers with multi-coloured wood and plastic handles. 'All types and sizes,' he said. 'Very cheap. Best quality,' and held them out like a posy.

Gustad shook his head. 'Why so crowded today? What is happening?'

'Bazaar is happening,' said the tool-seller. 'Friday is always the biggest bazaar day. After *namaaz* at the mosque.'

Then, among the tools, Gustad spied something familiar. Red, rectangular metal plates with holes along the borders. And green perforated strips. 'Is that a complete Meccano set?'

'Yes, yes,' said the man eagerly. In a trice he disentangled the pieces from the jumble of tools and placed them in Gustad's hands.

And as Gustad felt the metal under his fingers, smelled the metallic smell of rust from the little wheels and rods and clamps, the years fell away. He saw a little boy holding his father's hand and walking timidly down these lanes. His father talking enthusiastically about antiques and curios, pointing, describing, explaining. The shopkeepers calling, Mr Noble see this vase, you will like it, Mr Noble, very rare plate, saving it just for you, very cheap. And his father saying quietly in his ear, Listen to them, Gustad, listen to the thieves. And the little boy saying, Pappa, look, a Meccano set, such a big one. His father pleased, patting his head, saying, Yes, at least a number ten, sharp eyes you have, just like mine. Then his father bargaining, offering a preposterously low figure, haggling and dickering, are you crazy, walking away, come back sir, come back, yes, walking back, no, go to hell, please take, honest price, in God's name, don't blaspheme, final figure, truthfully sahab, OK you thief – and thus, the bargain sealed.

They took the Meccano home wrapped in newspaper, where, under Grandpa's supervision, Gustad made a wooden box for it, with sections to hold nuts and bolts, fishplates and right-angled brackets, discs and tyres, pulleys and flywheels, tie-rods and cranks, platforms and curved plates, all in their separate compartments. Afterwards, to the delight of the parents and grandparents, various models emerged from Gustad's room: fire-engine, crane, racing car, steamboat, double-decker bus, clock tower. His greatest triumph was a drawbridge that could be raised and lowered. Every time he completed something, Pappa would say, this boy will make the name of Noble great.

'Excuse me?' said the stall owner. 'You want to buy the Meccano?' He touched Gustad's shoulder.

'Oh,' said Gustad. 'No, no. Just looking.' He handed back the set, ran a hand through his hair and surveyed the series of lanes running perpendicular to the main road, all littered with a miscellany of goods, as though a convoy of lorries had symmetrically spilled their loads. Much of it was metal and glass, gleaming in the hot afternoon sun. Worthless junk lay side by side with valuable objects: chipped cups and saucers, Meissen ware, Sheffield cutlery, vases, brass lamps, Limoges porcelain, solder-repaired cooking utensils, ewers, wind-up gramophones with shining conical horns, silver trays, walking-sticks, weights and measures, cricket balls in varying stages of wear, refurbished cricket bats, umbrellas, crystal wineglasses.

He picked a lane at random and entered. An earwax remover was busy at the corner, his customer wincing occasionally as the slender silver instrument entered, explored, and emerged. Gustad stepped carefully around them. What would happen, he wondered, if someone jostled the man's arm while he was excavating? The thought made him shudder.

And what had become of the Meccano set? Lost with everything else, no doubt, during the bankruptcy. The word had the sound of a deadly virus, the way it had ravaged the family. All because of one proud man's stubbornness. Pappa putting off his operation for months, finally having to be rushed to hospital. And before going under the anaesthetic, handing charge of the business to his younger brother, against everyone's advice. For Pappa hated being given advice.

The brother had a formidable reputation for drink, and for frequenting the racecourse. The speed with which he mortgaged the assets and fuelled his vices was astonishing. Gustad's father emerged from hospital to the shambles of what had once been the finest bookstore in the country, and the family never recovered. The strain of it all sent his mother to hospital. And then, there was no money to pay for a private room and nurse, nor for Gustad's second-year college fees. His father called him to explain and fell to pieces. He wept and begged forgiveness for failing him. Gustad did not know what to say. Seeing his once invincible father behave in this broken manner did something strange to him. He began to utter scornful things, while silently swearing to himself, then and there, that he would never indulge in tears – not before anyone, nor in private, no matter what suffering or sorrow fell upon his shoulders; tears were useless, the weakness of women, and of men who allowed themselves to be broken.

It was a tough vow to make at seventeen, but he had kept it. True to his word, he did not cry for his mother when she lay in the general ward, uncomplaining and uncomprehending, nor when she died after her brief sojourn there. His father had gone so far as to ask him, 'Not one tear for Mamma?' and Gustad had stared back in stony silence, although his eyes were on fire. The final ignominy for his father was that he could not afford even the four days of prayer at the Tower of Silence.

One thing that gave Gustad some satisfaction during this time was the death of his dissolute uncle, whose liquor-marinated liver, scarred and cirrhotic, finally succumbed. But Gustad's father had insisted on looking after the worthless brother as best as his impoverished state permitted, which again raised Gustad's scorn.

He came to the corner of the lane without passing any bookstalls. How little it took, he thought, to wake up so many sleeping memories. '*Chumpee-maalis! Tayel-maalis!*' called a voice at his elbow. The man fell in step beside him, swinging his little rack of oils and unguents, a towel slung over his shoulder: 'Head *maalis*? Foot *maalis*?' Gustad shook his head and quickened his pace to discourage the roving masseur.

Working his way through the crowds, he came at last upon two bookstalls spread out on the pavement. Next to them, a barber clipped away vigorously, oily black locks descending hard and fast on to the white sheet. Gustad stopped, but the titles were in Hindi, Gujarati, or scripts he was unable to identify. 'No *Angrezi* books?' he asked a man who sat on a trunk.

'Oh yes, *Angrezi* books.' He rose and opened the lid of the trunk. Inside were issues of *Life* dating back to the early sixties, tattered Superman comics, *Reader's Digest*s, and *Filmfare*.

Gustad looked at his watch: past three. Had to hurry. Between two and four, Jimmy had written. The next lane had several stretches of book-strewn asphalt. Mainly paperbacks: westerns and romances. The remaining stalls were selling motorcar parts, glass jars, and wooden stools, so he turned the corner into the next lane and came upon a collection more respectable than any he had seen so far. A richly bound *Great Dialogues of Plato*, volume seven of the *Encyclopedia of Religion and Ethics*, edited by James Hastings, and Henry Gray's *Anatomy of the Human Body* caught his eye. He picked up each in turn and leafed through it.

'Very good books,' said the owner. 'Very difficult to find. Only in Chor Bazaar you can find.'

Gustad bestowed a studied disregard upon him, remembering his father's bargaining style. He badly wanted the three books. What a wonderful way to augment my small collection. How fine they will look in the bookcase that Sohrab and I . . . that I will build. 'How much?' He waved vaguely at the books.

'Different-different prices,' said the man.

Smart fellow. Going to be difficult. Gustad pointed at random to various titles to confuse him. When the performance was over, his three selections came to nine rupees. He tossed them back disinterestedly and turned to leave: 'Too much.'

'Why walk away? You say how much.'

'Four rupees.'

The man stooped to pick up the books, and Gustad thought he had won. 'Listen, *seth*, listen to me. Make a *boni* with me. Seven rupees.'

'Four rupees.'

The man pointed to the sky. 'By the light of the sun, in the shadow of the mosque, I tell you honestly my last price. Less than that I cannot go, or what will I feed my children?' He paused. 'Six rupees.'

Gustad paid. 'Are there others selling English books?'

'Oh yes. One new fellow came recently. Good stock. At the end of this same lane, keep walking straight.'

Gustad's arm encircled the three books. The mass of the weighty volumes began to tell reassuringly, and he felt less guilty about spending the money. What was six rupees for three classics. Must visit Chor Bazaar regularly from now on. One or two books at a time, and eventually I will have enough to fill that bookcase. It's all a family really needs. A small bookcaseful of the right books, and you are set for life.

At the corner, he saw a tea stall. Next to it was the bookstand. Scores of volumes were in wooden crates, with the spines facing up, and more were displayed on a plastic sheet upon the pavement. He went closer. At the rear, leaning against a packing crate, bound in red cloth with gold lettering, stood *The Complete Works of William Shakespeare.*

iii

He looked around nervously and peered inside the empty tea stall.

This corner of the lane was strangely quiet, compared to the chaos and hubbub he had wandered in for over an hour. A boy stood by the bookstand. Gustad bent to get the volume, but the others under his arm made it difficult. 'Which one?' the boy asked. He followed Gustad's finger, skipped nimbly over the front rows and retrieved it.

Gustad knew he was at the right place. He opened the volume to *Othello*, nevertheless, and turned to the end of act I. Yes, there they were, underlined in red, all five repetitions: 'Put money in thy purse.' Thorough as usual, was Jimmy.

He shut the book, looked up and saw a man with a white turban watching from the shadow of the tea stall. Gustad's pulse skipped a beat. He stepped out of the shadow, and now Gustad observed that the turban was not a turban at all, but a heavy bandage of white surgical gauze. And as the man approached, he recognized him despite the bound head. What a coincidence! He went forward eagerly, raising his hand in greeting.

'Mr Noble. It is good to see you again.' He was a tall man, as tall as Gustad, and clean-shaven.

Gustad shook his hand joyfully. 'You remember me? For nine years I have waited to thank you for your kindness. If I had known that you and Major Bilimoria –' What a tough man, he thought, to be up and about, hale and hearty after such a nasty crack on the head. The way he had flown over the handlebars of the Lambretta – made him shudder just to think of it.

'And how is the hip?'

'Almost good as new. Thanks to the Major, we went to Madhiwalla Bonesetter. A gifted man, performed a miracle for me. But,' puzzled Gustad, 'that day, when I had my accident – you and Major Bilimoria – in the taxi . . . you said nothing. You did not know him in those days?'

'Oh, I knew him. Sometimes, though, we have to pretend, because of the kind of work we do. Sometimes it is safer to be just a taxi-driver and passenger.'

Gustad understood. 'But it looks like you also had an accident recently?'

'Yes. Not exactly an accident. Come, let's have a little tea.' He led him inside.

'I am sorry, I know your face so clearly, but I have forgotten your name.'

'Ghulam Mohammed.'

'Now I remember. In the taxi you told my son.'

'And how is Sohrab?'

Gustad was amazed. 'You remember his name even?'

'Of course. How can I forget? Major Bilimoria has always talked to me about your family. Says it's like his own. Even before your accident I knew about you. Any friend of Bili Boy is a friend of mine.'

Gustad chuckled. 'Bili Boy. That's a nice name for Jimmy.'

'In the army all his friends called him Bili Boy.' Ghulam Mohammed paused, looking into the distance. 'We had some good times then. It's all very different now, in RAW.'

'You both joined RAW at the same time?'

'Yes. Wherever Bili Boy goes, I go. He will always have me with him. Least I can do for the man who saved my life in '48. Kashmir, you know.'

'He never told me about that.'

'Well, that's Bili Boy, never likes to boast. Yes, he came alone, looking for me after orders to retreat were given. Or I would be lying in the hills in seventeen separate pieces, nicely carved up by those tribesmen.' The tea arrived in glasses; Ghulam took one and sipped. 'That's the story. And that's why Bili Boy can always depend on me. His friend is my friend.'

Then Ghulam Mohammed put down his tea, leaning forward so his face was very close. 'And his enemy,' he said, almost in a whisper, 'will have to answer to me. Anyone who harms him, I will go after them, whatever it takes: knife, gun, my hands, my teeth.' He bared his clenched teeth and spoke through them.

Gustad moved back uneasily: 'He is lucky to have a friend like you.' Strange fellow. One instant warm and friendly, the next, chilling my spine. He reached for his tea. The hot, steaming liquid was murky through the transparent glass. Tea leaves, ground almost to a powder, rose to the top and returned to the bottom, riding the convection current. He braved a sip. It was bitter. 'But what about your accident?'

'Not an accident. They were aiming for my scooter.'

'Really?' Gustad could not help feeling a thrill of excitement. 'Who do you suspect, Pakistani spies?'

He laughed. 'Nothing so simple. Let's just say, occupational hazard.' He drank some more and pointed to Gustad's glass. 'You are not drinking?'

'Needs more sugar.' Ghulam Mohammed waved. A woman appeared from the back, listened, and returned with a bowl of sugar. Gustad added some and tasted. He nodded approvingly. 'You are leading a really dangerous life. But what about Jimmy, is he OK in Delhi?'

'We don't need to worry for Bili Boy. He is smarter than you and me put together.'

Gustad wanted to hear more about Jimmy, but knew from the tone of Ghulam's voice that no information would be forthcoming. 'What happened to your taxi, why were you on a scooter?'

'Sometimes taxi, sometimes scooter. In RAW you have to do all kinds of things. Today I am a bookseller. Tonight, I leave Bombay to do something else for one week.' He laughed and drained his glass of tea. 'OK. I better give you the parcel that Bili Boy sent.'

He stepped outside to the bookstand and opened a crate. Inside was a bulky package the size of a large overnight bag, wrapped in brown paper and tied with thick string looped at the top to form a handle. 'That's it,' said Ghulam Mohammed. He eyed Gustad's three volumes. 'But you have a lot to carry.'

Gustad was thinking the same; it would be tricky on the bus. 'This is yours,' he said, handing back the Complete Shakespeare. Then, 'Mr Mohammed, since today you are a bookseller, will you sell me that one?'

Ghulam laughed. 'Sure, sure.'

'How much?'

'For you, compliments of the management.'

'No, no, I must pay you something.'

'OK, the price is your friendship.'

'But that you already have.'

'In that case, you have already paid for the book.' They both laughed and shook hands heartily. 'Wait, I will get the boy to wrap all four in one parcel. Easier to carry that way.'

While the package was being prepared, Ghulam Mohammed wrote an address where Gustad could reach him. 'You know where it is?'

'House of Cages,' read Gustad. 'Yes, Dr Paymaster's dispensary is in the same locality. Our family doctor.'

'A man sells *paan* outside the House. Peerbhoy Paanwalla, he is called. You can leave a message with him any time.'

Gustad knew who Peerbhoy Paanwalla was. The man had been selling *paan* for as long as Dr Paymaster had practised medicine, perhaps longer. Childhood illnesses had enabled Gustad to observe Peerbhoy at his trade, during periodic visits to the dispensary for measles, chicken-pox, mumps, vaccinations and booster shots. And later, during his schooldays, Gustad sometimes used to sneak away from class with his friends and hang around the House of Cages to listen to Peerbhoy Paanwalla. Peerbhoy's droll histories of the place, about the encounters between the ladies of the House and their clientele, entertained his *paan*-buying customers endlessly.

'Very reliable friend,' said Ghulam. 'Any message will get to me from him.' The boy returned with the book parcel. Gustad noticed that it was tied in the same way as Jimmy's, with the clever handle of twine at the top.

After shaking hands again with Ghulam Mohammed, he retraced his steps through the lanes. The streets were gradually being cleared of tools, sockets, plates, lamps, dynamos, rugs, vases, utensils, watches, cameras, electric switches, stamp collections, transformers, magnets, and all the nameless, numberless assort-. ments that covered the asphalt. The earwax remover was still working, cleaning out the orifices of one final client. As Gustad passed them, the man extracted the long, thin, silver instrument and held it up for the customer to see. A glistening brown pellet, the size of a pea, was perched in the tiny scoop.

'*Sabaash!*' said the customer, proud of his ear's performance. Like an impresario, he turned the other ear to the instrument, eager to show what this one could produce. Gustad was tempted to stand and watch, but that would have been rude. Besides, Jimmy's package was quite heavy, the twine handles were cutting into his fingers.

The bus arrived, very crowded, and Gustad had a hard time of it. Negotiating with his loads, he accidentally prodded a woman in front of him. She turned with a stream of angry words. 'What is he doing, not watching where he is going. Coming on the bus with his big-big packets, poking disrespectfully, just like that. With so much luggage he should take a taxi, no? Why come on bus and harass us.

Poking and pushing us as if we are not buying a ticket and he is the only one buying a ticket . . .'

Gustad was in such good humour after meeting Ghulam Mohammed that it did not bother him. He bowed deeply to the woman and said, as elegantly as he could, 'I am so sorry, madam, for the inconvenience. Please accept my apology.' He smiled charmingly at her scowling face.

The woman, who had probably never been called madam or received so gallant a bow, was flattered and mollified. 'That is all right,' she said, cocking her head to one side, 'please don't mention.' During the rest of the journey they exchanged smiles whenever their eyes met. 'Bye-bye,' she said when her stop arrived, which was one before his.

*

Tehmul-Lungraa was waiting impatiently in the compound. 'GustadGustadletme. Gustadletmehelpletmecarry.'

He gladly handed over the book parcel. Tehmul was proud of the honour. 'Thank you,' said Gustad when they reached the door, and took it back before turning the key.

Tehmul raised a finger to his lips: 'Gustadquietveryquiet.'

'What?'

'QuietquietGustad. Notwellnotwellsleepingnotwell.'

'Who is not well?'

'RoshanRoshanRoshanissleepingRoshan. Nonoisequietnotwell.'
Gustad frowned and waved him away as he opened the door with his latchkey.

i

'You are waiting for sunset before doing it, like I told you?'

'Always,' said Dilnavaz.

Miss Kutpitia leaned against the wall, favouring one leg. 'Ohh! This rheumatic foot.' She pondered, her chin in her hand. 'There can be only one reason. The black spell has gone so deep and strong inside Sohrab, the lime cannot pull it out.'

'Are you sure?'

'Of course I am sure,' she said indignantly. 'Listen. When a spell goes very deep inside, it requires another human being to pull it out.'

'And how to do that?'

'There is a method. First, the same seven circles round his head. But instead of throwing the lime in the sea, cut it, squeeze the juice, and make someone – anyone – drink it. That person will pull the spell out of Sohrab.'

Simple enough, thought Dilnavaz. 'And where does the spell go afterwards?'

'Inside the one who drinks the juice.'

'That means someone else will have to suffer?'

'Yes. I myself don't like that.' Miss Kutpitia shrugged and continued: 'But it is the only way.'

'I cannot make an innocent person suffer, baba.' Assuming it works, of course. 'Who can I give the juice to, anyway?'

'We have someone right here in Khodadad Building.' The old woman smiled mysteriously.

'Who?'

'Tehmul-Lungraa, of course.'

'No, no!' Dilnavaz shrank from the idea; it seemed utterly callous to her. 'Maybe I should drink it myself. After all, Sohrab is my son.'

'You are talking rubbish.' Dilnavaz said nothing to that, struggling with the dilemma, and Miss Kutpitia continued. 'Listen, I am not a wicked person. You think I like to harm innocent people? But look at Tehmul. How much brains does he have to begin with?' Dilnavaz listened silently. 'So what difference will it make? Tehmul himself will not notice anything. What I say is, we should be happy that for the first time he will do something good for another person.'

'You really think so?'

'Would I say it otherwise?'

No, Miss Kutpitia would not say it unless she believed it. But what am I supposed to believe? 'OK, thank you. I will do it. And thank you also for giving the newspapers to Roshan. Her class now has highest collection for refugees.'

'Good,' said Miss Kutpitia, opening the door for her to leave.

In her kitchen, Dilnavaz took a lime from her hiding-place, sliced it and squeezed the juice into a glass. Then a spoonful of sugar. A pinch of salt. 'A spoonful of sugar helps the medicine go down, the medicine go down, the medicine go down . . .' She filled it with water and stirred, watching for Tehmul through the front window. Hope he comes before Gustad.

The compound was empty. 'Just a spoonful of sugar helps the medicine go down . . .' The pneumatic honking of the school bus sounded, and Roshan appeared in the compound. 'In a most delightful way . . .' Looking so unwell. Her cheeks pale and her brow dotted with perspiration. 'What's wrong? Are you feeling sick?'

Roshan nodded. 'I had to keep going for chhee-chhee.'

'How many times?'

She thought for a moment. 'Four. No, five times.'

'Change your clothes and lie down. I'll give you medicine.' When will this chronic diarrhoea leave my poor child alone? She went to fetch the pills. Roshan followed, and saw the glass of lime juice.

'What's this, Mummy?' She lowered her nose to smell.

'Stop!' Dilnavaz leapt to take it away.

'But what is it?'

'Nothing, nothing.' She tried to sound calm. 'Something for cooking. If you drink it your stomach will get worse.' Shivers went up and down her spine. Dada Ormuzd! What would have happened if my child swallowed the spell-filled lime juice? Even the thought is scary.

Roshan made a face at the pills. 'Brown ones again? They taste so bitter at the back of the throat.' She swallowed them expertly and went to bed.

Dilnavaz did not have to wait long, for Tehmul soon hobbled by the neem to look up into its branches. She beckoned through the open door. 'Come in.' He approached shyly. A hand went to his groin for the circular scratching. 'Don't do that, Tehmul.' Obedient, he removed the hand and stuck it in his armpit. 'Look what I have for you.'

He sniffed the glass of lime juice, watching a floating pip with great interest. 'Drink, drink,' she said. 'Very tasty.'

He took a tentative sip. His eyes lit up and he licked his lips. 'Veryveryverytasty.'

'Drink it all,' she encouraged. 'All for you.'

Tehmul tilted the glass and drained it without pause, then smacked his lips and burped. 'Verytastypleasemorepleaseplease.'

'No more.' It had been so easy. 'I will call you again when there is more, OK?'

He nodded eagerly. 'Callpleasecall. Morepleaseverytasty.'

'Now go.' He swivelled on his good leg and flung the other around, kicking the door. 'Shh,' said Dilnavaz. 'Quietly. Roshan is sleeping, she is not well.'

Tehmul put his finger over his lips. 'Quietquietquiet. Quiet-Roshansleepingquiet.' He shuffled carefully through the doorway and returned to the compound.

ii

The sound of the door latch drew Dilnavaz from the kitchen. 'What is all this *ghumsaan*? How much did Jimmy send?' she asked, nettled by the two bulky packages Gustad placed on the desk.

'*Ghumsaan*? Without even knowing what is inside? This is the Major's parcel. And these are four beautiful books. Art and wisdom and entertainment.'

She clapped a hand to her forehead. 'Books! More books! You are crazy. Where will you put? And don't repeat your nonsense about the bookcase you and Sohrab will build one day.'

'Calm down and leave it to me. But first listen to who I met at Chor Bazaar.'

She looked at him disbelievingly. 'You are not going to say Major Bilimoria.'

He laughed. 'No. But someone who knows him. And me.' He told her about his conversation with Ghulam in the tea stall.

'A hundred times I've said not to eat or drink from the roadside. You behave like a child sometimes.'

'I just had a few sips of tea, for the sake of courtesy.'

'One sip is enough to cause sickness.'

That reminded him. 'What is wrong with Roshan?'

'Stomach is a little bad,' she said. 'But who told you?'

'Tehmul-Lungraa. How did he find out?'

Oh no, she thought. What else did the idiot say? To her relief, Gustad did not wait for an answer. He had had evidence before of Tehmul's ability to ferret out information ahead of others with whole minds and bodies. He went to Roshan, and returned promptly. 'Asleep. Gave her medicine?'

'Two Entero-Vioform.'

'Good,' said Gustad. 'Will soon settle. And if motions are still loose after tomorrow, then Sulpha-Guanidine.' He always kept a ready supply of these pills at home. Before Roshan, it had been Darius who, till he was thirteen, constantly fell victim to bouts of diarrhoea. At first, Dilnavaz used to object to Gustad's dispensing the pills, insisting that their doctor must be consulted. She had faith in Dr Paymaster despite his shabby office with the board outside which read: Dr R. C. Lord, MBBS, MD Estd 1892. Dr Lord was the predecessor from whom Dr Paymaster had purchased the closed-down dispensary almost fifty years ago, but the latter didn't bother to change the board when he first started in practice because money was scarce. If his timid, new patients referred to him as Dr Lord, he did not pay much attention to it.

In a very short while, word spread of the young doctor who was wise and kind, humorous and considerate, who could cure half the sickness just by making the patient laugh it away. Dr Paymaster's practice began to grow. Soon there was a little money to spruce up the dispensary, buy a decent couch and chairs for the waiting area, and subscribe to the foreign medical journals he so badly wanted in order to keep up with new medicines and research. He was even able to afford a board with his own name.

But this last purchase was an enormous blunder.

The very next day, the dispensary was in turmoil. Patients were marching in and marching out, demanding to know who this Dr Paymaster was. What had happened to the funny, jovial Dr Lord? When would he return? They refused to listen to explanations or be examined by the young upstart. The few who risked treatment were unanimous in their verdict: the medicine did not cure as well as before; and the news spread.

In desperation, Dr Paymaster went to the sign-painter to bring back the old board. Fortunately, the sign-painter still had it, lying under a heap of discarded shingles and nameplates he was saving for firewood. It was rehung over the entrance, and the confusion vanished overnight.

And overnight, Dr Paymaster sorrowfully realized something they never taught in medical college: like any consumer product, a doctor's name was infinitely more important than his skills. In time, however, he grew reconciled to the fact and did not hold it against his patients, nor did he resent his predecessor's signboard. Besides, he felt, the year 1892 on it had a touch of dignity, and everything else that longevity and endurance suggested, especially in the doctoring business. And so, only a small inner circle of patients such as the Nobles knew his real name and addressed him correctly.

With the passing of years, Dr Paymaster became a grandfatherly individual, bald and round-faced, with the countenance of a sad clown. He still conducted the doctoring at his dispensary in his jesterly way: clowning with hypodermics or enemas, sniffing at jars of vile-smelling chemical compounds and making funny faces, or just keeping up an endless patter of amusing nonsense – things which would seem silly to a healthy person, but not to the sick and desperate and frightened, who were grateful for everything.

For all his buffoonery, however, Dr Paymaster was not a spontaneous individual. His act was carefully controlled, and outside the clinic he was solemn, even grim, when encountered in a non-professional capacity at the market or fire-temple. Once Gustad teased him, asking if his real name was not Dr Jekyll. Dr Paymaster replied, unamused, that it was the sick and the worried who needed gladdening, and since his supply of cheerfulness was not endless, it was wise to conserve it.

The Nobles never abandoned Dr Paymaster, nor did they lose faith in him. But over the years they began to accept his limitations. First they gave up on miracles, then on his ability to effect permanent cures, and finally, on the hope that he would recommend newer, more effective remedies he might come across during his perusal of medical journals from famous research centres abroad.

But Dr Paymaster's subscriptions to the foreign journals had run out a long time ago. Like everything else about the government, foreign exchange regulations involved convoluted rules and tortuous procedures, and Dr Paymaster decided to spare himself the agony. After Lal Bahadur Shastri became Prime Minister upon Nehru's death, it seemed for a while that the stagnant waters of government would at last be freshened and vitalized, despite the sceptics who said that such a short man would not be able to command respect on the world stage. Then along came the twenty-one-day war with Pakistan in which he fared much better than Nehru had in the war with China, and silenced the unbelievers. 'Short in height but tall in brains is our Lal Bahadur,' Dr Paymaster told all his patients, bending his knees and walking like a dwarf with an enema syringe in the bayonet-charge position. 'A pukka purgative he gave the Pakistanis.'

While the crowds cheered, Shastri boarded a plane for Tashkent where Kosygin had offered to negotiate a peace between India and Pakistan. The night the Tashkent Declaration was signed, Shastri died on Soviet soil, less than eighteen months after he became Prime Minister. Some said he had been killed by the Pakistanis, and others suspected a Russian plot. Some even claimed it was the new Prime Minister's supporters who poisoned Shastri, so that her father's dynastic-democratic dream could finally come true.

Whatever the truth, once again the government was in chaos. Streamlining foreign exchange regulations ranked very low on the country's list of priorities, and Dr Paymaster's subscriptions remained unrenewed. Thus, when it came to diarrhoea, the same two names, Entero-Vioform and Sulpha-Guanidine, kept appearing on his prescriptions.

These repetitive prescriptions made Dilnavaz finally agree with Gustad that it was a waste of time and money to go to the dispensary. Medicinal names now began to roll as trippingly off her tongue as they did his. The left-hand section of the sideboard filled up with the pills and syrups most in demand. There was Glycodin Terp Vasaka for sore throats, Zephrol and Benadryl for coughs, Aspro and Codopyrine for colds and fevers, Elkosin and Erithromycin for septic tonsils and inflamed throats, Sat-Isabgol for indigestion, Coramine for nausea, Veritoi for hypotension, Iodex for bruises, Burnol for minor cuts and burns, Privine for stuffed noses, a Yunani cure-all for external use (which looked like plain water but was meant to eradicate every ache and pain) and, of course, Entero-Vioform and Sulpha-Guanidine for diarrhoea. All these were on the first shelf. On the second, the collection was somewhat more eclectic.

As Dilnavaz's confidence grew, she began recommendations outside the family. When diarrhoea struck some of the more populous families in Khodadad Building, like the Pastakias, who had one toilet in their flat and five children ranging from four years to nine, the situation was critical. They would have to resort to the water-closets of accommodating neighbours, running up and down the stairs to find the nearest vacant ones. With so much movement and urgency, accidents were inevitable; then the air in the building changed, and Dilnavaz's nose told her that her medicinal advice would soon be indispensable.

She felt sorry for Mrs Pastakia – five children to look after, and on top of that, a father-in-law with high blood-pressure who shouted regularly at the sky. She would ask Mrs Pastakia for an accurate description of the symptoms if she had not already glimpsed them on the stairs or in the hallway, and advise, in her most confidence-inspiring, doctorly voice, 'Two Entero-Vioform, three times a day.' Or 'One Sulpha-Guanidine, powdered in a spoonful of sugared water,' because it was a pill with bulk and the taste of profoundly bitter chalk. Experience with Sohrab, Darius and Roshan had taught her what it took to dispatch various pills.

Gustad did not approve of these neighbourly prescriptions. Sooner or later, he said, free advice was seen as interference, and impoverished everyone involved. But Dilnavaz replied that if someone could save on doctor's bills, it was her duty to help.

She waited impatiently as Gustad unwrapped the parcel of books and wound the string evenly around the ball in his desk, tossing it from hand to hand. 'Don't you want to first see what Jimmy has sent?' she asked.

He smiled in a superior manner. 'All in good time.' He held up the Plato: 'What a beautiful book,' and passed it to her, doing likewise with the others. She looked at them perfunctorily and placed them on the desk. The Major's parcel was undone in the same meticulous manner. Under the brown paper was another wrapper, of black plastic, sealed firmly with tape. He tried to tear it, underestimating the strength of the tape, then rummaged in the desk for his penknife and noticed Tehmul outside the window, waving frantically. 'What is it?'

'Gustadpetitionpleasepetition. Signsignpetitionplease.'

He remembered. He had left it for a week on the sideboard. 'But did you go to all the neighbours?'

'GustadGustadyousignfirst. Gustadfirsttheneveryone. Seeseesee-Icansay. SeeseeseeGustadNoblesigned.' Tehmul was right, he knew, people were always afraid to be the first to get involved.

Tehmul received the signed petition as though it was a magnificent trophy, beaming all over his trusting face. 'GustadGustad. ThankyouGustad.' He shushed with his finger at his lips. 'Quietquietquiet. Nonoisenonoise.'

Gustad answered with a finger to his own lips, imitating the shushing sound. Tehmul was overjoyed at their conspiracy of silence. He burst out in a fit of giggling and left.

'Veryquietverytastyverytastyjuice.'

Smiling, Gustad resumed attacking the tape. 'Poor fellow. What will become of him if something happens to his brother, I don't know. Why was he saying very tasty juice?'

Dilnavaz shrugged. 'You people say poor fellow, but you keep encouraging his crazy ways. No one even helps to find him some simple job.' The wrapping litter reminded her of the earlier vexation. 'So much rubbish in this house. And you bring more books.'

He worked the penknife through the last piece of tape and unwound the black plastic which went around and across four times. She began clearing up: 'With so much junk I cannot clean or dust properly, and all that paper still on the windows and ventilators. God know when . . .'

The plastic slipped off and silenced her in mid-sentence. Stacks of currency notes, of hundred-rupee denomination, in neat bundles, now sat before their eyes. Crisp new bundles, with shiny staples, and a little encircling band of brown paper.

She found her voice first: 'What is it? I mean, what is the meaning of it? Can it be a mistake?'

He gaped at the pile of money. Gradually, his gaze took in the background, the window, the compound. Outside, in the dusky light, was a mouth as open as his own, but the face around that mouth was Tehmul's, looking in at the little hill of money.

That broke the spell for Gustad. With a roar, he slammed shut the window, cutting off from Tehmul's vision the sight that made his eyes shine as they had on the day he saw the naked doll.

iii

Gustad realized that shutting the window was not enough. He rushed to the door. Tehmul, still agape, had not moved from the spot. 'Come here!' Anger did not work; he tried again, soft and coaxing. 'Come, Tehmul, come. Let us talk.' But Tehmul began backing away fearfully. 'OK, OK,' said Gustad, and shut the penknife, making sure that Tehmul observed it sliding into his trouser pocket. 'See? No knife. Now you will come?'

'OK, OK Gustad. Comingcomingcoming.' He swayed and stumbled. 'GustadGustadchickenneck.' With one finger he traced a line across his throat from ear to ear, then shuddered. 'PleaseGustadpleasenotmyneck.'

'Don't be silly, Tehmul. Knife is for opening the package.' He smiled, and Tehmul smiled back. 'You remember what you saw through the window just now?'

Tehmul's frantic hands delineated hills and mounds in the air. 'Moneymoneymoneymoney. Somuchsomuchsomuchmoney.'

'Shh!' He regretted the question, and looked around to see if anyone was approaching. He brought his face close to Tehmul's, towering over him. 'Talk softly.'

Tehmul cringed, then remembered they were partners in silence and his face broke into a grin. He raised his finger to his lips. 'QuietquietGustad. Roshansleepingnonoise.'

'Yes. Good. Now listen.' Tehmul nodded vigorously. 'What you saw is our secret. Your secret and my secret. OK?'

'SecretsecretGustadsecret.'

'Yes. Secret means you must not tell anybody. Tell no one what you saw.'

'NoonenooneGustadnoone. Secretsecretsecret.'

117

'Yes.' He checked again – the compound was clear. 'And I will give you one rupee for keeping the secret.'

Tehmul's eyes lit up. 'YesyesGustadoneoneonerupeesecret.' He held out his hand while Gustad opened his wallet.

'Remember. Tell no one.' He handed over the note.

Tehmul examined the rupee, turned it over, held it up to the light, sniffed it. He grinned and began to scratch himself. 'Gustad-Gustadtwotwotworupees. Secretpleasetworupeessecret. Pleaseplease-please.'

Gustad brought the wallet out again. 'OK. Two rupees.' Then he put a hand on Tehmul's shoulder and said, in what he hoped was a menacing whisper, 'Two rupees for not telling. But you know what will happen if you forget? If you tell someone?'

Tehmul's grin vanished. He tried to squirm away, but the steel vice on his shoulder kept him from moving. He shook his head from side to side with all his might, as though the more forcefully he did it, the better he could appease Gustad.

'If you forget, I will catch you like this.' Gustad moved his hand from the shoulder to Tehmul's nape. 'Then I will take my knife.' With his free hand he fished for the penknife in his pocket, as Tehmul trembled in his grasp. 'I will open it.' He sprang the blade with his teeth. 'Like this.' The effect of gleaming white incisors on the shiny blade was sinister. 'And when it is open, I will cut your throat, like the *goaswalla* cut the chicken's. Like this.' He moved the knife across Tehmul's throat from ear to ear, keeping the blade safely covered with his index finger. Tehmul started to whimper, and his eyes filled with tears.

'Will you forget?' Tehmul shook his head. 'Will you tell anyone?' The head shook again, and Gustad snapped shut the penknife. 'Good. Now put the money in your pocket.' He released his neck.

Tehmul folded the two notes till they were down to a square inch. He pried off his right shoe and tucked the square into his sock, under the heel. 'GustadGustadthankyou. TworupeesGustad. Tworupeessecret.' He started backing away slowly.

Gustad watched him go, sorry that he had to frighten the poor fellow. But it was the only way, nothing remained in Tehmul's mind except fear. He forgot for a moment that the real problem still sat inside, on black plastic, upon his black desk.

The bundles of currency had tumbled when the plastic was unwrapped, and Dilnavaz restacked them. 'What trouble is Jimmy trying to bring down on our heads, God only knows. Sending all this money in a package, like onions and potatoes.' She began wrapping the plastic.

He stopped her. 'What are you doing?'

'Packing it. To send it back before there is any trouble.'

'What are you saying, what trouble? You don't even know whose money it is or what it is for.'

'Trouble does not come with a big advertisement giving reasons and explanations. It just comes. And with idiots like Tehmul-Lungraa watching and blabbing, it comes faster. Take the money to Chor Bazaar, baba, give it back to your taxi-driver.'

He dismantled the neat stacks. 'Not a word will pass from Tehmul's mouth. I have spoken to him.' He checked the first and last serial numbers in a few of the bundles: yes, there were a hundred notes to each. He counted the number of bundles: again a hundred. And yes, they were all in the hundred-rupee denomination. 'My God!' he whispered. 'Ten lakh rupees!'

The vast sum, spoken, served to renew her fears. 'Take it back, I beg you!' She reached for a corner of the plastic, but he snatched it from her.

'Take it back is the only thing stuck in your head. Makes you forget everything else.' He began to fan through each bundle. 'Jimmy said there would be a letter.'

She joined the search for the letter; the sooner they found it, the sooner this trouble could be sent back. 'Nice smell,' she said, bringing her nose closer to the bundle, to the pleasantly sharp odour of new banknotes.

'Very nice. For twenty-four years I have worked with this smell in my nose. Never get tired of it.' He paused to reflect. 'Wonderful thing is, five-rupee bundles smell different from ten-rupee bundles. Each amount has its own smell. I like this hundred-rupee smell the best.' He riffled, and a small folded paper fell out. 'Here it is!'

The letter was very short. They read it together:

Dear Gustad,

Thanks for going to Chor Bazaar. Now all that remains is to deposit the money in a bank account.

Since you are savings supervisor, it will be easy to avoid all the rules and regulations about large deposits. But don't worry, this is not black-market money, it is government money I am in charge of.

For the account, use the name of Mira Obili, and if you need an address, yours, or my post office box in Delhi. It does not matter, I trust you completely. The only reason for secrecy is that there are many people in our own government who would like to see my guerrilla operation fail. I will send more instructions when necessary.

> *Your loving friend,*
> *Jimmy*

PS Forget Iago's advice. Ten lakh won't fit in your purse. Good luck.

Gustad smiled. 'I was wondering why Jimmy chose that line.'

'Forget your wondering and help me pack this.'

'Don't you understand what this is about? He is trying to save the poor Bengalis being murdered by Pakistan.'

She was exasperated; sometimes he was like a little child, refusing to acknowledge reality. 'Surely by now it's gone into your brain that you cannot do this. Unless you want to do dangerous illegal things and lose your job!'

'What about Jimmy? Do you know what dangerous things he must be doing in RAW?' But even as he tried to imagine Jimmy's heroics, he knew she was right.

'For him, it is his job, he joined the secret service. Let him do all his secreting and servicing himself, without making us starve to death. That is what will happen if you ever lose your job, remember!' Then, wishing she had not uttered the words, she added in a subdued voice, *'Owaaryoo,'* and performed the God-forbid gestures, snapping her fingers three times while sweeping her hand outwards, away from Gustad, to ward off the bad vibrations of that dire possibility.

Reluctantly, he began putting the package together. She helped him stack the bundles. 'I gave him my word. In my letter I said he could rely on me.'

'It was before he told you what he wanted. To ask for a favour without telling what favour is not nice.' She brightened. 'I know.

Refuse it in a way that won't look bad. Write to him that you lost your bank job.' She caught herself too late and performed the *owaaryoo* again. 'No, no, don't say that, say you got transferred to some other department, different duties. So you cannot do deposits.'

He considered her plan and liked it. 'You are right. That way he won't feel I let him down.' He pushed the unfinished package to one side of the desk and wrote the letter.

There was a knock. Dilnavaz ran to the bedroom and came back with a sheet, throwing it over the heap of money before opening the door. It was only Sohrab. 'Thank God,' she said and removed the sheet.

'Oh boy!' said Sohrab. He started to laugh at the sight of so much money. 'Daddy robbed his bank?'

Gustad turned to Dilnavaz with a face black as thunder. 'Warn your son right now, I am in no mood for his senseless jokes.'

She knew it was not an empty ultimatum when he spoke in that tight low voice, as though his throat were choking. She cautioned Sohrab with a look. 'Money is from Major Uncle, but we are sending it back.' She handed him the note, as well as Gustad's reply. 'It's too risky for Daddy.'

He read it and said, 'How childish, this anagram.'

She did not know the word. 'Anagram?'

'You take a name, mix up the letters, and form a new name. Mira Obili is an anagram of Bilimoria.' Gustad pretended not to listen. He verified the letters mentally, however. Sohrab fingered the bundles of currency and toyed with the notes. 'Jimmy Uncle says this is government money, right? So let's spend it on all the things government is supposed to do. Wouldn't it be nice to fix the sewers in this area, install water tanks for everyone, repair the –'

Gustad sprang from his chair without warning and aimed a powerful slap at his face. 'Shameless!' Sohrab managed to deflect the blow. 'Talks like a crazy rabid dog! My own son!'

Shaken and bewildered, Sohrab turned to his mother. 'What's the matter with him these days? I just made a joke!'

'You know what the matter is,' she said quietly, and silenced him as he tried to say something. He left the room, trembling with emotion.

Gustad continued wrapping the package as though nothing had

happened. But he could not pretend for long. 'Changed so completely, it's hard to recognize him.' The disquiet about the strange parcel, disappointment with Jimmy's unseemly request, now mixed with the other, deeper sorrow, of filial disrespect and ingratitude. The pernicious mixture filled his mouth with wormwood. 'Who would have thought he would turn out like this?' He pulled on the twine and it snapped. She patiently knotted the pieces together.

'Every year at exam-time we fed him seven almonds at daybreak.' His bitterness turned to the past for nourishment. 'With holes in my shoes I went to work, so we could buy almonds to sharpen his brain. At two hundred rupees a kilo. And all wasted. All gone in the gutter-water.' She put her finger on the string to hold it in place while he tied the knots. 'Remember,' he said, loud enough for Sohrab to hear inside, 'I kicked him once to save his life, and I can kick him again. Out of my house, this time! Out of my life!'

She extricated her finger from the tightening knots in the nick of time. O God, no, please no! Please don't make him talk like this! The lime juice will work, I know. It must work, or what will happen?

'It is too late to go back today to Chor Bazaar,' she said. 'Will you go next Friday?'

He accepted the change of subject: 'No, not Chor Bazaar,' and explained the new arrangement. But Ghulam Mohammed had said he was leaving Bombay for a week. For the duration, they agreed to hide the money in the kitchen, in the coal storage alcove under the *choolavati*.

v

Darius returned from cricket practice just before dinner-time, and so did the mosquitoes. Gustad said not to dally, to shut the door before the nuisance filled the whole house. Darius dropped a bundle of newspapers to the floor, received another pile from someone in the compound, and said, 'Bye.'

'Who was that? Where did you get all the papers?' asked Gustad, swatting mosquitoes left and right.

'Jasmine. She gave me the papers,' he mumbled.

'Who? Say loudly, I cannot hear!'

He repeated the name fearfully, and Gustad was furious. 'I

warned you not to talk to the dogwalla idiot's daughter. What is that fat *padayri* up to, anyway, giving you newspapers from her house? If he comes here again to complain, even your mother won't be able to save you from the terrible punishment I will give.' Then Gustad's full attention was devoted to the mosquitoes. He suggested to Dilnavaz that she consider sewing mosquito nets for their beds. He could easily make a frame over which the nets would hang like a canopy. 'In Matheran,' he said, 'my father took the whole family for a vacation when I was very small, and the hotel had mosquito nets for every bed. It was wonderful, not a single bite all night long. Never in my life have I slept so beautifully. At dinner-time there was no nuisance either. The manager used to put a dish –'

He stopped, electrified by the memory. 'Yes! That's it! Quick get a big dish. The biggest we have.'

'For what?' asked Dilnavaz.

'Just bring it, I will show you.'

She ran to the kitchen and ran back. 'How about this German silver *thaali*? It's the biggest.'

'Perfect,' said Gustad, clearing the dining-table. He placed the round shallow dish under the bulb and filled it with water. When the surface grew still, the light bulb's reflection steadied and shone brightly, tantalizingly, under water. Then the mosquitoes started to dive in. One by one, abandoning the real bulb, they plunged, unswervingly suicidal in their attempts to reach the aqueous, insubstantial light. Somehow it was a greater attraction than the one hanging from the ceiling.

Gustad rubbed his hands in satisfaction. 'See? That's how the hotel manager in Matheran used to do it!' Even Dilnavaz watched gleefully as the vicious little insects were roundly vanquished.

'Now we can eat in peace,' said Gustad. 'Let them come. As many as want to. We have water enough for them all.' The surface was covered with little twitching brown specks. He emptied the *thaali* down the drain, refilled it from the drum, and was ready for dinner.

But Sohrab refused to leave the back room and come to table. Dilnavaz pleaded with him not to make matters worse. When she told Gustad, he said, 'What is it to me?'

They ate without Sohrab, while the mosquitoes continued to

dive, some with such force that they caused tiny splashes. For the first time in weeks, dinner concluded without a single mosquito falling in anyone's plate.

*

Two days later, while Gustad was at work, Sohrab packed a few of his things and left. He told his mother that he had made arrangements to live for a while with some college friends.

Dilnavaz refused to accept it, said no, it was impossible, this was his home. She started to weep. 'Your father wants the best for you, he is just upset right now. You cannot go away because of that.'

'I'm fed up with his threats and everything. I'm not a little boy he can hit and punish.' He promised to visit her once a week. When she saw nothing would change his mind, she wanted to know how long he would stay away. 'That depends on Daddy,' he said.

In the evening, she told Gustad what had happened. He hid his surprise and hurt, and blandly repeated his harsh words from two nights ago: 'What is it to me?'

NINE

i

Two things swirled and spun through Gustad's mind the following week while he said his prayers at dawn, swirled like the whirling wind-tossed leaves fallen in the compound: Roshan's enervating diarrhoea, and the forbidding package in the dingy *choolavati*. There was a third thing, but that, he pretended, did not exist.

The pills were powerless this time, both Entero-Vioform and the more potent Sulpha-Guanidine. Why? My poor child, missing school day after day. And Jimmy, of all people, asking me to do something criminal. The wind was strong, Gustad nudged and settled his black prayer cap. After last night's brief shower, a light-hearted reminder of the approaching monsoon, the vinca's leaves were green and fresh. He never ceased to wonder at the vinca's endurance, surviving in the small dusty patch, year after year, despite the fenders of cars that ripped and clawed at its stems, or children who tore wantonly at its blooms.

He crouched to pick up an empty Char Minar packet entangled in the branches and heard a car approach. Without looking over his shoulder he knew it was the Landmaster. Inspector Bamji's police duties called him out at all hours. Sometimes, if Gustad was up reading late at night and heard the car, he would smile and picture Soli Bamji rushing with his magnifying glass to find clues. People had named him Sherlock Bamji many years ago. Once, there had been a particularly gruesome murder, and Bamji, in the course of neighbourly chitchat, was asked how the police had solved the case. Without stopping to think, he replied, 'Elementary, my dear fellow.'

The inevitable followed. Everyone knew Soli was not a private investigator, nor did he smoke a pipe. And whereas the archetype was always elegantly correct in speech and diction, Bamji was fond of verbal colour and ribaldry. But he was tall and thin, with a gaunt face and high forehead, and this, together with those ill-chosen words, was sufficient glue to make the name stick permanently.

Bamji beeped and stopped. 'Hullo, bossie! Hope you said a prayer for me.'

'Of course,' said Gustad. 'Crime is calling you very early today?'

'Oh, nothing much. But seriously, bossie, it's going to be a big problem if the *maader chod* municipality cuts our compound in half. How will my car get in?' Good, thought Gustad, serve him right; Bamji was one of the worst offenders when it came to inflicting wounds on the vinca. 'You think the landlord's petition will be strong enough to bugger the municipal arses?'

'Who knows? My feeling is, when government wants something, it gets it, one way or another.'

Inspector Bamji adjusted the rearview mirror. 'If the bastards break down this wall, it will completely fuck up our privacy. You better pray every morning, bossie, for the good health of our wall.'

That reminded Gustad. 'Have you noticed how much it stinks, and all the mosquitoes?'

'Naturally, with the amount of piss that flows there. Every sisterfucker with a full bladder stops by the wall and pulls out his *lorri*.'

'Can't you use your authority to stop it?'

Inspector Bamji laughed. 'If the police tried to arrest every illegal pisser, we would have to double-triple our force.' He put the Landmaster in gear, waved goodbye, and hit the brakes again. 'Almost forgot. When that Tehmul-Lungraa came with the petition, he was talking some nonsense. About seeing a mountain of money in your flat.'

Gustad feigned laughter. 'How I wish.'

'I said to him, Scrambled Egg, don't tell lies. Then I gave him one solid *chamaat* across his face.'

'Poor fellow.'

'If his nonsense reaches the wrong ears, it would simply cause trouble. Temptation for bad elements. You don't want thieves to come looking for imaginary money.' He drove off.

That Tehmul. How to seal his drooling, babbling lips? Thankfully, Soli did not believe him, and others would also assume that Tehmul was gibbering as usual. Tonight I will warn him again.

When he is loitering in the compound.

But when Gustad returned from work in the evening, the compound was deserted. He came out thrice before dinner, and was thwarted each time by Tehmul's absence. He tried once more, after changing into his pyjamas. It was almost ten o'clock and still windy. Bits of newspaper and ice-cream wrappers had been blown into the bushes. Should I go up to his flat? But the older brother might be there.

A window opened noisily, and Gustad looked up. It was Cavasji, his white hair shining. He inspected the sky, cocking his head from side to side like an exotically plumaged bird. 'Monsoon is coming, so You be careful! Year after year, Your floods are washing away poor people's huts! Enough now! Where is Your fairness? Have You got any brains or not? Flood the Tatas this year! Flood the Birlas, flood the Mafatlals!'

When Cavasji was a young man once, he used to be called Cavas Calingar because he was round as a watermelon. But as he grew older he lost weight drastically, which made his height seem to increase, week by week, month by month. Tall he grew, and thin as an ancient prophet, as severe as a soothsayer, while his hair turned into a gleaming white halo. And the nickname was shed for ever, forgotten like a dry, shrivelled scab.

His daughter-in-law ran down the stairs to Gustad. 'Sorry to disturb you at night,' said Mrs Pastakia, 'but the *subjo* in Motta-Pappa's garland is very dry. Please can I get some more?'

Gustad fetched his pruning shears. He disliked Mrs Pastakia intensely, but tolerated her for the sake of Mr Pastakia and his old father. She was as inquisitive, short-tempered and manipulative as her husband was high-minded, upright and patient. One wondered how the two had managed to stay together so long and raise five children. Of course, Mrs Pastakia blamed all her shortcomings, including her occasional ill-treatment of old Cavasji, on her migraine. This invisible assailant struck at convenient intervals, sending her to bed for the day, where she suffered in silent agony and caught up on her back issues of *Eve's Weekly*, *Femina*, or *Filmfare*, and Mr Pastakia did the housework after coming home from office. He must have the soul of a saint, thought Gustad, to have endured her these many years.

'Congratulations,' said Mrs Pastakia.

'What?'

'I heard you won a big lottery. How nice!'

Gustad handed her the *subjo*, told her she was sadly mistaken, and bade her goodnight. He broke off some flower spikes and took them inside. Dilnavaz silently watched him separate the seeds to soak in water. She knew he had been prejudiced against the *subjo* because it was Miss Kutpitia who had identified and broadcast the plant's hidden powers. Now he gave the drink to Roshan, and she was grateful.

The next day was even windier. When Gustad returned from work, the compound's solitary tree was swaying wildly. 'Roshan is better, touch wood,' said Dilnavaz. '*Subjo* was a good idea.'

He nodded, pleased. And Ghulam Mohammed will be back this week, I can send him a message then. Ask him when and where I can return the parcel.

He prepared the note and sealed the envelope. Tomorrow he would deliver it to Peerbhoy Paanwalla.

ii

Seven days later he went again to the House of Cages to see if there was a reply. Peerbhoy, sitting cross-legged on a wooden box before his large brass tray, said Ghulambhai had collected his messages, and that was all.

Three weeks passed. No word came from Ghulam Mohammed, but the monsoon arrived in full force on a Friday night, preceded by a severe lightning storm. Gustad stepped outside to examine the sky. He looked to the west, at the clouds over the Arabian Sea, and sniffed the air: yes, it was getting closer. He sat awhile after the others had gone to bed, reading the newspaper. The refugees were still coming. The official count put the figure at four and a half million, but the reporter who had returned from the refugee camps said it was closer to seven. The prediction was for ten million by next month. Four and a half or seven or ten, thought Gustad, what difference. Too many to feed, in a country that cannot feed its own. Maybe the guerrillas will soon win. If only I could have helped Jimmy.

He checked the cricket scores, then abandoned the paper. He went to his desk and picked up the Plato. The new books had sat on one corner of the desk since they were brought home four Fridays ago. And my plans for the bookcase – turned to dust. Like everything else.

Around midnight the rain commenced. He heard the first drops chime against the panes. By the time he got to the window the rain became a downpour. The wind was sweeping it inside. He took a deep breath to savour the fresh moist earth fragrance, feeling great satisfaction, as though he had had a hand in the arrival of the monsoon. It will be good for my vinca bush. And I remembered to push the rose to the edge of the steps – it will get the rain slanting into the entrance.

He shut the window and sat again to read but could not concentrate. The advent of the monsoon was exciting – and it was always like this with the first big storm, even in his earliest memories, back to a time when the torrential rain coincided with the new school year, new classroom, new books, new friends. Sloshing in new raincoat and gumboots through flooded streets of floating bottle caps, empty cigarette packets, ice-cream sticks, torn shoes and slippers. Watching the normally vicious traffic paralysed and drowned, which had a marvellous sense of poetic justice about it. And the ever-present hope that it would rain so hard, school would be cancelled. Somehow, that childhood excitement blossoming with the first rain had never faded.

The thunder was sporadic now, but the crashing torrents made up for the noise. He could distinguish, within the large sound of water, the individual ones: on the asphalt strip in the centre of the compound, a flat, slapping noise; on the galvanized awnings, loud and reverberating, like a huge tin drum; against the windows, the soft tap-tap-tap of a shy visitor; and the biggest sound of all from the five rainspouts on the roof, which delivered their accumulations like cataracts plunging mightily to the ground. It was an orchestra in which he could separate the violins and violas, oboes and clarinets, timpani and bass drum.

He felt a twinge in his left hip. Yes, a sure sign the monsoon had arrived. It came again, the pain. Sharp enough to bring back the agonizing weeks I spent in bed. Jimmy, God bless him, had been such a help.

Like a baby Jimmy carried me inside the hall, in his arms. What a busy place it was, where Madhiwalla Bonesetter was holding his clinic – volunteers helping with patients, carrying them in on stretchers or pushing their wheelchairs, others preparing bandages. Two men were sorting various types of fragrant herbs and bark into little packages. The glue for their labels was homemade – a mucilage of flour and some foul ingredients, but the herbs and bark covered up the smell.

And at the centre of it all stood the great Bonesetter himself, surrounded by his loyal helpers. In appearance he was so ordinary, no one could have guessed what extraordinary powers he possessed. He wore a long white *duglo* and a prayer cap, resembling one of those men in charge of serving dinner at a Parsi wedding: the chief of the *buberchees*, who supervised everything from making the dinner announcements to dispatching busboys with washbowls, soap and hot water ewers down the rows of sated guests after the feasting ended.

But Madhiwalla was revered like a saint for his miraculous cures. He had saved shattered limbs, broken backs, cracked skulls – cases which even specialists and foreign-trained doctors (with degrees from famous universities in England and America) who worked in well-equipped hospitals had looked into, seen nothing worth saving, and shaken their heads despairingly. And Madhiwalla Bonesetter redeemed them all, all those hopeless cases, with no more than his two bare hands, his collection of herbs and bark, and, in the case of slipped discs, his right foot, with which he delivered a carefully controlled kick to the lumbar region that promptly restored the wayward disc.

No one knew exactly how he did what he did – magical was his footwork, magical the passes with his hands: feeling here, kneading there, bending, twisting, turning, and setting. Quickly, quietly, painlessly. Some said he first mesmerized the patient into not feeling pain. But those who had watched him closely knew this could not be, because he never bothered to look into the patient's eyes, which were often closed to begin with. The Bonesetter's eyes followed his hands: they could see deeply, piercingly, through skin, through fat, through muscle, bearing down to the very bone, down to where the damage was. It was no wonder that X-ray laboratories rued the day of his arrival.

Setting Gustad's fractured hip would be child's play for Madhiwalla, the onlookers had said. (Always, there were onlookers when the Bonesetter was in attendance: well-wishers, admirers, patients' relatives, the merely curious, all were welcome to watch – his skills and accomplishments were open to public scrutiny.) But it was a hideous and pitiful sight to behold, certainly not for the faint of heart. Broken bodies were everywhere – laid out on stretchers, bundled on the floor, collapsed in chairs, huddled in corners, their moans and shrieks filling the air. Splintered fibulae and tibiae that had ruptured the skin; a cracked humurus grotesquely twisting an elbow; the grisly consequences of a shattered femur – all these awaited their turn with the Bonesetter, awaited deliverance.

And Gustad, seeing and hearing such horrors as he had never witnessed before, soon forgot about the pain coursing through his own body. He wondered what could have inflicted such injuries on these people. In his grandfather's furniture workshop he had seen the occasional severed finger or pulped thumb, but nothing like this. It seemed to him that somewhere, in a factory, someone was churning out these extravagant mutilations with great deliberation.

But along with the agony suffusing their screams and groans, he also detected a strain of hope, hope such as had never been expressed in the words of the most eloquent. Hope pure and primal, that sprang unattended and uncluttered from the very blood of the patients, telling Gustad that redemption was now at hand.

Later, he tried to remember what Madhiwalla had done to set the fractured hip. But all he could recall was his foot being grasped and the leg swung in a peculiar way. From that moment, the pain decreased. The setting was complete, and the bone would be healed by repeated application of a paste made from the bark of a special tree. The Bonesetter wrote down a number for Jimmy. The two who were labelling packets with smelly glue matched the coded number and gave him what was prescribed. Madhiwalla never charged a paisa for his treatment, nor did he reveal the names of the trees and herbs, in order to keep the unscrupulous from commercially exploiting his knowledge at the expense of the ailing poor. The rich were welcome to make donations. His secrecy was applauded by all, but it was also a source of concern: Madhiwalla was an old man, what would happen when he was no more, if his knowledge died with him? It was believed, however, that he was secretly training a successor who would emerge and heal when the need became evident.

Dilnavaz made the paste according to the Bonesetter's prescription: by soaking the bark in water and grating it against the rough stone slab they used for grinding *masala*. It was hard work, making enough paste to coat the entire hip. And no sooner had she finished than it seemed to be time for the next application. Gustad felt guilty to see her sweat and pant over the stone, disregarding her back and shoulders that were screaming for rest, and with little Roshan also to take care of, just three months old. But for twelve weeks she gritted her teeth and carried on, refusing the help of outsiders, determined that her efforts alone would get her husband back on his feet.

A car door slammed in the rain. The Landmaster. What bad luck for Bamji, to have night duty on a night like this. But the car seemed to be idling outside. There was a burst of thunder, and then a splash. Was he having trouble with the engine? Gustad went to the window.

The car drove off before he could undo the clasp. The clock showed almost one. He opened the glass and stopped the pendulum with a finger, groping for the key. The shining stainless steel felt cool in his palm. He wound the clock and went to bed.

He slept fitfully, dreaming that he was walking to the bank from the Flora Fountain bus stop. Something struck him from behind. He turned and saw a hundred-rupee bundle at his feet. As he bent to pick it up, several more hit him, painfully hard. He asked his tormentors why. They refused to answer and continued their barrage. His spectacles were knocked off. 'Stop it!' he shouted. 'I'll complain to the police! I don't want your rubbish!' He flung back the money, but it returned as fast as he threw it. A police van drove up and Inspector Bamji stepped out. Gustad was overwhelmed by his good fortune. Bamji, however, without showing any sign of recognition, went to the crowd of money-throwers. 'Soli, listen to me, let me tell you what happened!' begged Gustad. Inspector Bamji, speaking in Marathi, to Gustad's astonishment, told him to shut up: '*Umcha* section *nai*.' 'He's a bank worker and he won't take our money,' the others complained, while Gustad watched, bewildered. 'Where are we to go if the bank refuses it?' 'No!' yelled Gustad, 'I cannot take it, I have no place to put it! What will – ' Out of nowhere appeared Mr Madon, his gold snuffbox in one hand and his Rolex chronometer in the other: 'What is going on, Noble?

Opening a branch operation on the pavement, hmm?' He crunched Gustad's fallen spectacles, brushed aside his explanations, and said it was past ten o'clock. 'I give you thirty seconds to be at your desk.' He held up the chronometer and said, 'On your mark. Get set. Go.' Gustad ran, elbowing his way through the crowds who were all headed in the other direction. How can that be, he wondered, it is not evening. As he reached the bank entrance, limping wildly, a sardonically smiling Mr Madon materialized in the doorway and showed him the chronometer: 'Thirty-four seconds. Sorry,' and handed him a termination notice. 'Please, Mr Madon, please. Give me one more chance, please, it was not my fault, I . . .'

Dilnavaz shook him by the shoulder: 'Gustad, you are dreaming. Gustad.' He grunted once, turned over, and slept soundly the rest of the night.

iii

A grey drizzle filled the melancholy dawn. Gustad could not go outside for prayers. He opened the window a little. Swollen with water, it resisted, moaning ominously. A flock of startled wet crows half scuttled and half flapped their way to a safe distance. Some flew into the branches of the neem. He looked at the sky and concluded there was at least another day's worth of rain in those clouds.

The bedraggled crows watched balefully, then began hopping back towards the window. By the time Gustad finished two cups of tea, the sky was lighter and the crows much louder. The shrieking and cawing finally got to Dilnavaz: 'What *is* going on in the compound?' He buttoned up his pyjama top, put on his rubber slippers and went out with an umbrella.

Crows had gathered from miles around. Besides the multitude teeming in the compound, there were clusters on the entrance steps, shaking out water from their feathers. Another disciplined black line perched along the awning. 'Psssss!' said Gustad, flapping his hands and stamping. He stepped around a large puddle outside the entrance, hissing and waving the open black umbrella like a giant crow. Then he saw the vinca bush, and his stomach turned. Bile-bittered tea rose to his mouth. The crows waited, wondering if they were about to lose their banquet. 'Dilnavaz!' he roared through the open window. 'Come quickly!'

133

She was outside within moments, her feet flopping in Darius's rain shoes which she had donned in her haste. 'O God!' she said, and covered her eyes. 'Why ask me to look at it? What good is it to make me sick in the morning?'

A headless bandicoot lay in a dark, red-brown puddle that had collected at the base of the vinca. The cleanly severed head was beside the body. Despite the progress made by the crows' beaks, it was immediately apparent that the cause of decapitation had been a sharp instrument of human design.

'This is the absolute limit!' said Gustad. Simultaneously, the two thought of Tehmul, of his fascination with rats. But Gustad said, 'No, I don't think so. Even if he did it, he would never throw it in the vinca. He would go to the municipality for his twenty-five paise.'

Dilnavaz was more anxious to be rid of the half-eaten carcass than to find the culprit. 'I'll call the *kuchrawalli* right now to sweep it away.'

'Who is it that hates my vinca so much?' wondered Gustad. 'And where was that bloody Gurkha, what kind of watchman is he?' Meanwhile, wakened by the noise, Darius came to the window. He was ordered to summon the Gurkha from the office building.

'But I am in my pyjamas,' said Darius.

'And what am I wearing, a wedding dress? Go right now!' Grumbling and frowning, Darius hurried through the compound, keeping well towards the inside so no one in the building saw him. Particularly the soft brown eyes of Jasmine Rabadi. If those melting, soft brown fourteen-year-old eyes were to spy him in his silly pyjamas, it would destroy his chances for ever, he was certain of that.

'You know where the Gurkha sleeps in the daytime?' Gustad called after him. 'In the little room, next to the lift.'

'Yes, yes, I know,' he said, scowling and jerking his head angrily. He returned shortly with the Gurkha, and conducted a cautious but dignified retreat.

The Gurkha was a small, bow-legged man whose calf muscles bulged powerfully, as did the sinews of his forearms. When he did his rounds at night for the office building next door, he included the compound of Khodadad Building in his circuit, and for his pains, each tenant paid him two rupees a month. He had not yet changed out of his uniform: khaki shirt and khaki short pants, with a khaki cap. Round his waist was the leather belt carrying the ceremonial Gurkha kukri: a short broad-bladed sword, and nestling near the hilt, two tiny daggers in their separate sheaths.

He saluted smartly, his almond-shaped Nepali eyes twinkling. 'Salaam, *seth*,' he said, and then to Dilnavaz, 'Salaam, *bai*. How is baby?' He was very fond of Roshan. Sometimes, when she was dropped off by the school bus across the road, he would, if he was awake, race over and escort her safely into the compound. Roshan called his family of daggers mummy-knife and the twins.

'Baby is all right,' said Dilnavaz.

'And what is the meaning of this?' said Gustad, pointing at the torn, crow-eaten bandicoot.

'*Arré baap*! What a very big rat!'

'That I know, thank you,' said Gustad. 'But who cut its head, who threw it in my flowers, that I don't know. And that is what *you* should know, because you are night-watching in the compound.' He paused. 'Or are you taking money from us for sleeping all night?'

'*Arré* no, *seth*. Not like that, never. Every night I walk here, banging my stick on the black wall. One o'clock, two o'clock, three o'clock. All night. But I heard nothing, saw nothing.'

Gustad looked at him disbelievingly. Dilnavaz said, from the corner of her mouth, using the Gujarati *asmai-kasmai* code so the Gurkha would not understand, 'M*as*m*ay*b*is*m*e* h*is*m*e* w*as*m*as* sl*eas*m*e*p*is*m*ing* b*eas*m*e*c*aus*m*a*use *is*m*it* w*as*m*as* r*ais*m*ai*n*is*m*ing*.'

So Gustad tried a different approach to the cross-examination. 'How do you make rounds when it rains?'

The Gurkha smiled, revealing perfect neem-nurtured white teeth. 'Office people have given me very good long raincoat. I wear that when rain is falling. And plastic cap, with flaps to cover the ears, which go like this, over the cheeks, then there is a button under the chin which –'

'OK, OK. So last night you walked in your long raincoat and cap. But I heard no banging of stick.'

'O *seth*, so much noise of rain and thunder, how can you hear my stick?'

Gustad had to concede the point. 'But from now on, I want to hear the stick, rain or no rain. Bang harder, bang under my

135

window, but bang, I am warning you. I must hear it every night.'
The Gurkha nodded vigorously to placate him, sensing that the
matter was almost concluded. 'And on your way out, tell the
kuchrawalli to clean this at once.'

The crows began converging again when Gustad and Dilnavaz
turned to go in. He decided to stay. 'You will be late for work,' said
Dilnavaz. 'I'll wait till *kuchrawalli* comes.'

'It's OK. There is enough time.' By now, he was feeling bad about
having made her view the bandicoot's torn entrails.

iv

It rained through Saturday but stopped during the night. Gustad
lay awake to hear the Gurkha's nightstick. By and by, the reassuring knock of wood against stone started to punctuate and measure
out the hours of darkness. Satisfied that the scolding had worked,
he turned over and fell asleep.

Sunday dawned with a clear sky. Gustad was wakened by a ray
of light entering through a corner of ventilator glass where the
blackout paper had come untacked. No rain, he thought. Prayers in
the compound? It will still be soft and squelchy. Better stay inside,
took too long to clean mud from slippers yesterday.

He sat up, stretched, and rubbed his eyes. The cawing started.
Just one crow at first, as though it was calling the faithful to prayer,
but soon joined by others, fervent recruits who lent their eager
throats. Then the sound grew frantic, the entire assembly raising its
voice in a strident chorus of ecstasy, and Gustad bounded out of
bed.

The mattress lurched wildly in reaction, waking Dilnavaz. 'What
happened?'

He pointed to the window. 'You can't hear?' The cawing made
her sit up; she reached for her duster-coat.

The morning was windless, and the rain puddles were still as
glass, reflecting a cloudless sky. But only a few feet away, by the
vinca bush, was a different world. The competition was rough, and
the crows, in their urgency, were flapping and pecking, sometimes
attacking one another. A few withdrew now and then to gird their
loins, then re-entered the fray. It was hard to see what was in the
bush because of the frenetic, fluttering multitude of grey-black
wings and feathers.

'Aaaaahhh!' roared Gustad, waving his arms wildly. 'Caaaah! Caaaah!' Like a black curtain lifting, the crows ascended and settled some distance away. He saw the dead cat: brown with patches of white, its eyelids not shut, and the eyes still unpecked. The mouth was slightly open, displaying a pink tongue. Wet whiskers skimmed the water surface. Were it not for the fact that the cat's head, like the rat's the morning before, was severed from its body, it would have seemed that the creature was thirsty, lapping water from the puddle. Gustad realized with detachment that this was how he used to imagine the sliced-off heads of dragons in his childhood *kusti* fantasies: intact, looking as if they were capable of continuing a separate existence.

'Don't look,' he said to Dilnavaz, too late. She retched twice, then was in control. 'What is going on, I'd like to know,' he said quietly. 'Darius!'

Rubbing the sleep out of his eyes, Darius came. 'What?'

'Quick, call the Gurkha.'

'I'm not going again in my pyjamas. Yesterday also you sent me,' he protested. 'It's not fair.' Besides, the map of his teenage lust, charted during the night, was printed starchily on the fabric over one thigh.

'Don't argue with me! Go right now!'

'I'm not going!' Darius yelled back, and returned to bed.

Gustad said to his receding figure, 'You will have an unhappy life if you take your rascal runaway brother's example and shout at your father! Remember that!'

'Never mind,' said Dilnavaz. 'I will go.'

'It's shameful. How quickly he learns the bad things. But wait. Tehmul! My friend! Tehmul!' It was the first time Gustad had seen him since that Friday after Chor Bazaar. He waved and smiled, coaxing him close, making no sudden moves lest he flee.

Tehmul approached shyly, scratching cautiously, and smiled at Dilnavaz. 'GustadGustad.'

'How are you, Tehmul? You enjoyed the rain?' Tehmul spied the beheaded cat and burst out laughing. He edged closer and bent to pick up the head.

'No, no, Tehmul, don't touch. It's bad, it bites.' Tehmul drew back, grinning. 'Will you do something for me? You know the Gurkha who sits in the building next door? Go and call him, say that Noble *seth* wants to see you.'

Tehmul scattered the crows with his hobble. When he returned with the Gurkha, he imitated the salute by slapping his forehead briskly with his palm. Gustad kept a blank face and pointed silently to the bush.

'O Bhagwan,' said the Gurkha. 'What is happening?'

'Why ask Him? You should know. What time did you fall asleep? Two o'clock? Three o'clock?'

'*Arré*, Noble *seth*, all night I was walking.'

'Lies!' shouted Gustad, pointing to the evidence. 'This will not do! Enough is enough!' Windows opened and curious faces peered out. 'Yesterday a rat with head chopped off. Today a cat! Somebody is doing mischief, and what are you doing? Not doing your job! What comes tomorrow? Dog? Cow? Elephant?'

'R-a-tratc-a-tcat,' said Tehmul. 'R-a-tratc-a-tcat.'

'I am warning you, I will stop your pay. And all the neighbours also, I will tell them to stop, that you are a useless watchman.'

The Gurkha panicked. 'O *seth*, your feet I will touch, don't do that. How will I put food in my children's stomach? First-class night-watching I do, first-class. One more chance, please.'

'R-a-tratc-a-tcatd-o-gdog.'

Inspector Bamji's Landmaster turned into the compound and halted by the foursome. 'What's going on, bossie?'

Glad to see a figure of authority, Gustad appealed to him. 'Soli. You say what you think. Somebody is throwing dead animals in my flowers. And this wonderful watchman does not know anything about it.'

The Gurkha stood at attention while Inspector Bamji got out and took a good look at the cat. Tehmul imitated the inspector's hands-behind-back pose. 'R-a-tratc-a-tcat,' he said.

Inspector Bamji smiled a small, grim smile. It was a professional smile. 'Somebody's knife is very sharp. A very skilful knife. Anyone has a grudge against you, wants to harass you?'

Gustad shook his head, and looked at Dilnavaz. She reinforced his denial with hers, adding, 'Sometimes people kill animals to do magic. They use the blood in *puja* or something.'

'That's true,' said Inspector Bamji. 'All kinds of lunatics out there. I think whoever is doing this, for whatever reason, is throwing it here because it's a quiet, convenient place for disposal – in the bush, hidden by the black wall. If our watchman did some watching, the problem would be over.'

'One more chance, *seth*,' said the Gurkha. 'Only one more.'

Inspector Bamji winked at Gustad and nodded. 'OK,' he said. 'One more chance. But no more sleeping.'

'Never on duty, *seth*,' he said. 'Swear on Bhagwan's name.'

'Useless,' said Bamji, meaning the fellow would never admit to it, and got into his car. The Gurkha threw a salute in his direction, then presented one each to Dilnavaz and Gustad. Tehmul saluted the Gurkha. 'C-a-tcatr-a-trat,' he said, and began following him to the gate. Halfway there, he switched to a yellow butterfly, stumbling to keep up as it glided gracefully before him. Sometimes it paused upon a blade of grass till Tehmul all but reached it.

Gustad watched him sadly, remembering Sohrab. With his butterfly net fashioned from a broken badminton racquet. On Sunday mornings I used to take him to Hanging Gardens.

Dilnavaz knew what he was thinking. 'He will come back,' she said. 'Shall I tell him you want him to come back?'

He pretended not to understand. 'Who are you talking of?'

'Sohrab. Shall I tell him you want him back?'

'Tell him what you like. I don't care.' She said nothing. It would have to wait till they were inside, for down the compound came Mr and Mrs Rabadi with Dimple.

The two were muttering between them, deliberately loud. 'People think we are stupid. Fooling our little girl, saying fund-raising for refugees. God knows where the money goes.'

Gustad said to Dilnavaz, so the Rabadis could hear, 'I cannot bother replying to every lunatic ranting by the roadside.' When they were gone, he added, 'Would not be surprised if that idiot was responsible for the cat and the rat.'

'No, no,' she said, clinging to common sense. 'He does not like us, true, but I don't think he would do this.'

And she was right. What Gustad found next morning put everyone in the building beyond suspicion.

Up bright and early, he was determined to say his prayers in the compound. A good way to start the new week. The Gurkha was by the vinca bush. 'Salaam, *seth*. No dead animals in the flowers, not even an insect.' His relief was great.

Gustad inspected for himself. He circled round, and noticed a piece of paper, curiously positioned. It was folded and inserted snugly between two adjacent branches, as though in a letter-holder.

Not something done by a random breeze. He pulled it out. There were two innocuous lines written in pencil, a child's rhyme that made the colour drain from his face:

Bilimoria chaaval chorya
Daando lai nay marva dorya.

The Gurkha looked over Gustad's shoulder. 'What language is that, *seth*?' Since he had been forgiven, it would not hurt to solidify things with a little friendliness, he felt.

'Gujarati,' said Gustad shortly, wishing he would leave.

'You can read Gujarati?'

'Yes, it's my mother tongue.'

'What does it say, these funny-shaped letters?'

'It says: "Stole the rice of Bilimoria, we'll take a stick and then we'll beat ya."'

'Means what?'

'It's something that children sing when playing. One child runs, the others try to catch him.'

'Oh,' said the Gurkha. 'Very nice. Salaam *seth*, time to sleep now.'

Gustad went inside with the rhyming couplet. There was no doubt now. No doubt at all about the meaning of the two decapitated carcasses. The message was clear.

TEN

i

Gustad sat with the scrap of paper before him, seeing not words or calligraphy, but an incomprehensible betrayal, feeling that some vital part of him had been crushed to nothingness. Years of friendship swam before his eyes and filled the piece of paper; it taunted him, mocked him, turned into a gigantic canvas of lies and deceit. What kind of world is this, and what kind of men, who can behave in such fashion?

He knew he must arise and go now to the coal-storage alcove. Jimmy Bilimoria had trapped him, robbed him of volition. If I could let the rotten world go by, spend the rest of life in this chair. Grandpa's chair, that used to sit with the black desk in the furniture workshop. What a wonderful world, amid the din of hammering and sawing, the scent of sawdust and sweat and polish. And in Pappa's bookstore, with its own special sounds and smells, the seductive rustle of turning pages, the timeless fragrance of fine paper, the ancient leather-bound volumes in those six enormous book-filled rooms, where even the air had a special quality, as in a temple or mausoleum. Time and the world stretched endlessly then, before the bad days came and everything shrank. And this is how my father must have felt, in this very chair, after the profligate brother had destroyed all, after the bankruptcy, when there was nothing left. He, too, must have wanted not to move from this chair, just let what remained of time and the shrunken world go by.

'You finished praying already?' Dilnavaz emerged from the kitchen, her water chores done. The front and sleeves of her nightgown were soaked as usual. 'Is the vinca all right today?'

'The vinca is all right,' he said. But the habit of twenty-one years, to share all with her, was too powerful. He could not block out of his voice or keep from his face the brokenness he felt.

'What has happened?' He handed her the scrap of paper. 'O my God,' she said feebly. 'Jimmy . . .?' Gustad nodded.

'But to us . . .?' He nodded again.

'Maybe the taxi-driver . . .?'

'That makes no difference.'

She squeezed her wet nightgown desperately, as though wringing out the water would rid them of this painful treachery. 'I think we should take the money and go to the police, tell them the whole story,' she said. 'How you got it, what you were told to do with it, the rat and the cat, everything.' Proposing righteous action lent her strength as she tried to fill the empty space inside with spurious baggage. 'Give them Major Bilimoria's address also – the post office box number. He can burn in *jhaanum*! He and his national security!' The ruthless edge creeping into her voice surprised her. 'Or tell Inspector Bamji. Then he can look after everything.'

Gustad shook his head. He resisted the temptation to join in her way of filling the emptiness. 'You don't understand. Inspector Bamji, the police, have no power over RAW.' He shook his head again. 'We are dealing with heartless people – poisonous snakes. It could have been Roshan and Darius instead of the bandicoot and cat.' He crumpled the note vehemently, tossing it from him with loathing. 'I suppose we should be grateful to Jimmy for that.'

'*Owaaryoo*,' she said, frantically snapping her fingers towards the door, outwards, away from her home and family.

'There is only one thing to do.' He removed his prayer cap. She followed him to the kitchen where he got on his knees by the *choolavati* and pulled out the package. He opened a corner of it, enough to insert a hand, and withdrew one bundle. She watched anxiously, hoping he would not notice the limes or Sohrab's application forms. 'Don't worry,' he said, 'I will be careful. After twenty-four years I know the place and procedures inside out. One bundle for deposit every day. Ten thousand rupees. More than that will be suspicious.'

'But it means to finish the whole parcel will take . . .'

'One hundred days. I will write and tell him that's the best I can do.' He put the money in his briefcase. 'I don't understand this world any more. First, your son destroys our hopes. Now this rascal. Like a brother I looked upon him. What a world of wickedness it has become.'

The air-raid siren started its keening lament as Gustad got off the bus at Flora Fountain. Like some gigantic bird of mourning in the skies above the city, circling, diving and wheeling, it drowned the traffic noises. Ten o'clock already, he thought. Should have been at my desk by now.

For several weeks the threnodic siren had been wailing every morning at exactly ten o'clock: a full three-minute warning, followed by the monotonic all-clear. There had never been any official announcement, so the public assumed that in preparation for war with Pakistan, the government was checking to see if the air-raid sirens were in working order. Others believed it was to familiarize people with the dirge-like sound – they would not panic when an air raid was signalled in the middle of the night if they became acquainted with the wail during their daylight hours. Cynics said it seemed more like a conspiracy, because if the Pakistanis ever wanted to carry out a successful bombing raid, all they had to do was make sure they reached the skies overhead at exactly ten o'clock. But perhaps the most wishful explanation was that the siren sounded to let people check their watches and synchronize them at ten, as part of the pre-war effort to improve punctuality and productivity in government offices.

With ten thousand rupees in his briefcase, Gustad was tense as he walked with the crowds flowing from bus stops to office buildings. Some scuffling suddenly broke out at the corner, and he tightened his grip on the briefcase. That was the corner where the pavement artist worked with his crayons. Gustad had often stopped to admire his portraits of gods and saints.

The pavement artist did not restrict himself to any single religion – one day it was elephant-headed Ganesh, giver of wisdom and success; next day, it could be Christ hanging on the cross; and the office crowds blissfully tossed coins upon the pictures. The artist had chosen his spot well. He sat cross-legged and gathered the wealth descending from on high. Pedestrians were careful with this square of pavement, this hallowed ground, as long as it displayed the deity of the day. They flowed around the image like a stream of ants, diverging and converging automatically around it.

Sometimes, accidents happened, like the one this morning. Someone stumbled and left his shoe-print on the drawing. Justice was dispensed summarily. The crowd refused to let the hapless fellow depart till he had made reparation by leaving a generous gift for the god. Then the artist took his crayon and touched up the god's shoe-printed face. And watching the artist, Gustad suddenly perceived a mutually beneficial proposal in the holy drawings. But he was late for office; he would speak to him one evening when it was not so crowded.

The all-clear faded as he climbed the steps into the bank. He stopped by Dinshawji's desk and whispered, 'Meet me outside in the lunch break. Very urgent.' Dinshawji nodded, pleased. He loved secret compacts, privileged information, clandestine conversations, though they came his way far less often than he would have wished.

Three months had gone by since Dinshawji's return to work after his illness, and it troubled Gustad that he still looked as pale and washed out as on the night of Roshan's birthday. But how jolly his conduct had been, singing and laughing and joking as if he hadn't a worry in the world. Who would have thought he had recently come out of hospital then? Gustad wondered if he was taking proper treatment. Anyway, hats off to Dinshu, for going on so cheerfully, without ever complaining.

At one o'clock they met as arranged. Dinshawji had cauliflower sandwiches, and noticing Gustad's briefcase, asked, 'You also got dry lunch today?'

'No, no, something more important than food. I will have to miss my lunch.' Whereupon Dinshawji insisted that he have a cauliflower sandwich. He accepted.

'And what is the urgent matter?'

Gustad told him everything, from Major Bilimoria's letter about the guerrilla operation, to the money package from Ghulam Mohammed. But he left out the bandicoot, the cat, and the rhyming couplet. Scaring Dinshawji would not help anything. Instead, he emphasized how their effort would help the Mukti Bahini's liberation struggle, which Dinshawji found very stimulating. The more enthusiastic he became, the worse Gustad felt at having to dupe his sick friend who was now willing to break banking laws and jeopardize his job and pension this close to retirement.

At the end, Dinshawji was so inspired, he would have agreed to join a bayonet charge against Pakistani soldiers. 'Absolutely, *yaar*.

One hundred per cent we will help the Major. Somebody has to do something about those bastard butchers.'

'That's how I feel,' said Gustad.

'And did you read today about what America is doing?' Gustad confessed he hadn't read the papers for the last three days. '*Arré*, CIA bastards are up to their usual anus-fingering tactics. Provoking more killings and atrocities.'

'Why?'

'It's obvious, *yaar*. If there is more terror, then more refugees will come to India. Right? And bigger problems for us – feeding and clothing them. Which means we will have to go to war with Pakistan, to solve the refugee problem.'

'Right.'

'Then, the CIA plan is for America to support Pakistan. So India will lose the war, and Indira will lose the next election, because everyone will blame her only for the defeat. And that is exactly what America wants. They don't like her being friends with Russia, you see. Makes Nixon shit, lying awake in bed and thinking about it. His house is white, but his pyjamas become brown every night.'

Gustad laughed and opened the briefcase. 'Time to get back,' he said, and handed over the money in a plain envelope.

Dinshawji wrapped his empty lunch bag around the bundle. 'Yes. Have to be on the dot these days. Remember the olden times? When they took attendance just by counting the jackets hanging on the chairs? No bloody time-book nonsense. *Arré*, they trusted you in those days to do your work. Honour system. Jacket on the chair, hat on the rack, and you could go out for one-two hours, take a nap. Nobody minded. Age of honour and trust is gone for ever now.'

Gustad checked if the lunch-boxes were still there. 'You go in,' he said. 'I'm just coming.' He scribbled a note to Dilnavaz: 'My Dearest, Everything OK with Mira Obili. But did not have time to eat. Love & xxx.' The aroma from the tiffin box intrigued his nose. He pulled out the rack of containers and saw pumpkin *buryani*. His mouth watered. Never mind. I can taste some tonight. And Darius will have the rest – he always likes rice at night, in addition to the main dish with bread. Needs it, too, with all the body-building.

It was three minutes to two. Dinshawji was utilizing the time around Laurie Coutino's desk. He had become bolder over the

145

weeks, egged on by the other men. Now he was insisting that she dance with him. He sang 'Rock Around the Clock', prancing about her chair as she sat demurely, waiting for the lunch-hour to end. The beads of sweat were not long in appearing on his bald pate. He wiggled and jiggled, waved his arms, threw back his head, and added a pelvic thrust occasionally.

Gustad looked on, concerned that trapped under the spell of his pitiful clownery, Dinshawji would forget the crucial envelope on Laurie's desk. Day by day, he worried more and more for Dinshawji, for his ailing appearance, the face like parchment, the eyes battling to hide pain. But he also despaired about his embarrassing ways and the demise of his self-respect. Dinshawji was acting with abandon, in the manner of a medieval plague victim who knew that since the last vestige of hope was lost, clinging to dignity and other precious luxuries affordable by the healthy was of little use.

He stopped singing, and said, panting, 'Laurie, Laurie, one day I must introduce you to my little *lorri*.' She smiled, ignorant of the Parsi slang for the male member. 'Oh yes,' he continued, 'you will love to play with my sweet *lorri*. What fun we will have together.'

She nodded pleasantly, and around them, the men guffawed, digging one another in the ribs. Gustad winced. Dinshawji was going too far. But Laurie smiled again, a little puzzled, and uncovered her typewriter.

People drifted reluctantly to their work-stations as the minute hand crept upwards. Gustad followed Dinshawji, and reminded him as they parted, 'Don't forget. Bring me the deposit slip for initialling.'

The scheme worked perfectly. 'All done without a hitch,' said Dinshawji next day at lunch. Gustad passed him the second bundle, and suggested slowing down with Laurie while they were helping the Major, just to avoid drawing attention.

'On the contrary, *yaar*, on the contrary,' said Dinshawji. 'Safest thing is to behave this way. As long as I do my nonsense, I am the normal Dinshawji. If I become serious, people will start watching and wondering what's wrong.'

Gustad had been ready to tell him he was a stupid old fool. But when Dinshawji said what he did, Gustad did not have the heart to scold. How true, he thought. And the more ill he becomes, the harder he will work to be the normal Dinshawji.

So Gustad let him continue in his way, praying that nothing would go amiss with the deposits. Slowly, the package in the coal-storage alcove emptied. Sometimes he wondered what else Major Bilimoria would demand once the money was deposited. But he did not dwell on that; instead, he looked forward to the day when the black plastic would collapse completely upon itself.

iii

Early in August, a few hours after Gustad left for work with the twenty-seventh bundle of money, Dilnavaz was surprised by the doorbell. She had just finished cooking the day's meals. The *dubbawalla*, on the run in the pouring rain, had picked up Gustad's lunch-box, and she hoped the food would not be cold when it reached the office. Now she was not expecting anyone else.

The morning stream of vendors had ended with the arrival of the ashes-and-sawdust-man's handcart, who had sold her a sack of each; her supply of the cleansers was running low. She was resisting the recent popular change to detergents and nylon scrubbers. Not that Dilnavaz had anything against modern technology – she always looked for the Sanforized label when shopping for fabric: it was a blessing not to lose three or four inches per yard to shrinkage. And those new Terylene and Tery-Cotton shirts were a miracle, never needed ironing. But she drew the line at fancy soaps and scrubbers; not only were they expensive, they did not do as good a job as *raakh-bhoosa* and a twist of coconut coir. Nothing worked better than the centuries-old method when it came to scouring pots and pans greasy with *vanaspati* and ghee. Some people claimed it was unhygienic, because you never could tell what ashes these fellows were selling – could be from cremation grounds, for all you knew. But Dilnavaz had faith in her man, trusted the quality of his *raakh* and *bhoosa*.

After the sacks were emptied in the *chawl* outside the WC, Tehmul-Lungraa arrived to dutifully drink his glass of lime juice. He swallowed the mixture with a burp and a grin, as she watched anxiously to see if he was behaving more brainlessly than usual. She both dreaded and wished Tehmul's deterioration: the erosion without which it would be impossible to redeem Sohrab. Tehmul returned the glass: 'Thankyouthankyouverytasty,' and left,

147

scratching his groin with one hand, waving with the other.

And it was while she was washing out the glass that the doorbell surprised her. Through the peephole she saw Roshan with one of the school nuns. Dilnavaz's hand trembled as she fumbled with the latch.

'Good-day, Mrs Noble,' said the nun, shaking water off her umbrella. Then she started, and dropped the umbrella, for Tehmul suddenly materialized behind her. He examined her cagily from head to toe, from the folds of her wimple to the rain-muddied hem of her white habit, gazing long and hard at the crucifix shining upon her flattened bosom. He scratched his head and circled around her, never having seen such a strangely attired creature during all his cloistered life in Khodadad Building and its surrounds.

'Yes, Sister,' said Dilnavaz, taking Roshan's hand. 'What is wrong?' But the question was unnecessary; the child's wan countenance and clammy hand revealed all.

'Roshan is not feeling well today, so we decided to bring her home.' The nun squirmed under Tehmul's gaze and eyed him suspiciously. 'She has been to the bathroom several times already, and brought up her breakfast.'

'Thank you for coming, Sister. Say thank you, Roshan.'

'Thank you, Sister.'

'You are welcome, child. Now get well soon, we want you back in class.' She stroked Roshan's head and said a short, silent prayer before leaving.

Dilnavaz took off Roshan's raincoat, dried her hands and feet. 'Sleep a little. I will phone Daddy and tell him.'

'Ask Daddy to come early today. Please.' Her pale, beseeching face made Dilnavaz want to hold her tight, but she did not let it show.

'Now you know Daddy has work to do in the office,' she said briskly, covering her with a sheet. 'He cannot leave it just like that.'

'Only once,' she pleaded.

'OK, I will ask him. Sleep now.' She locked the door and went to telephone.

Miss Kutpitia took a while to reach the door. Dilnavaz could hear talking inside the flat. Visitors for Miss Kutpitia? Impossible. She put her ear to the door. 'I made *bhakras* today for your tea. And if you finish all your lessons quickly, I will take you to Chaupatty, you can dig in the sand with your spade. Hurry, hurry now, be a good boy, don't waste time.' Then a door slammed inside. Dilnavaz stepped back as footsteps approached.

Miss Kutpitia opened the peephole, asking coldly, 'Who?'

'Dilnavaz.'

The cover fell into place and she unbolted the door. 'Forgive me, day by day eyes are getting worse and worse.'

'It's all right, sometimes I also have trouble seeing. What to do, years pass and make us old.'

'Rubbish!' said Miss Kutpitia spiritedly. 'Many years before you will have my kind of problems. Your three children will get married, make you a grandmother first.'

'All in God's hands. But can I use the phone?'

'Of course.' She unlocked the receiver and stepped aside. While waiting for the bank receptionist to locate Gustad, Dilnavaz looked around her. No sign of any visitors. Unless they were hidden behind the two locked doors. She finished and offered thirty paise.

'I cannot take money for phoning about Roshan's sickness,' said Miss Kutpitia. Insisting was useless, it was impossible to get past the adamant years between their ages. 'Put it away in your pocket. Put it away or you will make me angry.' She looked for the key. 'Poor Roshan. What a sweet and gentle child she is.' The lock clicked back on the receiver. 'Can I tell you something? You will not mind taking an old woman's advice?'

'Not at all,' said Dilnavaz.

'Listen. I heard you talking about the doctor. What I am saying is: go, get the medicine. But don't forget there are causes of sickness for which doctor can do nothing.'

'I don't understand.'

Miss Kutpitia raised a hand with the index finger extended. 'When a laughing-playing child like Roshan suddenly becomes sick, there can be other reasons. Such as evil eye. And doctor's medicine is no prevention or cure for that. There are special ways.'

Dilnavaz nodded.

'Oh, you know about them?' She shook her head, and Miss Kutpitia was irritated. 'Then why are you nodding? Listen. Take your needle and thread, a nice strong thread with a big knot at the end. Select a yellow lime, and seven chillies. Chillies must be green,

149

not turning red. Never red. String them all together with the needle. Lime goes at the bottom. Then hang the whole thing over your door, inside the house.'

'What will it do?'

'It is like a *taveej*, a protection. Each time Roshan walks under it, the evil eye becomes less and less powerful. Actually, once you hang it, everyone in your family will benefit.'

Dilnavaz agreed to prepare the talisman immediately. 'But you know, Sohrab is still refusing to come back home.'

'Naturally. You want a miracle or what? You want Seem-Salamay Foofoo and Abracadabra? Then go to a magician.' But her annoyance passed easily, and she reassured Dilnavaz. 'Patience. These things take time. Tehmul comes for the juice?' She thought for a moment. 'There is one more thing you can do, if you like, to make it a little faster. You will need Tehmul's nails.' She explained the full procedure. 'But after this, there is only one remedy left. And it's too dangerous, Tehmul could completely lose his mind, become a madhouse case. It is so terrible, I am not even going to tell you about it. Just do what I have said.'

'Thank you. So much of your time I've taken.'

'What have I to do anyway? Sit and wait till the One Up There calls me.'

'Don't say that, you have many years left with us.'

'Such a curse you are putting on me? What will I do with many years? I wish them for you and your children instead.' It was difficult to get the last word on the subject of death and dying with Miss Kutpitia, as on any other subject. Dilnavaz tried again, unsuccessfully, to give her thirty paise, then returned home.

A smile like a sunburst shone briefly on Roshan's drawn face when she heard that Daddy would be home early to take her to Dr Paymaster. 'Early? Then I'll sleep now,' she said, and closed her eyes. Dilnavaz stroked her hair, remembering that when the boys were little, they waited just as anxiously for their Daddy to return from the office. How Sohrab and Darius used to race to the door to open it for him. Now they are grown, and things are so different.

iv

Gustad's early arrival coincided with Dimple's walk, and he came face to face with Mr Rabadi. The Pomeranian yapped and darted at his ankles, fetching up short thanks to the leash, but Gustad burst out, 'If you must keep an animal, at least train your bloody bitch!'

It provided Mr Rabadi with the opening he had been waiting for. Recently, Dustoorji Baria had given him two new sets of prayers: one for Dimple's health; the other to weave protective vibrations around his sweet child Jasmine, safeguarding her from the savage lusts of wild boys like that son of Noble. The prayers made Mr Rabadi feel invincible. 'You are talking of training an animal? First teach manners and discipline to your own son! Walking away with somebody else's newspapers!'

'Go, go! Ask your daughter about it! And take your bitch with you, before I lose my temper!' Gustad went inside, leaving him to mutter among the bushes.

'Is Roshan ready?' asked Gustad, his rage straining his determination to keep his voice down.

'Almost.' Dilnavaz wondered what the matter was.

'Good. I will be back in two minutes.' He went to the WC *chawl* and picked up *The Times of India* and *Jam-E-Jamshed* stacks, one under each arm. He asked Dilnavaz to open the door. 'That dog-walla idiot is saying my son stole his papers, so I'll give him papers!'

She blocked his way. 'Calm down a little. That man is a crackpot, why are you being like him?'

'I am telling you, open the door and move aside!'

'But how will we pay next month's bill without these?'

'That's OK, we will stop the papers! Every morning brings nothing but bad news, anyway.'

She gave up and let him pass. His teeth were clenched tight. The weight under his arms hampered him, making him limp more than usual. Tehmul hurried over to help. 'GustadGustad. Pleasepleaseplease. Iwillcarrythankyoupleaseverymuch.'

'Shut up and get lost!' he said without looking at him.

Tehmul froze. Not till Gustad entered the building at the other end did he dare move. Blubbering and sniffing, he went to stand at a safe distance from the neem tree.

Gustad climbed the two floors to Mr Rabadi's flat and dumped the papers outside. Inside, Dimple yipped and yapped a few times, but no one came to the door.

The needle refused to pass through the lime. Dilnavaz pushed, and it snapped in two. From the china hen where her sewing things were kept, she selected a longer, fatter needle. It entered smoothly; the lime slid along the thread and stopped at the knot. Threading the chillies was much easier; the needle met no resistance.

She climbed on a chair to examine the ventilator over the front door. The blackout paper had come undone at one corner. She lifted it and tied the thread to one of the horizontal bars behind. The paper fell back over it.

No need to rush, Gustad and Roshan would be gone for an hour or more. Now for the lime juice. The last time Sohrab came to visit, she had circled his head with several limes at once, to have a ready supply. But only three remained. Please God, make Sohrab come soon. His visits becoming less and less frequent. And he promised me, once a week, he said. A wonder he even lets me do the lime, the way he says no to everything else.

She went to the window for Tehmul. He was still standing near the tree. 'Come,' she said, 'juice is ready.' In the kitchen he held out his hand for the glass. 'What big nails. Don't you cut them every week?' He shook his head bashfully.

'Come, I will do it for you.' She picked up the nail scissors. He shook his head again and put his hands behind his back. 'Come on, come on,' she coaxed, 'not nice to have such big nails. All dirty collects inside.' He would not budge. 'Then, no juice today. First nails, if you want the juice.'

Gazing longingly at the glass, he put out his fingers. She grasped them before he could change his mind. His hand was sticky. The edges of the nails were rough, jagged where he had bitten them, and underneath was greenish black stuff. Overcoming her revulsion, she began, collecting the clippings in a little plastic dish.

Once, she glanced at his face and saw him smile. Not his usual grin, but more innocent, a child's smile. What was he thinking? Perhaps a memory of his long-dead mother, kindled by the nail scissors? Something left over inside his damaged head, from his happy childhood years before the fall?

A lump came to her throat, and her eyes moistened. Suddenly

she felt an intense loathing for herself. No. She would not go on with this. Regardless of what Miss Kutpitia said.

She looked up again after finishing the other hand. Tehmul was digging his nose and transferring the pickings to his mouth. No, I must have been imagining. Not possible for anything to remain inside this skull – definitely an empty shell. He held out his hand for the lime juice.

'Not yet. Must do toes also.' He removed his shoes without untying the laces, and pulled off his socks. Two rupee notes, folded small, fell out of the right one. He carefully reinserted the money, then rubbed his toes urgently, kneading dirt, dead skin and sweat into little black bits which flaked off and fell to the floor. A smell like vomit now filled the kitchen.

Battling back the nausea that threatened to overcome her, she tackled the brittle, greenish-yellow crescents. But the light, ticklish contact of her squeamish fingers made him squirm and giggle. She had no choice other than to grasp the reeking foot, hold her breath, and complete the task.

He drained the juice eagerly. His old grin returned. 'Thankyou-thankyouverytasty.' He repeated his thanks as she shut the door. She thought she heard him say 'thankyouthankyoumummy'. No, probably something else. Hard enough to understand him when he is in front of me, leave alone behind a closed door.

After washing her hands thoroughly, she prepared coals on a small grate over the stove, the way Gustad did for the *loban* thurible after his evening prayers. Miss Kutpitia had insisted on that, it had to be a coal fire – neither the kerosene stove nor a candle flame would do. When the coals were glowing, she turned off the stove, packed the chunks together, and emptied the plastic dish over them. The nail clippings came alive with hisses and crackles, shrivelling and curling inwards, then turned quickly into shiny black, bubbly residues.

A horrible stench stabbed at her nostrils, acrid and miasmic, making her recoil. Like the smell of the devil himself, from the depths of *dojukh*, she thought. With a hand over her nose, she went to the spice rack for turmeric and cayenne. They would open wide Tehmul's channels, Miss Kutpitia had explained, through which his spirit would reach and yank the evil out of Sohrab's brain. Dilnavaz sprinkled a pinch of the yellow and red powders on the black molten mass.

Now the smell grew worse. A harsh pungency was added to the terrible fetor. Coughing and choking, she opened the window and stood by it, tears running down her face, till Tehmul's nails vaporized completely and became one with the firmament.

i

Dr Paymaster's dispensary was located in a neighbourhood that had changed in recent years from a place of dusty, unobtrusive poverty to a bustling, overcrowded, and still dusty, nub of commerce. Crumbling, leaky warehouses and rickety-staired, wobbly-balconied tenements had been refurbished and upgraded, from squalid and uninhabitable to squalid and temporarily habitable. The sewer system remained unchanged, broken and overflowing. Water supply continued to be a problem. So did rats, garbage and street lighting.

But the neighbourhood decided to make the best of it. Gleaming new signboards, featuring names like Fit-Tight Nuts & Bolts, A-1 Music, and Stylo Hairdressers, started going up over dingy old shops and *kholis*. The new owners sold transistors, toasters, tyres, auto parts, plastic crockery – everything essential for the magic which swallows up a hundred years of history and propels a country stuck in the nineteenth century directly into the glories of the twentieth. Sometimes, swallowing a hundred years in one gulp caused acute indigestion. But the troubled populace was assured by its venerable leaders that it would pass; for the interim they offered free of charge wordy anodynes which mitigated no one's suffering.

Soon, there appeared in the neighbourhood enterprising individuals who serviced motorcars, retreaded tyres, restored refrigerators, and allowed the waste products of their enterprise to run where they would. The barefooted now had to skip and hop over grease slicks, oil puddles, razor-sharp fins of broken cooling coils, and long, twisting snakes of vulcanized rubber disgorged by tyre retreaders. The black rubber strips were particularly frightful during August, with the Naagpanchmi festival approaching, when every street corner featured snake-charmers collecting alms from devotees anxious to feed the cobras a little milk in exchange for reptilian blessings. In the dark, it was easy to mistake a six-foot strip of black rubber for an escapee from the snake-charmer's basket.

These sordid footpaths provided one reason why Gustad hated coming to Dr Paymaster. But with the failure of *subjo*, Entero-Vioform, and Sulpha-Guanidine, he had no choice.

Over the years, as the neighbourhood underwent its peculiar transmogrification, only four establishments were able to resist change and endure. The nature of their businesses satisfied needs too deep to be displaced by builders, speculators, or government planners.

The first two were cinema houses, located at the crossroads not far from the beach. Despite their proximity, the proprietors enjoyed peaceful coexistence because the supply could never satiate the voracious demand. When a new film arrived, it roused the neighbourhood and awakened an industry that was seldom fast asleep. Black-marketeers and scalpers began buzzing around the theatres, bombinating ceaselessly, very like the mosquito clouds that rose from Khodadad Building's urine-soaked wall, droning tunefully: 'Ten-for-five, ten-for-five, ten-for-five . . .' Price ratios could keep soaring, depending on the stars and number of songs on the soundtrack. The black-market usually slowed after the first mad rush, then lay dormant like larvae waiting to hatch with the next celluloid release.

By and by, one of the cinemas decided to renovate, in keeping with the neighbourhood's and the country's aspirations, and the other had no choice but to follow suit. After the work was completed, both cinemas announced on the same day, with full-page newspaper advertisements, the first movie theatre in the country with 70mm capability, Todd-AO and Six-Track Sound. Soon, people were thrilling in their plusher, softer seats to the wide-screen spectacle, where the hero and heroine loomed like giants, where the massive trees round which they danced and sang grew ever taller, and where the black-hearted villain's evil dagger was bigger and sharper, and glinted more wickedly than was ever thought possible for a dagger to glint. Audiences emerged in awe, their confidence renewed that nothing could now stand in the way of the country's progress and modernization.

The first film to be shown after the renovations was an epic of kings and warriors, and Gustad had taken his family to see it. This was before Roshan was born, when Darius was three and Sohrab seven. For close to four hours, the kings and warriors spoke in thunderous voices, while gallant steeds and shining armour clashed with deafening clangour. Cudgels bashed, swords slashed, cymbals crashed. Maces bristling with ferocious spikes landed and shields were dented. At suitable intervals, hordes of women descended upon the battlefield, and the warriors and kings ceased their military pursuits: in bloodstained, battered armour, they sang and danced with their womenfolk. But the musical encounters seemed as terrifying as the battle scenes, and soon, Sohrab was shrieking in terror while Darius sobbed, though neither would turn away his eyes. Dilnavaz had to force them to put their faces in her lap, where they eventually fell asleep.

While the years went by to the rolling thunder of film reels, there was a third establishment nearby that did not alter its basic business. It was the oldest house in the locality. A skeleton staff was ready all day to provide service, but after six o'clock the cages filled up with painted women in saris wrapped impossibly low over their bellies, in blouses skimpier than brassières, or in little-girl frocks, fingers holding the cigarette of the wanton. Strands of fragrant jasmine and *chamayli* hung in their hair, bangles tinkled on their wrists, and the soft chhum-chhum of anklets could be heard when they moved. Scented oils and perfumes from Bhindi Bazaar – extracts and attars that enveloped them in dense, erotic clouds – filled the evening air and cloyed the senses of passers-by.

The House of Cages offered a full range of services, from the brisk, no-nonsense handjob even the poorest of day labourers could afford, to the most intricate contortions from a standard *Kama-Sutra* or *The Perfumed Garden*: something to suit the tumescence of every customer and wallet. The locals dreamed about soft scented sheets, air-conditioned rooms, hot and cold drinks, dancing-girls, various exotic liquors, food fit for a king from the brothel's delectable kitchen, and aphrodisiacs like the notorious *palung-tode* – bed-breaker – *paan*. The House of Cages catered for every one of these luxuries, with the exception of the last. *Paan* had to be purchased from the stall outside.

The stall outside was the domain of Peerbhoy Paanwalla, the

grizzled old man whose lips were perpetually reddened, doubtless from sampling his own wares. Rain or shine, he wore nothing more than a loongi. His wrinkled, old-woman dugs hung over a loose-skinned belly equipped with a splendid, ageless navel that watched the street tirelessly, an unblinking, all-seeing third eye. Sitting cross-legged on his wooden box, he seemed more swami or guru than paanwalla, his high forehead furrowed with creases bespeaking ancient wisdom, his large authoritative nose flaring brahminically as he dispensed slices of sagacity in direct discourse or wrapped between betel leaves.

Like an artisan of antiquity, Peerbhoy took great pride in his products. Besides the notorious bed-breaker *paan*, he sold various others: to ward off sleep, to promote rest, to create appetites, to rein in an excess of lust, to help digestion, to assist bowel movements, to purify the kidneys, to nullify flatulence, to cure bad breath, to create seductive breath, to fight failing eyesight, to make well the deaf ear, to encourage lucidity of thought, to improve speech, to alleviate the stiffness of joints, to induce longevity, to reduce life expectancy, to mitigate the labour of birthing, to ease the pain of dying – in short, he had a *paan* for all seasons. But among neophytes, tense because it was their first time, or first in a brothel, the one most in demand was the bed-breaker.

When they gathered, drawn by the large brass tray Peerbhoy rang like a gong, he soothed their anxieties with aphrodisiacal anecdotes. *Palung-tode paan*, he would say, as he chose a betel leaf, snipped off its stem, and began mixing chopped betel nuts, chunam, and tobacco – the *palung-tode*, he would say, had a long and honourable history, popular with Hindu rajas and Mogul emperors alike. In the old days, when it was time for the annual procession in which the raja had to walk naked before the public with erect phallus, to convince his subjects that the right to be ruler still belonged to him, it was the *palung-tode* he relied on. The secret was told to a few courtiers only, who, each year after the ceremony, were executed to guard the deception.

Mogul emperors also used *palung-tode*, said Peerbhoy, but in a less pedestrian way: when they wanted to service their harems. Though even here, reasons of state intruded, because the emperor's sexual prowess was invariably linked to his popularity, and, for his enemies, was a reliable indicator of how deeply he had penetrated the hearts and minds of his subjects. Coups and palace plots were inevitably on the rise when word came from the *zanaankhana* that the emperor was flagging.

All this, no matter how true or false, said Peerbhoy Paanwalla (as he extricated herbs from unmarked jars and added mysterious powders from dented metal cans) – all this was a long time ago, and now has become history or fable. But not so long ago, a man calling himself Shri Lokhundi Lund, Mister Iron Cock, had arrived and, flashing his money, ordered the most expensive, undiluted *palungtode*, determined to take unfair advantage of the House policy: satisfaction guaranteed. He paid (in the old days, it was cash in advance) and made his choice.

For a full hour the selected one toiled over him, rode him mercilessly, till, exhausted and ashamed, she dismounted and excused herself. And he? He lay upon his arrogant back, erect as at the moment of mounting. There was a brief consultation in the manager's office, and Lokhundi Lund was asked to choose again, compliments of the House.

The second one was younger, and in the firm roundness of her succulent thighs and buttocks she showed promise and the capability of bringing to fruition the sweat and labour of her colleague. She bestrode the customer and galloped for two hours, two hours non-stop, while he lay laughing at her efforts. Two hours, and she collapsed, her frothy juices running copiously down her defeated thighs. What kind of monster was this, the others wondered, what kind of monster who could be ridden endlessly, unyieldingly?

Now it was a question of the House's reputation. A third woman took over, grim and sinewy as a battle-hardened Rani of Jhansi, saying a quick prayer before she rode into combat. But her wiliest tricks astride that battering ram, that pillar of stone, that annihilator of maidenheads – her wiliest tricks were doomed to failure. And so it went through the night, till all the women in the House impaled themselves to no avail, one by one, upon the indomitable lance. The clock struck four a.m. and the manager began preparing a refund voucher for Lokhundi Lund.

But wait, said the first woman, who had just returned rested and strengthened, having made her invocation to Yellamma, Protector of Prostitutes, Goddess of Lust and Passion. Stand aside, she told her colleagues, casting off her garments. Then she who had first trustingly allowed the monster into her leafy haven, into her sheltered nook, into her friendly pleasure-gap: she once again took the place that was rightfully hers. And who says there is no poetry or justice in brothels? For just as the first cock crowed in the shacks of the destitute, she who had started it, now ended it. Lokhundi Lund shrieked once, then lay moaning, wilted at last.

That day, the House of Cages was closed for rest and recuperation from the havoc wrought within its walls. But its honour was inviolate for it had fulfilled its guarantee, concluded Peerbhoy Paanwalla, handing over the green triangles of *paan* and collecting his money. The nervous novices knew what they were chewing was not the original *palung-tode*, but they were not on a record-breaking quest like Lokhundi Lund. Besides, Peerbhoy's stories worked wonders, the same stories for which Gustad used to bunk school with his classmates and come to gape at the women in the House of Cages.

Gustad's first memories of this locale were linked to Dr Paymaster's dispensary, the periodic visits with his father for inoculations against smallpox, cholera, diphtheria, typhoid and tetanus. His father was especially concerned about the last, since Gustad spent so much time in the furniture workshop playing with Grandpa: one rusty nail, Pappa used to say, could produce that peculiar sardonic grin of lockjaw which would bring grief to the family. To reach the dispensary they had to pass by the brothel, and Gustad was intrigued by the lolling women. Once, he asked Pappa why they were half-dressed. Pappa said that these were not women, they were just men playing a game, like the ones they saw on the streets on Fridays, clapping their hands and dancing and begging. But Gustad knew these were not *hijdaas* in the House of Cages; he knew Pappa was lying.

Then the current of passing years brought Gustad to teenage shores, where anything was more challenging than being in class. His friends and he would stand outside the girls' school, watch cricket practice in the *maidaan*, or go for long aimless walks. Their favourite pastime was to loiter near the House of Cages, listening to Peerbhoy's tales of the power and glory of *palung-tode*. One day they decided to join the queue for this concoction. Waiting like students with the jitters before the big examination, their fifteen-year-old heads spinning with unmanageable emotions, they did their best to look poised and experienced. When their turn came, Peerbhoy laughed away their demands, preparing instead a *paan* which would cleanse their heads of boyish impurities and help them concentrate on their studies.

A long way now from those teenage shores, Gustad had almost forgotten Peerbhoy's fantastic stories. But it was always a visit to Dr Paymaster that brought him to the neighbourhood, and, over time, illness and the forbidden pleasures became entwined in his mind. It disgusted the core of Gustad's being, the stream that led his thoughts from one thing to the other, as he led his sick child by the hand to the dispensary.

The dispensary, of course, was the fourth establishment in the neighbourhood that never altered its function. Barring the brief, impolitic substitution of a new sign for Dr R.C. Lord's old board, Dr Paymaster had resisted all changes. Due to his peculiar location, his patients and their ailments fell into four distinct groups. First were the victims of workshop injuries. Mechanics came to him regularly with severed digits wrapped in newspaper, waiting stoically for treatment as though at the post office to mail a parcel. Radio repairers were carried in when they suffered a severe electrical shock. And periodically, a group of car painters arrived to get their lungs overhauled and cleansed of paint and turpentine.

The tyre retreader was also a regular patient. He had the misfortune of working directly opposite the House of Cages. Gripping a tyre between his knees while the sharp tool in his hands zigzagged the circumference, he sometimes let his eyes stray to the women lounging spread-leggedly across the road; sometimes, he gazed too long, and then the tool slipped.

Dr Paymaster's second group of patients were a by-product of the cinema industry. When tickets were in great demand, tempers rose rapidly, and once in a while an irate crowd would beat up an usher or ticket-clerk who was then delivered to the doctor for mending. The occasional scalper, if excessive greed clouded his finely-tuned instincts, also ended up at the dispensary via this route. But usually it was the ticket buyers who came for treatment after long queuing under the hot sun, collapsing from sunstroke and dehydration.

The House of Cages provided the clientele that constituted the third group. The women came for periodic check-ups as required by the municipal licensing authorities, and Dr Paymaster was never able to get used to them. They came in their business outfits and jested with him: 'Doctor, need to check if all machinery in good condition,' or 'We give you our business, you don't give us yours,' which embarrassed him terribly.

The patients Dr Paymaster looked forward to most were in the fourth group, made up of families like the Nobles. He yearned to cure the childhood illnesses, the middle-class maladies, of which he saw fewer and fewer as the years went by and the neighbourhood changed. Measles, chicken-pox, bronchitis, influenza, pneumonia, gastro-enteritis, dysentery – these were the things he wanted to treat. He wanted to lance boils painlessly for children who ate too many mangoes, and then see their grateful smiles. He wanted to bandage the fingers of little boys who cut them on kite-strings, on razor-sharp *maanja* stiffened with powdered glass and glue which they employed in kite fights up in the clouds. He longed to comfort youngsters scratched by dogs and terrified by their parents' tales of fourteen big injections in the stomach, though usually a penicillin shot was enough if the dog was an inoculated household pet.

He knew that the disorders he yearned to treat were there in the city, in vast numbers. Somehow, they just never found their way to the door of his dispensary. When one of them came along, it was like an answer to a physician's prayer.

ii

The tiny, crowded waiting-room was separated from Dr Paymaster's inner sanctum by a partition with a door. Large panes of green ground glass in the partition showed vague outlines of what went on inside.

When the door opened for the next patient, Dr Paymaster glimpsed Gustad and Roshan. He wished he could usher them in ahead of the rest. It had been a typical, lacklustre day: knocking, tapping, listening, peering, then signing his approval, so the painted ladies could continue in business. Sometimes he felt like a building inspector – all that was missing was a rubber stamp: *Safe for Human Habitation*. He handed Hemabai a clean bill of health as she emerged from the back, tall and bristling with daunting curves, called Hydraulic Hema by the neighbourhood mechanics because of a unique, ecstatically fluid movement she had perfected.

The doctor brought his hand down on the silver desk bell and waved at the Nobles. In the next half-hour, he dispensed with the half-dozen who were waiting, then rose to shake Gustad's hand and pinch Roshan's cheek. 'Seeing you after a long time. Which is very good, medically speaking, but not so good, socially speaking. Something cold to drink?' He went to the tiny Kelvinator whose inadequate innards refrigerated vials of serum and unstable compounds, plus some Goldspot and Raspberry for special patients. 'Or shall I send the boy for tea?'

'Nothing. Nothing, thanks,' said Gustad. 'I just had tea. And I don't think Roshan should.'

'Why, why? What's wrong? Ate brinjals?' Dr Paymaster habitually euphemized sicknesses and things medical.

'Stomach. Loose motions for a few days.'

'How many?' Gustad knew what he was about to say would not go down well. He cleared his throat and plunged into it. The doctor masked his exasperation but not wholly: 'Tch-tch-tch. You waited so long before coming?'

Gustad looked sheepish. 'Entero-Vioform and Sulpha-Guanidine usually works very well.' Better not to mention *subjo*.

'Those are medicines – not to be gobbled like sweet *papee* or *chana-mumra*. Come on, Roshan, lie down. I have to tickle your tummy a little bit.' While he listened with his stethoscope, he asked about school.

She mentioned the raffle. 'I won a big doll, but she is sleeping naked in the cupboard just now.'

'Why naked?' She explained about the voluminous wedding dress and described the articles of clothing. 'You know what I think?' said the doctor. 'Your doll is ready to be a bride, so we should find her a bridegroom. A nice young Parsi boy. Fair and handsome like me.' He pretended to be injured when Roshan laughed. 'What? Am I not young and handsome?' He stroked the few wisps of white on his head. 'See my fine black curly hair. And my face. So good-looking. Even handsomer than your daddy.'

Roshan laughed again, but after more persuasion it was agreed the doctor was the best match for her doll. Dr Paymaster made her turn on her side to face the partition while he prepared an injection. He winked at Gustad to say nothing. 'Now we must plan the wedding. I love accordion music. Does Dolly?'

'Yes,' giggled Roshan.

'Very good. Then we will have Goody Seervai's band. But if he is booked, we will call Nelly's orchestra.' He selected a needle from the sterilized tray and went to the Kelvinator. 'The next thing is the caterer. I always enjoy Choksy's food.' Choksy Caterers was unanimously approved. He enumerated the items he wanted on the menu, starting with a carrot-and-mango pickle, wafers, *murumbo*, and Choksy's special wedding stew, while directing a cold ether spray over the spot to be injected. Next, there was to be leaf-wrapped fish steamed in green chutney, succulent chicken legs fried Mughlai-style, and mutton pulao.

'Ow!' said Roshan. By the time he came to the dessert, which would be pistachio kulfi, the needle had been withdrawn. He rubbed the spot with cotton wool.

'OK,' he said. 'All finished. Now you can sit on the sofa outside while I talk to Daddy.'

After the door was shut, Gustad asked, 'It's not diarrhoea? How serious?'

'Not diarrhoea. But no need to worry.' He began writing a prescription. 'Sometimes, of course, even a case of diarrhoea can be worrying. Look at East Pakistan – a patient with a simple sickness, but very difficult to cure. A patient in critical condition, needing the intensive care unit. But no one in the world cares.' Dr Paymaster believed that politics, economics, religious problems, domestic strife, all could be dealt with methodically: observe the symptoms, make the diagnosis, prescribe medicine, offer the prognosis. But he also believed that just as some diseases of the human body were incurable, there were diseases of countries, of families, of theological dogma, that had fatal outcomes.

'East Pakistan is suffering from a diarrhoea of death,' he continued. 'Death is flowing there unchecked, and the patient will soon be dehydrated.' The smooth gliding of his fountain-pen was interrupted; the nib scratched and produced half-formed letters. He held it up to the light, peering through the reservoir's transparent plastic. 'Empty again.' He unscrewed the cover, dipped it in the bottle of Parker Ink, and squeezed the bladder. 'East Pakistan has been attacked by a strong virus from West Pakistan, too powerful for the Eastern immune system. And the world's biggest physician is doing nothing. Worse, Dr America is helping the virus. So what's the prescription? The Mukti Bahini guerrillas?' He shook his head.

'Not strong enough medicine. Only the complete, intravenous injection of the Indian Army will defeat this virus.'

He finished the prescription and handed it to the compounder in the little cubicle at the rear. Gustad knew from experience that Dr Paymaster had the wit and stamina to sustain medical metaphors endlessly. He interrupted. 'Will she be all right?'

'Absolutely. I am sitting here, no, if anything goes wrong. I think it's an intestinal virus. Keep her home for a few days. Only boiled rice, soup, toast, a little boiled mutton. And bring her again next week.'

The compounder finished mixing the prescription. He presented the dark-green bottle along with the bill. Gustad looked at the amount and raised his eyebrows. 'Refugee tax,' the compounder explained apologetically.

iii

The doctor's calm manner and reassuring talk kept at bay Gustad's fear about the virus. He led Roshan to the bus stop past the rows of shops, past Cutpiece Cloth Centre, Bhelpuri House, Jack of All Stall, Naughty Boy Men's Wear. Peerbhoy Paanwalla was busy outside the House of Cages. The women stood in the doorways or leaned against windows, displaying what they could between the bars. Loud music, a popular film song, blasted from within: *Mere sapno ki rani kab ayegi tu*, O Queen of my dreams, when will you arrive . . . It could be heard all the way to the bus stop.

Later, as they neared the gate of Khodadad Building, the effects of Dr Paymaster's salutary presence were wearing off. At the black stone wall, the stink had been growing from strength to strength, with pools of urinous ordure multiplying as the evening darkened. When the stench hit Gustad, the last of the doctor's reassurances drowned helplessly. The insidious stink in his nostrils left no room for optimism.

He began to blame himself for Roshan's illness, wished he had never heard of Entero-Vioform or Sulpha-Guanidine. His limp slipped its usual containment, and by the time they reached the door, he was swaying wildly from side to side.

'What did the doctor say?' asked Dilnavaz.

Gustad shut and opened his eyes meaningfully, and she understood. 'Everything is fine, Dr Paymaster is going to marry Roshan's dolly.'

'Yes,' said Roshan. 'Choksy Caterers will cook the wedding dinner.' He gave her one dose from the mixture. They sent her to bed, and he quietly told Dilnavaz what the doctor had said.

She sat silent a few moments while the lines on her face rearranged for a storm: 'Now you are satisfied? Now will you admit it? I repeated it till I was exhausted, till my lungs were empty. But you treat my words as if a dog is barking.'

'What idiotic-lunatic thing are you saying?'

'Neither idiotic nor lunatic! I am talking about water, what else? I said it over and over. That we should boil the water, boil the water, boil the water. But it would not go into your brain only!' she said, ferociously digging her fingers into her skull.

'Yes! Blame me! That's the easiest thing.'

'If not you then who? Your dead uncle? No, no, you said, potassium permanganate is enough, no need to boil. You Nobles think you know everything.'

'That's right! Don't blame me alone! Blame my father also, and grandfather and great-grandfather. You ungrateful woman! Why do you think I said not to boil? For your sake! As it is, you are so busy in the morning, running from bathroom to kitchen, with no time even to sit and drink your tea!'

Their voices rose steadily, though neither seemed to notice. She said, 'There is a remedy for that, if I have no time in the morning. But you just sit and read your newspaper, while my insides are heaving and aching with lifting the tubs and buckets. And two big sons you have, like *lubbhai-laivraas*, who have never helped me once.'

'Correction, you have two sons. I have only one. And what has happened to your mouth? Why must I say everything when – ?'

'Everything? What everything have you told them? Always I shout and scream, while nice Daddy watches quietly. To finish their food, to do homework, to pick up their plates. Without a father's discipline what can you expect now but disobedience?'

'Yes! Blame me for that also. It is my fault that Sohrab is not going to IIT! My fault that Darius is wasting his time with the dogwalla idiot's fatty! My fault that Roshan is sick! Everything wrong in the world is my fault!'

'Don't deny it! From the beginning you have spoilt the boys! Not for one single thing have you ever said no! Not enough money for food or school uniforms, and *baap* goes and buys aeroplanes and fish tanks and bird cages!'

They did not notice Roshan standing in the door till she started to sob. 'What is it, my darling?' said Gustad, bringing her to sit beside him.

'I don't like it when you fight,' she said through her tears.

'No one is fighting. We were just talking,' said Dilnavaz. 'Sometimes grown-ups have to talk about these things.'

'But you were shouting and angry,' sobbed Roshan.

'OK, my *bakulyoo*,' he said, putting his arm around her. 'You are right, we were shouting. But we are not angry. Look,' and he smiled: 'Is this an angry face?'

Roshan was not convinced, especially since her mother sat rigidly at the dining-table, with her arms stiffly folded in front of her. 'Go kiss Mummy.'

He looked at Dilnavaz's wrathful countenance, still struggling to soften. 'Later. But you I will kiss now, you are closer.' He kissed her cheek.

She would not give up. 'No, no, no. I cannot sleep till you kiss. Mummy will come here.' When Dilnavaz did not move, she went and began tugging at her arm, leaning on it with all her meagre weight. Dilnavaz gave in. She looked coldly at Gustad and brushed his cheek cursorily.

'Not like that!' said Roshan, frustratedly pounding the arm of the chair. 'That's not a real Mummy-Daddy kiss. Do it like when Daddy goes to work in the morning.' Dilnavaz rested her lips against Gustad's. 'Eyes closed, eyes closed!' yelled Roshan. 'Do it properly!'

They obeyed, then separated. Gustad was amused. 'My little kissing umpire,' he said.

Roshan somehow sensed that it took more than the joining of lips and closing of eyes to get rid of anger and bitterness. But she did not know what else to do, and went to bed.

iv

Mr Rabadi gathered up the newspapers outside his front door. He was unable to lift the lot in his arms, and insisted that Mrs Rabadi help him. She was all for selling them to the *jaripuranawalla* but he would not listen. 'I will show that rascal! You just do as I say!'

'Yipyip! Yipyipyipyip!' Dimple ran excitedly round the papers, tumbling the piles Mr Rabadi had made. He dragged her inside, bade Mrs Rabadi come out, then shut the door. 'Carry,' he ordered, pointing to one stack, and took the other himself.

In the compound, they ran into Inspector Bamji. 'Hallo, hallo!' he said. 'Selling old papers? But shop will be closed now.' He looked at his watch in confirmation.

'I'll show him!' muttered Mr Rabadi. 'I came out to take Dimple for a walk, and tripped on them! Almost fell down the stairs and broke my neck! Outside my door he threw them!'

'Who?' asked Bamji.

'That – that rascal!' he sputtered. 'Noble in name only!'

'Gustad?'

'Trying to kill me, laying a trap like that outside my door! What does he think in his own mind of himself?' He dropped the papers close to the bushes. Mrs Rabadi looked at him questioningly, clutching tight her stack, whereupon he grabbed her hands and pulled them apart. From his pocket he withdrew a matchbox.

'Are you sure?' said Inspector Bamji.

Mr Rabadi struck and dropped a match. 'First his son steals my papers!' The newspapers caught. 'If he thinks he can throw this outside my door and I will forget everything, he is mistaken!' Within seconds the stacks were burning fiercely, which added fuel to Mr Rabadi's inflammation. His face turned a bright orange. 'It is not the newspapers I care about! There are manners, apologies, respectfulness at stake! There are principles involved! Let him learn once and for all who he is tangling with!'

Inspector Bamji had nothing to say. Tehmul came to watch the flames. 'Hothothothot.' He edged closer, and Inspector Bamji pulled him back. 'Careful, you Scrambled Egg. Or your face will get fried.'

Suddenly, there were yells of fire! fire! *'Aag laagi! Aag laagi!* Help! Call the *boombawalla!'* Cavasji, leaning out the window upstairs with the *subjo* garland around his neck, gave the alarm. Mr and Mrs Rabadi melted away to their flat. Cavasji turned his attention to the sky. 'Once again You have done it! Inflicting suffering on the poor only! The stink, the noise, the flood – now the fire! Have You ever burnt the homes of rich *sethiyas?* Have You ever, tell me!'

Gustad heard the shouts and simultaneously saw the orange

glow through the window. When he got outside, only Tehmul was there. 'GustadGustad. Hothothothot.'

The blaze was dying. Charred bits of newspaper lay by the bushes. Soon the breeze carried the scraps through the compound, and Tehmul began chasing after them. Gustad went inside, amused that the dogwalla idiot had been provoked to such lengths.

But something more had been provoked, Gustad soon realized. Mosquitoes, stirred up as never before, and maddened by the smoke. They descended in clouds of blind fury, bent on vengeance – stunning themselves against walls, pinging into the hot glass of the light bulb, ricochetting, alighting in his hair, stinging his face.

He ran to switch on the lights in the house, shouting to Dilnavaz to fetch all the large flat dishes she could find. But when he went to the drum and turned on the tap – nothing. He got up on a stool and looked inside. The drum was empty, it had sprung a leak where the spout was soldered to the side. And there was barely enough water left in one of the buckets to last till morning. There would be no mosquito traps tonight.

It was back to swatting and slapping, back to Odomos.

i

Gustad went to the bed-with-the-door with the new mixture and pills. Dr Paymaster had changed Roshan's prescriptions four times in the last fortnight, and ordered blood tests, stool tests, and barium X-rays. Last week, Gustad had sold his camera to pay the bills.

When Roshan sat up to take the medicine, he wanted to hold her for ever in the safety of his arms. Instead he stroked her forehead and rubbed her back gently. But she already knew that her strong and broad-shouldered Daddy (with his big biceps which he could wriggle up and down like living creatures) was scared, helpless in the face of her illness. Sometimes, when he came to look at her in the morning, she thought he was going to cry, and it ushered the beginning of tears into her own eyes. Then she forced herself to think of nice things, like Major Uncle visiting on Sundays for Mummy's delicious *dhansak*, when Daddy and he, with Sohrab and Darius cheering them on, would place their elbows on the table and try to push down each other's hand. Their muscles swelled so big, it seemed they would burst. It was such fun to watch them sweating and struggling and laughing at the same time. Major Uncle was also a very strong man, even taller than Daddy, but Daddy usually won, he was so tough.

'How is the injection, my little *bakulyoo*?' said Gustad. 'Still paining?'

'Aches a little.'

He went to the sideboard and got the tube of Hirudoid ointment. 'This will dissolve the swelling.' He rubbed it over the spot. 'Now. What else would you like? Would you like your big Italian doll to come out of the cupboard?'

'Oh yes.' Her eyes brightened at the prospect.

'When I come home this evening, we'll take all her clothes from the suitcase and dress her up. Then she can sit with you on the sofa. Or sleep here beside you. OK?'

'Yes, but don't be late, Daddy.'

'No, I promise. Now go to sleep. Lots of rest. Come on, close your eyes. Or shall I sing for you, like a little baby?' Teasing her, he began, to the tune of 'Ta ra ra boom dee-ay' the song she used to hear as an infant:

> Roshan is a good girl,
> A very, very good girl,
> See how well she goes to sleep –

'No, no! Not that song!' Roshan protested. 'Sing my favourite.' So he sang a verse of the 'Donkey Serenade', then kissed her cheek and said goodbye.

'Goodnight-Godblessyou,' she said.

'But it's not night now.'

'I am always sleeping. For me it's always night,' she said, and they both laughed.

He collected the thirty-ninth bundle from the kitchen. Will soon be halfway there, he thought. The sky clouded while he rode the bus, and the rain commenced when he reached Flora Fountain. The final rallies of a departing season. The monsoon was over the hump. He debated: bicycle clips or not? Air-raid siren not yet gone off – enough time. Hate sitting all day with damp trousers clutching my calves. He fished inside the briefcase for the clips, and raised a foot to the bus shelter's bottom stile. The trouser cuff was wrapped tightly round his shin and the clip snapped on: first one leg, then the other.

From the bus stop he could see the dome of the bank building. How whitely it gleams, against the grey sky. Rain washing it clean, day by day. He reached the bank portico and snapped off the bicycle clips. The water ran off his umbrella ferrule as it leaned against the pillar. He pinched each trouser leg at the knee and cuff, to restore the crease, then shook water off the umbrella. Someone touched his elbow from behind.

'Good-morning, Mr Noble,' said Laurie Coutino, with a hint of singsong. The way convent schoolgirls rise and greet the teacher. Roshan also had the habit.

'Good-morning, Miss Coutino.'

'Mr Noble, may I talk to you sometime today?'

He noted with approval her use of 'may' instead of 'can'. But the request surprised him. 'Sure. Eleven o'clock, after I finish checking the ledger?'

She shook her head. 'I'd prefer privately.'

His surprise grew, he looked at his watch. 'Still ten minutes to ten. We can talk now. Or lunch-time.'

'Lunch-time, yes.'

'Good, I'll meet you in the canteen. One o'clock.'

'Not in the canteen, please. Maybe somewhere outside.'

She brought her head close, speaking softly. Whiff of some nice perfume. What is she up to? 'Meet me here at one o'clock.'

'Thank you so much, Mr Noble,' she whispered, and went inside. He watched her receding form appreciatively, puzzled but flattered, and followed.

Since it was not yet ten, the tellers' cages were unoccupied. Some early customers waited, moving their eyes rapidly from clock to counter to idle employees, as though sufficient repetitions of their visual cycles would hasten the conjunction of the three. Behind the counters, not oblivious of the restless customers but sharply aware the time was still their own, a few clerks were reading newspapers; others were lounging with their feet on a desk or file cabinet. Dinshawji was describing something animatedly to an avid group of listeners.

Gustad could hear his voice: '. . . and then the second fellow said, "Changing gears? That's nothing, *yaar*."' He broke off when he saw Gustad: 'Come quick! This is a good one.'

Gustad had heard the story before, but listened patiently as Dinshawji started again. 'The first man says, "*Yaar*, ever since my wife started driving lessons, new-new things she does in her sleep. Grabs my *lorri* and says, first gear, second gear, reverse – this way and that way she keeps twisting it." Then the second fellow says, "Changing gears? That's nothing. My wife, in the middle of the night, catches my *lorri*, puts it in, and says, twenty litres petrol, please."'

Roars of laughter filled the space behind the counter. The men slapped Dinshawji on the back. 'One more, one more,' said someone, but the clock's slow, solemn bonging dispersed them.

Gustad opened his briefcase and casually handed over the

172

bundle of money. 'Won't meet you for lunch, Dinshu. Going out for some work.' He closed and opened his eyes slowly. Dinshawji understood: explanations not possible, others present. He assumed it concerned the secret mission, as he liked to call it.

At eleven, Gustad left his desk for a cup of tea, then changed direction and went the long way, past Laurie Coutino's desk. He was not sure why he did that, but after this morning, he wanted to look at her again. Their eyes met in passing, and she smiled. He felt foolish at the quickening of his heartbeat. Like a schoolboy.

ii

He waited under the portico. No danger of being observed, everyone busy with lunch. There she is. 'Thank you for coming, Mr Noble.'

'My pleasure, Miss Coutino. Where would you like to go?'

'Please call me Laurie.' He smiled, nodded. 'Anywhere, Mr Noble, as long as it's private. I don't want people to see us together and get the wrong idea.'

'Quite right. There is a nice restaurant at the corner.'

'I've seen it from outside,' said Laurie.

'They have private rooms, maybe we can talk there.'

They walked to the corner, stepping carefully. The rain had left fresh, deep puddles. 'Mr Noble, were you in the army?'

'No. Why?'

'I've seen you limping. I wondered if that's what it was. Somehow, the way you walk, your shoulders, your moustache, make you look like a military man.'

Flattered, he modestly laughed away what he assumed was a compliment, in the manner that an army man would. 'No. This injury was not received in the service of my country. It was in the service of my family.'

Intrigued by his way of putting it, she asked how. 'To save the life of my eldest,' he said, 'nine years ago I jumped from a moving bus in the path of a car.' He told her about the rainy morning, the bus conductor, Sohrab's fall, the visit to Madhiwalla Bonesetter.

'Does this bonesetter still practise?' she asked.

'Oh yes. But he is very old now, he does not hold his clinics as often as before.'

'I must remember his name, in case I ever break a bone.'

'You must take good care of them.' He felt bold enough to add, 'They are too beautiful to break.'

She blushed and smiled. 'Thank you, Mr Noble.' The convent-girl lilt in her voice again. They walked silently past the great traffic circle. He thought of the last time he had been at the restaurant. Just over three months ago. With Dinshawji. But it seems like years. Time's tricks. And Ghulam Mohammed's accident. Wish the bastard had died. Those heads neatly sliced ... Like a *goaswalla's* knife – bhup! And Tehmul trying to pick up the cat. And Jimmy's bloody letter.

The restaurant was crowded downstairs, the waiters spreading the usual odours and noises as they dashed back and forth. Fried samosas, overboiled tea, pungent *rugdaa*. Clatter of plates and glasses slammed before customers. Orders yelled to the kitchen. Kitchen yelling back. 'Three teas, *paani-kum*, one paneer mattar! Idli dosa, sambhar, lassi!' And over the cashier's head, two more handwritten signs had been added, beneath the *Rice Plate Always Ready* sign. One said, *No Combing Hair In Restaurant*. The other injunction was sterner, and more sweeping: *Don't Discuss God & Politics*.

Upstairs, the private rooms were empty. A flight of stairs steep as a ladder led to the mezzanine. He followed Laurie, her bottom undulating at his eye-level, ascending at the same rate as his eyes. Dinshawji should be watching. Bum within nibbling range. Omelette sandwich, and Laurie's bum for dessert.

The stairs gave on to a very small landing that led to six doors. He opened the nearest one. Another sign greeted them: *Please Ring Bell For Waiter Under Table*. 'Now why would they put the waiter under the table?' said Gustad.

'You have a sense of humour just like your friend Mr Dinshawji,' she said, laughing appreciatively. It was the first time he had heard her laugh. Started with a snort, segued into a bray. Such a pretty girl, but the ugliest laugh I ever heard.

The room contained four bentwood chairs and a glass-covered wooden table identical to the ones downstairs. The menu was under the dirty glass. The extras, for the five-rupee minimum charge, were air-conditioned privacy and a worn, beaten sofa with stains on the covers. The room spoke blatantly of the single sordid purpose it was meant for. He saw her eyes examining the well-used sofa. 'I'm sorry about this place. I have never been here. Upstairs, I mean. Didn't know it was like this.'

'That's all right. At least we can talk privately.'

'Yes,' he said. 'We better order something. Then you can tell me what the problem is.'

'It's not really a . . . yes, it is a problem.'

Their heads converged to share the menu. Pretending to read, he watched her from the corner of his eye. Dinshu was right, very attractive girl. Her upper lip had an exquisite curve, the hint of a pout that accounted for her sexiness.

'Ready?' he asked. She nodded. 'Now where's the bell for the waiter?' He groped under the table. She felt around too, and their hands met. He pulled away quickly, as though jolted by electricity. 'Sorry,' he said awkwardly.

'It's all right,' she smiled. The bell button was located on the leg at the far side, and she rang. Moments later, the waiter knocked discreetly, not to endanger his tip. He knew from experience that anything could develop in these rooms between the bell and his arrival.

'Yes, yes, come in,' said Gustad irritatedly, to show Laurie that he was offended at the waiter's assumptions. They sat erect, very formal, with arms folded.

The waiter took the order, fearing that things were not passionate enough. No pre-luncheon concupiscence here. Unhappy men gave small tips. Perhaps they needed reassuring. 'Please sir, in exactly five minutes with the food I will return. I will be knocking, then afterwards you will have complete privacy.'

Gustad shook his head as the door shut. 'One-track mind.'

'Not his fault,' said Laurie. 'It's a one-track room.'

An audacious remark, he thought. 'Now tell me why you wanted to see me.'

'Yes.' She passed a hand over her hair, and adjusted her collar. 'It's difficult to talk about it, but I think the best thing is to tell you rather than the manager.'

'Mr Madon? What's wrong?'

She took a deep breath. 'It's your friend, Mr Dinshawji.'

Oh no, thought Gustad.

She continued, 'You know how he carries on all the time, playing the fool.'

'Sure. Dinshawji does that with everyone.'

'I know. That's why I did not mind it. Joking, dancing, singing, all that is OK.' She inspected her nails. 'I don't know if you heard, but one day he began telling me he wants me to meet his *lorri*.' She bit her lower lip, hesitating. '"You can play with my little *lorri*," he said, "such fun two of you will have together."' Now she looked him in the eye. 'You know, at first I thought it was his daughter or niece, or something like that, and I would smile and say, "Sure, I would love to."'

Gustad coloured. It was difficult to continue meeting her eye. But he said nothing, let her go on.

'Then recently, I found out what it really means. Can you imagine how I felt?'

Gustad searched desperately for words. Embarrassed before Laurie, furious at Dinshawji, fearful about Madon, he could only say: 'I am so sorry about it. I did try to make him stop.'

'You know how I feel when I think of those men laughing every time he said it? It's so difficult to come to work, I want to resign and tell Mr Madon why.' Her tone, even and controlled so far, grew emotional. 'If someone speaks my name now, no matter who, I feel bad. It reminds me of the dirty meaning. Mr Dinshawji has ruined my own name for me.' She touched her hanky to the corner of one eye.

She is really upset, Dinshu's had it. Gone too far this time. And if it reaches Mr Madon's ears . . . Casanova of Flora Fountain castrated. He leaned forward earnestly. 'Please don't say that. Laurie is a beautiful name. That will never ever change just because of some silly slang word.'

'You know, I don't mind his jokes and all his acting. I used to think it was so sweet. A cute old man, trying to impress me. The things he says. He was telling me he works for the secret service, that he is in charge of ten lakh rupees, to fully equip the Mukti Bahini guerrillas. Can you imagine that? Mr Dinshawji in the secret service?' She laughed a little.

'Ha! Ha! Ha! In the secret service? Too much!' said Gustad, restraining his urge to slam his fist on the table and scream, or do something to Dinshawji that would make him scream with pain. The stupid idiot! Absolutely brainless and . . .! After I told him how quiet the whole thing has to be kept! What a complete, what a total – !

'Isn't it funny?' said Laurie.

'Ha! Ha! Ha! I don't think the secret service would hire him to clean their toilets even.'

'Anyway,' she said, 'I was so upset about the dirty joke, I wanted to go and tell Mr Madon.' She looked at her watch. 'Then I thought Mr Dinshawji would get into serious trouble, and I didn't want that. Is he close to retirement?'

'Very,' said Gustad. 'Just two years left. He's also very sick, though you wouldn't think so from his jovial attitude.'

'I didn't know that.' She paused, fingering a tiny paper-cut on her left hand. 'I decided to tell you all this because you are his best friend. But if you already tried to stop him – '

'I'll convince him. Just leave it to me.' But right now, I have to convince her, or he and I will both get buggered. 'This evening after work. I will make sure he never upsets you again.'

'Thanks, Mr Noble. I knew talking to you would help.'

Just wait till I see him. The stupid fool. With all his idiotic-lunatic nonsense. The bloody fool.

iii

The *dubbawalla* had departed with the lunch-boxes. To let Dilnavaz know he would be late, he telephoned Miss Kutpitia. The connection was bad. 'Hallo! Hallo, Miss Kutpitia! This is Gustad Noble!' No one paid any attention to the bellowing. With the roulette wheel of the telephone exchange, the odds of getting a bad connection were as good as they were bad for getting a good connection. He hung up, then remembered his promise to Roshan about dressing the doll. Now I am going to be late, and she will think I forgot. Which I did. His head began to hurt, a sharp pain, as though something was trying to break through the skull. He realized what Mrs Pastakia meant when she described her migraine for all and sundry: like someone poking about inside with knitting needles.

He returned to his desk, kneading his forehead. It was becoming too much to bear, Roshan's sickness, Dilnavaz blaming him for potassium permanganate, Jimmy's treachery, Dinshawji's stupidity, Laurie's complaint, Sohrab's betrayal, nothing but worry and sorrow and disappointment piling up around him, walling him in, threatening to crush him. He moved his massaging hand from the forehead to his nape and closed his eyes.

177

When he reopened them, rubbing them like a sleepy, tired child, Dinshawji was leaning against the desk. The fist he had wanted to slam on the restaurant table, he indulged now, upon the desk. Bhum! it came down, and Dinshawji took a great leap backwards, alarmed. 'Easy, boy, easy!' His sudden movement was painful. He clutched his sides and winced.

Gustad put his elbows on the desk, face resting in his hands. At least the danger of bursting a blood vessel had been averted, he thought. He spoke softly, and Dinshawji had to draw close again in order to hear. 'You make the blood in my brain start to boil, you stupid fool.'

Dinshawji was hurt. 'How are you talking, *yaar*. What's wrong? First at least tell me my crime.'

'I will. I promise you I will. Meet me under the portico at six.' He turned his chair away, kneading his forehead again. Dinshawji waited a few moments, quite forlorn, then left.

For the rest of the day Gustad could do no work. Having enumerated his worries, disappointments, and betrayals, he was tormented by them. When he thought of Roshan, his heart went cold: for a second, he imagined the worst, then mentally performed Dilnavaz's *owaaryoo* gesture which he had often ridiculed. How can she blame me, potassium permanganate worked so well all these years. Jimmy said they always used it in the army. Damn Jimmy, the bastard. Once like a brother . . . and now? Those Bible stories, that Malcolm used to tell me. When we went to Crawford Market. One about Cain and Abel . . . Fairy tales, I used to think. But from the distance of years, how true. My own father's case. His drunken, gambling brother who destroyed him as surely as crushing his skull. And Jimmy, another kind of Cain. Killed trust, love, respect, everything. And that other story, about Absalom, son of David. By now Sohrab would have been finishing his first term at IIT, if only . . .

What was left, he asked himself, after the very purpose he had struggled and worked and waited for all these years – after that very purpose was callously shattered by his own son, and the shards kicked aside, dropped clattering in the rubbish-pail, like his application forms. All I wanted was for him to have a chance at a good career. The chance wrenched away from me. Now what is left? What is left in life? Tell me, Dada Ormuzd, what?

And so it went all afternoon: from Sohrab to Roshan, then back to Jimmy, and Dilnavaz, and Laurie, and Dinshawji. Circles, U-turns, reverse circles, till he was dizzy with thought, exhausted from anxiety, and close to being broken by despair.

But at six o'clock he was saved by anger. He saw Dinshawji under the portico, and his fury returned. The stench from Dinshawji's mouth was unbearable. Good. Serves him right if he has been fretting and agonizing, now he will come to his senses.

Dinshawji smiled weakly. 'Your smiles will vacate the premises,' said Gustad, 'when you hear what I have to tell you.'

'You keep shouting at me,' he complained. 'All afternoon you have been drowning yourself in anger. But why not say what has left its sting poking in your heart?'

'I want you to be able to enjoy your cup of tea first. It may be the last thing you will ever enjoy.'

Dinshawji laughed, a poor copy of his usual incorrigible laugh. 'What suspense you are creating, *yaar*. Taking tuitions from Alfred Hitchcock or what?'

They walked past the great circle, past the traffic of vehicles and humans. Like a vast river that had reversed its direction, the current was speeding northward – northward, the flow of tired humanity, from banks, insurance companies, shoe shops, textile shops, accounting firms, manufacturing offices, opticians, advertising agencies – northward, the weary flow, by crush of bus, by squeeze of train, by rattle of bicycle, by ache of feet – northward to suburbs and slums, to houses, hovels, apartments, tenements, one-room flats, corrugated-metal shacks, street corners, pavements, cardboard huts – flowing north till the current petered out, its waters still but not restful, lying in darkness, trying to scrounge enough strength to prepare for the morning tide southward, and the repetition of the endless cycle.

They waited for their tea. 'You know why I was not in the canteen for lunch?' asked Gustad.

'If you tell me I will know why.'

'Because Laurie Coutino wanted to talk to me privately. So we came here. Upstairs, to a private room.'

'Go, go! Really?' Dinshawji grinned. 'You lucky bugger.'

'No, you are the lucky bugger. Because the whole time she talked about you.'

'You are joking!'

Gustad minced no words, wanting them to be as deadly as the goaswalla's knife that went bhup! Dinshawji's pale countenance lost its last trace of colour; his mouth fell open, fetid breath billowed across the table. 'But there is more,' said Gustad mercilessly. Dinshawji gazed blankly at his hands in his lap, too ashamed to look up, too dazed to speak. 'Luckily, Laurie does not believe in your secret service and ten lakh rupees and guerrillas. She laughed when she told me. But if it reaches Madon's ears? And he gets suspicious about our deposits? What are we going to do then, you bloody fool?'

'What can I say, Gustad?' said Dinshawji feebly. 'You are absolutely right, I'm a bloody stupid idiot.' He worried the handle of his teacup with his forefinger: 'What shall we do now?'

'It's in your hands. If you stop bothering her she won't go to Madon. She told me.'

'Of course I will stop. Whatever you think is best.' He gulped from his cup. 'But . . .'

'But what?'

Dinshawji took another swallow, choked, and had a coughing fit. 'If I suddenly stop fooling with her, everybody will wonder what's wrong. Don't you think?' He coughed some more. 'Then they will start poking their noses to find out what happened. It won't be good if they see you giving me a packet every day.'

'I have thought about that, I have a plan. What you must do is stop your jokes and teasing with everyone. At the same time, I will start telling people that poor Dinshawji's health is not good again, he is feeling completely under the weather.'

'I would prefer to be feeling under Laurie's skirt.' The attempt at humour was frail, but it was a hard habit to break.

'No more jokes, you agreed,' said Gustad sternly.

'Sorry, sorry yaar. Just with you, privately.'

'OK. So I'll spread the story tomorrow. All the fellows will be sympathetic, everything will be fine. Can you manage it?'

'Of course. Let me tell you, it's more difficult to be a jovial person all the time than to be a quiet, sickly one.' The truth of Dinshawji's words was sharp and cruel. They finished their tea silently and left.

From the next morning, Dinshawji changed utterly. Everyone's heart went out to the grave individual, suddenly fragile and spent, who greeted them with only a quiet hallo. When Gustad came across him later in the day, he was surprised at how authentically Dinshawji projected his new image. Till he remembered that it seemed authentic because Dinshawji was no longer playing a role; reality, at last, had caught up with him; and Gustad felt awful for confiscating his mask.

iv

The tap was re-soldered to the bunghole. Gustad walked home from the Horaji's repair shop with the water drum upon his shoulder. Dilnavaz was waiting anxiously to tell him about the visitor who would call again at nine p.m. 'He was asking for you,' she said. 'Would not tell me anything. Very strange fellow. Barefoot, and all paint on his hand, as if he was playing Holi with coloured powder. But Holi festival is seven months away. I hope that shameless Bilimoria has not sent him with more troubles for us.'

Gustad could guess who it was. Later, he was able to reassure Dilnavaz, when the man returned as promised: 'Don't worry, I told him to come. To fix that stinking wall.'

He went with the pavement artist into the compound. 'So. You finally made up your mind to leave Flora Fountain?'

'What to do,' said the pavement artist. 'After the trouble that day, police began harassment. Making me move from here to there, this corner to that corner. So I decided to come and see the place you were telling about.'

'Good,' said Gustad, 'you will like it.' They went outside the gate and the artist inspected the wall. He ran his hand over the surface, feeling with his fingertips. 'Smooth black stone,' said Gustad encouragingly, 'perfect for your pictures. Wall is more than three hundred feet long. And lots of people pass by every day.' He pointed to the twin towers next to Khodadad Building: 'To go to those offices. Then there is a bazaar also over there, further down. With expensive jewellery shops. Lots of rich people travel this road. On that side, about twenty minutes away, there are two cinemas. Monday will be no problem, I can guarantee.'

The pavement artist completed his inspection by taking a crayon from his satchel and sketching briefly. 'Yes. Quite good.' He wrinkled his nose. 'But stinks very much.'

'That's true,' said Gustad. He had been wondering how long before the artist said something. 'Shameless people treat the wall like a roadside lavatory. Look! There's one now!'

At the far end, a figure stood motionless in the shadows, silent except for a soft hiss. From his centre flowed a liquid arc glinting by the light of the street lamp. 'Hai!' shouted Gustad. '*Bay-sharam budmaas*! I'll break your *huddi*, you rascal!' The arc terminated abruptly. The man's hand shook twice and performed a deft movement in his trousers before he slipped away.

'You saw?' said Gustad. 'Shameless. That's the reason for the stink. But once you draw your holy pictures, no one will dare.' He glimpsed hesitation on the other's face and hastened to add, 'First we will have the whole wall washed and cleaned.'

The pavement artist thought for a bit, then agreed. 'I can start tomorrow morning.'

'Good, good. But one question. Will you be able to draw enough to cover three hundred feet? I mean, do you know enough different gods to fill the whole wall?'

The artist smiled. 'There is no difficulty. I can cover three hundred miles if necessary. Using assorted religions and their gods, saints and prophets: Hindu, Sikh, Judaic, Christian, Muslim, Zoroastrian, Buddhist, Jainist. Actually, Hinduism alone can provide enough. But I always like to mix them up, include a variety in my drawings. Makes me feel I am doing something to promote tolerance and understanding in the world.'

Gustad was impressed. 'How do you know about so many religions?'

The artist smiled again. 'I have a BA in World Religions. My speciality was Comparative Studies. Of course, that was before I transferred to the School of Arts.'

'Ah,' said Gustad. They agreed to meet next morning, very early, when the street-sweeper arrived. Later that night, he said to Dilnavaz, 'Tell that worthless son of yours who kicked IIT in the face. Tell him when he comes next time to visit you – that poor wandering pavement artist has two BAs.'

At dawn, after the street-sweeper cleaned up the nocturnal deposits, Gustad convinced him with the help of a five-rupee note to wash down the wall. He got him a stiff wire brush to scrub it well. The artist arrived with his satchel, a Petromax lamp, and a small roll of bedding. 'The sun will come out now,' said Gustad, 'wall will soon be dry.'

Three hours later, as he left for the bank, the artist was hard at work on his first drawing. He watched, trying to identify the subject, and finally interrupted, 'Excuse me. Which one is that, if you don't mind my asking?'

'Trimurti. Of Brahma, Vishnu and Shiva, the gods of creation, preservation and destruction. If that is all right with you, sir? Or I can do something else.'

'Oh no, it's fine,' said Gustad. He would have preferred a portrait of Zarathustra to inaugurate the wall, but realized that this triad would have a far-reaching influence in dissuading the urinators and defecators. When he returned in the evening, the artist had lit the Petromax. The Trimurti was complete, as well as a grim, sanguinary Crucifixion. A representation of the Jumma Masjid was in progress – since Islam prohibited portraits, he restricted himself to drawings of the famous mosques.

'Hope it does not rain,' said Gustad. He tested the air with a deep breath. 'So far, no stink.' The artist nodded without looking up from his work. 'But you will have to be careful tonight. It's the first night, people do not know yet that there are holy pictures here.'

'That's OK, I will warn them,' said the artist. 'I am going to work all night.' He set down a green crayon which started to roll away down the pavement. Gustad stopped it, replaced it in the box. 'Excuse me sir. Please, one request. Is it OK if I break a twig from your neem every morning? To brush my teeth?'

'Sure,' said Gustad. 'Everybody does that.'

During the night, the artist completed two more pictures: Moses descending with the Ten Commandments, and Ganpati Baba. As the sun was rising he added some flourishes to the latter's flesh-coloured proboscis, then took up his white crayon to write in the commandments on Moses's stone tablets.

Over the next few days, the wall filled up with gods, prophets and saints. When Gustad checked the air each morning and evening, he found it free of malodour. Mosquitoes and flies were no longer quite the nuisance they used to be; with their breeding grounds drying up, the numbers diminished dramatically. And in Khodadad Building, Odomos became a thing of the past. Dilnavaz and Gustad put away the flat dishes, *khumchaas*, *tapaylis* from under the light bulbs; there was no further use for those mosquito traps either.

The holy countenances on the wall – some grim and vengeful, some jovial, some compassionate, others frightful and awe-inspiring, yet others kind and avuncular – watched over the road, the traffic, the passers-by, day and night. Nataraja did his cosmic dance, Abraham lifted his ax high above Isaac, Mary cradled the Infant Jesus, Laxmi dispensed wealth, Saraswati spread wisdom and learning.

But the artist began to have misgivings as the wall underwent its transformation. Bigger than any pavement project he had ever undertaken, it made him restless. Over the years, a precise cycle had entered the rhythm of his life, the cycle of arrival, creation and obliteration. Like sleeping, waking and stretching, or eating, digesting and excreting, the cycle sang in harmony with the blood in his veins and the breath in his lungs. He learned to disdain the overlong sojourn and the procrastinated departure, for they were the progenitors of complacent routine, to be shunned at all costs. The journey – chanced, unplanned, solitary – was the thing to relish.

Now, however, his old way of life was being threatened. The agreeable neighbourhood and the solidity of the long, black wall were reawakening in him the usual sources of human sorrow: a yearning for permanence, for roots, for something he could call his own, something immutable. Torn between staying and leaving, he worked on, ill at ease, confused and discontented. Swami Dayananda, Swami Vivekananda, Our Lady of Fatima, Zarathustra, and numerous others assumed their places on the wall, places pre-ordained by the pavement artist; together, they awaited the uncertain future.

THIRTEEN

i

The air-raid siren poured its howls into the bank through the open window. To Gustad's ears, the rising and falling wail heralded better days, dismissing the chilling ululation of impending disaster it had been so far. At dawn, he had offered up special thanks. The halfway mark was crossed, today the fifty-first bundle would be deposited. Dada Ormuzd, my gratitude. For keeping trouble away. And for Roshan, so much better, some colour back in her cheeks at last.

The morning flew by. He met Dinshawji, passed him the bundle. 'What's the news, Dinshu? What about the Pakistanis?'

Dinshawji turned both hands palms up. 'Who knows? I have not yet seen the paper.' He stood, and Gustad glanced at his stomach. There it was, what he had been noticing for the past few days: a swelling, as though something was growing in there. He turned away before he was caught looking.

Dinshawji dragged himself painfully to the bathroom. Though he had renounced his clowning, people continued to expect one of his innumerable jokes when they exchanged morning greetings with him or asked how he was. They held themselves in readiness for laughter, but now there was one stock answer for everyone: 'Thussook-thussook, my cart rumbles along.' The first few times, people assumed that since it came from Dinshawji, it must be funny, perhaps some kind of subtle deadpan humour. Stubborn perceptions of the jovial man and his quick tongue persisted in their minds. So they chuckled or smiled broadly and slapped his shoulder.

But when he repeated the response morning after morning: 'Thussook-thussook, my cart is rumbling along,' they had to give in to the reality demanding acknowledgement. Now they wanted to hold his hand and comfort him, but all they said, morning after morning, was: 'How are you, Dinshawji?' and he answered with the words which let them share his pain.

Gustad had suspected the truth about Dinshawji's illness ever since Roshan's birthday. But when it became known to everyone in the bank, the truth seemed to multiply in intensity, following some perverse undiscovered law of physics, whereby the burden grew directly in proportion to the number of people carrying it. He prayed for Dinshawji every morning. That he was responsible for forcing him to abandon his comic ways gnawed at his conscience. After all, if Roshan could feel better because of her doll, perhaps Dinshawji got worse because he had to give up his games. But besides guilt, there was also shame – his prayers had a selfish motive: should Dinshawji stop coming to work, it would interrupt the deposits, delay the riddance of the package in the *choolavati*.

In the evening the pavement artist, his unease and restlessness having disappeared, was happily whistling 'You Are My Sunshine'. He greeted Gustad and said that today, a small bunch of flowers had been left before the drawing of Saraswati. 'Must be someone sitting for an exam.'

'That means respect for the wall is increasing, thanks to your beautiful pictures,' said Gustad. The artist smiled modestly, bowing his head, and said that in the last few days, passers-by had left enough money to pay for a new set of clothes and a pair of shoes. He planned to go shopping soon. Gustad inspected the latest deities and entered the gate, whistling the tune that had been on the artist's lips. He saw Dilnavaz on the steps outside, hushing and scolding the children, urging them to go to the far end of the compound and play without making any noise. The whistle ceased, his mouth went dry. He walked faster.

'It's started again,' she said. 'Very loose motions, seems worse than before.'

He dropped his briefcase on the desk. The fledgling bits of hope he had been nurturing all day took wing. Like the sparrows that chirped in the compound's solitary tree, but flew away if the Landmaster backfired, Gustad's hope circled once over his head and departed. If it were possible to, he would have leaped up to hold on to it. 'Is she asleep?'

'No. Stupid children outside, making so much noise.'

He went to Roshan's bedside and leaned over the slatted door to kiss her forehead. The doll lay beside her, arrayed in the bridal finery that seemed so funereal now. It sent a shiver down his spine. He raised its head to make the eyes open, and left it leaning against the headboard. 'There,' he said. 'Now the doll can look after you when you sleep. If she sleeps all day, she'll become lazy and fat, like the dogwalla idiot's daughter.'

He squeezed her hand and returned to the dining-room. 'I'm going to the doctor, Roshan doesn't need to come. And he better refer us to a specialist.' Dilnavaz suggested a cup of tea before leaving. He untied his shoelaces and rested his feet on the teapoy. 'At least this proves it could not have been bad water,' he said. 'You have boiled it every day.'

'Who knows? Once an infection, virus, gets in the body – '

'You still want to blame me? Fine!' He retied his laces and dramatically poured the tea down the drain.

She regretted her words. For him to leave now, without anything having passed his lips after mention of tea, was extremely unpropitious. 'OK,' she said, 'you hate me and you hate my tea. But at least drink a little water before going.'

'Drink it yourself.' He knew of her superstition, and was determined to make her suffer.

ii

Dilnavaz debated whether to consult Miss Kutpitia while he was gone. The partial recovery, followed by this worsening, was most mystifying.

But then the doorbell rang. It took her a moment to recognize Dinshawji. She was surprised how much he had changed since Roshan's birthday. All the same, she was not prepared to tolerate any of his silly jokes or rubbish, and made her greeting as stiff as possible: 'Sahibji'. But there was nothing to fear. The man who had laughed and sung that night, drunk beer and recited rhymes, and done numerous small things to annoy her, was not the man who stood before her with a newspaper under his arm and a bulky envelope in his hand.

'Forgive me for disturbing you,' said Dinshawji, very soft. As soft, she thought, as the muted midnight clucking of the chicken Gustad had brought home. 'Could I speak to Gustad please? It's very important.' His voice shook, and his rheumy eyes wandered nervously as he fidgeted, moving the newspaper from one armpit to the other.

'He went out just two minutes ago.' Her resolve to chasten him with a cold shoulder and sharp tongue weakened somewhat.

'Out?' He looked as if he would burst into tears. 'Ohhhh. Now what will I do?' He began to twist and tug at one of his shirt buttons. 'It's very, very important.'

That melted Dilnavaz's remaining resistance. 'Come in,' she said, 'if he is still at the bus stop I'll call him back.'

'No, no, no. How can I give so much trouble?'

'It's OK, bus stop is just outside the compound. Just come in and sit, baba.'

As if threatened by her note of impatience, he immediately made his way to the sofa. 'Thank you, thank you. Sorry for the trouble, please forgive.' The teapoy caught him on the knee as he stumbled past, making him wince. He lifted his trouser leg to examine the spot whiie Dilnavaz called Tehmul.

'HowareyouIamfinehowareyouthankyoupleaseveryverytastyjuice.'

'Quick, go to the bus stop. If Gustad is there ask him to come back. Tell him very important. Quickly.' Leaving the door open, she went inside to sit with Dinshawji.

But Dinshawji was no longer alone. His timid whispers had reached into the back room and awakened Roshan to the visitor's presence, the visitor who had once made her laugh, made her birthday glow with merriment for a while, before everything became noise and quarrel and unhappiness. Now, with her doll, she waited on the sofa beside Dinshawji and hoped he would soon start being funny again.

'Will you drink something?' Dilnavaz asked him.

'No, no. Enough trouble I have given you.' She brought the glass of water that Gustad had refused a few minutes ago.

Tehmul appeared in the doorway. 'GonegoneGustadgone. Bus-goneGustadgone.'

'Gone?' Dinshawji repeated helplessly.

'Gonegonegonegone.'

'It is very, very important to talk to him,' he said, rolling the newspaper desperately, tighter and tighter. His distress was acute; Dilnavaz could not let him leave.

'He went to the doctor for Roshan. It won't take long.'

'So much trouble I am giving,' he said timorously, but was relieved at being allowed to stay.

Tehmul dragged his bad leg slowly into the room. His shining eyes were fixed on the doll. 'Pleasepleaseplease. Letmetouchplease. Pleaseonceonlypleasepleaseplease.'

'No!' Roshan clutched the doll about the waist.

Dinshawji smiled. 'Such a small girl and such a big voice.'

'Tehmul,' said Dilnavaz sternly. 'Go play in the compound.'

He stopped his forward movement, his lower jaw working as though in search of words to protest. But there were no words, and no one to complain to. He left. A leaf fell from the neem tree, gracefully sailing earthwards on the breeze. He followed the leaf. It floated to the left, turned to the right, then spun with the current. He stumbled, tripped, and fell. Dilnavaz sighed and shut the door.

'Your voice is not sick,' said Dinshawji to Roshan. 'Nice and strong it came out just now, didn't it?'

'Touch wood,' said Dilnavaz, reaching for the teapoy with one hand and guiding Roshan's with the other. Dinshawji obligingly followed their example.

'Come on, Roshan,' he said. 'Let's hear your voice again.' She smiled, embarrassed, and fussed with the doll's veil. 'How about a little song? They must be teaching you songs in school. Come on, no, please,' he cajoled.

She hesitated, then said, to Dilnavaz's surprise, 'We sing "Two Little Eyes" for assembly every morning.'

'Perfect,' he said. 'I would love to hear that. Do it just like in school.'

'OK.' She sang softly:

> Two little eyes to look unto God,
> Two little ears to hear His words,
> Two little hands to work every day,
> Two little feet to walk in His way,

performing each line with all the actions taught by her teacher – pointing to eyes and ears, holding out her hands, indicating the feet.

Dinshawji clapped. 'Very good, very good. What else does the assembly sing?'

She stood and clasped her hands, bowing in each direction as she sang:

Good morning to you! Good morning to you!
Whatever the weather, we'll make it together!
In work and in play, a beautiful day!

'Bravo, bravo,' said Dinshawji, holding the doll's hands and bringing them together in a clapping motion.

'Enough singing,' said Dilnavaz, 'or you will get tired.' She went to the kitchen to check if the potatoes were done. When she returned, they were playing games with their hands spread flat on the teapoy. Dinshawji was counting out the fingers for *Arrung-Darrung*. As he reached the end, Roshan joined in with *'Bhum dai nay bhooski!'* That was the cue to raise their hands and slam them down, pretending to collapse where they sat.

'You are too old for that game now, Roshan,' said Dilnavaz. 'We used to play it when you were four or five.' She detected some slight envy in herself.

'She played it for my sake,' said Dinshawji. 'I am still young enough for it. Now we will play *Kaakerya Kumar*.' They stacked their fists upon the teapoy, Dinshawji's at the bottom, then Roshan's then his again, with Roshan at the top. They went through the questions and answers: *'Kaakerya Kumar, ketlo bhaar?'* *'Munno bhaar.'* *'Ek utari nay bagalma maar,'* taking turns and coercing each other with dire threats to retract the fist and stick it in an armpit. Imaginary chairs, cupboards, beds, cars, lorries were hurled at each other, till the imaginary pain was so much that someone capitulated. The denouement came when Dinshawji's final fist resisted all threats, including the wrathful flames of Small God, until Roshan hurled the all-consuming fire of Big God. Dinshawji removed his fist amidst howls of pain: 'O, I'm burning! I'm burning! Burning in the fire of Motta Dadaji!'

Even Dilnavaz laughed at his antics. Then she insisted that Roshan really must lie down again. 'One more game, please Mummy, before I go.' She got her pack of cards and played *Ekka-Per-Chaar*, in which she was trouncing Dinshawji, till she got sleepy and abandoned the game. She went to bed smiling, leaving the doll on the sofa.

Dinshawji's anxiety and nervousness returned once she left. He began toying with his newspaper again, rolling and unrolling it. Its edges were in tatters, his clammy hands covered in black smudges.

iii

Gustad insisted that the compounder deliver his message immediately to Dr Paymaster: it was an emergency. He waited by the tiny cubicle in the little storage space, amid medicine bottles of green glass, foul-smelling powders, and boxes containing pharmacological paraphernalia. Everything covered with dust. Unused for God knows how long. Why does he bother to store all this? Always prescribing his same standard four-five remedies. And calls himself a doctor. God knows why we keep coming to him.

The patient inside emerged, and through the ground glass the doctor's figure could be seen walking towards the cubicle. An ill humour had settled upon Dr Paymaster after a day of dealing with fools and misguided militants. All morning, he had spent his energies convincing his neighbours that the way to make the municipality repair and improve things was through the democratic process, through petitions, through the ballot box, or the judiciary. Just because the gutters stank was no reason for them to sink to the gutter-level rowdyism of the ruling party, or take out a big *morcha* to threaten the municipality. Finally, they agreed to try his way. But after they left, he had to argue for an hour with the gas company, to get a replacement cylinder – explaining to the idiots that if he could not light his burner and sterilize his equipment, the clinic would shut down. But the idiots would not understand. How was the country going to fight a war at this rate, he wondered.

He was not in a pleasant mood as he listened to Gustad. 'Hope you followed my instructions properly. Or did you modify the prescription? Any more Entero-Vioform? Sulpha-Guanidine? I know how much you like those.' His grouchiness surprised the compounder too. 'But you know what the biggest problem is? Everybody wants to be a doctor. Worse, everybody thinks he *is* a doctor.'

Shortly after, Gustad left with a new list of pills. How dare he say such things! Taking advantage, just because he knows me for so many years. What does he think of himself? First virus, now colitis. Easy to keep throwing out new names. Doctors think everyone else is stupid.

191

By the time he passed the House of Cages, he was yawing wildly, battling to stay afloat in the storm of Dr Paymaster's making. There was a temporary lull at the House. Here, as in any business, things were wont to happen in spurts and starts. Peerbhoy Paanwalla waited idly for the next round of customers, arranging and re-arranging his trays and tins. When Gustad hurried by with a leg that seemed lame, he could not resist calling out, '*Arré*, gentleman, hallo, how are you!'

Gustad thought he was being solicited by one of the many pimps who lurked in these doorways. Peerbhoy had used the favourite greeting of the pencil-thin moustachioed, oily-haired, gaudy-neckerchiefed individuals with ingratiating smiles, who sidled up at the least opportunity. Doubtless Peerbhoy had picked up the line from them. Gustad turned, saw him wave, and realized his error.

'Hallo, gentleman! You did not come back for Mr Mohammed?'

'No, it's all right. That problem is OK now.' What else to say about that rascal? And bloody Bilimoria.

'Just this morning Ghulambhai was here,' said Peerbhoy. 'He was looking very worried, very upset. I asked him what was wrong, but he would not say anything. Do you know what hap-pened?' Gustad shook his head and started off.

'Wait, wait,' said Peerbhoy. 'I will make a *paan* for your leg. Make your bones strong. No more lameness.'

'No need. It's fine.'

'No, *huzoor*, it's not,' he insisted. 'Just now you were swaying so badly. Up and down, and side to side. Like a launch at Apollo Bunder in the monsoon sea.'

Gustad trimmed his sail, straightened the rudder, and demon-strated with a few steps. 'See? It's OK.'

'Ah, yes, I can see it is OK now. Means the trouble is in the head. And for that, also, I have a *paan*.' Without waiting for consent, his hands began to whizz around, opening cans, trimming a leaf, crushing a nut.

Why not, thought Gustad. 'OK. But not too expensive.'

'All my *paans* are reasonably priced. All except one. That one you need only if you are going to the House.'

'You still make the *palung-tode*?'

'While there are men, there will be *palung-tode*.'

How old he has grown, thought Gustad. The large hands had

lost none of their skill or dexterity, but his fingers were gnarled, the nails yellowing like old newsprint. 'I remember you selling *paan* here since I was a child.'

'Oh yes. A very long time.'

'May I ask how old you are?'

Peerbhoy laughed. 'If you can count all my years to the day of my death, and subtract the number left from now till then, you will have my present age.' He folded the betel leaf and tucked in the corner. 'Eat that and tell me.'

Gustad opened wide, pushed it in. His mouth could barely contain the *paan*. 'Very nice,' he mumbled indistinctly. 'How much?'

'Only one rupee.'

Before getting on the bus, Gustad spat out half. The taste was a mixture of sweet and sour. Slightly pungent. Also tart and bitter. And mouth starting to feel funny.

Outside Khodadad Building, he jettisoned the rest. By now, the numbness had spread to his mind, which was not unpleasant, but made it difficult to think about Dr Paymaster's advice. He opened the door with his key. 'Dinshawji? What brings you here?'

'Forgive the trouble,' he murmured. 'It's very important.'

Dilnavaz saw the red on Gustad's lips and got a whiff of the bitter-sweet odour. She was disgusted. 'You smell horrible! Behaving like a *mia-laanda!*'

'Sorry, Dilnoo-darling,' he said feebly, and went to the bath-room, gargled, used toothpaste. That got rid of some of the smell and colour. But the numbness continued to clutch at his mind as he returned to the front room.

'What did doctor say?' she asked. 'And whatever made you eat a *paan*?'

'Peerbhoy Paanwalla said it would be good for my leg.' He rubbed his forehead. 'A cup of tea, please?'

'Like children, you men are. Doing stupid things.' She remembered the tea he had poured down the drain. 'You are sure this time you want one?' But he was too far gone to catch the sarcasm, and nodded meekly.

'What about doctor?'

'Saying idiotic-lunatic things. That we are not giving proper rest and diet. Blaming us! Wants to put Roshan in hospital. Everyone knows what happens in hospital. Blunders and botches, wrong injections, medicine mix-ups.'

Dinshawji nodded in agreement. 'Go to a hospital when you are ready to die, is what I always say.'

'Absolutely correct,' said Gustad. '*Bas*, with doctors, any time they don't know what to do – throw the patient in hospital. Who is there in the world that can take better care of my Roshan than I, I would like to know. He made the blood in my brain start to boil!'

'Few months ago,' said Dinshawji, 'my doctor wanted to admit me to Parsi General. I said to him, General is no, and Field Marshal is also no. Then my Alamai took his side, so what to do? I had to go.'

'Would have been hundred times better to rest at home.'

Dilnavaz set out three cups. Dinshawji waited, rolling and unrolling the newspaper. The edges were peeling in thin strips.

Gustad gulped his tea scalding hot, soon as it was poured. 'Slowly, slowly,' cautioned Dilnavaz. 'It will burn up your blood.' She appealed to Dinshawji: 'Won't listen to me when I say it's not good to drink it so hot and so black. Blood burning is not the only problem. It can also cause stomach cancer.' Dinshawji shuddered when she said this. He sipped his tea slowly, the cup trembling at his lips.

'My sister-in-law's father had the same habit,' she continued. 'Drank the tea soon as it was poured, boiling from the stove. By the time he was fifty, the whole lining of his stomach was completely gone. They had to feed him through a tube in his arm. Luckily, poor man did not suffer very long.'

Gustad asked for a second cup. She said, 'Dinshawji is waiting, he has something very important to say.'

'Say it, Dinshawji. I am ready.'

Dinshawji's hands shook as he opened the newspaper. He folded it and gave it to Gustad, along with the bulky white envelope. Gustad recognized it and flared up. 'Are you crazy? You did not deposit?'

'Please read,' he implored, close to tears. 'You will understand.' The piece was fairly short, titled 'CORRUPTION RIPE IN RAW', which made Gustad snort:

> Acting jointly on the basis of an anonymous tip, the CBI and city police yesterday arrested in the nation's capital an officer of the Research and Analysis Wing, Jimmy Bilimoria, on charges of fraud and extortion.

He turned disbelievingly to Dinshawji, feeling as if the *paan*'s numbness was returning to lay its icy fingers on his brain. 'Impossible! What kind of rubbish is this?'

'Please read,' he pleaded again, but Gustad had already lowered his eyes:

> The police report stated that, based on the accused's confession, the facts were as follows. Some months ago in New Delhi, Mr Bilimoria, impersonating the Prime Minister's voice, telephoned the State Bank of India and identified himself as Indira Gandhi. He instructed the Chief Cashier to withdraw sixty lakh rupees from the bank's reserves for delivery to a man who would identify himself as the Bangladeshi Babu. The next day, Mr Bilimoria, this time in the persona of the Bangladeshi Babu, met the Chief Cashier and took delivery of the sixty lakh rupees.
>
> The police report goes on to state that Mr Bilimoria has admitted he perpetrated the fraud in order to expedite aid to the guerrillas in East Pakistan. 'The Mukti Bahini are brave and courageous fighters,' the RAW officer is said to have written in his confession, 'and I was growing tired of watching the bureaucrats drag their feet.' He claims the idea was entirely his own, and his zealousness in helping the Mukti Bahini is to blame.
>
> A Footnote: While the alleged facts of this case are certainly unique, what strikes this reporter as even more unusual are the circumstances surrounding this highly imaginative crime. For example, assuming that Mr Bilimoria has the talent of voice impersonation, is it routine for our national banks to hand over vast sums of money if the Prime Minister telephones? How high up does one have to be in the government or the Congress Party to be able to make such a call? And was the Chief Cashier so familiar with Mrs Gandhi's voice that he accepted the instructions without any verification whatsoever? If yes, does that mean that Mrs Gandhi has done this sort of thing frequently? These questions cry out for

answers, and till the answers are heard, clearly and completely, the public's already eroded confidence in our leaders cannot be restored.

Dilnavaz handed Gustad the second cup of tea as he finished reading. It slipped through his fingers to the floor. The cup shattered, the hot liquid splashing his right foot and ankle.

'What's the matter? Are you feeling all right?' She felt his forehead in alarm, thinking it was the *paan*.

'Of course I am all right,' he said irritatedly, 'you are the one who dropped the cup.' He made no attempt to pick up the broken pieces or wipe his foot. 'Jimmy has been arrested.'

'What?' She took the paper and sat beside Dinshawji who was much calmer now. Gustad wondered what he was thinking. 'Believe me, Dinshu, I had no idea, or I would never have done it. I would never have asked you – '

'Where is the question of that?' said Dinshawji gently. 'There is no doubt in my mind about you at all.'

'He lied. Major Bilimoria lied from the beginning. About everything! To me!'

'Yes, but I am wondering what to do now,' said Dinshawji.

'We took such a risk. For his stolen ten lakh rupees. For a bloody crook, thinking we were doing something good!'

'Yes, yes, Gustad,' said Dinshawji calmly. 'But we cannot change that now. *Fait accompli. Jay thayu tay thayu.* Now we have to think about what to do with the money.'

'Dinshawji is right,' said Dilnavaz, surprised to hear him speak so sensibly.

'I'd like to burn it all. The way that dogwalla idiot burned the newspapers,' said Gustad bitterly.

'First of all, I think we should stop depositing it,' persisted Dinshawji, still on the rational track.

'But what about the money already in the bank?'

'Just leave it the way it is. Maybe Ghulam Mohammed will contact you. Or you can contact him.'

'But he could also be in jail,' said Dilnavaz. 'We don't know how far he was involved in it. Maybe we should go to the police with everything.'

Gustad remembered: 'Ghulam Mohammed is not in jail. I'll go to him tomorrow. Peerbhoy Paanwalla told me he saw him today, looking very upset and worried. No wonder. Yes, he is definitely involved in this. Too risky for us to go to the police. You know what kind of dangerous fellow he is.'

'Is he?' asked Dinshawji.

'Of course,' said Gustad, then remembered in time that Dinshawji knew nothing about the cat and bandicoot. 'That is, I am assuming.'

'I still cannot believe,' said Dilnavaz, 'our Jimmy would do something so crooked.'

'People change,' said Gustad. 'In his confession it says money was for guerrillas. Then why did he send ten lakh to me? My right hand I will cut off and give you if this is not something crooked. What kind of guerrilla pipeline is that, from Delhi to Chor Bazaar to Khodadad Building?'

'True,' said Dinshawji. 'But we don't know the whole story. And I think the reporter is asking some good questions. Everyone says Indira and her son – the motorcar fellow – are involved in all kinds of crooked deals, that they have Swiss bank accounts and everything.'

'That's right,' said Dilnavaz. 'And there has been talk of worse things. When Shastri died.'

'I remember that,' said Dinshawji. 'It was the time I had my gall-bladder operation, almost six years ago. I was in bed when the news came on the radio.'

'Yes,' said Dilnavaz. 'And before that, when her father was still alive, there was poor Feroze Gandhi. Nehru never liked him from the beginning.'

'That was tragic,' said Dinshawji. 'Even today, people say Feroze's heart attack was not really a heart attack.'

Gustad got annoyed. 'What does all this gossip and rumour have to do with the Major? He is the one who tricked me! If politicians are crooks and rascals, how does that change what Jimmy did?'

Dinshawji saw it was time to leave. He shook hands with them both. 'Sorry for bringing so much bad news.' He plodded to the door.

'On the contrary, thanks for coming. Without your newspaper we would never have known about it,' said Gustad. After Dinshawji had gone, he sat on the sofa for a while, worrying the doll's veil. 'My *bakulyoo* didn't take her doll to bed tonight.' Then he went and stood by the window. 'What kind of evil spell are we caught in, I wonder sometimes. How long is this *punoti* going to last?'

Tehmul saw his figure framed in the light. 'Gustad. Please-Gustadplease. Theywouldnotletmetouchnotoncenotonce. Please-pleaseplease. Onlyonceonly.'

Gustad raised his arm and waved it vaguely. He drew the curtain, having no time or compassion to spare tonight. There was the sound of sniffling outside, and a sob; then the sound of footsteps: a light step first, then heavy and dragging, alternating till they faded.

FOURTEEN

i

Nearing the crossroads, Gustad saw the cinema billboard lights blaze in the dusking sky. Synchronized bulbs flashed around gigantic cut-outs of hero and heroine, guardians of the city's evening chaos; behind them loomed a bearded villain, nastily twisting his villainous lips.

Outside the Aarey Colony milk booth, three boys in tattered vests and a little girl in scavenged ankle-length blouse scrambled round the wire racks, examining the used bottles. The booth attendant bellowed to leave the bottles alone. Bad for business, he said, nuisances staring with big-big eyes as if they never saw milk in their lives.

The children waited till he was absorbed in his work, then sneaked up again. The attendant heard the tinkling of bottles. He silently opened the door at the rear of the booth and leaped out as Gustad reached the corner.

The three boys escaped. The little girl was caught by the sleeve of her blouse-frock. '*Budtameez!*' said the man, and whacked her over the head. 'Won't listen when I tell you nicely!' Whack, again. The child squealed and struggled. The boys watched helplessly. The man lifted his hand for the third blow, which never landed.

Gustad grabbed his collar from behind and the shock made him lose his grip. The boys clapped, and the girl quickly ran to a safe distance. Gustad spun the man around. 'You have no *sharam*, a big donkey beating a tiny girl?'

'All day they make nuisance,' he whined. 'Harassing my customers, grabbing their bottles before they even put them down.' Gustad released the man's collar. The little girl watched gratefully from her place of safety. She wiped her runny nose on a sleeve. How thin she is. Even skinnier than Roshan. 'People don't like to stop where there are beggars,' the attendant continued. 'If I don't sell my quota, this booth will shut down. Then what will I do?'

'Give me one bottle,' snapped Gustad, taking out his wallet.

'What kind? Chocolate, mango, pista, plain?'

Gustad beckoned to the little girl. 'Come, baby. What milk you like?' She made a shy movement with her head and shoulders. He insisted she choose.

'Plain white,' she said timidly. The attendant grudgingly placed a bottle before her and inserted the straw. After a few sips she called the boys, holding out the bottle towards them.

'Wait wait, what is this?' said Gustad. 'Milk is for you.'

'My brothers. They also like milk,' she said shyly, looking down and tracing a design in the dust with her toe.

'Oh,' considered Gustad. 'What kind they like?'

'Chocolate!'

'Chocolate!'

'Chocolate!' came the replies in quick succession, and then, in unison, 'But any kind is OK.'

'Three chocolate,' he told the attendant. He waited while they drank, not willing to trust the fellow alone with them. When the straws gurgled emptily, he left. They tagged behind for a little distance, skipping along, pushing one another, bursting into film songs now and again, not quite certain how to show their gratitude. Eventually, they disappeared in the rush of movie-goers.

Past the cinema junction, the crowds thinned. The Wheeler-Dealer Tyre Mart was taking in its display from the pavement. The car mechanics (All Makes–Local & Foren) collected their tools and spare parts from the curb and locked the cars. Near the House of Cages were the usual loiterers, come to gaze at the exotic birds in their skimpy, colourful plumage. The genuine customers entered and emerged without dilly-dallying.

'Hallo, gentleman!' said Peerbhoy. 'Leg is fine today?'

'Yes, yes, very fine,' he replied, pre-empting offers of another *paan*. 'Is Ghulam Mohammed coming today?'

'Already he is inside.'

'And I can go in? They won't mind?'

'The women? *Arré*, they like it if a man comes. Ghulambhai is on top floor, exactly opposite the staircase.'

A radio or record-player somewhere was playing an old film

song: '*Dil deke dekho, dil deke dekho, dil deke dekhoji* . . .' Try giving your heart away, give your heart away and see, exhorted the singer. Gustad entered the place hesitantly. Down the passage, into the cheap perfume smells and nauseating attar mingled with body odours. The women waiting for customers. Bosoms thrusting. One dropped a hand to the hem of her skirt and raised it so the thigh was exposed. Gustad glanced quickly: hairy. He climbed the stairs. At the next landing, the exhibition repeated. Cleavages and navels framed in doorways. One in shorts (Hot Pants, said the print on the back), turned sideways, showing squeezed-out half-moons. He looked without staring, hoping his face showed a blank disinterest. Have to be desperate to . . . that one needing a good shave. Elongated *baatli* mangoes. Wheeler-Dealer tyres. This place looking better from outside than in. But they say at Colaba, beautiful high-class whores. Colaba call-girls, making lots of money with Middle East tourists, Arbaas, fond of AC-DC, both ways . . .

The rooms he could peek into were sordid. Bed, thin lumpy mattress, no sheet, ceiling fan, chair, table. In one corner, a basin and small mirror. Where were the scented silk sheets, the air-conditioned rooms, drinks, refreshments? The luxuries that they talked of in their stories of this place? Where were the dancing-girls, the skilled practitioners of the art said to possess secrets that could drive a man insane with pleasure? The way these women moved and displayed themselves, there was as much chance of going insane with pleasure as recovering from heart surgery performed by a beef-carving Crawford Market *goaswalla*. He climbed the third and final floor. It's always the same. Always, things look wonderful from afar. When the moment arrives, only disappointment.

The music ended, then the same song started again. '*Dil deke dekho, dil deke dekho, dil deke dekhoji*' . . . must be someone's favourite record. He knocked on the door opposite the stairs. It opened a crack. He did not recognize the man with a full beard who peered out. Then the man spoke and let the door open wide: 'Mr Noble. Please come in.' The voice was familiar. In the months since Chor Bazaar, Ghulam Mohammed had lost his bandage and gained a beard.

Gustad entered cautiously. The room was like the others he had glimpsed, down to the wash-basin, but instead of a bed there was a desk. Framed pictures of Mahatma Gandhi and Jawaharlal Nehru hung on the wall behind the desk.

'Please have a seat. I was expecting you. Thanks for coming so promptly.' Polite and courteous as ever, thought Gustad. As though nothing had happened. 'You read it in the newspaper?'

'Yesterday,' said Gustad.

'You must be wondering what's going on.' He swivelled from side to side in his chair, then became very still. 'It's true. Our dear friend is really in jail. But the rest is lies. Dirty lies. You know everything that appears in newspapers is not the truth.'

Salt and pepper, ginger and garlic, came to Gustad's mind, what he used to tell Sohrab about propaganda and falsehoods. 'I know how to read a newspaper,' he said. 'But you tell me the truth. Why Jimmy sent ten lakh to me for deposit. You say what the truth is.' He felt his anger rising, though he knew this man had to be dealt with cautiously. 'And tell me also about the cat and the huge rat thrown in my bush. With the heads chopped off.'

He watched him closely, but Ghulam betrayed no trace of emotion. 'I don't know what you are talking about, Mr Noble. In RAW, we have no time for playing with cats and rats. But I can tell you this. Bili Boy has enemies. This whole story was cooked up by people at the very top to cover their wrongdoings.' He leaned closer. 'I'm glad you asked about the money. Sadly, I am not in a position to answer your questions. Bili Boy will tell you himself, at the proper time. You have to trust him.'

'I think I have trusted him too much already.'

'Now, Mr Noble. No sense being upset with your friend when he needs you most.'

'What do you mean?'

'His life is in danger,' said Ghulam Mohammed. 'He is –'

Screams and shouts drowned the *Dil deke dekho* record. Ghulam jumped up from his chair and checked the back alley outside his window, then opened the door to listen. The women were yelling abuse at someone – a male, judging by the derision and taunts concerning his manhood which flew thick and fast. The two men went to the landing. The attar-clouded air of the brothel filled with the women's colourfully obscene speech.

Then, through all of that, penetrated an unmistakable high-speed utterance: 'Pleasepleaseonceonly. Onceonlyonce. Fastfastrubbing-

pleaseonceonly. Pleasetakemoneypleaseplease. Letmetouchletme-
pressonceonly.'

'I can't believe it!' said Gustad.

'What?'

'That voice! It's Tehmul-Lungraa, lives in my building. Poor
lame fellow with a half-cracked head.'

'You are sure?'

He seems relieved, thought Gustad. 'Completely sure. What is
he doing here, but?'

'Same thing that other men do, I think.'

'Cannot be, he's like a child. Sounds like he's in trouble.'

The row was proceeding on the ground floor. Hydraulic Hema,
favourite of the mechanics, with lips like blood and eyes black as
coal, was savagely shaking Tehmul by the ear. Women surrounded him, taking turns to clip him on the head, pinch, pull his
hair. They were enjoying the sport, staying out of his reach as he
continued to make a grab at a breast or tried to reach inside a skirt.
'Pleaseletmetouch. Pleasepleaseonceonlyletmetouchplease. Take-
moneyplease.' He held out a round cigarette tin that jingle-
jangled, but there were no takers.

'Tehmul!' shouted Gustad. 'Stop it!'

Tehmul dropped his hungry hands. He looked around, trying to
locate his beloved Gustad, and found him, halfway up the stairs.
'GustadGustadGustad.' He waved the cigarette tin, with the
blood-lipped amazon still clutching his ear. A well-placed blow
dislodged the tin. It burst open on the floor and scattered the
coins. Most of them twenty-five paisa pieces. The women fell
silent.

'What is all this shouting and screaming like a madhouse?'
demanded Ghulam Mohammed. 'This is a respectable establishment, not some third class *rundi-khana.*'

The women protested, all speaking at once: 'It's not our fault,
this fellow – !'

'He keeps wanting to touch and – !'

'There is no law that we have to lift our skirts for anyone who
can pay!'

'They say madmen have very big ones, built like horses! We
don't want to get hurt!'

Hydraulic Hema held on to Tehmul's ear while her sisters

poured out their grievances. 'Enough!' said Ghulam Mohammed. 'I have heard enough! Let go of his ear!'

'*Arré*, he'll start grabbing again, he's a complete gone-case!' she said, her voice like sandpaper.

'No, he won't.' Ghulam Mohammed looked at Gustad. The women moved away as Tehmul was released. He stood motionless, contrite.

'What is all this, Tehmul?' said Gustad reproachfully. 'What have you done here?'

'GustadGustadverysorryGustadpleaseGustad.' He stooped to pick up his empty cigarette tin. 'Somuchmoneyallgonegonegone. Moneyforrubbingfastfastfastfast. Nicenicefeelingallgone.' He looked forlornly inside the tin.

'Where did money come from, Tehmul?'

'Ratratratdeadratmunicipalrat.'

Of course. 'He is OK now,' he told Ghulam. 'I'll take him home with me.' Tehmul began to gather his coins.

'*Chulo*, everybody back to your rooms,' ordered Ghulam, '*tamaasha* is finished.' The women dispersed, save a couple who stayed to help Tehmul refill his tin. Tehmul slipped his hand in Gustad's as they walked outside to Peerbhoy Paanwalla. The latter had already gathered what the commotion was about. He agreed to watch Tehmul till Gustad finished his business.

*

'I was telling you that Bili Boy's life is in danger.'

'First you say he is in prison, then you say his life is in danger.' What does he take me for.

'I know you are upset, Mr Noble,' said Ghulam patiently. 'But please try to understand. People at the very top are involved. They can do whatever they like with Bili Boy. In this country, laws don't apply to the ones at the top, you know that.'

'So what can I do?'

'First of all, the money must be sent back.'

'Sure. But I have already deposited half. You can have the remaining fifty bundles any time.'

'All of it, Mr Noble. Withdraw the rest if you have deposited it.' The voice was sharper now.

'Do you know how difficult it is to deposit and withdraw these big amounts? How dangerous? The law is being broken.'

'Better than bones being broken, Mr Noble.' Whose bones does he mean? Unemotional, the bastard's voice. 'Do you know how dangerous it is for Bili Boy? They are using their usual methods to make him say where the money is. The only reason he has not confessed is that he wants no trouble for his friends.'

What part of this to believe? How to trust him or Jimmy? 'Now Bili Boy has made a deal with them,' Ghulam continued. 'If the money is returned in thirty days, they will ask no more questions.'

For all I know, this bastard could take the money and disappear. But if Jimmy is really being tortured? 'Thirty days is impossible. I can only withdraw one bundle a day.'

'Withdraw two, Mr Noble.' A smile appeared suddenly on his face. 'Or I will have to come and rob your bank.' Disappeared just as suddenly. Poison again, in his voice. 'I will do whatever is necessary to help Bili Boy. You have thirty days to return the full package.'

Gustad tried to protest again, but the man was hard as steel. 'If the money is not delivered on time, things will go badly for *all* of us, Mr Noble.' Bloody bastard. With one hand I could flatten him. He knows I dare not.

They fixed the delivery date. 'But if you are ready earlier,' said Ghulam, 'please come. I will be here every evening.' He led him to the door. 'So you were saying someone threw a dead cat and rat in your bushes?'

'Yes.' With one hand. Just one blow.

'Hope you catch him, whoever he is.'

On the way downstairs most of the doors were shut. Brisk business. The record-player was spinning another song, about undying love, constant for over a hundred years, for eternity . . . '*Sau saal pahalay, mujay tumsay pyar tha, mujay tumsay pyar tha, aajbhi hai, aur kalbhi rahayga . . .*' the melody warm and syrupy, dripping nostalgia. And no way out for me. Have to withdraw. Involve poor Dinshawji also in the risk.

Outside, Peerbhoy told him Tehmul had left. 'Don't worry, he is all right. Poor fellow tried to explain what happened. But speaks very fast. I gave him a *paan* to reduce his juice production.'

ii

Miss Kutpitia could offer no explanation about Roshan's relapse without examining the lime and chillies. So Dilnavaz went back with those neutralizers of evil eyes.

'Yes,' said Miss Kutpitia. 'Yes, just as I thought. Look at this. You know what usually happens to a yellow lime?'

'It turns brown, becomes soft and smells sour.'

'And see this one,' she said triumphantly. 'Hard as a rock and black as the devil! And no smell at all.'

Dilnavaz felt a cold draught slink through the passage. Then Miss Kutpitia pointed out how peculiarly the chillies were also behaving, all still green as Satan's emeralds instead of turning red. She kept passing them between her fingers like beads on a rosary. 'Shows us how much damage the evil eye can do. The poor child has received the full force of it.' She sniffed the chillies. 'Fortunately, it is not difficult to be rid of. The seven will do it.'

'But why did Roshan first improve, then get worse?'

'Will you wait? I am coming to that. Listen. Inside the child, two forces are attacking: evil eye, which is unintentional; and something else, something dark, something deliberately inflicted. Now, when the evil eye is crushed, the child recovers. Then the dark force arises, and the child is sick again.' She picked up the lime. 'This,' she said. 'This black stone reveals the dark force.'

Dilnavaz wrung her hands. 'So medicine is of no use?'

'Some use. Will keep her from getting worse. But won't cure. We have to find the one responsible for the dark force.'

'O God! That will be impossible!'

'Not with alum.' A rare smile, of quiet confidence, strayed across Miss Kutpitia's lips. 'Wait.' She went to her kitchen and returned with two chunks the size of pigeon eggs. 'Take these. And Roshan must be present when you do what I will tell you, or it's no use.' She detailed the procedure, then returned the chillies and lime. 'From now on, learn to be more cautious. And teach your children also. Teach them to fear the nights of the full moon; and with Kalichovdas approaching, keep them indoors after sunset. Tell them not to step on, or over, strange objects placed in the road. Beware of anything that looks like a little packet of flowers, or broken eggs or shattered coconuts. Those things come from black-magical *kaarestaan*, believe me.'

Dilnavaz nodded, trying to memorize her instructions. 'But what about Sohrab? When will he return to me?'

'Patience.'

'Is there nothing more I can do?'

Her persistence vexed Miss Kutpitia; then, as a matter of compromise, she said, 'Do Tehmul's nails again. Add a lock of his hair this time. On the day after the new moon. His channels will be open widest that day.' Wagging her bony forefinger, she admonished her again: 'But you must be patient.'

Dilnavaz ventured timidly, 'You had said there was a final remedy we could try if everything failed –'

Miss Kutpitia cut her off sharply. 'I have told you not to think of that. Put it out of your mind. At once.'

'Whatever you wish. You know best, that's why I come to you.' She thanked her humbly and left.

iii

Dinshawji's advice to Gustad was to comply with everything Ghulam Mohammed said. 'Don't defy him. Just do it quietly, then we can forget about the bastard.'

'But we'll have to withdraw two bundles a day. That's the only way we'll finish in thirty days.'

'Don't worry, leave that to me.' Dinshawji went about the task quietly, confidently. Each evening he passed two bundles to Gustad, who took them home and stuffed them back into the hateful black plastic under the *choolavati*.

The bank was abuzz with the remarkable case in New Delhi. It was not very often that a Parsi made the newspapers for a crime. The last sensation had been more than a decade ago, when a naval commander had shot and killed his wife's lover. In the canteen, they debated Major Bilimoria's dubious confession, and the plethora of startling facts that the investigation was uncovering. Most of them refused to believe he could have imitated the Prime Minister's voice, there was something very fishy about the whole thing, they said.

Dinshawji and Gustad took part in these discussions, trying to show a normal interest. Dinshawji handled it so well, thought Gustad, filling with admiration for the cool courage and good sense. Here was no clown or buffoon, but a solid, dependable friend. How badly I misjudged him. And how will I ever repay him for all his help?

Before long, the thirty-day deadline reached the halfway mark. Gustad emerged to pray at dawn and found the rose plant, the vinca, and the *subjo* bush hacked to the ground. Every stem, every branch had been slashed off, chopped into little pieces.

No point in calling the Gurkha, he thought. Why make a fuss? But Jimmy loved the vinca, sometimes he would come to water the flowers in the morning.

He stood there for a minute or two, then fetched the rubbish pail and quietly gathered up Ghulam Mohammed's bloodless reminder.

*

Dinshawji stepped up the pace to withdraw three bundles a day, and Gustad wished he had not mentioned Ghulam's threats. But the least he owed Dinshawji now was complete honesty. 'Isn't that dangerous, Dinshu? Thirty thousand will be highly noticeable on the ledger, don't rush it.' Dinshawji said there was nothing to worry about, he knew what he was doing. So the account was emptied five days ahead of the deadline.

That evening, Gustad shook his hand fervently. 'Thank you, Dinshu, thank you. I don't know how to thank you enough, so much you've done for me.'

'Forget it, *yaar*,' he smiled. 'It's nothing.'

But it was only the next day, after Dinshawji had expunged all traces of the fictitious account, that Gustad learned the truth. Dinshawji collapsed just before lunch, and was rushed to Parsi General. Mr Madon sent a messenger to Dinshawji's wife, and granted Gustad's request to ride in the ambulance.

As it sped through the streets, its siren wailing, Dinshawji regained consciousness. 'It's OK, Dinshu, everything will be all right,' said Gustad. 'Your wife has been informed, she will come to the hospital.'

'My domestic vulture,' said Dinshawji, smiling weakly. 'God bless her, she will come flying.' The ambulance weaved in and out of traffic, at times grinding to a halt, making Gustad curse and fret. He gazed upon Dinshawji's face and noticed how the dewlaps under his chin had, in repose, collapsed into little rolls of skin along the throat.

Dinshawji opened his eyes again. 'Now you know, Gustad, why such a big rush. I could feel that not many days were left. So I began to take out three, to finish the job. Before it was too late.' Gustad took his hand in both of his. The thing in his throat made it impossible to speak. The hand felt cold, and very smooth.

Dinshawji's wife was not there when the ambulance reached Parsi General. 'Traffic is bad,' said Gustad reassuringly. 'Alamai must be caught in the jam.' He stayed with him while a bed was found in the male ward and the formalities were completed. It was the same ward where Dinshawji had spent time six months ago.

Dinshawji urged him to get back to the bank. 'Or else that Madon will start marching up and down, asking why Mr Noble is taking so long to come back.'

'Don't worry about Madon. I am going to stay here till the doctor sees you.'

'Not necessary, *yaar*. This place is like a vacation home for me.' His eyes twinkled the way they used to before Laurie Coutino's complaint. 'All the comforts and conveniences I can imagine.' Then he sang softly, out of tune:

> O give me a home where the nurses' hands roam,
> Where they all have big beautiful tits;
> But where seldom is heard an encouraging word,
> And the patient is treated like shit.

Gustad laughed. 'Shh! If they hear you, they will give you a tough time. These people don't know how to appreciate a Poet Laureate. You know their favourite way to harass patients?'

'What?'

'When you ask for the bedpan, they make you wait and wait till you think you cannot hold it any more.'

Dinshawji chortled, holding his stomach where it hurt. '*Arré*, let them try that with me. I will just let go, dhuma-dhum, dhuma-dhum. Right in the middle of the bed. And make the whole hospital stink. More work for them only.' They laughed again. Then Gustad shook his hand and left. At the registration desk, he made the clerk note Miss Kutpitia's telephone number next to Alamai's, just in case.

He did not return immediately to the bank. Outside, in the hospital grounds, the sun was shining on the lawns. He found a bench along a path between flowerbeds. A butterfly flitted among the flowers. He saw its brilliant orange and black patterns before it floated away. Sohrab had one like that in his collection. Monarch, he said its name was. I can remember perfectly. After the rain, at

Hanging Gardens. Everything was in bloom. Sohrab all excited the night before, making plans. And so shy in the garden, with his *sudra*–and–racquet net. But he caught five that day. Monarch was first. He removed it from the killing-tin with his tweezers, its antennae crippled, thorax contorted. A cloud had passed over Sohrab's face when he saw that twisted butterfly, and Gustad knew his son would not pursue the hobby for long.

How much of all this does Sohrab remember, he wondered. Very little, I think. For now. But one day he will remember every bit. As I do, about my father. Always begins after the loss is complete, the remembering.

The butterfly returned, gliding on a slow breeze. He watched till it became a speck and disappeared from sight.

iv

When the lumps of alum fell on the hot coals, they fused into a single blob. The blob bubbled and frothed, making a hissing, gurgling sound as it perched viscously atop the coals. Roshan watched with interest till the coals lost their red heat and the seething activity ended.

'Now back to bed,' said Dilnavaz. 'You will feel better after these prayers.' She observed curiously, fearfully, the smooth, white contours the alum had assumed. How wickedly it sits on the coals. This evil thing. It separated easily from the embers, light and brittle. Like a fresh *khaari* biscuit, she thought, concealing it in a paper bag – the clue to the dark force harming her child.

Miss Kutpitia was delighted with the results. 'Good, very good,' she said. 'What a nice, complete shape. Often it crumbles, and then it's difficult to read. But you have done it so well.' She placed the indeterminate mass on the telephone table and inspected it. 'Come, you also look,' she said. 'But look at it without seeing it. That way it will take on different meanings. Look with the eyes you use when you dream.'

Dilnavaz tried, unsure of the instructions. 'Reminds me of the Sister who brought Roshan home when she was sick.'

'What?' said Miss Kutpitia disbelievingly.

'See, looks like the long white *jhabbho* the nuns wear.'

'But would they want to hurt Roshan? They are good and godly people.' She explained again. 'Listen. If you use only your eyes, you will only see the things of this world. But we are dealing with forces from another world.' They studied the alum again, silently, turning it this way and that.

'Wait a minute, wait a minute,' said Miss Kutpitia. 'Yes, definitely. Stand here,' she said, pulling Dilnavaz over to the other side. 'Now what do you see?'

'A hat? No. A house? A house without windows?'

Sorely disappointed with Dilnavaz's hamstrung imagination, Miss Kutpitia dismissed the suggestions with the contempt they deserved, then guided her eyes with the benefit of her own expert vision. 'Look, what is this? A tail. And this, this, this, and that? Four legs. And over there?'

'Two upright ears!' said Dilnavaz, excited, catching on at last, to her mentor's relief. 'And that, that's a snout!'

'Right!' said Miss Kutpitia. 'What does it all add up to?'

'A four-legged animal?'

'Of course. A dog, I think.'

'A dog? Sending out a dark and evil force?'

'You are not remembering what I said before.' Miss Kutpitia was impatient. 'I said the alum shape will give us a clue. That does not mean it will show the culprit. Someone who owns a dog could be the one we are looking for.'

Dilnavaz clutched her face with both hands. 'O my God!'

'Now what is it?'

'Mr Rabadi! He has a white Pomeranian! He was – !'

'Calm down. First of all, does he have a reason?'

'Yes, yes! He and Gustad have been fighting all the time, since the time of the big dog. Tiger, who used to do his chhee-chhee in Gustad's flowers. And now the small dog also barks at him. Then there was trouble with newspapers, and he thinks my Darius is after his daughter. Rabadi really hates us!'

Miss Kutpitia picked up the crucial shape. 'You know what you have to do next.'

v

A fragrance was in the air near the compound wall. 'Where is it coming from?' asked Gustad. The artist was fixing up his pictures. Some people had the annoying habit of touching the wall when they performed their obeisances. This had never bothered him in the past: during his years of wandering and drawing, he had learned that impermanence was the one significant certainty governing his work. Whenever the vicissitudes and vagaries of street life randomly dispossessed him of his crayoned creations, forcing him to repaint or move on, he was able to do so cheerfully. If short-panted, knobbly-kneed policemen did not stamp out his drawings with regulation black-sandalled feet, then eventually they became one with the rain and wind. And it was all the same to him.

But of late, something had changed, and he became very protective of his work. 'Hallo, sir. Not seen you for many days,' he said, putting down the crayon. 'Lots of new pictures are complete.'

'Beautiful.' Gustad sniffed the air again. 'Such a nice smell.'

'It's coming from Laxmi,' said the artist, and Gustad walked towards the goddess of wealth. Someone had stuck an *agarbatti* in a pavement crack next to the picture. The incense stick was down to the final inch, its vital end glowing a bright orange. Frail wisps of grey-white smoke rose gently, floated towards Laxmi's face, then vanished in the evening air. Gustad enjoyed the delicate fragrance. As the *agarbatti* burnt itself out, a length of ash dangled momentarily before falling in a sprinkle around the stub.

'The wall is getting more and more popular,' said Gustad. 'But what about money, you are getting enough?'

'Oh yes,' said the artist. 'This is a very good location.' He showed off his new clothes. 'Terylene pant – latest fashion, bell-bottoms, with seven belt loops. And Tery-Cotton shirt, drip-dry.' He tugged at the collar to display the label on the inside. But his feet were still bare. 'I went to Carona, Bata, Regal Footwear. Tried lots of different-different styles. Shoes, sandals, chappals, but they all pinch and hurt. Barefoot is the best.' Then he led Gustad to his most recent artwork: Gautama Buddha in Lotus Position under the Bodhi Tree; Christ with Disciples at the Last Supper; Karttikeya, God of Valour; Haji Ali Dargah, the beautiful mosque in the sea; Church of Mount Mary; Daniel in the Lions' Den; Sai Baba; Manasa, the Serpent-Goddess; Saint Francis Talking to the Birds; Krishna with Flute and Radha Holding Flowers, the Ascension; and finally, Dustoor Kookadaru and Dustoor Meherji Rana.

The artist was far from his usual reticent self; he confided that he was going to save up to buy new painting supplies: 'From now on, no more crayons. All pictures in oil and enamel only. Completely permanent. Nothing will spoil them.' Then he introduced Gustad to brief hagiographies of saints such as Haji Ali, who had died while on pilgrimage to Mecca. The casket containing his mortal remains floated miraculously across the Arabian Sea, back to Bombay, till it came to rest on a rocky bed not far from shore. Devotees constructed his tomb and a mosque on the very spot, as well as a causeway to the mainland which could be walked at low tide.

Then there was Mount Mary, another place of miracles. A band of frightened fishermen, caught in a violent storm, were certain they would drown. But the Blessed Virgin Mary appeared and assured them they would be safe, for she would watch over them. In return, they were to build a church atop a hill in Bandra, and place in it a statue which would wash ashore at the foot of that hill. The fishermen reached dry land safely. Next morning, when the seas grew calm, a statue of Mother Mary with the Infant Jesus in her arms floated ashore at the very beach.

The artist unfolded one story after another, and Gustad listened, engrossed. What a wealth of knowledge, he thought. And apart from the way the wall had been transformed into a clean place, there was such a sense of goodness about it, about the holy pictures.

When it got too dark to see, Gustad went into the compound. Inspector Bamji's Landmaster rolled in. '*Arré* bossie! Amazing thing you have done, really. In one shot all the fucking pissers gone. No more *goo-mooter*, no more stink. Just like a bloody miracle, bossie.'

'With so many saints and prophets on the wall, one miracle should be easy.'

'Too good, bossie, too good!' said Bamji. 'You have made it pisser-proof. But you know, I don't understand the *maader chod* mentality of our neighbours. Can you believe it? Some of them (I won't say names) are grumbling – that why should all *perjaat* gods be on a Parsi Zarathosti building's wall. I'm telling you, sawdust in their brains.'

'I think I can guess who they are.'

'Oh, forget it, bossie. Not worth thinking about. Instead of being happy that smell is gone, nuisance gone, mosquitoes gone, *saala maader chods* find something else to cry about.'

'Anyway,' said Gustad, 'the artist has drawn Zarathost Saheb. And also Meherji Rana and Dustoorji Kookadaru.'

'Of course, bossie. More the merrier. A good mixture like this is a perfect example for our secular country. That's the way it should be. The *ghail chodias* will complain even if God Himself comes down. Something they will find wrong with Him. That He is not handsome enough, or not fair enough, or not tall enough.' Inspector Bamji waved and drove off. Gustad entered with his latchkey, laughing quietly to himself. Roshan was sobbing on the sofa.

'She won't stop,' complained Dilnavaz. 'Being so silly.'

'Is it paining somewhere? What's wrong?' He rushed to the sofa and held her.

'Nothing is paining. Her doll is lost, that's all.'

'What do you mean, lost? Such a big doll? It's not a needle or button.'

'We can't find it anywhere in the house.'

'Then say stolen. Lost!' He wiped Roshan's eyes. 'Where was it left?'

'On the sofa, for many days.'

'*Bas*, you must have left the door open. So many times I have warned you. How long does it take for the fruitwalla or biscuitwalla or anyone to grab something and run?'

'I never leave the door open,' Dilnavaz stated emphatically, simultaneously remembering her frantic rushings to and from Miss Kutpitia's.

'Don't worry,' he comforted Roshan. 'We will find it.' Where on earth, he wondered helplessly. A miracle would be required, like the wall. Why did miracles and misfortunes always come hand in hand?

i

'The money is all here. You better count it.'

Ghulam looked hurt. 'Please don't say that, Mr Noble. I trust you with my life. You are Bili Boy's friend, and mine.'

Bastard hypocrite, thought Gustad. Last time, menacing and vicious – like a cobra spreading its hood. Now all sweet and grateful. Bloody actor. 'I hope the need to be your friend and the Major's is ended.'

Ghulam sighed and opened a newspaper. 'You saw this report from Delhi today? About Bili Boy.' Curiosity got the better of Gustad's bitterness.

'See?' said Ghulam. 'They are out to get him. Three different magistrates in three days, to dispose of Bili Boy's case.' He mauled the paper angrily. 'People at the very top are involved, believe me.'

The bastard is right. Something funny going on. 'Major Bilimoria lied to me from the beginning. How can I believe or not believe? Who can I trust? You? The newspaper?'

Ghulam looked pained again. 'Please, Mr Noble, things are not what they seem. He is trapped by the ones at the top.' Gustad's face showed scorn for his words. 'And what's hurting him most in prison is not his enemies' blows, but his friend thinking he has been betrayed. That's why he wants to meet you and explain.'

'What? But you said he is in prison.'

'It can be arranged. If you will go to Delhi.'

'Impossible. I have no leave, and my child is sick, besides, with – '

Ghulam reached inside his jacket. 'He has written to you. Please read.' Gustad opened the envelope:

My dear Gustad,

Where shall I start? Things have gone wrong. So hopelessly wrong. And I almost got you into trouble. Can you forgive me?

I have only one request to make now. Shameless of me to even mention the word request, but I want you to come to Delhi, so I can tell you what happened. It is a long complicated story, and you will not believe words on paper, because I sent you words on paper before and could not keep them from turning false. Please visit me. I want you to know and understand, hear from your own lips that you forgive me. Ghulam Mohammed will arrange everything. Please come.

Your loving friend,
Jimmy

Gustad folded the note and slipped it in his pocket.

'Will you go?' asked Ghulam.

'I was tricked by him once.'

'You are making a mistake, he is really your friend. But not for long if his enemies finish him off.'

'Come on, now.' Bloody actor. Will say anything to convince me.

'No, really. Not exaggerating. If you dealt with these people, you would know. Please go.'

'OK, let me think about it,' said Gustad, making the concession solely to get away from the persistent entreaties.

The night air was thick. Stifling as that rascal's presence was. Smelling like the black stone wall before the artist came. The gutters were overflowing again, the stench and noxious gases bubbled steadily. Gustad wondered if Dr Paymaster, the shopkeepers, whores and mechanics were getting results from their complaints to the municipality. He hurried along, holding his breath and, when he had to, inhaling as shallowly as possible.

Tehmul was waiting in the compound when he got back. 'GustadGustadveryveryimportantletter.' It was from the landlord, thanking the tenants for signing the petition against road-widening. He promised to keep them informed about the lawsuit. Of the thirty copies, Gustad kept one and instructed Tehmul to deliver the rest. Way the courts work, we will all be old and dead. By the time there is a verdict. Thank God.

Through the remaining days of October, Dinshawji's condition did not improve. He seemed to shrink in his hospital bed. His arms, legs, neck, face – everything withered, except the lump in his stomach, that insidious mound under the sheet. And his size twelve feet, erect, like twin sentries at the foot of the bed.

Gustad visited as often as he could, at least twice a week, and thought it curious that he never came across Dinshawji's wife during the bedside hours. He brought Dinshawji up to date on bank news and personalities. To amuse him, he narrated Mr Madon's row with an employee, or described what Laurie Coutino had worn to work. 'Down to here, her blouse was today,' he said, undoing the top three buttons of his shirt and tucking the fronts in sideways to make a deep plunging V.

'Go, go! Couldn't be,' Dinshawji chuckled.

'Swear,' he said, pinching the skin under his Adam's apple to validate the oath. 'Down to here. Without exaggeration. When she walked, her boblaas shivered like mounds of Rex Jelly, I am telling you.'

'Arré, stop torturing me, yaar. Please, I touch your feet!'

'All day long, the fellows kept going to her desk with some excuse. Those buggers. Even Goover-Ni-Gaan Ratansa. You won't believe it, finally old Bhimsen also, tottering and crawling. Memsaab, he said, you want tea-coffee? Some cream-cracker biskoat? That was just too much.'

Dinshawji shook with laughing. 'What about Madon?'

'He got his share in his private cabin. In the Officers' Enclave. Said his own secretary was busy, so he wanted to give Miss Coutino some dictation.'

'Sure,' said Dinshawji. 'He must have given her the d-i-c and forgotten about the t-a-t-i-o-n after seeing her Rex Jelly.'

The subject exhausted, Gustad told him the money had been returned to Ghulam Mohammed, and showed him the Major's note. 'So what do you think of that?'

'Difficult to say,' said Dinshawji, 'but if I were in your place I would go.'

'And if it is another trick?'

Dinner arrived, and the bed-table was positioned over Dinshawji. The ward boy briskly served a bowl of soup and a covered platter, then wheeled the food trolley to the next bed. Dinshawji looked quite helpless, pinned under the trestle.

'Shall I raise the head a little?' asked Gustad. He wound the handle but the feet began to rise. He inserted the key in the next slot and tried again; the top half slowly elevated. 'Comfortable?'

There was a grateful nod, and he flipped the lever to lock the bed in place. Dinshawji dipped the spoon in the bowl and conveyed it to his mouth. But his hand shook wildly, the soup dribbled throatwards down his chin. He smiled sheepishly, trying to wipe it with the back of his hand. Hesitantly, Gustad unfolded the napkin and cleaned him up. When Dinshawji let him do that without protest, he took the spoon and began feeding him. 'A little bread with it?'

'Yes, please.' Gustad broke a slice into the soup. He sank the floating pieces, then fished them out one by one.

The covered dish held a mutton cutlet and a small helping of boiled vegetables. '*Bas*, I am full,' said Dinshawji.

'No, no, you must eat.' Gustad divided the cutlet into manageable mouthfuls, forked a piece and held it to his mouth. 'Come on, come on. Open up. It's very tasty.'

'Please *yaar*, the soup filled my stomach and my chest.'

'Be a good boy, now, Dinshu.'

'OK, on one condition – we eat half-half.' Gustad agreed. Midway through the meal he tried to pass on an extra piece. 'Cheating, cheating,' said Dinshawji. 'Your turn.' After they had emptied the plate in this way, he drank a little water through the spout of his feeding cup. He watched Gustad put the tray aside for the ward boy and wind down the bed slightly. 'Sorry for all this, Gustad.'

'Rubbish. I got to enjoy your tasty cutlet,' said Gustad. Unless he kept up the façade, he knew he would descend into gloom and sadness, which would not be good for Dinshawji.

Later, as he was leaving, Dinshawji thanked him again. His voice was almost tearful. 'Don't know what I would do without your visits.'

'Forget it, *yaar*. It's nothing. Actually, helps to pass my time also.' He straightened the pillow. '*Chaalo*, good-night. And don't do any *ghaylaa-chayraa* with the night nurse.'

'Have you seen her? Real *futaakro*. My Lady with the Lamp. She can borrow my candle any time her lamp is out of order.'

Gustad walked down the cold, clattering corridor, wondering

how Dinshawji managed when he did not come. Did the ward boy or nurse feed him, or was he left to spatter and spill? And where was the domestic vulture? He had wanted to ask, but it would have embarrassed Dinshawji.

So all through the rest of October and the first half of November, he visited regularly. On Sundays, he spent the entire afternoon and evening with Dinshawji. Towards the middle of November, his condition worsened, and he was fed intravenously. Now Gustad could only sit, helpless, and watch as the bottles, hanging cold and spiritless from the rack, poured their indifferent fluids into his friend. He suddenly realized how much he had come to look forward to feeding Dinshawji. Now the transparent tubes and shiny needles had taken over.

But he did not falter in his visits, especially the Sunday afternoon ones, which, for some reason, meant more to Dinshawji than all the weekday ones. Sundays had become extremely busy days for Gustad. Dr Paymaster's new strict diet for Roshan forced him to resume his hated Sunday morning Crawford Market routine. She had to be fed a variety of boiled foods, not even a hint of spice. Also, coconut water every morning, chicken soup for lunch and dinner, the juice of three sweet lemons in the afternoon, and a drink of Bovril as and when desired in between.

The money from the sale of Gustad's camera was swallowed by the medicine bills. And the special diet was proving very expensive, especially the Bovril, which could be bought only on the black-market. He wondered whether to sell his watch or his gold wedding cuff-links next. But while he was at work one day, Dilnavaz got Mrs Pastakia to keep an eye on Roshan, and went to Jhaveri Bazaar. She checked at three different shops and accepted the best offer for her two gold wedding bangles.

She gave the money to Gustad, and it was too late for his objections. She added, 'For God's sake, don't bring home the chicken alive again.'

If it had not been for his child's sake, nothing could have induced Gustad to endure the sights and smells of Crawford Market; it still repulsed him as much as ever. Every Saturday night he went to bed with a trace of nausea that grew stronger towards dawn. But one morning, when he entered the great crowded hall and made his way towards the back where the chickens were, he was pleasantly surprised. The sharp, importunate smells of provisions and spice shops came first, then the fruit stalls, where a huge pile of discarded pineapples and oranges, on the verge of putrefaction, emitted a sickly sweet odour. In the open space near the egg shops, next to the poultry, a tall, lean man was approaching. He looked so familiar that Gustad stared, trying to place him. When their eyes met, the tall man had the same look of partial recognition on his face.

'Oh my gosh!' said the tall man. 'It's Gustad Noble, isn't it?'

'Malcolm! After how many years!'

'I don't believe it!'

'Where have – !'

They put down their shopping baskets and shook hands, all four of them, and laughed and hugged, and slapped each other's backs. Then Malcolm placed his left hand on Gustad's shoulder to squeeze it – he still had that habit – and shook hands all over again. Overcome by the chance meeting, it was a while before they could talk sensibly and exchange news, catch up in some meagre way on their decades of separation. Malcolm was still single, and had fulfilled his early ambition of earning his living by music. 'But who can afford pianos and lessons these days? With the refugee tax and all? Remember, supply and demand – too many teachers around.' Now he had barely enough pupils to keep him in sheet music and scores, and to pay the piano-tuner to come regularly. 'Records also getting difficult to buy. Bloody smugglers charge more and more. Even at Stanley & Sons, the selection is hopeless now, and prices so high.' In the end, he had had to take a job at the municipality, he confessed.

'What a shame,' said Gustad. 'You have such a gift.'

'Only ones who make money in music are those monkeys who play for recording studios. Rubbish like jingles or Hindi movie soundtracks. But I cannot sell my soul that way. Bloody ting-ting-ting-ting all day on the piano? After my years of classical training? Forget it.'

Finally, the conversation came to the present. 'So that's great,' said Malcolm. 'You still come here for your beef.'

'No, not really. We buy from the *goaswalla*. More convenient, comes to the building every day.' He did not reveal his main reason for abandoning Crawford Market; it would sound silly, his fear of riots and bloodshed.

But cliché or no cliché, thought Gustad, better to be safe than sorry where fanatics were concerned. Like all riots, it had started with a peaceful rally. A vast congregation of sadhus wielding staffs, tridents, and various other equally sanctified religious instruments, staged a demonstration outside Parliament House to protest against cow slaughter. Familiar with modern trends in political campaigning and public relations, they also brought along a herd of cows. Slogans were raised, banners unfurled, curses showered on government personnel; drums, bells, horns, cymbals added to the clamour; and the gentle creatures in their midst began lowing nervously. The wrath of the gods was invoked upon the murderers of sacred Gomata, and suddenly, quite inexplicably (some claimed it was the Hand of Providence), the gathering turned violent. The police opened fire. Cows and sadhus stampeded. Staffs and tridents, hooves and horns, bullets and truncheons, all took their toll. And there was also a political death: the Home Minister who sympathized with the sadhus and encouraged their demands had to hand in his resignation. Then the Registered Trade Union of Sadhus and Holy Men sanctioned country-wide agitation, and it was a long time before cow-slaughterers and beef-eaters could breathe freely again. Gustad stayed clear of Crawford Market; his beef-buying trips were never resumed.

'Buying from *goaswalla*?' said Malcolm. 'Chut-chut, man, it's just not the same thing. That *goaswalla* will never get you the neckie part. But then what brings you here today?'

Gustad told him about Roshan's illness. Despite the gap of thirty years, he felt as comfortable with Malcolm as he had during their college days. He also confided the disappointment about Sohrab, the heartache, the blighted future. Then the subject of Dinshawji came up: 'It's so sad, so painful, to see this wonderful character lying helpless. My one true friend ever since you and I lost touch.' While Gustad said this, he was also thinking of Jimmy Bilimoria, but kept that story untold – the Major was to be expunged from his life.

Malcolm was touched by his friend's troubles. 'There is a way to help your child,' he said. 'And your sick friend. Have you heard of Mount Mary?'

Gustad started. What a coincidence! 'Yes, I have.'

'I don't mean the joke we used to tell in college,' Malcolm said laughingly. 'You know, asking the girls the way to mount Mary. I am talking about the Church of Mount Mary.'

'Oh, so that's what the joke meant. But yes, I know the church also. Just recently a pavement artist told me the miracle of Mount Mary.'

Malcolm was impressed by Gustad's account of the brilliant artist who had transformed the black stone wall. 'But come with me to Mount Mary,' he said. 'Ask Mother Mary for help. She will cure Roshan and your friend. Miracles are happening every day, I have personally witnessed so many.' He offered to help pick out a chicken first, and they started walking in that direction. Gustad learned more about the church, how it had a tradition of welcoming Parsis, Muslims, Hindus, regardless of caste or creed. Mother Mary helped everyone, She made no religious distinctions. And as they made their way through the chicken coops, Gustad felt it was like their college Sundays again, those long-ago mornings of church and beef and Christianity. He listened to his friend while examining the fowl the shopkeeper held out.

'Wait, wait,' Malcolm interrupted, 'see that?' He pointed to a misshapen foot. 'Must have had a fight. Never buy a chicken that's been in a fight.' He made the man put it back, admonishing him: 'You think we are blind or what?' He took over the selection process, and Gustad was glad. Malcolm reminded him of Pappa during the prosperous days – in his element at Crawford Market.

'Damn good chicken,' said Malcolm, finding one that pleased him. 'Feel here. Under the feathers, man.' Poking perfunctorily with one finger, Gustad agreed. The man took his knife and went to the back. Malcolm followed, beckoning to Gustad to come too. 'Have to be very sharp with these buggers, or they exchange it.' The man asked if they wanted the head. Gustad declined, and it was tossed into the gutter, to the waiting crows.

'Come with me,' said Malcolm, as they retraced their steps to the bus stop. 'We can go to Mount Mary this afternoon.'

In the old days, Gustad would have promptly dismissed such an invitation. Dabbling in religions was distasteful and irreverent, an affront to the other faith and his own. But Mount Mary was different – a feeling almost of pre-ordination about it. First, the pavement artist, describing the miracle. Then suddenly meeting Malcolm today. And hearing the same thing. Like divine intervention. Maybe Dada Ormuzd is telling me something.

'OK, we will go.'

'Good,' said Malcolm, pleased. 'See, I will catch the two o'clock local from Marine Lines. You wait on the platform at Grant Road and watch for me.'

'Right,' said Gustad. 'What's the time now?' It was ten-thirty, ten-thirty by the hundred-year-old clock in Crawford Market's façade, faithfully keeping the hours (except during power cuts) for butchers and pet-shop owners, merchants and black-marketeers, shoppers and beggars, all under one vast roof.

Gustad watched Malcolm walk home down the road to Dhobitalao where Sohrab's old school was. From the bus stop he could see the walls and railings around the police station near St Xavier's. They used to train police dogs in that yard. Once, he and Sohrab had watched through the barred gate, as the Doberman pinschers attacked dummies and mauled their trainers' heavily padded arms.

The bus came, and Gustad cast an anxious glance at his basket. The old dread about dripping blood still haunted him. Although in the last few weeks he had perfected his basket technique: layers of newspaper at the bottom and sides, and a polythene bag within – if the polythene leaked at the seams, then the newspaper would soak up the effluence. It was performing flawlessly, but as though to justify his anxiety, the woman in front turned and eyed him nastily. She reached for a sari corner to cover her nose and mouth. Her eyes continued to swivel from the basket to his face.

She knows what's in there. Smells my fear, like a dog. Eyes of a Doberman. These bloody vegetarians. A sixth sense for meat. No luck on buses . . . that time from Chor Bazaar. Bumped into Madam Wide-Arse. How upset. But how quickly I charmed her.

He smiled at the memory, and the vegetarian woman read arrogance into it. She made her eyes spit venom.

iii

'I'm off to see Dinshawji,' Gustad told Dilnavaz after lunch. He hoped to return early enough to stop at the hospital and convert his lie into a half-truth. He felt guilty, using up Dinshawji's afternoon visiting hours.

At two o'clock, a fast train to Virar pulled into Grant Road station. The surging, jostling exchange of bodies commenced, then the train pulled out: the overflowing third class; the cushioned first class; the Ladies Only, windows covered with special metal grills, with chinks so tiny, not one molesting, Eve-teasing finger could poke through. On the platform, the sign changed to show the next arrival. Gustad examined the display, trying to unravel its intricacies. Meanwhile, the train came in, and Malcolm called to get his attention. In a few minutes, at Bombay Central, the two were able to get window seats. 'Slow train,' said Malcolm. 'Supply and demand, always.'

Gustad read the station names as the blue, white and red signs on the platforms periodically swept past his window. Mahalaxmi. Lower Parel. Elphinstone Road. Dadar. 'Dadar,' said Gustad. 'I had to come here with Sohrab when he was in seventh standard. To get his textbooks at Pervez Hall.'

'What's that?'

'They do social work, helping students.' He smiled as he remembered. 'Sohrab was so excited with all the books there. He wanted to see everything, the books for eighth standard, ninth standard, tenth standard, SSC, all of them. The old lady said to him, *dikra*, do it slowly, one year at a time, gobbling too much will give you indigestion.' Malcolm laughed at the imitation of the old lady's voice, as Gustad continued: 'I used to be the same way, when I first began going to my father's bookstore. Trying to examine every book immediately. As if they were all going to vanish.' His face clouded over at his inopportune words. 'But they did. With the bailiff.' Matunga station.

'But you remember how we took my uncle's van to hide the furniture? In the night?'

'Yes, just one day before the bloody bailiff's truck.'

'You still have that furniture?'

'Of course. What superb quality. My grandfather made it, you know. Still in perfect condition,' he said proudly. The train passed over Mahim Creek, and the stink of raw sewage mingled with salty sea smells made them wrinkle their noses.

'How much longer?' asked Gustad.

'Next one is Bandra.'

*

An old woman shuffled towards them on the platform. Her shoulder was weighed down by a khaki cloth bag crammed with candles. Rheum, like stubborn tears, lingered at the corners of her eyes. Out of the bag's fraying mouth, the white candlewicks peeked clownishly, a silent cluster of tiny tongues supplicating on the old woman's behalf. Her wizened face and grey-streaked white hair reminded Gustad of the bird-woman in *Mary Poppins*, on the steps of St Paul's. Poor thing, how old and tired . . . *feed the birds, tuppence a bag, tuppence, tuppence, tuppence a bag* . . . special film première, it was. St Xavier's High School's gala night, to raise funds for the new gymnasium. And that other song. Such a long word. Sohrab was the only one who could remember it when we all got home. 'Superca . . . superfragi . . . Supercalifragi . . .'

'What?' said Malcolm.

'Oh, nothing.' What a memory, what a brain the boy had. And such a waste.

'Candles for Mount Mary,' the old woman murmured, pulling a handful out of the khaki bag.

Gustad hesitated. 'Keep walking, man,' said Malcolm. 'Cannot trust these people. They mix impurities, then the candle does not burn properly. Near the church you get better quality.'

The old woman hawked feebly, spat her reproach, and called after them: 'If everybody buys near the church only, what will happen to me, henh? How will I put a morsel in my mouth?' She said more, but the words were lost in a fit of coughing.

Outside the station, Malcolm negotiated the fare with an unmetered taxi. When they were off, the driver reached under his seat and came up with a bunch of medium-sized candles. 'For Mount Mary?' he asked eagerly.

'No,' said Malcolm.

The driver persisted. 'You want bigger? I have all different-different sizes in the dickey.'

'No man, we don't need your candles.' He gave the I-will-handle-it look to Gustad, who was preoccupied with the partly-raised window rattling violently. The handle was missing, so the glass could not be wound up or down.

'I have everything for Mount Mary in the dickey,' said the driver. 'Complete set. Hands and feet, legs and thighs. Full heads. Separate fingers and toes.' The litany of body parts distracted Gustad from the clattering window. 'Knees and noses, not to forget eyes and ears. Everything that you – '

'How many times to say no before you understand?' snapped Malcolm. Sulking, the driver shifted gears vengefully as the hill approached. The car began to climb. Gradually, between trees and buildings, they glimpsed slices of the sea, coruscating like shards of a mirror. The rocky beach became visible now, shining hot and black in the sun. 'We can go there,' said Malcolm, 'after church. It's so pleasant to sit on the rocks when the tide comes in with the breeze. So peaceful.'

Children clutching candles ran up to the taxi as it halted by the gates. The driver shooed them off. Gustad offered to share the fare but Malcolm refused: 'You are my guest today.' They turned their attention to the two carts by the gates, seeing which, the taxi-driver-cum-spurned-candleseller flung his arms in the air. He drove off, spinning his wheels and turning sharply. A cloud of dust enveloped the two men. 'Bastard,' said Malcolm.

The four-wheel carts were stacked with everything for the church-goer. They had tarpaulin roofs supported on a frame of metal rods. One was being attended to by an elderly woman, portly and in black, who sat like a statue on a wooden stool. A smartly dressed young fellow looked after the other cart. Their inventories were virtually identical: rosaries, holy pictures, plastic Jesuses, pendant-size silver crosses on silver chains, desk-size crucifixes, wall-size crucifixes, Bibles, framed photographs of Mount Mary, souvenirs of Bombay for out-of-town pilgrims. But all these items occupied the peripheries of the carts. The central display was dedicated to the wax products.

Arranged in neat rows were fingers, thumbs, hands, elbows, arms (inclusive of fingers), kneecaps, feet, thighs and truncated legs. The hands and feet came in left and right, in two sizes: child and adult. Skulls, eyes, noses, ears, and lips were grouped separately from limbs and digits. Complete male and female wax figures were also available. There they all lay, corresponding to the catalogue the taxi-driver had recited, divisions and subdivisions of limbs and torsos anatomically organized.

A vision of Madhiwalla Bonesetter's clinic swam briefly before Gustad's eyes, of limbs hanging lifelessly, limp and defenceless as these waxen ones. His left hip twinged sharply with a forgotten pain. He passed a hand over his brow and looked to Malcolm to be guided through this world of wax. This unfinished Madame Tussaud's, he thought.

'You see,' explained Malcolm, 'suffering people come to Mount Mary and offer up the part that is troubling them. Think of it as a repair shop. Mother Mary is the Mechanic for all sufferers, She mends everything.' His earthly correlatives made Gustad smile appreciatively. A repair shop, yes, that was good. Like the mechanics on Dr Paymaster's street.

'Some people do it differently,' continued Malcolm. 'They first come and pray to Mother Mary, and promise to return with the part after it is cured. But that makes no sense to me. If your watch is not working, can the watch-repairer fix it unless you give it to him?' The conclusion was irrefutable. The portly woman was moved to nod in agreement. 'Also,' said Malcolm, 'it's too much like bargaining, don't you think? I trust Mother Mary completely with advance payment.' The woman quivered on the stool. It was difficult to tell if she was shaking with mirth: her face was still impassive.

Malcolm picked out a female child's torso and gave it to Gustad. 'For Roshan. Next, your friend in hospital. If the cancer has spread, maybe best thing is to buy the full body.' He indicated the male figure in the last row. The woman in black grudgingly got off her stool. 'Who else?'

Gustad hesitated. 'Can Mother Mary help with the head? I mean the mind? For someone not thinking straight?'

'Oh yes, I think Sohrab will definitely benefit.' Malcolm picked out a male head. 'Now what about your hip?'

'No, no, that's OK.'

'What rubbish, man. This morning only you were limping at the market, I saw myself. Come on, don't be shy.' The portly woman bent sideways on her stool to see around the cart, and examined Gustad. Having sized him up, she expertly picked out a wax leg. 'Good,' said Malcolm. 'You will see how it helps. Who else?' Gustad thought of Jimmy. The pleading note he sent me. All those scary things uttered by Ghulam Mohammed. Jimmy's enemies, wanting to get rid of him and . . .

'Anyone else?' asked Malcolm again.

'No. No one else.'

The portly woman in black totalled the purchases. 'The offerings will work,' explained Malcolm, 'only if you pay. My money is no good.'

227

'Of course, naturally.'

'Four candles now,' said Malcolm, moving to the other cart. 'I always buy from both, to be fair.'

Gustad paid, and they went inside the hot crowded church. Devotees with offerings were slowly making their way towards the altar. The ceiling fan made a woman's veil caress Gustad's face. Candles in their hundreds were burning fiercely in flat metal trays. The collective light cast a brilliant orange glow towards the sanctuary. Around the trays were strewn countless limbs and figures, a waxwork universe petitioning on behalf of the suffering multitude. The intense heat from the candles was robbing the offerings of their shapes. Gustad knelt, following his friend's example, then Malcolm indicated that the wax purchases should be relinquished and the candles lit. But it was difficult to find a bare spot amid the scorching blaze in progress. Malcolm looked around to see if anyone was watching. He made room by quickly knocking over a few candles that were down to half their size. Like a backhand table-tennis smash, thought Gustad. 'Is that allowed?' he asked in a whisper.

'Oh, it's OK. Someone will later do the same to yours. Important thing is to light them.' He drew Gustad's attention to the main icon. 'That's the statue found by the fishermen.'

It was draped in rich, gold-embroidered fabrics; what seemed like precious or semi-precious stones glinted by candlelight. 'Did they also find those clothes?'

'No, no, they were made much later, from donations.' Gustad wondered what the statue was wearing when it came ashore.

'You see Baby Jesus on Mother Mary's left arm? Once a year, He moves. Next year He will be on the right arm. No one knows how it happens. A true miracle.' Then Malcolm fell silent. He crossed himself and started to pray. Gustad joined his hands, bowed his head and thought of Roshan, wishing her healthy and well again; of Dinshawji, that his suffering may ease; and of Sohrab, that his good sense be restored to him. He did not bother with his hip; it was really not that important.

*

The sea was steadily working its way to high tide. The two men selected a dry flat boulder to sit. 'Such a beautiful place,' said Gustad.

'Yes, especially this part of Bandra. But the buggers have plans for reclamation and development.'

'Roshan would really enjoy it. When we go to Chaupatty or Marine Drive sometimes, she loves to sit and watch the waves.'

Now and again, the salt spray touched their faces lightly, like the woman's errant veil had touched Gustad's cheek. After a while they had to pick another rock. 'The sea is pushing us back,' said Malcolm.

They talked fondly of the old days, of college, and the crazy old professors and padres. Gustad said he had never forgotten how kind Malcolm's family had been to him, welcoming him in their home every evening, letting him share the music, even offering him a place to study. They tried to fill in for each other the lacunae in the scanty outlines exchanged earlier at Crawford Market. But to reclaim suddenly the gaping abyss which had swallowed up time was well-nigh impossible. They had to be content with wisps and strands that came to hand as they groped or stumbled their way through the vaults of memory.

'That sonata you used to play with your father,' said Gustad. 'Da dee da da dee dum, Ta ta tum, Ta ta tum, Ta ta tum . . . You remember it?'

'Of course,' said Malcolm without hesitation. 'Last movement of César Franck's Sonata for violin and piano. In A. It was Daddy's favourite.'

'Mine, too,' said Gustad. 'Sometimes you two played it when it was getting dark in the evening. Before the lights came on. It sounded so beautiful, tears would almost spring to my eyes. I still cannot decide exactly whether it made me feel sad or happy. So difficult to describe.' So difficult. Like Tehmul, all of us. Even with proper tongues, words are hard to find.

'You won't believe this,' said Malcolm, 'but after Daddy's stroke, in such bad condition that he couldn't hold his violin or remember his own name, this sonata was always in his head. He could only make sounds with his mouth, no speech. But he would keep humming the last movement.'

Malcolm whistled the theme as Gustad smiled encouragingly. 'You know, I used to love to see your father put rosin on the bow, his face was always frowning with concentration when he did that. Then he would start to play, his bow moving up and down with so much life and power – gave me a strange feeling. As if he was searching desperately for something, but always disappointed. Because the piece ended before he found it.'

Malcolm nodded vigorously, he understood exactly. Gustad continued: 'And the funny thing is, my father had the same kind of look in his eyes. Sometimes, when he was reading – a kind of sadness, that the book was finishing too soon, without telling him everything he wanted to know.'

'That's life,' said Malcolm. The encroaching waves made them move again. Gradually, their conversation shifted to the present, to politics and the state of the nation. 'Look at it. Indira has visited every country in Europe, they all say they sympathize. But nobody does a damn thing to make Pakistan behave decently. What is left but war?'

'That's true. This Refugee Relief Tax is terrible,' said Gustad. 'It's killing the middle class.' He described how, working at the bank, he could see the trend: more and more people had to draw on their savings. Then he asked what it was like to work for the municipality.

'Very boring,' said Malcolm. 'Not worth talking about.' He looked at his watch. 'Ready to go?'

But the rush of the approaching tide, the blue-pink sky filled with comforting white shapes, the dancing foam and sea-glistened rocks, the touch of salty breezes on his face: all this was working to bestow gently upon Gustad a serenity he had not known for a very long time. He decided to stay. Malcolm had to leave for a piano lesson, but they promised to keep in touch, and shook hands on that. He thanked Malcolm for bringing him to Mount Mary; Malcolm replied it was his pleasure.

Alone, Gustad gazed at the horizon. There, the sea was calm. The tidal hustle and bustle could only be perceived near the shore. How reassuring, the tranquillity at the far edge, where the water met the sky. While the waves crashed against his rock. He felt an intense – what? joy? or sadness? did it matter? Like the sonata. Or dawn in the old days, the rising sun, its rays streaming happy golden tears into the compound, the sparrows chirping in the solitary tree.

The sun sank in the ocean, its journey done for the day. And all things that mattered in life were touched by this sweet, sad joy.

One after another he remembered them. The workshop, the cheerful sound of tools, but also the silence of the end of day. Rides in his father's four-horse carriage with the shiny brass lamps, it did not matter where to, for it was magic just to go clip-clop, until the ride ended and the horses were led away to the stable. Pappa's wonderful parties, the food and music, the clothes, the people, the toys. And yet, always, at some point in the evening, the thought would surface – that the food would be consumed, the guests would leave, the music would stop playing, then he would have to go to bed and the lights switched off.

The opening bars of the sonata continued to obsess him, and the tears he could not permit now scalded his eyes. A wave touched the tip of his shoe, barely wetting it. The next one soaked both toes. If a person cried here, by the sea, he thought, then the tears would mix with the waves. Salt water from the eyes mixing with salt water from the ocean. The possibility filled him with wonder. He stood watching till the sea covered his rock. Then he followed the directions Malcolm had left him to get to Bandra station.

Later, as he emerged at Grant Road to walk home, the word came to him. 'Supercalifragilisticexpialidocious.' He repeated it softly. He would amuse Dinshawji with it tomorrow. Make up for missing today's visit.

SIXTEEN

i

Dilnavaz answered the door without checking the peephole, as it was Gustad's time to return from Parsi General. She was startled by the bearded man. When he introduced himself as Ghulam Mohammed, her first impulse was to slam the door in his face, lock and bolt it from inside.

'Mr Noble, please?'

'He is out.' Such everlasting woes that *bhustaigayo* Major dumped on our heads. When will it end? 'He has gone to hospital to visit a very sick friend.' Not that I need to explain to this *sataan*. But maybe he will feel sorry. If he has a heart.

'I will wait in the compound.' Good, she thought, don't want him in my house. How dare he come here so shamelessly, after the things he did to us.

But she changed her mind: 'You can sit inside.' That way, I can warn Gustad at the door.

'I am grateful. Thank you.'

She stayed in the kitchen, casting nervous glances into the front room. If she could only tell the black-bearded thief exactly what she thought of him. He smiled politely towards the kitchen door, curious about the black-out paper on the ventilators and the glass everywhere.

'GustadGustadGustad,' Tehmul yelled through the window. 'PleasepleaseGustadplease.'

'Excuse me,' said Ghulam Mohammed. 'I think someone is asking for Mr Noble.'

She went to the front. 'Yes?'

'GustadGustadplease.'

'Gone out.'

He scratched his armpit, deliberating, then remembered the rest of his message. 'Phonephonephone. Veryimportantphone.'

'Miss Kutpitia sent you?' Tehmul nodded, using both hands under his arms like claws. 'Stop it!' she said, and the hands dropped. 'Say that Gustad will come later.' Cannot leave this black-bearded scoundrel alone. But who can be phoning on Sunday?

She did not have to wonder long, for shortly after, Gustad arrived. At the door, she whispered about the visitor. 'Shall I stay here or go for the message?'

'You go,' said Gustad. 'Better if I talk to him alone.'

Ghulam Mohammed stood up when he entered. Ignoring the outstretched hand, Gustad said, 'Last time I made it clear. I want nothing more with you or Mr Bilimoria.'

'Please don't get upset, Mr Noble, I am sorry to disturb you and your wife. Promise, this is the last time. But remember you said you would consider Bili Boy's request? To go to Delhi?' He spoke appeasingly, almost cajoling. No trace of threat or hardness. 'More than six weeks I waited for you, Mr Noble.'

'No, it's impossible to go, I –'

'Please Mr Noble, let me show you this.' He opened his briefcase. Not another newspaper, thought Gustad. It was.

Ghulam indicated the article. 'About Bili Boy. If I tell you, you will think I am lying. See for yourself in the paper.'

It was still light outside, but the covered glass had let darkness overtake the room. Gustad switched on the desk lamp:

SENTENCING SOON IN RUPEES-FOR-RAW CASE
Following the recent judgement in the case of voice-impersonator Mr Bilimoria, the RAW officer who defrauded the State Bank of sixty lakh rupees, the defendant's request for a retrial was denied yesterday.

It is now learned that the head of the Special Investigation Team, appointed to determine if a retrial was necessary, had asked for more time to conduct a thorough review of the evidence. Soon after, he was killed in a car accident on Grand Trunk Road.

His replacement has brought the investigation to a rapid conclusion. The report finds that a retrial is not necessary. Sentencing is expected to follow shortly.

Gustad folded the newspaper and handed it back.

'It was his last chance,' said Ghulam Mohammed. 'But the courts are in the pockets of the ones at the top. Those bastards think we are stupid, that we don't understand what it means when the chief investigator suddenly dies in a car accident.' He clenched and unclenched his fist. 'Now it's just a matter of time. Please go and meet Bili Boy. Before they finish him off. Please.'

'Why do you keep saying finish him off? This is not Russia or China.' But something funny going on, for sure.

Ghulam shook his head sadly. 'I don't know how to convince you, Mr Noble. But it's true.'

'OK, suppose it's true. Does it matter whether he sees me?' Gustad tried to sound hard. 'He did not care about me, lying, and using me for his purposes.'

'You are wrong, he did care. He made sure you did not get into trouble after he was arrested.'

'But it's impossible to go to Delhi. My office –'

'Mr Noble, please,' he pleaded. 'Three days is all it will take. You leave by train, arrive next morning, and go to the prison. I will arrange for the visit. You will be back on the third day.' He pulled a small envelope out of his shirt pocket and held it towards Gustad.

'What's that?'

'Return ticket. Please.'

Gustad opened the envelope and saw a sleeping-berth reservation for Friday. The prison address, too. He pushed it back at Ghulam. 'I don't think –'

'Please, Mr Noble. For the sake of your friend. Who still loves you like a brother.'

Like a brother. Yes. That's how I loved him. All these years in the building. Our prayers at sunrise, the children growing up, so many kindnesses, the fun and laughter we shared. And what has it all come to now? Jimmy sitting in jail. Asking for me. What can I say?

'OK.' He accepted the train ticket. And as he said the word, his hatred of Ghulam sublimated as well.

'Thank you, Mr Noble. Bili Boy will be so happy to see you. But one thing. Please don't tell him what I said. If he still has some hope, please let him keep it.'

On his way to the door he noticed the empty bottle of Hercules XXX on the sideboard. Gustad had not been able to throw it away.

'That was Bili Boy's favourite. Right from the very old days, in Kashmir.'

'I know,' said Gustad. 'He gave me that bottle.'

Dilnavaz returned from Miss Kutpitia and let herself in. She was surprised to hear them chatting pleasantly as Ghulam left. 'What did he want?'

Gustad explained. She was suspicious about the whole arrangement but did not argue, as the telephone message was very urgent: 'Parsi General phoned. They could not get Alamai's number.'

He looked up, and knew. 'Dinshawji . . .?'

She nodded. 'About one hour ago.'

He covered his face with his hands. 'Poor Dinshu. Was it peaceful? Did they say?'

'He became unconscious late in the afternoon.'

He stood up. 'I must go at once. If they could not get Alamai, it means he is alone.'

'But I don't understand. You were there. What time did you leave him?'

His lie, his attempted half-truth, was no longer of any consequence. 'I did not go to Dinshawji today. I went to a church in Bandra. Mount Mary.'

It baffled her. 'Church? All of a sudden?'

He sat again, supporting his chin. 'Don't worry, I have not converted or anything. I met Malcolm Saldanha at Crawford Market this morning. It was amazing – we talked like we never lost touch.' He narrated the story of Mount Mary. 'And Malcolm says miracles are still happening every day.'

She understood perfectly. After all, Gustad and she desired the same destination, only their paths were different.

'But,' he said bitterly, 'one thing is sure. There was no miracle for Dinshawji.'

She touched his shoulder gently. 'You tried your best. It's not your fault.'

Her attempt to comfort struck like the arrowhead of an accusation. He thought of the illegal deposits, of Laurie's complaint, and then Dinshawji's silence. It *was* my fault. Everything changed when Dinshu became quiet. I silenced him.

'He was sickly for so long,' Dilnavaz tried again. 'Remember how he looked when he came for Roshan's birthday?'

'Yes, I remember.' Thussook-thussook, my cart rumbles along. Over and over he heard it in his mind, thussook-thussook, my cart

keeps rolling. Now, finally, the cart had come to a rest, its wanderings halted. Peace at last, my Poet Laureate.

'It's all right if the crying comes.' She leaned against his chair to
put her arm around him. He raised his eyes, burning with the tears
that could not flow. He lifted his eyes defiantly to her face, so she
could see them dry, observe them dry and unblinking. Only then
did he put his arm around her. And while they were thus, Roshan
entered the room and rejoiced to see her parents hugging. She tried
to encircle them both with her skinny arms. Gustad lifted her into
his lap.

'How are you feeling, sweetoo?'

'OK.' She examined their faces. 'But why are you looking so sad,
Daddy?' She put her fingers to the corners of his lips and tried to
stretch them into a smile, giggling at her efforts.

'Because we received some sad news,' said Dilnavaz. 'You know
Dinshawji who came for your birthday?'

Roshan nodded. 'He kept tickling me and making me laugh, with
gilly-gilly-gilly. He said, "I wiss you health, I wiss you wealth, I wiss
you gold in store."'

'What a memory. My clever little *bakulyoo*.'

Dilnavaz continued: 'He was very sick, in hospital. Today he
passed away and went to Dadaji, to heaven.'

Roshan considered this gravely. 'But I'm also very sick. When
will I go to Dadaji?'

'What idiotic-lunatic talk.' Gustad used the phrase of anger to
mask his dread. 'You are not very sick, you are much better. First
you will grow up and get married, have children. Then they will
marry and have their children, and you will be an old, old *dossi*
before Dadaji is interested in calling you to heaven.' He looked at
Dilnavaz reproachfully: she should not have spoken like that. He
hugged them both again before leaving for the hospital.

In the compound, Cavasji's voice was ringing: 'Tomorrow is
Monday morning, do You know that? And the Tatas will have their
board meeting! When You bestow Your bounties on them, remember us also! Be fair now! *Bas*, it is too much for – !'

Mrs Pastakia screamed: 'Shut up, you crazy old fellow! My head
is bursting into a thousand pieces!' Gustad wondered where her
husband was, allowing her to talk this way to his father.

Visiting hours had ended. He explained to the nurse on duty why he was there, and she accompanied him to the ward. 'When did he pass away?'

She consulted the watch pinned to her chest. 'For the exact time I have to check the records. But about two hours ago. His pain was too much just before he became unconscious. We had to give him lots of morphine.' Her voice was sharp, it echoed along the cold corridor walls. A chatty one. Usually they have no time for the simplest question. Rude as rabid bitches. 'Very unfortunate, no one was here with him,' she said accusingly. 'You are brother? Cousin?'

'Friend.' Poking her nose. None of her business.

'Oh,' said the nurse, in a tone that withdrew the accusation. But the barb remained, goading his flesh, along with the others he had twisted in himself. On Dinshawji's day I went with Malcolm. Left him to die wondering why I did not come.

'Here we are,' said the nurse.

'He's still in the ward?'

'What to do? If empty room is available, patient is put there.' She pronounced it 'avleble'. 'Otherwise nothing we can do.' He wondered about the way she used patient – he would have expected 'deceased' or 'body'. 'That is why we like relatives to come soon to make arrangements. Beds are in such short supply.'

'His wife is inside?'

'Yes, I think so,' said the nurse, halting at the ward entrance.

Gustad entered hesitantly and looked towards Dinshawji's bed. The figure of the woman he expected to see, seated in vigil, was missing. He gazed absently upon the rows of sleeping patients, heard their breathing and snores.

And if I did not know Dinshawji is gone, he would also have the sleeping look. Strange feeling. To stand beside his bed, and he cannot see me. Unfair advantage. As though I am spying on him. But who knows? Maybe Dinshu is the one with the advantage, spying from Up There. Laughing at me.

The straight hard chair was by the bed. He had grown so used to it over the weeks. Dinshawji's sheet rose in a sharp incline at the nether regions of the mattress. He glanced under the bed to see if the size twelve Naughty Boys were there by his trunk. Only the bedpan, its white enamel stark in the dark space. Beside it, the transparent flask-shaped urinal.

Not all patients were asleep. Some watched intently, keeping an eye on this healthy one visiting after hours, when he had no business to be here. In the dim night light of the ward their eyes focussed fearfully, drifted, then refocussed. When would it be their turn? How would it happen? And afterwards . . . ? Down an old man's face, tears were rolling slowly. Silently, on to the pillowcase dull white like his hair. Others were peaceful, reassured, as if they knew now that it was the simplest of things, was dying. After all, the one who had joked and laughed in their midst for several weeks had shown them how easy it was. How easy to go from warm and breathing to cold and waxen, how easy to become one of the smooth white figures in the carts outside the gates of Mount Mary.

Dinshawji had been stripped of all the appurtenances with which he had clung to life. The metal stand, gaunt and coldly institutional when the saline solution bottle used to hang from it, now stood empty. Now it looked just like a wire coat-rack, harmless and domestic. The various tubes had grown in number with the passing weeks: one through the nose, two in the arms, somewhere under the sheet a catheter. All withdrawn. As if he had never been sick. Were the tubes removed carefully, the way they were inserted: skilfully, by steady hands? Or just yanked out – the useless wires of an old broken radio, like my Telerad. And then the tubes thrown away in the rubbish, like the coils and transformers and condensers littering the pavements outside the repair shops.

Dinshawji dismantled. And after the prayers are said and the rituals performed at the Tower of Silence, the vultures will do the rest. When the bones are picked clean, and the clean bones gone, no proof will remain that Dinshawji ever lived and breathed. Except his memory.

But after that? After the memory is lost? When I am gone, and all his friends are gone. What then?

The eyes of the wakeful patients were still on Gustad. He found it disconcerting if their eyes met. So he kept looking at Dinshawji's surgical bed. The iron frame, painted creamy white. Black in places where the paint had peeled. Three sockets for the wooden-handled crank. The first raises the head – I used to wind it when Dinshawji's dinner arrived. Crankshafts and gears, just like my Meccano set.

Second socket for the feet (I raised them once by mistake). And the third for the mid-section. Strange. Why should stomach or pelvis be higher than the rest of the body? Only one reason I can think of. And not a medical reason. Unless the interns and nurses use it for playing doctor-doctor. Wish I had thought of that earlier. To tell Dinshu. But he would have come up with a better one himself. His hospital song. O give me a home where the nurses' hands roam . . .

'Supercalifragilisticexpialidocious,' he whispered in Dinshawji's ear, and smiled.

Dinshawji's wife appeared in the doorway. She looked around, then strode into the ward in a way that made it clear she was not to be trifled with. She saw Gustad's smile before he had time to wipe it off, and gave him a withering look.

Alamai was a tall woman, far taller than Dinshawji had been, with a carpingly stern face that would willingly find fault with the world, especially its inhabitants. A termagant if ever there was one. Her scrawny neck deliquesced into narrow shoulders which were perpetually raised, slightly hunched. No children and a wife like Alamai, thought Gustad, and yet such a sense of humour. Or because of it. His domestic vulture. He almost broke into a smile again as he recalled the favourite line: 'No need to take me to the Tower of Silence when I die. My domestic vulture will pick my bones clean ahead of time.'

'Alamai, please let me know if there is anything I can do,' he offered, after expressing his condolences.

Before she could answer, a pasty-faced young man burst in. 'Auntie, Auntie!' he called in a high-pitched voice which disembogued in part through a nose eminently suited to the purpose because of its shape and size. 'Auntieee! You went away while I was still in the bathroom!' The patients in the ward opened their eyes. Gustad estimated the fellow's age to be at least twenty, and wondered who he was.

'Shh! *Muà* donkey! Close your mouth at once! You boy-without-brain, sick people are sleeping here. You were going to get lost in the bathroom or what because I left?' The boy-man pouted at the scolding.

'Come and meet Gustadji Noble. He was Pappa's best friend.' To Gustad she said, 'This is our nephew Nusli. My sister's son. We never had children, so he has always been like our own son. In private he calls us Mamma and Pappa only. I brought him along to help. Come on, come on, what are you standing and staring! Shake hands with Gustad Uncle!'

Nusli giggled as he offered his hand. He was skinny, and stood with stooped shoulders. A single-*paasri* weakling, thought Gustad as he shook the clammy hand, wondering how a vulture's sister could spawn a milquetoast like Nusli. Perhaps it was inevitable. He repeated his question to Alamai. 'Is there anything I can do to help?'

'I phoned the Tower of Silence while Nusli was in the bathroom. They said the hearse will come in half an hour.'

The patients who had decided to close their eyes after Alamai silenced Nusli, opened them again. For Nusli chose to speak once more with his high-pitched instrument. 'I am so scaaared, Auntie!'

'A-ra-ra-ra! *Now* what are you scared of?'

'Of the hearse,' he whined. 'I don't want to sit in it!'

'You boy-without-brain, what is there to be scared of? It's just like a van. Remember, we all went for a picnic in the van last year with Dorab Uncle's family to Victoria Garden? And saw all the animals there? A van, just like that one.'

'No, Auntie, please, I am so scared.' He cringed and wrung his hands.

'*Marey em-no-em*! God knows to collect what dust I brought you along! Thought you would be a help. Help, my head!' and she struck it hard with both hands.

Gustad felt it was time to intervene, before more patients were awakened to the nightmare in their ward. 'Alamai, I will be happy to come with you in the hearse. To help with everything.'

'See? See, you *lumbasoo-baywakoof*, listen to Gustad Uncle. He is not scared, is he?' Nusli gazed at his feet and pursed his lips as though to blow spit bubbles. She thumped him on the back, and he lurched forward. 'Look at me when I talk to you!'

'Yes, yes, he will come,' said Gustad. 'He will sit beside me. Won't you, Nusli?'

'OK,' said Nusli, and giggled.

'I don't want any of your khikhi-khaakhaa,' said Alamai. But Nusli permitted himself another short paroxysm of giggles before heeding her injunction.

She turned her attention now to Dinshawji's trunk under the

bed. 'Come on, come on, Nusla! Don't just stand there! Come here and pull it out for me. I want to check everything that Pappa brought from home. Cannot trust these hospital people.'

Gustad felt it was a good moment to disappear. He could return at the hearse's appointed time. 'Excuse me, I will be back in a few minutes.'

Alamai, engrossed in taking an inventory, granted him leave with an imperious wave of her hand. He caught a glimpse of Dinshawji's black Naughty Boys in the trunk. Empty of their owner's feet, they seemed larger than life.

He walked down the long cold corridor and down the stairs. Through the reception area, through the lobby, till he was outside, in the hospital grounds. The lawn was slightly damp, there was a pleasing fresh-cut scent in the grass. The grounds were dark except for the dim light from an ornate cast-iron lamppost by the walkway. He headed for the little garden with the arbor where he had sat many Sundays ago, when Dinshawji had newly arrived at the hospital.

The bench, like the lawn, was damp. Too early for dew, it must have been made wet when the *maali* watered the flowers. Gustad spread his handkerchief and sat. The exhaustion he had kept at bay now overtook him. He felt drained, emptied of the last bit of energy that had got him through the day, took him to Crawford Market and to Mount Mary, that kept his limp under control, that made him suffer Alamai with forbearance.

It was cool on the bench under the trees. Peaceful. Like the countryside. Or a hill station, with the nocturnal insect sounds. Matheran, when I was eight years old. Where Pappa had taken the entire family: Grandma, Grandpa, the younger brother's family (the one who was to betray Pappa's trust and ruin him), and two servants. They had reserved four rooms at Central Hotel. It was raining when they alighted from the toy train that chugged slowly up the hill. Everything was damp as they arrived by rickshaw at the hotel. The manager was Pappa's personal friend. He sent cups of hot Bournvita to their rooms. When it got dark and the lights went on, the mosquitoes came. It was the first time for Gustad, sleeping under mosquito nets. He slipped in through the opening, then his mother tucked the flap securely under the mattress. It was strange to say goodnight-Godblessyou through the gauze-like material and

241

then listen to her say it. Her voice came clearly, but she looked so insubstantial behind the enveloping veil, far away, beyond his reach, and he was all alone, under the canopy of white, entombed in his mosquito-free mausoleum. It had been such a long journey, and he fell asleep.

But that picture. That picture of my mother – locked away for ever in my mind: my mother through the white, diaphanous mosquito net, saying goodnight-Godblessyou, smiling, soft and evanescent, floating before my sleepy eyes, floating for ever with her eyes so gentle and kind. That was the way he chose to remember her, when he was eighteen and she was dead.

And there had never again been cornflakes as delicious as the ones he ate at breakfast in Matheran. Or toast, with roses of butter, and marmalade. With the jabbering brown monkeys always waiting to snatch what fell or was carelessly left around. One had even grabbed a packet of Gluco biscuits from his hand. There were pony rides. Long walks in the mornings and evenings, to Echo Point, Monkey Point, Panorama Point, Charlotte Lake. With walking-sticks. Pappa bought one for each member of the party: freshly carved, with the smell of the tree still strong upon it. The cool, crisp mountain air filled their lungs, driving out the city staleness. At dusk it was chilly, and they needed pullovers. The manager told them stories of tiger hunts he had been on in these hills. And on the last night, the chef made a special pudding for them. After it was eaten, he came out to say goodbye, then pretended to be disappointed that they did not enjoy his pudding. They thought he was joking, for the bowl had been licked clean. But the chef picked up the empty bowl, broke it before their startled eyes, and distributed the shards in their plates, eating one himself to demonstrate. Everyone laughed at how well they had been fooled, crunching the pieces moulded from sugar and gelatine. 'Now this is what you call a sweet dish,' said Pappa.

But Gustad sat silent and downcast throughout dinner, thinking of the morrow, the end of the holiday. His father had tried to cheer him up, saying they would come again another year. And then, the bowl was broken and eaten. There was something so final and terrible about the act. He refused to eat a single piece of the flavoured sugar and gelatine.

And when the bookstore was bankrupt and the bailiff arrived, I remembered the broken bowl. Watching helplessly as the shelves were emptied and the books were loaded on lorries. Pappa begging and pleading in vain with the bailiff. The cleats on the bailiff's shoes clattering brazenly on the stone floor. The men continuing their task, dismantling Pappa's life, breaking it up into little pieces, feeding the pieces into the bellies of the lorries. Then rolling away, leaving in their wake a noxious smell. Diesel fumes. And I remembering the dinner-table in Matheran, the crunching down of the broken bowl – such a terrible, final act.

But what pudding was it that night? Lemon? No, it was pineapple. Or maybe caramel? Perhaps. Even memories do not stay intact for ever. Have to be careful, scrupulous, in dealing with them. And Dinshu is dead. Tomorrow, the vultures. Then, nothing. Except memories. His jokes. About the two men whose wives. And the other one, the bicycle pump. O give me a home where the nurses' hands roam . . .

Gustad closed his eyes, nodded. Jerked his head up. But down it went again. And up. His spectacles slid a little bit lower. The third time he did not struggle to raise his head.

*

A loud honking across the dark, damp grass silenced the crickets and cicadas in the foliage, and ended Gustad's brief nap. He pushed up his spectacles. A car was blocking the hospital driveway; a van waited to get through. He stood up. The building lights illuminated the legend on the van: HEARSE, and then the rest: *Bombay Parsi Punchayet*. The unpainted body of the vehicle shone eerily, silvery-white in the darkness.

He hurried across the lawn. The chirr-chirr-chirr-chirr started up in the grass again, as the cicadas reasserted their shrill presence. Hearses can be impeded by cars and barricades, he thought. But death. Death gets through every time. Death can choose to be prompt or fashionably late.

The offending car drove away, and the hearse rumbled over the remaining few yards. He reached the entrance just as two men emerged and climbed the steps into the lobby. Alamai was waiting. 'A-ra-ra-ra! Where were you all this time, Gustadji? I was thinking that by mistake-bistake you forgot and went home.'

Who does she think she is speaking to? Her *mai-issi* Nusli? Outwardly calm, he said, 'I saw the hearse just arriving. Are you ready?'

The hospital formalities were completed, papers checked and handed over, and the two *khandhias* went to work. Nusli stood by with Alamai's handbag while she did some last-minute rummaging in Dinshawji's trunk. She asked the men as sweetly and politely as she could, 'Please, can you also put this little *paytee* inside? So we can drive by my house and leave it there?'

'*Maiji*, we are not allowed to do that. Straight back to Doongerwadi we have to go. Only one van is on duty.'

Alamai folded her hands meekly and bent her head sideways. 'Look, *bawa*, a helpless old widow will give you her blessings if you can do this.'

But the two men were adamant: they had already glimpsed her true colours. 'Sorry, not possible.'

She flung down her hands and turned away in a huff, walking stiff and straight as a ramrod to the door, muttering about the extra trip by taxi she would have to make. 'Lazy, stubborn loafers,' she said under her breath, to no one in particular. Nusli followed her with the handbag, then the *khandhias* with the bier of iron, and finally Gustad.

In the hearse, the bier was secured to one side. Along the length of the van was a bench seat for passengers. The driver started the engine, and Alamai motioned to Nusli to get in. Hunching his shoulders, he crossed his hands over his chest and backed away. 'No, Auntie! Not me first! Please, not me first!'

'You boy-without-courage! You will remain a *beekun-bylo* for ever.' She pushed him away with the back of her hand. 'Move aside, *muà* animal, move aside! I will go first.' Ignoring the attendant's hand waiting to help her up, she was inside in one bound. 'Now *muà* coward! You climb now and hide under my petticoat.'

But Nusli turned to Gustad and asked him, with pleading eyes and imploring hand, to go next. Gustad obliged. Finally Nusli crept in, cringing, sitting as far back as possible. The man outside shook his head, slammed the van's rear door shut and made his way to the front, next to the driver.

The journey was uneventful except when the van went over an extremely bumpy stretch. Everyone was badly shaken, and the bier received a rough jouncing. The dead man's head moved around a bit, and Nusli shrieked in terror. This incident affected Alamai too in some way; she started to sniff and dab at her eyes with a little

244

hanky, and Gustad was utterly disgusted. Better to stay quiet than to pretend. Shameless hypocrite. Have to hire mourners if she wants more tears. Thank God the quality of afterlife does not depend on the quantity of tears.

But he was wrong. After sniffing and dabbing for a while, Alamai showed how badly he had underestimated her histrionic capabilities. For as the hearse turned into the Doongerwadi gates and made its way up the hill, she was convulsed by a great sob that burst forth without warning. She rocked back and forth, her tall, thin trunk swaying alarmingly in the narrow space, as she clutched her head in her hands and wailed. 'O my Dinshaw! Why! Why! Why! O Dinshaw!' Like Tom Jones and his Delilah, thought Gustad. Dinshu would have enjoyed this. His domestic vulture, finally singing her torch song.

'You have left me? Gone away? But why?' Since Dinshawji refused to tell her why, she sobbed some more, then directed her efforts at the roof of the hearse. 'O Parvar Daegar! What have You done! You took him away? Why? Now what will I do? Take me also! Now! Now and now only!' and she smote her chest twice.

The driver slowed by the prayer bungalows on the lower level and, receiving no instructions, continued to the upper level. But Alamai had not made any arrangements. Gustad asked to return to the office.

'These people,' grumbled the driver to his companion. 'They think they are out for a Sunday drive at Scandal Point, making me go round and round.'

Alamai was still wailing and beating her chest as Gustad led her into the office. 'It is God's will, Alamai,' he said, a little weary of the business. He tried to calm her with all the *de rigueur* phrases he knew. 'Dinshawji has been released from his pain and misery. Thanks to the mercy of the Almighty.'

'That's true,' she moaned, the volume of her sobs quite respectable for one with so skimpy a chest. 'He is released! At least from his suffering he is released!' Then the man in the office offered information about rates and expenses.

'Let us think of Dinshawji now,' said Gustad. 'Prepare for his prayers.' He deftly guided his words in through little windows that opened between her sobs. 'Do you want four-day prayers? At upper *bungalee*? Or one-day at lower *bungalee*?'

'One-day, four-day, what does it matter? He is gone!'

'For upper *bungalee*, you will have to live here for four days. Can you manage that?' He suspected that a question of a practical nature would stem the tears.

It worked. 'A-ra-ra-ra! Are you crazy? Four days? Who will look after my little Nusla? Who will cook his dinner, hunh?' It was all very quick from here on. The time for the funeral next afternoon was scheduled, and Alamai agreed to have the announcement in the morning's *Jam-E-Jamshed*. The clerk promised to telephone the newspaper before the presses rolled.

Once more, they occupied their places in the van. The driver took them to the allocated *bungalee*. It had a little verandah in the front leading to the prayer hall, and a bathroom at the back, where the deceased would be given the final bath of ritual purity. Alamai, Nusli, and Gustad took turns to wash their hands and faces before doing their *kustis*.

Meanwhile, Alamai got into a passionate argument with the men who came to perform Dinshawji's *suchkaar* and ablutions. She forbade them to follow the traditional method of sponging the corpse with *gomez*. 'All this nonsense with bull's urine is not for us,' she said. 'We are modern people. Use water only, nothing else.' But she insisted that the water be warmed first, because Dinshawji, it seemed, had a habit of catching a chill if he bathed with cold tap water.

Embarrassed, Gustad left her to do his *kusti*. Nusli gladly went with him. However, Alamai soon finished dealing with the *suchkaar* and followed them to the verandah.

Here, it was discovered that Nusli had forgotten to bring his prayer cap. 'You boy-without-brain,' she said, gritting her teeth, softly, in deference to the place and the occasion. 'Coming to a place of prayer without prayer cap. To collect what dust, I am asking?'

Gustad tried to restore peace by pulling out his large white handkerchief. He folded it along the diagonal and showed Nusli how to cover his head with it. This was a perfectly respectable method. But Alamai uttered another imprecation: '*Marey em-no-em*. Which fire burned all his wits, I wonder,' then decided to let the matter pass.

Gustad fled the verandah as soon as he knotted the last knot in

246

his *kusti*. He did not know how much more of this woman he could tolerate. He went into the empty room and sat in a corner, in the dark. Two men entered with the body, white-clad now, and laid it on the low marble platform. The face and ears were left uncovered by the white sheet. A priest arrived and lit an oil lamp next to Dinshawji's head.

How efficiently everything proceeds, thought Gustad. All routine. As though Dinshawji died every day. Alamai and Nusli took their seats. The priest picked up a sliver of sandalwood, dipped it in oil and held it to the flame. He transferred it to the thurible and sprinkled *loban* upon it. The fragrance of frankincense filled the room. The priest started to pray. For some reason, the quiet prayers made Nusli restless and fidgety. He kept squirming, adjusting the handkerchief on his head. But Alamai soon settled that wordlessly, by directing her elbow and knee into his person.

The *dustoorji* prayed beautifully. Each word emerged clear and full-toned, pure, as if shaped for the first time by human lips. And Gustad, lost in his thoughts, began to listen. It sounded so soothing. Such a wonderful voice. Like Nat King Cole's when he sang 'You Will Never Grow Old'. Soft, smooth, rich as velvet.

The *dustoorji* was not praying loudly, yet, little by little, in ever-increasing circles, his voice touched every point of the prayer room. Now and again, he added a stick of sandalwood to the thurible, or sprinkled *loban*. A dim bulb burned outside on the verandah. So dim, the bulb, it barely outlined the entrance, hazy behind the veil of fragrant smoke. Inside, the oil lamp cast its soft glow on Dinshawji's face, the flame wavering sometimes, moving with any slight breeze. And the soft glow on Dinshawji's face moved in waves with the movement of the flame. On his face light and shadow played like little children, touching it gently, now here, and now there.

The prayers filled the dark room slowly. Slowly, the prayer sound was the dark room. And before he was aware of it, Gustad was under its gentle spell. He forgot the time, forgot Alamai, forgot Nusli. He listened to the music, the song in a language which he did not understand, but which was wondrously soothing. All his life he had uttered by rote the words of this dead language, comprehending not one of them while mouthing his prayers. But tonight, in the *dustoorji*'s soft and gentle music, the words were alive; tonight he came closer than he ever had to understanding the ancient meanings.

The *dustoorji* cantillated the verses of the ancient Avesta. And as the notes and syllables were intoned, they mingled with the sounds of night. Steadily, from the trees and bushes rose the voices of night and nature, and from all the lush vegetation that grew here on the hill, around the Tower of Silence. The murmurings of leaf-hoppers and tree-dwellers, winged and crawling, ascended Doongerwadi, up towards the Tower of Silence. Their murmurings blended with the sandalwood and *loban* and prayer music floating forth from the room with the oil lamp, and Gustad understood it all.

iii

Dilnavaz was asleep, her head thrown back on the sofa. He opened the door with his latchkey, waking her.

'Is it very late?' she asked.

The clock showed just after ten. The pendulum was still. He checked his watch. 'Eleven-thirty.' He opened the glass and felt for the key.

'What happened?'

He wound the clock, telling her about Alamai, Nusli, the hearse, their arrival at Doongerwadi. 'When I went to the *bungalee*, I was so tired and sleepy, I said to myself, I'll leave in five minutes. Then the prayers started and . . .' He stopped, feeling a little foolish. 'So beautiful. I kept listening.'

He moved the minute hand, waited for the ten-thirty bong, then pushed it to eleven. 'Dinshawji's face. On the marble slab. Looked so peaceful. And you will think I am crazy . . . I moved my head this way and that. Changed my way of seeing. Thinking it must be the light. But . . .'

'What? Tell me.'

'There was no doubt. He was smiling.' He checked his watch again, and adjusted the clock's minute hand. 'Go on. Tell me I am crazy.'

'Prayer is a very powerful thing.'

'I saw his face when he was still at hospital. Also in the hearse. But nothing.'

'Prayers are powerful. Prayers can put a smile on Dinshawji's face, or in your eyes.'

He put his arm around her. 'I hope when I go there will be a smile like that on my face. And in your eyes.' The clock was still silent. He pushed the pendulum gently, and shut the glass.

SEVENTEEN

i

Those who missed the funeral notice in *Jam-E-Jamshed* got the news at the bank, in a memo from the manager which included employees' names under two headings: Funeral – Monday 3.30 p.m. and Uthamna Ceremony – Tuesday 3.00 p.m. Only Gustad was given a choice before the memo was written. Mr Madon, who had also elected to attend the funeral, offered him a ride in his car.

There was a large turnout at Doongerwadi. Few relatives, but many, many friends and colleagues. The news had taken them by surprise, so they were neither dressed in white nor had their prayer caps. But they managed somehow, the women draping their saris over the head, the men using handkerchiefs or borrowing caps from the sandalwood shop at the bottom of the hill.

It was not yet three-thirty, and people were still arriving. The overflow was accommodated in a pavilion adjacent to the *bungalee*, along with the non-Parsis. Looking over the gathering, Gustad realized that Dinshawji had brought laughter into the life of almost every person now sitting there silently, waiting for the last rites to commence. Even Goover-Ni-Gaan Ratansa had been known to smile occasionally at Dinshawji's jokes.

Alamai was saving a place for Gustad in the first row facing the marble platform. Mr Madon accompanied him to the front, to offer his condolences to Alamai. She thanked him for coming and introduced Nusli. 'It was Dinshawji's hope that one day, before he retired, Nusli would start working with him, side by side, at the bank. Alas, now it is too late,' she said, doing the first spadeful of groundwork regarding her plans for Nusli.

She decided it would be politic to seat Mr Madon also in the first row, and offered him Nusli's chair. And Nusli, to his credit, quietly moved further down. In his white *dugli* and maroon prayer cap the boy-man blended with the congregation, except at the moment when the *dustoorjis* gave the cue for the ritual of the dog. The Doongerwadi dog was led to the bier, the *char-chassam* dog, who, with his preternatural eyes, would contain the *nassoo*, the evil of death, and assist the forces of good. Nusli craned and peered, rising excitedly from his chair like a child seeing a dog for the first time. He made soft kissing sounds and snapped his fingers lightly to get the dog's attention.

No one noticed Nusli, however, for when the dog walked round the bier, sniffed in silence and left, Alamai suddenly stood with her arms raised and wailed: 'O dog! Make some little sound at least! O Parvar Daegar! No barking? Now it is certain! O my Dinshaw, now you have really left me!'

Women in her vicinity hastened to calm her. Gustad and Mr Madon were only too glad to move aside, visibly relieved at not having to comfort Alamai. Gustad shook his head at the pathetic exhibition, more pitiful for its being based on her mistaken notions about the *char-chassam* dog. Poor Alamai, with her modernistic ideas and her orthodox confusions.

The women held her from rushing to the bier, hanging on to her arms, trying to wrestle her down into a chair. Of course, if tall, lean Alamai had really wanted to, she could have easily tossed aside the four or five gasping women. But she suddenly gave up and flopped back. The women hugged her, patted her cheeks, adjusted her sari and said variously comforting things.

'God's will, Alamai, God's will!'

'What can we do when Dada Ormuzd makes His Almighty Plans for us?'

'Stay calm, Alamai, stay calm, please, for Dinshawji's sake. Or he will have trouble getting to the Other Side.'

'God's will! God's will!'

'Peace, peace, Alamai! Too much crying makes the body very heavy. How will they carry him then?'

'God's will, Alamai, God's will!'

The *dustoorjis* waited patiently until silence was restored, then continued with the Ahunavad Gatha. The rest of the prayers proceeded without interruption. At the conclusion, they invited Alamai to place *loban* and sandalwood on the *afargan* fire. All eyes were on her, the women alert lest she needed restraining again. But she seemed quite calm now.

After family members and relatives finished their obeisances, the other mourners filed past for the *sezdoe*. While they bowed and touched the ground three times, the room suddenly grew dark. The sunlight streaming into the prayer hall was blocked by four shadows. The *nassasalers* had arrived. They stood in the doorway, waiting to carry the bier to the Tower, to the well of vultures.

It was Gustad's turn. He observed Dinshawji's face carefully and bowed three times. Wish I could be one of the four. Surely Dinshu would prefer his friends. Silly custom, to have professional pall-bearers. And on top of that, poor fellows treated like outcasts and untouchables.

The *sezdoe* ended. The *nassasalers* entered, clad in white from head to toe. They wore white gloves and white canvas shoes. People moved aside to give them a wide berth, fearful of contact. Dinshawji's face was covered and the bier of iron carried from the prayer *bungalee*.

Once outside, the *nassasalers* took a few steps and stopped. They waited for the men who would follow in procession to fall in behind them. The approach to the well of vultures was for men only. The women lined up on the *bungalee*'s verandah.

'Please Gustadji,' said Alamai, 'do one thing for my Dinshaw's sake. Take Nusli up the hill. He is afraid to go without me, but says if he can walk with you then it is all right.'

'Of course,' said Gustad. He took out his handkerchief and called Nusli. They joined the procession, holding the white kerchief between them. Every man from the bank had decided to take the last walk with Dinshawji. Many of them were weeping openly now. They stepped up in twos or threes, linked by white handkerchiefs, in keeping with the wisdom of the ancients – that there was strength in numbers, strength to repel the *nassoo*, the evil which hovered around death.

Mr Madon had a white silk kerchief. He approached Gustad. 'May I?' Gustad nodded, and grasped Mr Madon's hanky in his other hand. The subtle fragrance of expensive perfume rose from it. The four *nassasalers* shuffled their feet and shifted the bier-handles cutting into their shoulders. They looked around to see if the procession was ready. The *char-chassam* dog and *dustoorjis* took their place. The *nassasalers* started forward.

The long column of handkerchief-linked men followed. Gustad gave Nusli an encouraging smile, then glanced towards the *bungalee*. The women were gathered to watch the men accompany their friend on his final journey. He looked for Alamai, curious to see how she was taking it. He expected to see one last bravura performance, some wailing, beating of the chest, perhaps even a little tearing of the hair.

But he was surprised (and ashamed of his uncharitable thoughts) to see her standing with dignity, her hands clasped tightly together. She was gazing quietly after Dinshawji, and when Gustad looked again he realized that she was indeed weeping. At last, she was weeping silent tears. Rising, perhaps, from a deep well of memories. Memories of? Joys, sorrows, pleasures, regrets? Yes, all these must have filled Dinshawji's and Alamai's private lives. And never a clue, never a word except that line about his dear domestic vulture. But hidden behind it, who knew what love, what life?

The procession wended its way towards the Tower. On both sides of the path, from dense foliage and undergrowth came the rustle of scurrying creatures. Once, a squirrel ran in front of the *nassasalers*, froze, then scampered on. Carrion crows, large and glistening, watched the column curiously from tree-tops. Ahead, a muster of peacocks shuffled to the edge of the path, craning inquisitively before scrambling to safety in the bushes. Their necks flashed blue amidst the green of the shrubbery.

The paved road ended and the gravel path began. The crunch of footsteps got louder as the feet moved from asphalt to gravel, reaching a crescendo when the entire procession was marching on it. Now the sound was magnificent, awe-inspiring. Crunch, crunch, crunch. Grinding, grating, rasping. The millwheel of death. Grinding down the pieces of a life, to fit death's specifications.

Up the hill went the column, the *nassasalers* setting the pace. Crunch, crunch, crunch. A fitting sound, thought Gustad, to surround death. Awesome and magnificent as death itself. And as painful and incomprehensible, no matter how many times I hear it repeated. Crunch, crunch, crunch. A sound to stir the past, to stir up sleeping memories, to whisk them all into the flux of the present, all the occasions when I marched thus, up the hill, upon the gravel walk, as though to crunch, to grind, to crush all loss, all sorrow, into dry flakes, pulverize it into nothingness, be rid of it for ever.

But it always comes back. So much gravel to tread, so many walks to take. For Grandma: who insisted on live chickens, knew spices and half-nelsons, and the secret but universal connections between matchmaking and wrestling. For Grandpa: who made furniture as stout-hearted as his own being, who knew that when a piece of furniture was handed down, the family was enriched by much more than just wood and dowels. For Mamma: fair as morning, sweet as the music of her mandolin, who went gently through life, offending no one, whispered goodnight-Godblessyou through the gauze-like net, and departed much too early. For Pappa: lover of books, who tried to read life like a book and was therefore lost, utterly lost, when the final volume was found missing its most crucial pages . . .

The incline of the hill levelled off. The procession had arrived at the Tower. The *nassasalers* halted and placed the bier on the stone platform outside. They uncovered the face one last time and stood aside. It was time for the last farewell to Dinshawji.

The men approached the stone platform, still linked in twos and threes, the way they had walked up the hill, and bowed three times in unison without letting go of the white kerchiefs. Then the four shouldered the bier again and climbed the stone steps to the door leading inside the Tower. They entered and pulled it shut behind them. The mourners could see no more. But they knew what would happen inside: the *nassasalers* would place the body on a *pavi*, on the outermost of three concentric stone circles. Then, without touching Dinshawji's flesh, using their special hooked rods they would tear off the white cloth. Every stitch, till he was exposed to the creatures of the air, naked as the day he had entered the world.

Overhead, the vultures were circling, flying lower and lower with each perfect circle they casually described. Now they started to alight on the high stone wall of the Tower, and in the tall trees around it.

Nusli edged closer to Gustad. He whispered nervously, 'Gustad Uncle. Vultures are coming, the vultures are coming!'

'Yes, Nusli,' he said comfortingly. 'Don't worry, everything is all right.' Nusli nodded gratefully.

The mourners walked to the terrace of the nearby *atash-dadgah* where the attendant handed out prayer books. There were not enough to go around; the attendant muttered to himself, 'How many copies am I supposed to keep?'

At the Tower, the chief *nassasaler* clapped three times: the signal to start the prayer for Dinshawji's ascending soul.

While they prayed, the vultures descended in great numbers, so graceful in flight but transforming into black hunched forms upon perching, grim and silent. The high stone wall was lined with them now, their serpent-like necks and bald heads rising incongruously from their plumage.

The prayer books were handed back, the white handkerchiefs folded and put away. The mourners had to make one last stop: to wash their hands and faces, do their *kustis*, before returning down the hill to rejoin the world of the living. And there, amid the sound of water taps and the murmur of prayers, Gustad turned abruptly to Mr Madon: 'I need leave on Friday and Saturday.' It was wholly impulsive; he had prepared no excuses.

But Mr Madon assumed the request was relating to Dinshawji's death ceremonies. He was quite understanding: 'Of course. I will mark it on my calendar, first thing in the morning.'

At the *bungalee*, Gustad returned Nusli to Alamai. She thanked Mr Madon for coming. He replied it was his duty.

ii

The street lights were extinguished as Gustad's taxi arrived at Victoria Terminus. The white statue of the Queen hovered in the dawn before the main façade. Red-shirted porters with thick, head-cushioning turbans rushed to the taxi, turning away disappointed when they saw the small bag.

Gustad went to the huge display but no trains were listed. Nearby, the questions of hordes of disgruntled travellers were being fielded by a white-jacketed official who kept removing his black-visored white cap to rub his forehead. Gustad waited for an opening, a space to elbow himself into, and finally shouted over their heads, 'Please excuse me, Inspector!'

His words found a direct channel to the beleaguered ears. The 'please' was balm to that harried spirit: 'Yes sir.'

'Where are all the trains?'

'Railway is gone on strike since midnight, sir.'

255

Gustad felt relief: now I can cancel the trip with a clear conscience. 'There is no service at all?'

'We don't know that, sir. But please listen to loudspeakers, they will be providing all the latest news.'

Gustad thanked him and went to the Inquiry counter. A handwritten sign perched on the closed window: refunds were available, but all bookings would be honoured when service resumed. To return his ticket, give back the money to Ghulam Mohammed, would be the easiest thing. Forget Jimmy once and for all. But if I don't give him a chance. To explain . . .

The tea stall was doing brisk business. Dilnavaz had forbidden Gustad to consume anything not packaged by a reputable company, but it was too early for a bottled cold drink. The man was setting up a pyramid of cups and saucers: 'Hot chai! Hot chai!' At intervals he eschewed that prosaic call for a rhyme sung with great gusto:

> Drink from saucer, drink from cup!
> Forget your sorrow, drink it up!
> Train will run – today? tomorrow?
> Drink one saucer, forget your sorrow!

Gustad set down his bag and ordered. 'Wait!' he exclaimed as the man was about to pour from a vast kettle boiling atop a Primus stove at full blast. 'That cup is dirty.'

The man squinted into it: 'You are absolutely telling the truth. But why worry, in one second it will be clean.' Without warning he cuffed his helper violently over the ear. '*Budmaas*! Leaving it dirty? Wash properly or I'll throw you out!'

'The water only is dirty, what can I do, you won't let me get more,' mumbled the boy of eight or nine, dipping the cup in a bucket of murky water.

He was cuffed over the other ear for his efforts. '*Sooverka batcha*! Blaming the water? Wash! Wash properly or every *huddi* I will break.' He smiled ingratiatingly at Gustad while the child whisked the cup around in the brown fluid: 'Absolutely clean now,' then dried it with a flourish of the cloth doing triple duty: to wipe brow, counter, and crockery.

Gustad took the tea and moved away. He poured a little in the saucer, blew, and tried a draught. The scalding brew was strong and sweet. Felt good going down, despite the dirty cup. Ah, the unique pleasures of railway tea: not so much the drink but the act, the privileged observer status it conferred. He watched detachedly as a family of four made itself comfortable under the station clock. Bedding unrolled, the father was fast asleep, outmanoeuvring circumstances that laid waste to his plans. Wife by his feet, infant at her breast. An older child curled up beside his father. Around their temporary shelter stood walls of luggage. Not far away, a woman lit her portable kerosene stove to make chapaatis. Her family members ate a pungent breakfast stew from shiny stainless-steel boxes.

A railway security person approached the stove, bent over wordlessly and doused the flame. 'Oiee!' cried the woman. 'What are you doing?' Maintaining his arrogant silence, he pointed to the sign listing prohibited acts.

'I'm a poor person,' said the woman. 'How can I read?'

The guard deigned to speak, reading the law for her. 'What kind of law is this?' protested the woman. 'Not being allowed to make chapaati for my children?'

'For the sake of your children's chapaati if whole place catches fire, then what?'

The loudspeakers came alive with violent hissing and crackling, then a high-pitched hum. A hush descended upon the railway station. The tea-stall clatter ceased; the newsstand boys stopped calling; and the sudden quiet awakened the man on the bedding. He sat up with a start. Everyone waited for the voice from above to speak of deliverance. The hiss and crackle bore fruit: 'Checking checking checking. One two three four. Checking. *Ek do teen chaar.'* A painful whine. Then the voice again, hoarse and indistinct, the malfunctioning system devouring most of the words. The survivors emerged like grape seeds spat carelessly through the loudspeaker mesh: 'Passengers are req . . . to vacate the plat . . . and wait in the . . . trains arrive . . . at which time . . . ssengers with tickets may . . . platforms.'

A small trickle relinquished the platforms; most stayed put with their luggage. Railway security guards were dispatched to herd them out. Rifle-bearing soldiers patrolled the yards, examining the tracks and signal boxes.

Gustad returned his empty cup to the counter and bought a newspaper. The headlines were about the strike; the Minister for

Railways promised that essential services would be maintained by managerial staff and the army.

That means a Bombay-Delhi train will certainly run, thought Gustad. He lost himself in the paper, the first he had purchased since the quarrel with the dogwalla idiot, when the carefully balanced household budget had gone up in smoke.

*

There was an announcement: Platform seven now boarding – unreserved train leaving for New Delhi.

Gustad folded his newspaper and hurried to the bottleneck at the platform seven entrance. With his one small bag he had an advantage over families with trunks, beddings, stoves, cooking utensils, cradles, wooden crates, and fragile earthen pots of drinking water. The train was not yet at the platform. Red-shirted coolies were busy circulating among the crowds. 'Risvard! Risvard seat! Ten rupees risvard!' One of them approached Gustad. 'Yes sahab, risvard seat?'

'This is not a reserved train,' said Gustad.

'Yes, yes, but I will find you risvard seat. You pay ten rupees only if you are happy,' said the coolie.

Gustad looked around him, and saw crowds thick enough to fill five trains. 'OK,' he said. The coolie led him down the platform and gave him a place to wait.

'Your bogie will stop here,' he said, 'stand here only.' He indicated his brass armband. 'Remember – number three hundred and eighty-six.' Then he was off towards the railway yard.

Shortly, the empty train backed in, each window framing a red shirt and white turban. People threw their belongings inside and jumped on before it was at a standstill. The red shirts took voice, ransoming off seats they had possessed in the yard. 'Risvard seat! Ten rupees!'

Gustad's porter waved and pointed to his armband. 'Three eighty-six! Don't worry, sahab, come slowly, your seat is ready.'

The compartment was already full. Three eighty-six took the bag and slipped it under the seat without getting up. Gustad took out his wallet and parted with the requisite note. The porter rose, Gustad sat.

'We are at their mercy, no?' said a voice from above. A well-dressed man in his thirties was stretched out on the overhead luggage rack. He laughed. 'Coolies are controlling the whole show. Railway Ministry thinks it is in charge, strikers think they are in charge. But the coolies are the real bosses. I paid twenty rupees for this de-luxe sleeping-berth.'

Gustad smiled up at him between the slats and nodded politely. Half an hour later, when the whistle blew, the compartments, entrances, and aisles were crammed with luggage and humans. He wiped his perspiring face on a sleeve, his handkerchief being inaccessible. The luggage-rack man said, 'Almost twenty-four hours to go. But it will definitely get better.'

And he was right. As time went by, the compartment no longer seemed so packed; the aggression to establish territorial rights had melted. Food packages were opened and lunch was eaten. People even managed to find a way to use the toilet; the men travelling in the water-closet were obliging enough to step out when it was needed for other functions.

'First time to Delhi?' the luggage-rack man asked Gustad.

'Yes.'

'Bad luck. With the strike and all. But sightseeing in Delhi will be good now, the weather will be pleasant.'

'I am going for personal business,' said Gustad.

'Oh, but I am also going for personal business only.' He found the coincidence funny. 'My parents live there. They are saying at my age I should be married, and at their age, they could pass away without seeing their eldest son married, which would be cause of great sorrow. So I am going to select a wife,' he revealed from his horizontal position.

'I wish you good luck,' said Gustad, not pleased to be the recipient of his confidences.

'Thank you very-very much.' He sat up and bumped his head.

For lunch Gustad bought a glass of tea through the window when the train stopped at a station. He opened Dilnavaz's packet of sandwiches later, when it was almost seven o'clock. Omelette. Dinshawji's favourite. How I used to tease him. Two sandwiches every day, for thirty years.

Twilight began to fade, the train sped northwards through darkness. Gustad chewed his sandwiches slowly, looking out at empty fields where a faint light glimmered here and there. Would this long journey be worth it? Was any journey ever worth the trouble?

Then his thoughts were of Dinshawji. Random thoughts, crossing decades of their lives. The new recruit, he used to call me. Would lift his arm and say, under my wing you will be safe – little smelly, but safe. Pointing out who could be trusted, who were tattletales, backstabbers, management *chumchas*. And his trick of leaving the jacket on the chair. How he made people laugh. At lunch and tea-breaks. Even during working hours, one-liners every now and then. Yes, to be able to make people laugh was a wonderful blessed thing. And what a long journey for Dinshawji too. But certainly worth it.

The train rocked through the night. It was much cooler now. He dozed, his head knocking against the window.

iii

In the wake of Gustad's early-morning departure, one disaster after another had followed Dilnavaz. The milk boiled over, she burnt the rice, the kerosene overflowed the funnel when she filled the stove – the kitchen was a ghastly mess.

She was worried about Gustad, wished he had not decided to go to Delhi. But it's the only way to find out the truth. Or he will never know peace. And to be honest, neither will I. All the same, the thought of Gustad entering a jail, even as a visitor, was frightening.

And besides, she had not yet done what Miss Kutpitia had prescribed for Roshan's illness. Roshan was much better now, but Miss Kutpitia had repeated her warning: not to be lulled into a false sense of security, because that's how the dark forces worked, lurking like poisonous snakes, striking when least expected. I did everything else her way, no sense stopping now.

But why for Sohrab does she always say patience, patience? What is that final remedy she is so reluctant to tell? I can take it no longer, lying awake all night worrying about Sohrab, and it's affecting Gustad too, though he will admit nothing, keeps saying, I have only one son, with his pain showing in his eyes every time I look.

If Miss Kutpitia's instructions were to be carried out, now was the time. And still she vacillated, till, later that evening, Mr Rabadi finished walking Dimple in the compound and rang the Nobles's doorbell. The Pomeranian commenced with a series of shrill yips as Dilnavaz opened the door. '*Choop ré*, Dimple!' scolded Mr Rabadi, 'be nice to Noble Auntie.' He was nervous. 'Your husband is there?'

'No.'

'Oh,' he said, at a loss, but also relieved. Just before ringing the doorbell, he had recited Dustoorji Baria's latest Prayer to Strengthen the Righteous. 'I can talk to you then?'

'I am listening.'

Her curt response left him a little flustered. 'See, fighting-bighting I am not interested in. We live in one building, and it's not looking nice. I am talking straight, and I am hoping you will listen straight and stop your son.' His confidence grew in proportion to the number of words he spoke.

Dilnavaz shifted her weight to the other foot. 'Stop our son? From what?'

'Please, *khaali-pili* don't do acting. Your son holds the bicycle seat and runs after my daughter. The whole building is watching and that's not looking nice.'

'What idiotic-lunatic talk is this?' Gustad's favourite phrase fit quite precisely, she realized. 'I don't understand one word of your rubbish.'

'Rubbish? Then ask your son only! I am a fool or what? He holds the seat, and whole building watches him run after my Jasmine with his hand touching her buttocks! That is not looking nice, let me tell you now only!' He waggled a finger which upset Dimple; she started yapping again.

Darius emerged from the back room to see if his mother needed help. When Gustad had left early in the morning, he put his hand on Darius's shoulder and said, half-joking and half-serious, 'Listen, my Sandow. You are in charge, look after your mother and sister.'

'There he is!' yelled Mr Rabadi. 'Ask him now only! Ask him if he put his hand on her buttocks or not! Now only, in front of me!'

Enough was enough, decided Dilnavaz. 'If you ask me, you should leave now only. Too much nonsense we have heard from you.' She tried to shut the door.

'*Khabardaar!*' protested Mr Rabadi, pushing against it. 'Show respect for your neighbour! I have not finished talking and –'

Darius, taking his father's trust very seriously, heaved the door shut. Outside, Mr Rabadi was hurled back, tripping over Dimple. He dusted himself off and threatened through the door to lodge two complaints at the police station: one for assault, the other for molesting his Jasmine. He also made a mental note to visit

Dustoorji Baria at the first opportunity and narrate the contretemps.

'You shouldn't have shut it like that,' said Dilnavaz, secretly quite proud. 'But what is he saying about his *jaari-padayri* daughter?'

Darius looked a bit bashful: 'She's not really fat. She just needed help to learn bicycling. To balance while she pedalled. The other boys all got tired in only one round. No stamina, so she kept asking me.'

'You know what Daddy told you. Rabadi is a crackpot and we don't want trouble with him.' More than a crackpot, she thought, capable of anything. 'Promise me you will not go near her or her father. Especially her father.' The way he had looked when Darius came to the door – my God. What a crazy look.

And now it made sense! Roshan had been getting thinner and thinner, and where was all her health and weight going if not to the dogwalla idiot's daughter? Who got fatter and fatter, day by day! Miss Kutpitia was right, the alum pointed squarely at Rabadi!

The needle of suspicion had sewn up the case to Dilnavaz's satisfaction. She made her plans. First the mixture to prepare. That was easy. But Miss Kutpitia said his scalp must be wetted with it. That was the tricky part.

iv

After midnight, Gustad was awakened by a hand tapping his shoulder. 'Excuse me,' said the luggage-rack man. 'You want to lie up there?'

'What about you?'

'I slept enough. I will sit in your seat.'

'Thank you,' said Gustad. With his limbs fast asleep, aching in every joint, it was difficult to climb to the rack. The man helped; Gustad swung up successfully and stretched out. He wondered sleepily about the fellow's groping hands. But it felt good to lie down. The stiff bones relaxing. The train rocking, soothing. Reminds me of another train. Long time ago. With Dilnavaz. On honeymoon . . .

He slumbered, drifting in and out of sleep. Half-dreaming and half-imagining he was in the coupé with Dilnavaz, twenty-one years ago. The day after their wedding. Impatient in their little

262

mobile bedchamber, not willing to wait till their destination and hotel . . .

A hand stroked Gustad's thigh. It moved to the crotch, discovered his dream-stiffened member, and was encouraged to go further. Fingers groped, fumbled with his fly-buttons, pried and squeezed one through the buttonhole. Did the same with the next. And Gustad realized he was not dreaming any longer.

Pretending to be asleep, he grunted, turned over, and while turning, lashed out with his elbow. He was not disturbed for the rest of the night.

Towards dawn it got cold. The train had left behind the warmth of the lower latitudes. Wishing for a blanket, wishing he was home in bed, he wrapped his arms around himself, drew his knees into his stomach and fell asleep again.

Sunlight through a ventilation grill woke him. Feeling the rays upon his face transported him to another time. Suddenly, all his doubts about coming to Delhi vanished like the night left somewhere down the tracks. Jimmy and I in the compound, saying our prayers. With the first light bathing us. At last everything will be put right between us.

The engine could not devour the remaining miles quickly enough for Gustad. At the next station he alighted, rubbing his cold hands. Some passengers had got off during the night, and there was more room in the compartment. 'Good morning,' he said to the luggage-rack man, who had a black eye. 'What happened?'

'Oh, it's OK. In the night I was going to WC and tripped over a suitcase or something. Banged my face.'

'These crowded trains, what to do. But thank you very much for your bed. I had such a good sleep,' said Gustad.

A chaiwalla passed with glasses of steaming tea in a metal rack. Gustad took two. The luggage-rack man reached for money, but Gustad paid. The hot glass warmed his hands. Poor fellow, he thought. Forcing himself to select a wife, to please his parents. And the poor woman, whoever she will be.

The warning whistle blew. The chaiwalla came back for his glass. Gustad held it out, unfinished. 'Drink, drink,' said the chaiwalla. 'Still time.' The whistle blew again, and the train moved. He began running alongside: 'Drink, drink. Little more time.' Gustad took a few hurried sips, more anxious to return the glass than the chaiwalla was to get it back. The glass changed hands at the end of the platform.

EIGHTEEN

i

Oh what a pleasant ache, to walk again, thought Gustad, left-right, left-right. But Jimmy in jail must feel . . . And soldiers again. Left-right, left-right in the railway station. With their immense backpacks, leaning forward to balance. Huge tortoises going erect. Would be quaint if not for their guns.

He ran his fingers through his hair – hard as unwieldy wire – and looked down at his dusty clothes: reddish-brown, from the miles of countryside the train had come through. He tried to brush it off but it was everywhere. Under the collar, under the cuffs, sleeves, watch-strap. Stuck up my nose – hard and dry inside, sitting like a big fat *cheepro*. Throat feeling raw. Everywhere itching desperately. Inside my socks, inside my *sudra*. Gritty grains crawling busily, exploring the skin with countless little feet and claws, coarsely announcing their chafing, scratching, raging omnipresence. Like questions about Jimmy in my mind.

He entered the waiting-room and went to the back, to the lavatories. Skirting the dirty puddles made by leaky pipes, overflowing toilets and general carelessness, he waited his turn for the wash-basin.

The ice-cold water of Delhi's December morning stung sharply. But it was wonderfully invigorating. *This is the way we wash our face, wash our face, wash our face* . . . He cleared his throat and spat . . . *This is the way we spit out dust on a cold and frosty morning* . . . Good thing Dilnavaz overruled my hanky, insisted on a towel. He rubbed it over the chest and back. Felt good, picked up some still-clinging dust. He put on a fresh *sudra* and shirt, left the waiting-room, and got into an auto-rickshaw.

The three-wheeler swerved in and out of traffic, changing lanes willy-nilly, tossing him from side to side. Forty minutes of agitation later, they stopped at a nondescript grey building. The ride had churned his insides as thoroughly as the thoughts of Jimmy, his mind. 'This is the place?'

'Yes, sahab, this only,' the driver replied. Gustad stepped out unsteadily and paid, slightly nauseous. He felt very alone as the auto-rickshaw rattled away. Wish I was inside it. Heading back to the railway station.

At the reception area he consulted the note Ghulam Mohammed had given him, and asked for Mr Kashyap. He was told to wait.

After half an hour a peon arrived and said, 'Sahab is calling you.' Gustad rose and followed him down a stone-floored hallway, past dirty yellow walls, to a door with a name plate on it: S. Kashyap. The door was ajar.

'Come in, Mr Noble.' The man rose to offer his hand. 'Mr Bilimoria was expecting you many weeks ago.' Mr Kashyap was thickset, with a face whose propensity was to smile regardless of what was being said.

'I have been very busy.'

'Unfortunately, Mr Bilimoria is not here any more.' The smile on the man's face gave his words a sinister slant.

'Not here?'

'No, no, what I mean is, he is not in this building in his regular cell, we had to move him to the hospital section.'

'What happened?'

'High fever, and lot of weakness. Must be a jungle sickness.' He kept smiling his wide, meaningless smile. 'His duties took him into the jungles very often.'

'But can I still meet him?'

'Yes, yes, certainly. Whether hospital, jail cell, solitary – I only have to approve all visitors, so no problem. We can go now.'

A cold bleak corridor connected the main building to the hospital. Mr Kashyap had metal cleats on his heels, and his steps rang out on the stone floor. The footfalls echoed in Gustad's memory. A feeling of profound loss and desolation, of emptiness, swept over him.

Mr Kashyap had a word with a guard in the hospital lobby. 'OK,' he said to Gustad. 'Please wait here, someone will be coming for you.'

'Thank you.'

'Mention not,' said Mr Kashyap and departed, smiling at the dirty yellow walls. Soon, a white-jacketed official arrived to escort Gustad upstairs. They passed large, smelly wards and some single rooms outside which policemen were on duty.

'You are a friend of Mr Bilimoria?' Gustad nodded. 'Very very unfortunate, all these legal problems. And now infection. He becomes delirious sometimes. Don't worry if it happens when you are there, we are treating him for it.'

Gustad nodded, finding it hard to believe. Jimmy's mind, sharp as a Seven O'Clock stainless-steel razor blade, delirious? Not possible.

'How long are you staying? Visits are only thirty minutes.'

'But I came all the way from Bombay. My train leaves at four p.m.'

'Mr Kashyap told me you were a special case.' He considered. 'Till three o'clock?' They stopped outside a room where a policeman sat on a wooden stool with a long, heavy rifle he was clearly weary of holding. The medical person gave instructions, and Gustad entered hesitantly.

The room was stifling, its single window bolted shut. The figure on the bed seemed asleep with face turned away. Gustad could hear the laboured breathing. Not wanting to wake Jimmy with a start, he moved cautiously to the foot of the bed. Now he could see clearly. And what he saw made him want to weep.

On the bed lay nothing more than a shadow. The shadow of the powerfully-built army man who once lived in Khodadad Building. His hairline had receded, and sunken cheeks made the bones jut sharp and grotesque. The regal handlebar moustache was no more. His eyes had disappeared within their sockets. The neck, what he could see of it, was as scrawny as poor *behesti* Dinshaw-ji's, while under the sheet there seemed barely a trace of those strong shoulders and deep chest which Gustad and Dilnavaz used to point out as a good example to their sons, reminding them always to walk erect, with chest out and stomach in, like Major Uncle.

All this in a year and a half? This the man who once carried me like a baby? Into Madhiwalla Bonesetter's clinic? Who could beat me at arm-wrestling as often as I beat him?

Jimmy's right hand lay outside the sheet, emaciated like his face. It twitched twice, then his eyes fluttered open. He looked bewildered and shut them. His lips produced a weak, croaking sound: 'Gus . . .'

O God. Can't even say my name. 'Yes, Jimmy,' he said reassuringly, taking his hand. 'It is Gustad.'

'Injec. . .jec. . .injhecshun,' he whispered, slurring badly. 'Wait. Soon . . . little . . . better.'

'Yes, yes, slowly. I am here only, Jimmy.' He pulled the chair close without letting go of his hand. What kind of sickness is this? What have they done to him?

Anger, accusations, demands for explanations emptied from Gustad's mind. Only a monster could harass a broken man for answers. He would wait, listen to what Jimmy wanted, comfort him, offer his help. Everything else had to be forgotten. And forgiven.

For thirty minutes he sat with Jimmy's cold, trembling hand in his. Finally Jimmy opened his eyes again. 'Gustad. Thank you. Thank you for coming,' he whispered. The slurring was less, though his voice shook with the effort.

'No, no. I am happy to come. But what happened?' Then, remembering his resolution, 'It's OK, don't strain yourself.'

'The injections they give . . . for infection. Makes it difficult . . . to speak. But. After an hour . . . better.'

The words formed and faded like wisps of smoke in a breeze. Gustad moved his chair closer still. 'What is the infection? Do they know what they are treating?'

'Something. Caught in Sundarbans. First . . . yellow fever, they said, then typhus, malaria . . . typhoid . . . God knows. But I think . . . getting better. Injections . . . terrible . . .'

He was silent for a bit, his chest heaving. 'Thank you for coming,' he said again. 'You will stay?'

'They gave me permission till three o'clock.' Gustad looked at his watch. 'So we have four whole hours.'

'Have to hurry . . .'

'Now listen, Jimmy, talking can wait. What's happened has happened.'

'But I want to. I feel no peace. Thinking about it . . . thinking about what you must be thinking,' he whispered.

'It's OK, what's happened has happened.'

'Tell me first about yourself . . . Dilnavaz and children . . .'

'Everyone is fine. We were very worried when you disappeared, that's all. Then your letter came, and we were happy that you were all right.' Gustad chose his words carefully: nothing must sound like an accusation. He remembered the decapitated rat and cat; the rhyme: *Bilimoria chaaval chorya*; the vinca, rose and *subjo* slashed to bits. He did not mention Sohrab, or Roshan's illness, nothing to give Jimmy cause to worry.

'How I miss Khodadad Building. . .wish I never took Delhi posting. But I can come back . . . in four years.'

'Four years?'

'Yes, my sentence.'

Gustad remembered Ghulam Mohammed's advice: if Bili Boy is hopeful, let him hope. 'Plus you can use your influence.'

'No, Gustad, this is one case where influence won't help. Goes to the very top . . . the dirty work.' Despair filled his eyes again. 'But . . . you know what I miss most . . . since I left?'

'What?'

'Early morning. *Kusti* and prayers together, in the compound.'

'Yes,' said Gustad. 'I also.'

Jimmy raised himself on one elbow to reach the water on his bedside table. He sipped a bit. 'Let me tell you what has been going on . . . it's hard to believe . . .'

The injection's numbing clutches loosened, letting his words grow clearer, but he could still produce no more than a painful whisper and, coughing frequently, had to pause often. The damage inside, viral or man-inflicted, had left its mark. It made Gustad wince to watch and listen.

'The offer was so exciting . . . difficult place to join. Prime Minister's office called me.'

'You worked there?'

'My letter came from there. For the Research and Analysis Wing . . . in direct charge.'

Again Gustad was puzzled. 'You were in direct charge of RAW?'

'No, she was,' he whispered. 'Surprised me.'

After the first little while, Gustad learned to rearrange Jimmy's words and understand his slow, disconnected, rambling fragments. He remembered, sadly, the Major's thrilling stories which used to captivate Sohrab and Darius for hours.

'In RAW . . . new identity. Management consultant. I could not

269

lie. . .to you. Just went away. I am sorry, Gustad. Really sorry
. . .how are the children?'

'Fine, fine. Everything is fine, Jimmy,' he said, patting his hand.
'So you went to Delhi and joined RAW.'

'Big surprise . . . she was using RAW like her own private
agency. Spying on opposition parties, ministers . . . anyone. For
blackmail. Made me sick. Even spying on her own cabinet. One of
them . . . prefers little boys. Another takes pictures of himself . . .
doing it with women. Bribes, thievery. . .so much going on, Gustad. RAW kept dossiers. On her friends and enemies. Where they
went, who they met, what they said, what they ate, what they
drank . . .' Jimmy broke off, gasping. Despite his condition, his
fondness for rhetoric would not let him trim the story beyond a
certain point of leanness. Some fat had to remain, the way he used
to insist with Gustad about *dhansak* meat – *charbee* in the right
proportion added to the flavour.

'Her friends become enemies and her enemies become friends
. . . so quickly. So often. Blackmail is the only way she can keep
control . . . keep them all in line. Disgusting. I was fed up. Not
what I came to Delhi for. I applied for transfer.'

He drank more water, propping up his pillow to keep his head
raised. Gustad held him under the arms and pulled him up. The
sheet slipped a little. He saw how hollow Jimmy's chest was, as
though the lungs had collapsed.

'Remember the cyclone last year . . . in East Pakistan? Thousands killed . . . bastards in West Pakistan no help. Showed the
Bengalis once and for all. West only wants their sweat. And in
December elections Sheikh Mujibur Rahman won. Absolute
majority.'

'Yes,' said Gustad. 'Bhutto and the generals would not let him
form the government. Yahya Khan sent in the army when the
Bengalis began civil disobedience.'

'Soldiers slaughtered thousands of demonstrators. Refugees
came . . . My superior told me our government will help guerrilla
movement. Right away I said I was interested. So Prime Minister's
office called me for interview . . . What close control she keeps on
RAW. Strong woman, Gustad, very strong woman . . . very
intelligent. People say her father's reputation made her Prime
Minister. Maybe. But now she deserves – ' The pillow slipped, and

he did not wish to raise it again. He cleared his throat feebly. 'Sohrab? How is Sohrab?'

'Fine, fine.'

'And Darius? Body-building?'

'Solid muscles,' said Gustad. 'The Prime Minister.'

Jimmy was grateful for the reminder. 'She came to the point. She said . . . your record is excellent, Major Bilimoria, and you understand our objectives. Her voice . . . so calm, such confidence. Not like her political speeches . . . yelling and screaming. Hard to believe now she could be in such crookedness. Maybe people around her . . . who knows.' Gustad wanted to ask what crookedness, but waited. All in good time, at Jimmy's pace.

'She put me in charge. Training and supplying the Mukti Bahini . . . tough fighters, Bengalis. Learned quickly. Factories sabotaged . . . bridges toppled . . . railway tracks –'

'Hai!' Jimmy suddenly broke off, looking over Gustad's shoulder. He had barely raised his voice, but compared to his feeble whispers it seemed like a yell. 'Swine! Get out! Not your bloody latrine!'

Gustad understood. He leaned forward and patted his shoulder. 'It's OK, Jimmy, everything is OK,' he said, as Jimmy drifted back into the comfortable past.

'Gustad, what time?' he panted. The effort had taken a lot out of him. 'Time for *kusti*?'

'Not yet, Jimmy, rest a little.' He continued to pat his shoulder till he was ready to resume the story.

'There was a ceremony . . . birth of Bangladesh. Invited the press to Kushtia district, not far from our border . . . village renamed Mujibnagar. New flag . . . green, red, gold, in the mango grove. Singing . . . *sonar Bangla*. And Pakistani artillery not far away. *Joi Bangla* . . . proud moment for everyone. But bloody foreign press printed name of the village . . . Pakistani Air Force destroyed it next day . . .'

Without knocking, a sharp-faced nurse entered the room. It was time for Jimmy's next injection. Her forearms were sinewy, the veins standing out like braided rope. She roughly turned him on his side, carried out her task, and left wordlessly.

'Again it will start. Then how will I talk to you?'

'Don't worry,' comforted Gustad. 'There is lots of time. Rest. I will wait.' He looked at his watch and was surprised: almost one already. How much time and precious effort Jimmy had expended saying these few words. As though each one was being sculpted painstakingly, out of stubborn granite that deflected his strokes, blunted his chisel. But he persisted, and after the long wrestle, presented them to Gustad. One by one. Who received them reverently, with anguish, because of the pain that went into their making.

'Money. Money was the main thing for Mukti Bahini. Without money, no supplies, no explosives, no guns . . . nothing. We needed a regular allocation, a budget. I told her at next meeting . . . operation would shut down . . . We were alone, but she not attentive . . . as if dreaming of something else. Strange woman . . . very strong woman . . .

'I thought she had lost interest, Mukti Bahini finished. But I gave her my full report. Suddenly she said, I understand the situation, I will arrange more funds. She went inside . . . to her small private office. Gave me instructions. Next morning to go to State Bank, meet chief cashier, ask for sixty lakh rupees.

'She started explaining, when aid officially sanctioned, amount will be replaced. I thought, whysh . . . why she telling me all this, none of my bi-bi-bish . . . bisnesh.'

The injection was gripping his tongue in its pincers again. Gustad wished he would stop and rest; he leaned closer, till his ear was inches away from Jimmy's lips.

'She said . . . don't tell chief cashier name or RAW identity. Only, Bangladeshi Babu . . . come for sixty lakh.

'Next morning, got the m-m-money. Amazing . . . sixty lakh, just like that. Then, in a few days, she sent m-mess-message . . . Now ja-ja-just listen carefully . . . her pe-plans. Hu-how she was arranging. To protect herself . . . ta-ta-trrrap me . . .'

Jimmy closed his eyes; the mouth continued to make small movements but no sounds emerged. He fell into an unquiet state resembling sleep. Gustad pulled the sheet up to cover him properly and went outside, exhausted. Jimmy's agonizing struggle had drained him.

The policeman asked, 'How is he? Lot of pain?'

'Yes. But sleeping now.' The policeman said there was tea and snacks in the canteen downstairs. He pronounced it snakes.

The *bhaiya* had been reluctant to let Dilnavaz have an extra quarter litre of milk: '*Arré bai*, you should have told me yesterday. Suddenly how to produce more?'

Others quickly jumped in, taking her side. 'Leave all your acting-facting, *muà*. We know you will just add quarter litre of water, soon as you are out of here.' Protesting the charge indignantly as usual, he let her have the milk.

Dilnavaz took it home and separated the extra quarter for the mixture. First came the *taveej* from over the front door. She sliced the lime into thin wedges, chopped the chillies, then proceeded to grind it all to a fine paste. The round stone rumbled and groaned as she dragged it back and forth over the flat slab.

The paste blended well with the milk, giving it a pretty pale green tint. Next she measured seeds into the mortar – anise, bishop's-weed, poppy, fennel, mustard – and pestled them to powder. The remaining ingredients were already in powder or liquid form: *kunkoo, marcha ni bhhuki, harad, dhanajiru, papad khar, shahjiru, tuj, lavang, mari, ailchi, jyfer, sarko, garam masalo, andoo, lassun*. She stirred briskly; everything must be well-mixed, Miss Kutpitia had insisted.

Now for the mouse droppings. Dilnavaz was sure she could find the required amount, thanks to Gustad's black paper; even this nuisance finally had its use. Lifting the corners, she soon gathered a teaspoonful. In the pan the black bits remained suspended no matter how much she stirred. She let the mixture stand, and proceeded to procure the final ingredient: a spider's round white egg-case. Amazing, the things Miss Kutpitia knew.

Dilnavaz located a large black-brown specimen near the ceiling, where the paper met the top of the ventilator. She lunged with the long-handled broom. The paper tore away, while the spider glided floorward in graceful stages on silken thread. She waited, poised over the predictable landing spot, to finish the job with her slipper.

But the queasy part still lay ahead – the dead spider's several legs were folded rigidly over the abdomen, and the round egg-case was locked behind a radial grid of dark furry appendages. They reminded her of Inspector Bamji's hairy legs, in the old days when he wore short pants, before his promotion.

Using paper and a pencil from Gustad's desk, she bent back the legs, one by one. Some sprang closed again, and had to be held down. Many broke off at the thorax or a midway joint. The cocoon, soft and slightly sticky, though not as clingy as a web, was disengaged after a little poking with the pencil.

She put the pan on the stove. The mixture warmed and became a dark-brown homogeneous compound. Even the obdurate mouse droppings co-operated to blend with the rest. Finally, the carefully preserved alum shape was crumbled and added.

Dilnavaz was ready for the dogwalla idiot.

*

On Saturdays, Mr Rabadi always took Dimple for a midday stroll through the compound, supplementing the morning and evening walks. Aware of this extra airing, Dilnavaz had rehearsed her strategy. She reheated the thick mixture and added a spoonful of milk. Yes, that was the right consistency.

Shortly after one o'clock, Dimple's shrill bark was heard, faintly, from the far end of the compound. Dilnavaz tensed. Now if only her luck held and the stairs were clear. Timing was important. She waited till Mr Rabadi got closer to the bushes, then nipped out the back and up the stairs.

Her calculations were perfect. She peeked over the balcony. Dimple had called a temporary halt to sniff, searching for the right spot, and Mr Rabadi looked on approvingly. Dilnavaz extended her arm and turned over the pan.

Mr Rabadi's roar resounded through the compound. She primly descended the stairs and returned home by her back door, cautious about claiming success. There was no evidence that his scalp had been anointed; Mr Rabadi would shout no matter where it landed – even if it fell harmlessly on the ground beside him. She longed to look but had to be content with listening.

'Junglees!' he yelled. 'Living like animals!' Hearing her master hold forth, Dimple added her voice to his. 'Thousands are starving! And shameless people throw curry in the compound!' Dilnavaz grew optimistic; it must have fallen close enough for him to at least smell it.

Then shrieks of pain entered the angry litany of complaints, as traces of *marcha ni bhhuki, andoo, lassun, garam masalo* and other fiery spices trickled down Mr Rabadi's hair and forehead, into his eyes. 'Aaaaa! It's killing me! Aaaaaa! Dying, *bas,* I'm dying!' Now Dilnavaz was certain she had been on target.

274

'Ohhhh! *Mari chaalyo!* Blinded! Blinded completely! Look, you shameless animal! Whoever you are! Look at me! Eyeless in the compound! Blinded by your curry! May the same thing happen to you! And to your children, and your children's children!' He made his way to his flat, cursing, howling, calling on the world to witness his cruel fate. Dimple pranced and leaped around him, enjoying his unusually animated state.

Dilnavaz returned to the kitchen. It had gone exactly according to plan. Miss Kutpitia would be proud of her, she felt, as she scrubbed the pan clean of its magical *mélange*.

'Was that the dogwalla idiot shouting, Mummy?' asked Roshan.

Dilnavaz started, she had not heard her coming. 'Yes, but you shouldn't say such things. And why are you out of bed?'

'I'm tired of sleeping all day. Can I do something else?'

'OK, sit on the sofa and read your book.' She rinsed the *raakh-bhoosa* off the pan. It emerged shining from water. Was it possible? So soon? It was no less than a miracle! Or coincidence. But what did it matter, the result was the same. Besides, was there a person alive who, at one time or another, did not find it difficult to disbelieve completely in things supernatural?

*

Before Miss Kutpitia could fully savour the victory, Dilnavaz moved on to the next item of business. 'I know I have to be patient,' she said. 'But you must help. I cannot go on like this, my head is so full of worries all the time.'

'What are you talking about?'

'Sohrab. My head is spinning and spinning because of the worries. You had said there was another remedy. A final remedy. We *must* do it now, please!'

'Must-bust nothing!' said Miss Kutpitia, miffed. 'How much do you know about these things? Don't tell me what to do!'

Dilnavaz retreated meekly: 'Never would I think of telling you what to do. But this is the only chance, it seems to me.'

'You don't know what you are asking. Terrible things could happen.' Miss Kutpitia's eyes narrowed, her voice dire, full of unspeakable events. 'And not all your sorrow or regret later on will do any good, or change one single thing.'

'Then my son is lost for ever?'

Miss Kutpitia was familiar with the sorrow for a lost son. 'That is not what I am saying. If you insist, we will do it. But on your head will be the *parinaam*, on your head the weight of all the consequences.'

Dilnavaz shuddered. 'For my son's sake I take the risk.'

'Then it is settled. Wait.' She became businesslike. From a pile of cardboard boxes, tins, newspapers and torn clothes, she fished out an old shoe-box. 'This will do. Now we need a lizard. Can you manage?' Dilnavaz's face radiated no confidence.

'Never mind. I will get one, wait.' Miss Kutpitia opened one of the two locked doors and shut it behind her. There were sounds of scampering before she emerged triumphantly, panting a bit, and handed over the box. 'Be careful with the lid, or it will run away. Wait, better tie some string.' From the heap where she found the shoe-box, she extracted a length. 'Good. Now leave it till sunrise under the bed where Sohrab used to sleep. Below the head. And bring it back tomorrow.'

'Then what happens?'

'One step at a time. Do this much first.'

She knew Miss Kutpitia would not satisfy her curiosity. 'Is ten o'clock all right?' No later than that: Gustad could return any time after noon, depending on the train.

'Ten, eleven, anything. Bring the box, and bring Tehmul, that's all.'

'Tehmul?'

'Of course.' Miss Kutpitia was annoyed at the silly question. 'Without him the lizard is useless.'

Imagining bizarre possibilities around the Tehmul-and-lizard combination, Dilnavaz passed Dimple and Mr Rabadi in the compound, and thought she caught a whiff of garlic as he scratched his scalp. She was relieved he had not suffered permanent damage. His eyes were fine, glaring fiercely at her.

She placed the shoe-box below Sohrab's *dholni*. How long it has been, she thought, since he rolled it out from under Darius's bed. The ache in my heart will not leave. Not till I hear again, each night, the rumbling of the castors.

iii

Jimmy was still in the grip of the injection when Gustad returned from the canteen. He soundlessly drew the chair close and waited. Again, the hand was first to stir. 'Gustad?'

'Yes, Jimmy.' He stroked the hand. 'I am still here.'

'Makes me thirsty . . . injection.' He reached for the water. 'Till where . . . did I tell you?'

'Prime Minister called you again to her office. You said she had made plans to protect herself.'

'Protect herself . . . yes . . . trap me.' Once he located the place, he proceeded as though he had not stopped. 'She said, I arranged for money . . . because Mukti Bahini must be helped . . . but. Having second thoughts. She said, I have enemies . . . everywhere. If they find out about this money, they will use the information against me. No difference to them that money is for a good cause . . . our country will suffer if government destabilized. Very dangerous border situation . . . CIA, Pakistani agents . . .

'It made sense. Shall I bring the money back, I asked. She said no, Mukti Bahini must not suffer . . . should be another way.

'She said, only problem is my telephone call to chief cashier . . . he might talk. Must correct that. How, I asked, he had heard her voice. She said, yes, but he did not see me speaking . . . we can always say someone imitated my voice.

'Very clever woman, Gustad. She said, if my enemies try to make trouble, all you have to say is . . . you imitated my voice. I laughed . . . who would believe this? But she said, under the proper conditions, people will believe anything. She promised . . . nothing would happen to me.

'Like a fool I agreed . . . trusted her. Then she said, maybe we should make our plan watertight . . . you can write a few lines just now. A confession. That you imitated my voice . . . because you wanted to continue helping Mukti Bahini. This way, she would be prepared in advance . . . if any politician tried to make mischief. Any allegations, and she could stand up in Parliament. With the written confession . . . that she was aware, and government was in control of the situation.

'What can I say, Gustad? Even to this . . . I agreed. She gave me a blank sheet of paper and her own fountain-pen. I wrote my confession . . . like an idiot. My respect for her . . . grown so much over the months. Such a strong woman. Trusted her completely.'

It baffled Gustad. The worldly-wise Jimmy Bilimoria, the cynical Major he had known for so many years, whose motto in life was: when in doubt, keep doubting. Could he really have done the foolish things he is describing? What kind of woman is she?

'Sorry Gustad . . . talking so much, forgot about your lunch. You want to eat?'

'No, I had some tea while you were sleeping.'

Jimmy smiled, but upon his wasted face the smile became a painful grimace. 'So often I have thought of Dilnavaz's *dhansak* . . . those Sunday afternoons.' He stared into the distance, his eyes cloudy. With a visible effort he began whispering again.

'So my operation was in full swing, I thought . . . sent the good news to Mukti Bahini commander. But few weeks later . . . when I went to visit, total disappointment on his face. What happened to new financing, he said. Took me for inspection. I saw for myself. Ragged condition . . . bare feet, torn clothes, no helmets. A few had guns . . . rest drilling with sticks, branches. Something terribly wrong . . . I hurried back to Delhi . . .

'Did some checking, through my private channels. Ghulam also investigated . . . at his end. They tried to finish him off on his Lambretta. Their favourite way, traffic accident. He was asking too many questions. But we discovered something impossible to believe. I checked again . . . Ghulam also. It made no sense . . . why this way, all she has to do is ask me . . .' He choked and began coughing violently. Gustad supported his head till it stopped. He held up the glass of water but Jimmy waved it aside.

'I have seen so much . . . bribery, double-cross, blackmail. This one . . .' He paused, and now took the water.

'What happened to the money?' asked Gustad.

'Money I was disbursing for supplies . . . intercepted. By Prime Minister's office. Rerouted. To a private account.'

'Are you sure of it?'

Jimmy made a gesture of despair: 'Wish I could say no.'

'But for what?'

'That I am not sure of. One possibility – to finance her son's car factory. Or could be for election fund, or maybe . . .'

'What did you do then?'

'Not what I should have done . . . but something very stupid. Should have exposed the whole thing. Told the press, opposition parties. Started an inquiry. But I thought, everything is controlled by her. RAW, the courts, broadcasting . . . everything is in her pocket, all will be covered up . . .'

Suddenly, Jimmy screamed, covering his face with his hands. 'Stop! Please stop!' He thrashed around, legs kicking air. 'Stop! Aaaaa!' Gustad tried to hold him but Jimmy kept him off with his flailing arms. He subsided of his own accord in a few moments, then lay panting, cold sweat running down his face, knees drawn up to his stomach.

Shaken, Gustad knew it was the telling that brought back the prison nightmare. He put his arm around him: 'It's OK, Jimmy. No one will hurt you, I'm still here.'

Gradually, Jimmy unclenched his fists and let his legs straighten. But he continued to shiver, and Gustad soothed him till it passed. He opened his eyes. 'Gustad? Water, please.' Gustad propped up the pillow again.

'Whole day and night I sat in my flat. Doing nothing . . . just thinking. What hope for the country? With such crooked leaders? Whole day and night . . . I sat thinking of all the people I had come across in my life . . . men in the army, good men. And my Ghulam Mohammed. Khodadad Building . . . the families living there. You and Dilnavaz, the children, the ambitions you have for them. And those bastards, those ministers and politicians, those ugly buffaloes and pigs . . . getting fatter and fatter, sucking our blood . . .' Jimmy trembled, choking with vehemence.

'It drove me crazy to think of all this. But I decided – if they can profit from the sixty lakh, why not us? Her son, his Maruti car factory, whatever they use it for . . . we can also use some. You, your family, Ghulam, me. Why not? I put aside ten lakh, told Ghulam to expect a delivery . . . our usual channels in Chor Bazaar.'

As gently as he could, Gustad asked, 'But why did you not tell me what was really happening?'

'Gustad, I know you . . . your principles. Would you have agreed . . . if I told you the truth? My plan was to complete my assignment, resign. Return to Bombay and divide the money. You, Ghulam Mohammed, me. It was wrong, I know, two wrongs don't make a right. But I was disgusted. And I was absolutely sure . . . if fifty lakh reached PM's office . . . no one would bother about missing ten. Every pipeline has leaks.

'But . . . I was mistaken. They came for me . . . arrested . . . made a case based on my confession. What they really wanted was the ten lakh. You know how it is in our jails when you refuse to . . .'

'And you refused.'

'Had to protect you and Ghulam . . . did not want any trouble for you. Once money was returned, everything fine. Transferred to hospital, proper treatment . . .'

Jimmy fell silent, and Gustad sensed he wanted to hear his reaction. 'What shall I say, Jimmy? All this suffering. But can you not still talk to lawyers, or newspapers, tell them the truth about your ten lakh, and about the whole bloody crooked –'

'Gustad, it has been tried. Everything is in their control . . . courts in their pockets. Only one way . . . quietly do my four years . . . then forget about it.'

'Everyone knows there's corruption,' said Gustad. 'But to this level? Hard to believe.'

'Gustad, it is beyond the common man's imagination, the things being done by those in power. But I did not call you here to make you worry . . . feel sorry for me. What has happened has happened. I just wanted to talk to you. To make sure you don't think I tried to trick you. You were so angry, Ghulam told me . . . in your place I would also have been. But I was hoping . . . you will forgive me now.'

Gustad held his gaze. He saw his friend's need for absolution, the pleading in his eyes. 'Do you forgive me?'

There was only one answer to give: 'Rubbish. Nothing to forgive, Jimmy.'

Trying to reach Gustad's hand, Jimmy raised his, shaking with the effort. Gustad clasped it firmly. 'Thank you, Gustad. For everything . . . for coming, listening . . .'

For a while they were silent. Then their conversation was of the old times, when the boys were still very little, when Major Uncle taught them how to march, left-right, left-right, and how to present arms, using rulers for rifles.

The nurse came to administer another injection shortly before it was time for Gustad to leave. The sinewy woman turned Jimmy over – the other side, this time – and plunged in the needle.

They managed to finish what they were talking about, say goodbye, before the drug silenced him. Gustad sat awhile on the edge of the bed, listening to the troubled breathing. He pulled the sheet up, tucked it in, then bent over and kissed his friend lightly on the forehead.

*

While Gustad slept propped up between his fellow travellers, the Prime Minister, in a special radio broadcast, told the nation that Pakistani Air Force planes had just bombed Indian airfields in Amritsar, Pathankot, Srinagar, Jodhpur, Chandigarh, Ambala, and Agra. She said it was an act of naked aggression; and consequently, India was now at war with Pakistan. By the time the train neared Bombay, everyone aboard had heard the news, having picked up bits and pieces of information mingled with rumour at stations along the way. At Victoria Terminus Gustad tried to buy a paper, but the few remaining copies were going at five times the normal price, and he turned it down.

NINETEEN

i

For good measure Dilnavaz left the lizard under Sohrab's *dholni*
three hours past sunrise. When it was time to visit Miss Kutpitia,
she picked up the box gingerly and shook it. A reassuring rustle
came from within.

What possible conjunction of Tehmul and the lizard would bring
Sohrab back, she could not even begin to guess. Strange, that in
Miss Kutpitia's presence, inside that flat, doubts vanished so easily,
and all her remedies became paradigms of sound, judicious action.
And yet, I must be going mad, to have begged her to do this.

She pushed open the front window to look for Tehmul. He was
waiting for her. 'Limejuicelimejuice. Veryveryverytasty.'

'No, no. No more lime juice. But Miss Kutpitia has something
very nice for you. Go, she is calling.'

'Phonephonephoneupstairs.'

'Right, where the phone is. Go, I am also coming.'

'Goinggoingverytasty.' Grinning hard, he set off, right hand
under left armpit. She let him have a head start of roughly two
minutes before following with the box.

An air of impatience surrounded Miss Kutpitia. She bustled them
inside. 'Come on, come on, shut the door,' she muttered. 'Where
do you think I do these things, on the staircase?'

Dilnavaz awaited her instructions. Now that the time was here,
she felt trapped (helpless, she thought, as the lizard in the shoe-
box). Events were already in motion; she could but watch them
gather momentum and manifest the promised end. Grinding spices
on the *masala* stone was one thing, grinding events to a halt was
another. It needed a different sort of strength.

In a daze, she watched Miss Kutpitia go to one of the two closed
doors and unlock it with a key from the bunch around her neck.

There was a gleam in the old woman's eyes as, in the manner of an artist unveiling the *pièce de résistance*, she threw open the portal and bade them enter the forbidden chamber.

The windows were shut tight, the heavy curtains drawn. Thick, stubborn odours of mildew and disuse loomed in the doorway. But Dilnavaz was reluctant to penetrate the room's gloomy secrets. With the palpable truth behind years of rumours and stories awaiting her, she lingered timidly in the passage. Tehmul, wide-eyed and perspiring, scratched nervously.

Miss Kutpitia became impatient with the dawdling twosome. 'Nothing will get done if you hover by the door all day!' She pushed them inside and slammed her hand over the wall switch. A weak light came on.

Dilnavaz gasped. She was unable to decide whether to look, or look away; both desires were equally strong. So she did neither, waited till the room and its contents (with the look of things which had never been looked at) began to register gradually upon her consciousness.

Shades of grey and white shrouded everything. Cobweb wreaths and layers of dust made it difficult to identify objects, except for the ghostly furniture. But as her senses adapted to the eerie stillness and the crepuscular glow of the dim, dust-coated light bulb, the shadowy chamber started grudgingly to yield its secrets. She was now able to see that the rags hanging on the clothes-horse had once possessed the crisp, starched form of a boy's shirt and short pants, perhaps a school uniform. From the lower rod, two dark, holey rags dangling like moults of mysterious reptiles were definitely the remains of socks. And what seemed to be a strip of shrivelled leather had been a belt of the finest snakeskin. Yes, it was clear.

Yes, she could see now, this must have been the room of Miss Kutpitia's nephew Farad, who had once filled her cup to over-flowing. The one who had died with his father in the car accident on the mountain road. And when their broken bodies were recovered from the ravine, Miss Kutpitia's cup had shattered, as irreparably as their bones – beyond the reach of any bonesetter's art, beyond miracles.

But Miss Kutpitia had been trying to mend and fix, ever since, in her own peculiar way. Her three and a half decades of reverently observed isolation had allowed the tropical climate to work its rot and ruin. The damp of thirty-five monsoons, rampant humidity-loving fungi, numerous types of variegated moulds – all played their clammy, smeary parts in the process of decay and disintegration. There was the boy's desk, with an exercise book lying open, its pages curled and yellow. Next to it, a stack of textbooks, the one on top brown-paper-covered, with the title penned by a boy's yet-to-mature hand, in fading ink that had defied the intervening years: *High School English Grammar and Composition* by Wren & Martin. Fountain-pen and inkpot, dry as dust. A warped, cracked ruler. Pencils. Erasers like little chunks of hardwood. Draped over a chair, a green raincoat covered with fuzzy, grey growth; under the chair, black gumboots, gone furry grey. On the bed, the mattress's black-striped ticking showed through gaping holes in the bedclothes where generations of moths had feasted for ten thousand nights. But the sheet and blanket were neatly arranged, the pillow in position, awaiting the occupant's return.

The door to the adjoining room was open too, and Dilnavaz could glimpse parts of its interior. That must have been the room of Farad's father. His lawyer's robe, in shreds more grey than black, was suspended from the door latch on a wire hanger. Sheaves of legal documents, bundles of court papers, each tied correctly with pink cloth ribbon, were in neat piles on a metal desk. A hairbrush, shaving kit, attaché case, magazines, occupied a bedside table. And everywhere, the cobwebs hung densely, wreathing the light fixtures, curtains, doorframes, windows, cupboards, clothes-horses, ceiling fans. Like *tohruns* and garlands of gloom, the cobwebs had spread their clinging arms and embraced the relics of Miss Kutpitia's grief-stricken past.

'Stand aside, Tehmul,' she said, irritated for no reason. 'Don't keep coming in my way.' She took the box from Dilnavaz and placed it on Farad's desk, opening the lid just a crack. In due course the lizard poked out its tongue-flicking snout. Miss Kutpitia promptly whacked it over the head with the warped ruler. She turned the box over on the desk, and, pinching the lizard's wriggling tail between her thumb and finger, snipped off about two inches of the appendage with a pair of blunt, rusty scissors.

Dilnavaz blanched; like Tehmul, she watched in fascination. Everything Miss Kutpitia needed was at the ready in this room. Like a regular cotton wick, the tail was inserted into a wick-holder, dipped in oil, and floated in the lamp glass. Loaded with its strange cargo, the holder rocked on the oil surface as the tail continued to writhe and wiggle, but managed to stay afloat.

'Now,' she said to Dilnavaz, picking up her box of matches. 'You go and stand outside. You,' she said to Tehmul. 'You want to have some fun?'

'Funfunfunfunfunfun.'

'Then sit down and pay attention to this glass.'

Tehmul giggled at the squirming tail and sat. The rotted wicker seat gave immediately. He sank, his bottom sticking out below and rendering him helpless. 'Fallingfallingfalling,' he appealed with a drowning man's outstretched arms.

Dilnavaz helped to extricate him before she left the room. Outside the door, a whiff of acrid fumes told her Miss Kutpitia had struck the match. Within seconds the latter emerged, shutting the door behind her.

'Very dangerous to look at it once it is burning,' she said. 'That's why I had to send you away.'

'But what about you? You must have seen it.'

'Never. You think I am crazy? I know how to light it without looking.' For five minutes they listened to Tehmul's giggles through the odours of burning lizard skin and flesh. Then Miss Kutpitia opened the door and called him out.

He was reluctant to leave. 'Twistingburningtwistingburning.'

'Enough now,' said Miss Kutpitia, 'go play in the compound.' She would wait a little longer to clean the glass, she whispered to Dilnavaz, because she wanted to take no chances. Even a smouldering bit of tail could have devastating consequences. Like that (she snapped her fingers) you could lose your mind.

Dilnavaz immediately took a good look at Tehmul to see if there was any change. 'Don't be silly,' said Miss Kutpitia, 'it needs a few days.'

'Oh,' said Dilnavaz, relieved and disappointed.

'Twistingtwisting,' said Tehmul. He descended the stairs, leading with his good leg and letting the lame one drop heavily. 'Twisting-twistingfireturning. Funfunfunfun.' He waved and disappeared from sight, but his voice came from the stairwell below: 'Burning-burningburningburning.' That the lizard tail had wriggled its way out of the glass and on to Farad's tattered exercise book, he left unsaid.

As Gustad stepped off the bus from Victoria Terminus, he could see that the compound wall's last vacant spots had been filled while he was away. Pictures of prophets, saints, swamis, babas, seers, holy men and sacred places, in oils and enamels, covered every square inch of black stone. The bright colours glistened in the late morning light.

On the pavement, flowers had been left by the faithful: singly, or in posies and bouquets. There were thick garlands, too, of roses and lilies, *gulgota* and *goolchhadi*, filling the air with their heavenly fragrances. He could smell them as far away as the bus stop, faint as the touch of the woman's veil at Mount Mary. And the closer he came, the richer grew the sweet aromas. Zinnias, marigolds, *mogra*, *chamayli*, *goolbahar*, magnolias, *bunfasha*, chrysanthemum, *suraj-mukhi*, asters, dahlias, *bukayun*, *nargis* enveloped his senses in a fantastic profusion of colour and scent, making him smile dreamily and forget his exhaustion from two nights on the train.

What an amazing contrast to the wall of old, he thought. Hard now to even imagine the horrid shit-and-piss hell it was. Dada Ormuzd, You are wonderful. Instead of flies and mosquitoes buzzing, a thousand colours dancing in sunlight. Instead of the stink, this glorious fragrance of paradise. Heaven on earth.

Weeks had gone by since he last examined the wall properly. Everything in crayon had been erased and done over in oil, including the inaugural Trimurti of Brahma, Vishnu and Shiva. What a miraculous transformation. God is really in His heaven, and all is right with Khodadad Building.

Gustad remembered the evening, almost two months ago, when he had been surprised by the perfume of an *agarbatti* wedged in a pavement crack. Today there were bunches of them, in *agarbatti* holders, sending up their fragile wisps of white, sweet-scented smoke. Nearby, in a little earthen thurible, *loban* smouldered with its unique, pleasantly pungent fragrance. Candles and oil lamps were lit at intervals. And there was even a stick of sandalwood before the portrait of Zarathustra. The black wall had verily become a shrine for all races and religions.

'Your idea was great, sir,' said the pavement artist. 'This is the best location in the whole city.'

'No, no, credit goes to your talent. And with your new oil paints, the pictures look even more wonderful than before. But what is all that stuff in the corner?' Gustad pointed to the far end of the wall, where a few bamboo poles, corrugated metal sheets, pieces of cardboard and plastic were stacked.

'I am planning to build a small shelter for myself. With your permission, sir.'

'Sure,' said Gustad. 'But you used to say that you like sleeping on your mat under the stars. What happened?'

'Oh, nothing,' said the artist, embarrassed. 'Just for a change. Come, let me show you the new ones I painted.' He led him by the arm. 'See there: Parvati with Garland Awaiting Shiva; Hanuman the Monkey God Building the Bridge to Lanka; Rama Killing the Demon Ravana; and next to that, Rama and Sita Reunited. And here: Upasani Baba, Kamu Baba, Godavari Mata. And this world-famous church, St Peter's, designed by Michelangelo, you must have heard of it.' Gustad nodded.

'Some more Christian paintings over here. Baby Jesus in the Manger with Three Wise Men; Madonna and Child; Sermon on the Mount. And these are Old Testament: Moses and the Burning Bush; Parting of Red Sea; Noah's Ark; David and Goliath; Samson Between the Pillars Pulling Down the House of Philistines.'

'Beautiful, absolutely beautiful.'

'And here is the famous Blue Mosque. Next to it, Haji Malung's Durgah in Kalyan. That's the Kaaba. Over here, the two great synthesizers of Hinduism and Islam: Kabir and Guru Nanak.'

'What about these, on this side? You missed them.'

'Oh, sorry. I thought you had seen them before. This is Agni, God of Fire; Kali, the World-Mother; and Goddess Yellamma of the *devdasis.*'

'Yellamma?' The name was vaguely familiar.

'Yes. The deity of *devdasis* – you know, *rundees, vaishyas,* whores – same thing, for all practical purposes. They call her Protector of Prostitutes,' explained the artist, and now Gustad remembered. Long, long ago, during his school days. He had heard the name in the stories of Peerbhoy Paanwalla.

'And this one. You should recognize this one,' said the pavement artist, smiling mischievously.

Gustad looked closely at what seemed a very familiar place. 'Looks like our wall,' he said tentatively.

'Absolutely correct. It's now a sacred place, is it not? So it rightfully deserves to be painted on a wall of holy men and holy places.'

Gustad bent down to get a better look at the wall featuring a painting of the wall featuring a painting of the wall featuring a . . .

'That's everything,' said the artist. 'Except for one more. I saved it for the end.' He led Gustad to the section which used to be shared by Zarathustra, Dustoorji Kookadaru and Meherji Rana. A fourth figure had been added, also in the garb and head-dress of a Parsi priest.

'Who's that?' asked Gustad sharply.

'That's the surprise. Being a Parsi yourself, I was thinking you will find this incident very interesting. You see, few days back, a gentleman who lives in your building – one with the small white dog –'

'Rabadi,' said Gustad.

'He said to me that since I was doing drawings of holy men and prophets, he had a request. I said sure, there is room for everyone on this wall. He showed me a black and white photo, said it was Dustoorji Baria, Very Holy Man for Parsis. Does lots of miracles to help the sick and suffering, he said. And not just restricted to spiritual problems, because the philosophy of Zoroastrian religion encourages material and spiritual success.

'I knew all this. But I did not want to tell him that besides my Art School diploma I had degrees in Ancient and Present-Day World Religions. You never know when you will learn something new. So I listened. He said that Dustoorji Baria was famous for helping people with health problems, pet problems, stock-market problems, business-partnership problems, job-finding problems, merchant-banker problems, problems of distinguished civil servants, problems of chairmen of many committees, problems of industrial lords, problems of petty contractors, and so on.

'OK, I am convinced, I said to him, and took the photo. Began to draw the picture. When the sketch was finished, I started with the oil paint. But then in the evening, that police inspector who lives here went by in his car –'

'Inspector Bamji,' said Gustad.

'He went by, looking at the new drawing. Suddenly he braked hard and reversed, began shouting at me to stop painting. I was quite frightened, you see, I have had enough trouble with police.

No appreciation for art they have – treat me as a vagrant or beggar. With very much humility I told him, please sir, the man with the small white dog has respectfully requested it, because this is a Parsi Holy Man.

'The Inspector began to laugh. Holy man? he said, arré, that fellow is a charlatan and a disgrace to the Parsi priesthood. Fooling desperate people, selling his photo-frames and amulets and rubbish. That sort of thing is absolutely not encouraged in Zoroastrianism, said the Inspector.'

'Then what happened?'

'Mr Rabadi came out for dog-walking. He heard the Inspector and began to argue: Dustoorji Baria had never made one single paisa of profit from his Holy Powers, those who said so were filthy jealous dogs, lazy idle loafers unfit to lick the sacred soles of his sapaat. Besides, this was a secular country, people had the right to believe what they wanted to, and Dustoorji Baria had a right to be on the wall as much as anyone else.

'I had to agree with his last point. The Inspector must have felt embarrassed about squabbling in public. He said, do what you like, a charlatan will remain a charlatan even if you put him among prophets and saints. Then he went away.

'Mr Rabadi told me that there were lots of sceptics and maligners like Inspector Bamji but they would all see the truth one day. He said he had proof of Dustoorji Baria's saintliness. When his big dog, Tiger, died a few years ago, tears fell from the eyes of a framed photograph of Dustoorji Baria that he has in his house. Amazing.'

'But do you believe it?' asked Gustad, smiling broadly.

'You see, I don't like to weaken anyone's faith. Miracle, magic, mechanical trick, coincidence – does it matter what it is, as long as it helps? Why analyse the strength of the imagination, the power of suggestion, power of auto-suggestion, the potency of psychological pressures? Looking too closely is destructive, makes everything disintegrate. As it is, life is difficult enough. Why to simply make it tougher? After all, who is to say what makes a miracle and what makes a coincidence?'

'That's true,' said Gustad. 'But this wall is the kind of miracle I like to see, useful and genuine, rather than tears from a photograph. A stinking, filthy disgrace has become a beautiful, fragrant place which makes everyone feel good.'

'And it will get better and better, now that the war has started. At such times people become more generously religious.'

'True,' said Gustad. 'Look, that sandalwood has stopped burning. You got matches?'

The pavement artist had a box. While Gustad attempted to rekindle the stick, a fire-engine clanged past, slowed, and turned into the compound. He abandoned the sandalwood and hurried inside. Firemen were unwinding the hose as he got there.

Tehmul was watching them, engrossed. He waved excitedly: 'GustadGustadGustad. Dingdingdingdingdingding. Funfunfun. Twistingtwistingturningfire.'

'Not now, Tehmul,' he said impatiently. Smoke was emerging from Miss Kutpitia's flat. He wondered if she was all right.

iii

After the firemen left, everyone agreed it was a miracle Miss Kutpitia's flat had come through largely unscathed. That there had been more smoke than flame was easily overlooked.

Through tellings and retellings, the smoky little fire became a roaring blaze, then grew into an uncontrollable conflagration. Khodadad Building had been on the verge of turning into a morsel for the belly of the raging inferno. But divine intervention had come to the rescue, it was fervently affirmed.

Others ascribed the good fortune to the wall: with people stopping to pray, to utter their invocations and thanksgivings, they said, it undoubtedly created endless vibrations of a propitious nature. How could it be other than that goodness and virtue reside here, in constant compassionate watch over this exalted place?

Inside Miss Kutpitia's flat, the damage was confined to the locked rooms. The precious grief-nurturing reminders of her beloved nephew and brother had perished within the brick walls of those reliquaries. Grey ash now lightly lay, covering the floors and the furniture, mingled with the dust of thirty-five years. The soggy ash coated everything, as though a sackful had been bought from the raakh-bhoosa man and spread by diligent human hands to scrub and scour the two rooms.

Miss Kutpitia and Dilnavaz assessed the damage, the latter promising to get Darius to help clear the mess. She was surprised that Miss Kutpitia accepted the outcome so matter-of-factly. In fact,

Dilnavaz found her positively cheery, looking forward to the chores that lay ahead, enjoying the sympathetic attention of people who had decided to forget her reputation for meanness and crankiness. It was tacitly accepted now that a person so providentially delivered from the jaws of fiery death must have forces of goodness on her side.

Only Miss Kutpitia understood the mystery of the benign fire. For thirty-five years, the very essences of all the hoarded mementoes had worked like a gentle salve upon the unkind gashes of her sorrow. They soothed her grief with their secret marrow, and Miss Kutpitia understood this well.

But she also knew that the qualities which made these objects special, made them glow with the aura which their owners had imparted to them, were not eternal – that one day they would lose their luminescence and become worthless. When that happened, she would be on her own.

Now, with the fire, it was evident that the day had arrived. The fire's conduct made it plain – all that was healing and life-giving in her treasures had already been drawn forth by her, leaving feathery husks too insubstantial to feed the flames. It was no great matter of puzzlement for Miss Kutpitia that the fire died in such a docile fashion.

*

In between helping Miss Kutpitia and doing her own cooking and chores, Dilnavaz heard Gustad tell Jimmy's story. She was happy and light-hearted for the first time in months. All the terror and shame and guilt of dabbling in unspeakable things with Miss Kutpitia was cremated in the fire, along with Miss Kutpitia's past.

Gustad wished she would sit still and listen. He tried to convey his anguish at witnessing Jimmy's wretched condition. 'You know the wooden presses that roadside juicewallas use? To squeeze the fruit? When I walked into Jimmy's room and saw him, it felt like my heart was being pulped in one of those presses.' His voice shook, but Dilnavaz did not notice. The softening veil of hustle-bustle and relief that descended in the wake of the lizard-tail mishap blurred and distorted things, held out generous promises of happy endings.

She was certain that Jimmy would recover and come back to Khodadad Building after four years. 'Don't you think so?'

Gustad preferred to say nothing. He turned to Roshan. 'Now, my little monkey. Just because you are feeling better does not mean you should run around all day. Little by little, as you get stronger.' He rose and stretched. 'So sleepy. Two nights on the train. But such a lot of work to do.'

'You don't have to come to help Miss Kutpitia,' said Dilnavaz.

'That is not what I meant at all. The war has started.'

'So what work for you if the war has started? My husband will take a gun and go to fight?' She threw her arms around his neck and, laughing, pressed her cheek against his shoulder. Roshan's recovery, Gustad's safe return, Miss Kutpitia's bright new demeanour – what more could she ask for? The days of gloom and worry were far behind. Except, of course, for Sohrab's absence. But even that, she felt, would now somehow be put right.

'Very funny you are becoming,' said Gustad sternly. 'Total black-out has been declared from tonight. I have to prepare for that, and for air raids.'

'They are not going to come all the way to Bombay at once,' she said, still laughing.

'All the way? Do you know that with modern jet fighters the Pakistanis could be here in minutes? Or do you think they will send you a postcard when they want to drop a bomb?'

'OK, baba, OK,' she said good-humouredly. 'Do whatever you think is necessary.'

He said it was a good thing he had not removed the blackout paper, at least that was one less job. He reminded her how she had kept nagging about it nine years ago, after the China war, nagging on and on. But in '65, when there was war with Pakistan, was it not convenient to have the paper already in place? 'Same thing again. History repeats itself.'

'OK, baba, OK, you were right.'

He carried a chair to the front door to inspect the paper. 'Leave Darius with me,' he said, as she prepared to go with the long-handled broom and various assorted *jhaarus* and *butaaras*. 'I'll need his help for a little while.' There were several places where mend-ing was required. Darius stood by to hand him the hammer, nails, and paper patches. Gustad climbed up and realized there had been no air-raid siren at ten o'clock this morning. From now on it would sound only for the real thing.

When the front door was done they moved the chair to the window by the black desk. 'I'll do this one,' said Darius. He climbed up and put out his hand for the hammer. But his father was caressing the dark brown wood of the handle, a faraway smile on his face.

'OK,' called Darius, to get his attention.

Gustad felt a great surge of pride as Darius's fingers closed round the handle. 'You never got to see your great-grandfather. But this is his hammer.'

Darius nodded. He had listened when Gustad used to teach Sohrab carpentry. He hefted the ball-peen hammerhead by its perfectly balanced handle, and knocked in the nails. When he gave it back, the handle felt slightly damp to Gustad. From Darius's palms, he thought. But how bountifully my grandfather used to sweat. Even in the prosperous days, when there were others to do it, he loved the heavy work. And the runnels pouring off his forehead, coursing down his face and neck. Deep in the midst of a job, two huge patches under his arms, and his vast shirt all soaked at the back, clinging to his skin, the wet appearing in the shape of a big heart. Then it was off with the shirt and *sudra*. The sweat flowing in great streams now, falling on pieces of wood, on the work table, on tools around him, sprinkling the layers of sawdust, which turned dark where the drops landed like life-giving water, like parched soil vitalized by a gardener. And the sweat from Grandpa's palms, soaking the handle of this hammer. To darken and burnish the wood. His hands first, and then my hands. Making the handle smoother and smoother. Sohrab should have . . . but Darius will. He will add his gloss to the wood.

What did it mean when a hammer like this was passed from generation to generation? It meant something satisfying, fulfilling, at the deep centre of one's being. That was all. No need to wrestle further with the meaning of the words.

They moved to the next window, the next ventilator, mending the tears, patching the gaps, while he told Darius about the workshop in the days before power tools, where men expended sweat and muscle, and sometimes even blood, to transform wood into useful, beautiful things; about Darius's great-grandfather who was a huge, powerful man, kind and gentle, but with an unswerving sense of justice and fair play, who had once lifted his own foreman by the collar till his feet swung clear off the ground, threatening to toss him out in the street, because the foreman had mistreated one of the carpenters.

They worked their way from window to window, from ventilator to ventilator, while Gustad remembered, opening the fenestrae of his life for Darius to look through. Darius had heard all the stories before, but somehow, with Great-Grandpa's hammer in his hand, they sounded different.

After the blackout paper was mended, they made shades of stiff cardpaper for the light bulbs hanging bare. They switched on the bulbs to check that the light fell in neat circles on the floor. Next, Gustad decided that underneath the huge four-poster bed would be the air-raid shelter: the pure ebony of its construction, and solid one-inch Burma teak slats, would be able to withstand the rubble if the worst were to happen.

'It took two men with a crosscut saw a whole day. A whole day's work, just to cut the ebony beams for the bedsteads and posters. That's why the main frame of this old bed is strong as any old iron,' he said. But the four-poster was next to the window. 'It won't do, has to be on the other side.' The cupboard and dressing-table were pushed out of the way. Then they struggled with the bed's immense weight, moving it inch by inch.

Dilnavaz returned from Miss Kutpitia's and saw them grunting and labouring. 'What are you doing? Stop! Your *aanterdo* and liver will burst! Stop, listen to me!'

'Do you know how strong your son is? Show her, Darius. Show her your muscles,' said Gustad.

'Touch wood, baba, touch wood,' she said, reaching frantically for the bedstead, and let them complete the task.

The mattress from Sohrab's *dholni* was spread under the four-poster. Dilnavaz caressed the place where Sohrab's head used to lie. Gustad frowned at her. He rolled up two blankets and stored them underneath, along with a torch and a water bottle. In an old biscuit tin he placed a phial of iodine, another of mercurochrome, a tube of penicillin ointment, cotton wool, adhesive tape, and two rolls of surgical gauze bandages. 'From now on,' he said, 'whenever there is a siren, we must go under.'

Just like a young boy, thought Dilnavaz. How he enjoys all this excitement. Taking advantage of his good mood, she said, 'If you are finished, Miss Kutpitia is requesting your help.' The firemen had forced open her windows which had remained shut for thirty-five years. Now they would not close, not one of the three, and she was concerned because of the blackout.

Gustad and Darius went readily to tackle the swollen windows, taking a chisel, sandpaper, two screwdrivers and the hammer. When they returned after an hour, Gustad remarked how Miss Kutpitia had changed. 'Smiled at me, even made a joke, saying it was time I brought another rose for her. Earth-and-sky difference in the old woman.'

And in you too, thought Dilnavaz happily.

*

The evening grew dark earlier than usual. By the gate, the lamppost stood lightless, and the pavement artist extinguished all candles, *agarbattis* and thuribles at sundown. The main road resembled a street under curfew. A solitary taxi went by, passengerless, headlights blackened. With its eyes closed, thought Gustad, like a somnambulist. Even the crows and sparrows, usually raucous at this hour, seemed disoriented by the unlit city.

The grey compound exhaled an air of hopeless melancholy around the blacked-out flats. Gustad inspected his windows from the outside: no chinks, no cracks of light. He walked along and looked up at Tehmul's windows. The older brother was in town, he had done the necessary work. But tomorrow he would leave on another of his sales trips. An extra key in case Tehmul got locked out was now with Gustad – Tehmul's next-door neighbours refused to keep it any longer; they said he was driving them crazy.

'What news, bossie?' called Inspector Bamji. 'Ready for the war?' He was applying lampblack to the headlights, leaving only a thin slit.

Gustad went up to him. 'Night duty?'

Bamji nodded. 'That's why this *maader chod* black stuff.' He wiped his hands on a rag. 'Bastards want to fight, now they will get a fight. Bloody *bahen chod bhungees* think they can just come over and bomb our airfields. What did they expect, our planes would be sitting outside? Our boys are damn smart, bossie, damn smart. Everything in underground concrete hangars. Now they will be clean bowled – off stump, middle stump, leg stump – nothing left standing.'

Gustad pointed up at the building. 'Looks like all our neighbours have done a good blackout.'

'True,' said Bamji. 'But bossie, on first day everyone is enthusiastic. Then they get careless. And we get complaints at the police station. Same thing happened in '65. Any time a light is seen shining, it's a Pakistani spy.' The wet rag would not remove the black stuff off his fingers. He went home to try something stronger.

i

Mr Madon issued guidelines and directives concerning air raids and sirens. Wardens were appointed in each department to ensure, among other things, that those handling cash locked up before leaving their positions when the siren sounded. Employees were to retreat beneath their desks – only one person under one desk. Exceptions would be made for those sharing a desk if they were of the same sex; if not, they were to pair up with the nearest appropriate staff member. Wardens would supervise the propriety of the pairing. Mr Madon wanted no flirting-below-desk-scandal to arise and stain his bank's escutcheon.

The instruction list, like everything else at the bank, reminded Gustad of his departed friend. Dinshu would have had a field day in the canteen, mimicking Mr Madon. And speculating on the thrills of going under a desk with Laurie Coutino, mini-skirt and all.

Now there were no jokes in the canteen, or song sessions. Instead, people talked endlessly about the war, repeating grim, gruesome stories of what was happening across the border. Rumour, fact, fantasy – all were devoured with equal zeal.

The debauched and alcoholic president of the enemy was said to be organizing unceasing bacchanals to keep his ministers and generals occupied: he feared an ouster if they regained their senses for too long. Thus did the crazed syphilitic cling to power, growing ever more desperate as he saw, through his haze of liquor, the unyielding worm gnawing contentedly at his brain.

Stories about the demoniacal occupation of Bangladesh were balanced by accounts of the Indian Army's gallantry. On the radio and in cinema newsreels, the Jawans liberated towns and villages, routed the enemy, and took prisoners by the thousands. There was report after report of the citizenry's generous support for the fighting men: about an eighty-year-old peasant who travelled to New Delhi, clutching her two gold wedding bangles, which she presented to Mother India for the war effort (some newspapers reported it as Mother Indira, which did not really matter – the line between the two was fast being blurred by the Prime Minister's far-sighted propagandists who saw its value for future election campaigns); about schoolchildren donating their lunch money, their faces scrubbed and shining as they posed with a splendidly rotund Congress Party official; about farmers chanting *Jai Jawan! Jai Kissan!* and pledging to work harder by growing more food for the country.

Of course, in the newsreels, no mention was ever made of dutiful Shiv Sena patrols and motley fascists who roamed city streets with stones at the ready, patriotically shattering windows that they deemed inadequately blacked-out. Or the unlucky individuals mistaken for enemy agents and beaten up with great relish by personal enemies. Or the number of homes burgled by men posing as air-raid wardens come to inspect the premises. In short, no effort was spared to inform the country of its invincibility, unity and high morale.

So high was the morale that when, six days into the war, the USA heeded General Yahya's call and ordered its Seventh Fleet to the Bay of Bengal, the populace was ready to take on even the mighty Americans. The nuclear-powered aircraft-carrier *Enterprise* moved out from the Gulf of Tonkin and led the Seventh Fleet through the Strait of Malacca. Its glorious mission: to frighten a cyclone-ravaged, war-torn province into submission. No one was greatly surprised by this, for mighty America always did like having military dictators for buddies. But as the Fleet drew closer, the names of Nixon and Kissinger became names to curse with, names which, if uttered, had to be followed by hawking and spitting. The illiterate could not read about the latest villainy but they learned to recognize the two villains' pictures in the papers: the scowling one with rat's eyes and the bespectacled one with the face of a constipated ox.

Old Bhimsen the office peon brought fresh news from the slums to Gustad and the others at the bank. He lived in a little *kholi*, in a *jhopadpatti* near Sion. During pauses between fetching tea or coffee, he told them how, in the slums, where children squatted over newsprint inside their shacks (because they were too young to go out alone and find a spot in an alley or a ditch), mothers took great delight in searching through discarded papers for the faces of the rat and the constipated ox to place under their babies' behinds. The closer the Seventh Fleet came to the Bay of Bengal, the harder it was to find unadorned copies of the two pictures. Bhimsen decided to help his slum neighbours with their anti-imperialist toilet-training. He requested all bank employees to give him their daily news-papers whenever pictures of Nixon or Kissinger appeared. No one refused. They were happy to assist the war effort and keep morale high.

But it was not morale alone that dealt with the Seventh Fleet. Close on the heels of the US ships came an armada of Soviet cruisers and destroyers, sailing earnestly from the pages of the Indo-Soviet Treaty of Friendship. And true to the spirit of the treaty, there was no violence. Not even a harsh word. For the Soviets merely wanted to remind the Americans of the roles and identities which they had rehearsed for so long on all the important international stages: that Americans were a kind and friendly people, champions of justice and liberty, supporters of freedom struggles and democracies everywhere.

And the Soviet reminder worked. The Americans did not forget. There, in the Bay of Bengal, by the dawn's early light, as the sun's rays made the rippling blue sea to shimmer and the December sky to turn a perfect pink, they remembered every single one of their globally-famous, ever-sparkling virtues. With patriotic tears in their eyes, they put the dust-covers back on their mighty American guns and cannons.

*

When Gustad returned home through the darkened evening, he knew Cavasji's blood-pressure was high again. Allopathic medicine was just not as efficacious as the *subjo*-on-a-string that Cavasji used to wear. He was leaning out to shake his fist against the black sky. Any more vehemence, feared Gustad, and the old man would topple over.

But Cavasji maintained his equilibrium. Only the light, a beacon of reproach, tumbled willingly from the open window into the compound, framing his disapproving silhouette. 'I am warning You now only! If You let a bomb fall here, let one fall on Birlas and Mafatlals also! *Bas*! Too much injustice from You! Too much! If

Khodadad Building suffers, then Tata Palace also! Otherwise, not one more stick of sandalwood for You, not one sliver!'

Gustad debated whether to go upstairs and point out to someone that the blackout was being violated. But a figure appeared behind Cavasji. It was his son. He took his elbow and gently led him away, shutting the papered-over window.

ii

For the third night in a row the air-raid siren howled through the city. It was shortly after midnight. The wailing roused Gustad and Dilnavaz immediately. The first time, he had taken a little while to realize it was not a dream about the former ten a.m. practice siren.

'Should I wake Roshan and Darius?' wondered Dilnavaz. 'Or will it be like yesterday, all-clear in five minutes?'

'Cannot take a chance like that.' He switched on the zero watt night-light while they took their places below the four-poster. Guiding his way with the torch, he went to the rickety main switch and flipped the lever to the off position, as recommended by the authorities.

The siren's mournful wail died after he joined them under the bed. Roshan took the torch from him and held it under her chin, pointing upwards. 'Ghooost!' She burst out with peals of laughter, then jumped as the shelling began.

It startled everyone. 'Anti-aircraft guns,' said Gustad confidently, taking back the torch. 'Ours.'

'Pakistani bombers must be coming,' said Darius.

'Oh, I hope Sohrab is safe!' whispered Dilnavaz.

'Why shouldn't he? He is not stupid to stand in the street. Anyway, our guns will chase the planes away.' But the thought of Pakistani aircraft over the city made Gustad uneasy. What if some idiot in the building got nervous because of the guns, and decided to put on the light? Or opened a window to see what was going on? He raised his head, bumping it against the Burma teak slats.

'Where are you going?' asked Dilnavaz fearfully, as he switched on the torch and eased out. The guns boomed four times.

'Outside. To check the building.'

She wanted him to stay right here, under the bed, but knew he would not listen. 'Be careful.'

'I'll come with you,' said Darius.

'No. You stay here with them.' He found his slippers and keys, keeping the light aimed low. With one hand on the latch, he switched off the torch before opening the door.

There was a new moon in the sky, a mere paper-thin sliver. The crescent would be no help to the Pakistanis, he thought with satisfaction. The guns boomed again. Seconds later, a beam of light swept the sky. Then another, and another. Searchlights, crisscrossing, seeking, raking the night. Standing by the tree, he watched the display, almost forgetting why he had come.

Another volley, longer than any so far, reminded him. He strode down the compound towards the gate: the windows were dark, including Cavasji's. He walked back towards the tree, checking the other half of the building. His own flat, Kutpitia upstairs, Bamji, the dogwalla idiot . . . all OK. But then, through the branches, a narrow rectangle of light appeared and disappeared as a breeze played with the leaves: a half-open window at the far end. Tehmul's! The stupid! The bloody –! And why is he up so late anyway?

As Gustad ran, his limp exploded in an ungainly hobble. He bounded up the stairs and raised his hand to deliver a furious knocking. Then he remembered. Tehmul's brother left the key with me. He located it by touch upon his chain, its unfamiliar shape greeting his exploring fingers, and inserted it silently. Good to give Tehmul a fright. Teach him to be more careful.

He entered, then stopped to listen, mystified by the faint sounds from within. Of panting, heavy breathing. A low moan. Muted. Panting again. Tehmul? What was he doing? Gustad tried to shut the door noiselessly behind him, but the latch tumbled. A loud metallic click pierced the verandah darkness like a needle. He flinched, standing still.

The sounds started again. He crossed the verandah, stepping softly towards the lighted bedroom. A threadbare curtain of faded yellow organdie hung in the open doorway. He could see the room floating behind the gauze-like material, dreamlike and ephemeral. Like the mosquito net, through which I used to see my mother, in Matheran, when she came to say goodnight-Godblessyou. Far away, beyond my reach, fading . . .

With an effort, he pushed the curtain aside. At once, everything ethereal or impalpable about the room vanished. Without the magic film of organdie, the place turned solid, sordid, smelly. The curtain rings tinkled against the tarnished brass rod. The soft ting-ting continued as the curtain swayed.

Tehmul did not notice anything. His back to the door, he was stooping over the white-sheeted bed, lost to the world. A dirty cream-coloured *rajai* with red and black embroidery along the borders was gathered at the centre of the mattress. He was naked except for his brown cross-strapped leather slippers. The sweat was glistening on his back.

'Tehmul!' said Gustad sharply. He succeeded in scaring him more completely than he expected. Tehmul screamed and jumped around, his right hand clutching an enormous erection. Now Gustad was able to see what was on the bed, while Tehmul, still proceeding with the automatic movement upon his rampant penis, ejaculated with a whimper.

Half-hidden by the bunched-up *rajai* was Roshan's doll, as naked as Tehmul. Her wedding dress, petticoat, veil, tiara, bouquet of flowers, stockings and the rest were neatly draped over a chair by the bed.

'*Bay-sharam*! Stop that! At once!' Gustad was angry, embarrassed. 'You deserve to be thrashed properly!' he continued for lack of anything better to say, then noticed Tehmul's striped pyjamas on the floor. He picked them up and flung them at him. 'Put your clothes on! At once!' He could smell a heavy vinegary odour in the wake of the pyjamas' flight.

Tehmul started to blubber, his tears mixing with sweat. 'Gustad-GustadGustad. Verysorry. Veryverysorry.'

'Shut up! And put on your clothes, I said!' He went to the window and closed it. Tehmul fumbled with the pyjamas. His hands shook with sobbing and made the task more difficult for his normally clumsy fingers. The drawstring baffled him as he formed loops, twisted and turned them, passed them through one another, only to see the bow disappear each time he pulled the ends taut.

He finished at last, and Gustad sent him to wash his hands. He examined Roshan's doll with distaste. There was no damage done, except that its pink legs and stomach and groin were sprinkled with gobs of dry and half-dry semen. How many nights' worth, he wondered. It would clean up easily, and Roshan would not notice any difference, but what good was that? He could not give it back to her now. It sickened him to think of his child touching this doll so

302

violated by Tehmul. No, he would take it away and donate it to an orphanage.

Tehmul was still crying when he returned from the bathroom. He held out his hands: 'GustadGustad. CleanhandsGustadclean. CleanwashedwithLuxveryveryverycleanLux.' He lifted them to his nose and sniffed: 'Veryverynicesmell,' then offered them to Gustad for verification.

Gustad violently swept the hands away from him. Tehmul staggered backwards, cowering, his sobs rising with renewed anguish. 'You have no shame? Stealing Roshan's doll, doing such dirty things with it?'

'GustadGustad,' he cried. 'GustadGustadtheywouldnot.'

'They who?'

'Theytheythewomen. GustadGustadtworupeesIpaidtworupees. Notheysaidnonono.'

He understood. The House of Cages. That night, Tehmul among the prostitutes, who had teased and taunted him.

Tehmul pointed to the doll. 'Wantedrubbing. Fastfastfast. Good-goodfeeling. Fastfastfastrubbing.'

Gustad's anger began to ebb slowly. Poor Tehmul. A child's mind and a man's urges. Shunned by the whores, turning to the doll in desperation. Somehow, it seemed a fitting solution. He imagined Tehmul undressing the doll each night, caressing it tenderly. Gustad remembered the day he had come home with the doll by taxi from Sister Constance, and met Tehmul in the compound. How gently he had patted the cheek, stroked the tiny fingers, gazed wondrously into the deep blue eyes.

Poor Tehmul. What was to become of him? Gustad tried to sound severe: 'Why did you open the window? Your brother told you to keep everything shut.'

'VeryverysorryGustad. Feelinghothot. Feelingveryveryhot. Open-windowcoolnicecoolcool. VeryverysorryGustad.'

Gustad wished he had the power of miracles, the power to cure Tehmul's ills, restore to him all the rights and virtues of mortals. And as Tehmul stood there, shamefaced, tears running down his cheeks, Gustad realized he could not take away the doll. Somehow, the loss to Roshan would not be as great as it would to Tehmul. One day, when she was old enough, perhaps he would tell her what had happened.

'I am going now.' He cleared his throat to make the words emerge sternly, the way he wanted them to. 'Remember, no opening the window even if you are feeling hot. Take a newspaper and fan yourself. Window always stays shut at night.'

'AlwaysalwaysGustad. Alwaysshutalways. VerysorryGustad.' He seemed puzzled when Gustad turned to leave, and pointed at the bed. 'DollyGustaddolly.'

Gustad shook his head. 'You keep her,' he said gruffly.

Tehmul's eyes opened wide, comprehending but not daring to believe. 'Dollydollydolly. Gustaddolly.'

'Yes, yes. Dolly is for you.'

Now Tehmul was certain, and dared to believe. He knew exactly what to do. He shuffled forward with his arms outstretched, and put them round Gustad. 'GustadGustad.' He hugged him tightly. 'ThankyouGustadthankyou.' Then he lifted Gustad's right hand and slobbered a kiss on the knuckles.

Touched by the act, also repelled by the saliva glistening on his skin, Gustad was confused, uncertain about how to deal with this situation. But Tehmul was unwilling to let go his hand till he had responded. He looked perplexed, not understanding why Gustad should be embarrassed.

So, very tentatively, Gustad put an arm around him and vaguely patted his shoulder. Then, with another reminder to be good and keep the window shut, he left. He wiped his knuckles discreetly upon the worn organdie curtain while brushing it aside to pass.

After the closeness of Tehmul's room, it was a relief to be in the compound. The night air got rid of the sweaty, musky odours that seemed to be stuck in his nostrils. The guns were quiet now, though the searchlights were still combing the night as he let himself in and switched on the torch. 'Gustad? Everything is all right?' Dilnavaz's voice seemed strangely distant, disembodied, coming from under the bed.

'Yes.' He went to the basin and washed his hands vigorously.

'What happened? You were gone for so long, we were getting worried.'

'Tehmul's window was open. I had to go up.' He wished she would stop asking questions.

'But so long? Was something wrong?'

'Nosmot in frosmont of the chismildren,' said Gustad. Then the all-clear sounded.

iii

As the Indian forces got closer to Dacca and the liberation of Bangladesh was imminent, the mood everywhere grew optimistic. People had adjusted to the blackout, the city no longer retired into gloom after dusk just because the lights were off. Gustad felt it was time he went to Dr Paymaster's dispensary to tell him Roshan was well now, and to ask if all medication should cease. They had had their differences during the illness, but Gustad was still fond of his childhood doctor.

'Wonderful news, wonderful,' said Dr Paymaster. 'And the other patient is also recovering. Wonderful.'

'Other patient?'

'Bangladesh.' The waiting-room was empty, he had time on his hands. 'Correct diagnosis is half the battle. Proper prescription, the other half. Injection of the Indian Army, I said. And so the critical moment is past. Road to recovery.'

He lowered the blinds; it was well after sunset. 'Now if only we could cure our internal sickness as quickly and efficiently as this external sickness, we could be one of the healthiest countries in the world. Did you smell the gutters just now when you came?'

'Terrible,' said Gustad, wrinkling his nose.

'Unbearable, I tell you. Does the municipality listen? Yes. Does it do anything? No. For months and years now. Problems wherever you look. Leaking, broken water pipes. Sewer overflowing. Inspectors come and inspectors go, but the gutters overflow for ever. And police corruption on top of that. They want weekly *hafta* from people who are using the pavements. Harassment from health inspectors also. They want baksheesh from House of Cages, even though it's properly licensed. Everyone in this area is fed up and running out of patience.'

'You have a prescription for the internal sickness?'

Dr Paymaster raised his eyebrows and smiled with a corner of his mouth. 'Of course. Only one problem. Prescription is so painful, it might kill the patient before the sickness does.' Gustad nodded, understanding the gist if not the specifics of the doctor's remedy.

Suddenly, through the window came the sound of a gong.

Peerbhoy Paanwalla's brass tray? Was he still telling the old stories to his customers? Curious, Gustad took his leave at a suitable break in the conversation.

Outside the House of Cages, a larger than usual crowd had gathered around Peerbhoy Paanwalla, unmindful of the sewer stench that made Gustad cover his nose and mouth with his kerchief. But Peerbhoy was not spinning his time-honoured yarns about the House of Cages: the aphrodisiacal tales for tyros guaranteed to heat the blood, elevate flagging confidence and boost *paan* sales. No, there would be no more of that for a while. In deference to the mood of the country and the threat from without, Peerbhoy Paanwalla had mobilized his talents for the common good, using his skills to weave a tale that defied genre or description. It was not tragedy, comedy or history; not pastoral, tragical-comical, historical-pastoral or tragical-historical. Nor was it epic or mock-heroic. It was not a ballad or an ode, masque or anti-masque, fable or elegy, parody or threnody. Although a careful analysis may have revealed that it possessed a smattering of all these characteristics. But since things such as literary criticism mattered not one jot to the listeners, they were responding to Peerbhoy's narrative in the only way that made sense: with every fibre of their beings. They could see and smell and taste and feel the words that filled the dusk and conjured the tale; and it was no wonder they were oblivious to the gutter stink.

Gustad had missed the beginning, but that did not matter. 'By this time in the West Wing,' said Peerbhoy Paanwalla, 'the Drunkard's tool was maggoty, withered and useless, into which not even the most potent *palung-tode paan* could breathe new life. His Minister of State for Sex, and his deputy, the Orgy Organizer, continued to arrange lavish spectacles. But the Drunkard could no longer participate in these Carnivals of Copulation. Vile as a serpent choking on its own venom, he watched the ecstasies of others, and drank whisky. Only whisky, in vast quantities.

'His foul anger, his poisonous moods, his sadistic habits made life intolerable for those around him. They racked their brains to come up with a solution. How to amuse the Drunkard? How to cheer his spirits and thus deliver their own?

'New-new remedies were attempted. They gave him Ludo, Snakes and Ladders, Monopoly, and Draughts, but he was unable to remember the rules long enough to play and enjoy the games. The Minister of Imports and Exports even ordered Playboy Jigsaw Puzzles of foreign ladies with pink-pink nipples and fine blonde pubic hair. But the pieces evaded his spatial skills. He put them in his mouth, one by one, then spat them, coated with fetid, viscous spit, in the faces of his anxious sycophants. Everyone was close to despair.'

The women in the House of Cages peered outside to see if there was any sign of customers. To their dismay, nowadays the men preferred to listen to Peerbhoy Paanwalla and go home, rather than come inside.

'Then the military made a suggestion: guns, they said, was the answer. How? asked the others. The military explained. The Drunkard's personal pistol had putrefied and could fire no more – so simply remind him of all the other guns he possessed: fire-spewing, lead-spitting, death-dealing guns. To command as he pleased. To make him forget the failure of his own little derringer.

'It was not surprising that the military people found the proper solution. After all, the Drunkard was a military man himself, and they knew how to cure the ills of one of their own. Especially when the cure fitted their own plans. The therapy could begin soon, for the perfect setting was ready: the East Wing, where the Bengalis were just asking for it.

'So the Drunkard inspected his guns: the light artillery, medium artillery, heavy artillery, anti-aircraft, mortars, howitzers, tanks, bazookas. And they touched a tender corner somewhere, awakening happy memories. He began to drool. A peculiar grin came over his face, and the lackeys and toadies heaved sighs of relief. Call my Butcher, he said, and they fell over each other to fetch him.

'My dear Butcher, said the Drunkard, I have a job for you in the East Wing. The Bengalis are forgetting their place. Those dark-skinned shorties are using big-big words like justice and equality and self-determination, which makes them feel tall and fair and powerful like us. Go there and sort them out.

'The Drunkard himself would not journey to the East Wing, but he wanted to be kept minutely informed of how his guns were doing. The Butcher promised: he would click many pictures and write often. Hopping and skipping with excitement outside the presidential palace, he went off licking his chops.

'At first, the Butcher and his men had a real picnic. What fun, so many guns to play with, so many live targets. But there was not much variety to their days or nights. Then the monsoon started, and their nice-nice uniforms got muddied like their minds, and big-big mosquitoes began to bite.

'Blotting out the ideas of justice, equality and self-determination from the minds of Bengalis was harder than they expected. No matter how many Bengali skulls they shattered – one million, two, two-and-a-half million – there were always more heads to consider. More heads inside which those same troublesome ideas of justice, equality and self-determination flowered, blooming with a fragrance that drove the Butcher's men crazy, because their noses were not used to anything stronger than the base, cowardly smells of tyranny and despotism.'

In the House of Cages the women waited restlessly. This war was no good for business, what with the refugee relief tax forcing them to raise prices; the blackout sending men home early; and now these new stories, arousing patriotic passion and national pride instead of priming lust.

Peerbhoy Paanwalla cleared his throat, spat, and wiped his lips. 'So, my brothers,' he continued, adding 'and sisters' after waving at the barred windows, 'in the end, despite the many women still unravished and the numerous mass graves still left to fill, the Butcher and his men turn their backs and run for home: to their polo clubs, cricket-fields and swimming-pools. Especially since the Indian Army is drawing closer, and they can hear the strains of "Jana Gana Mana" playing in the distance.'

The listeners cheered spontaneously, clapping and shouting 'Sabaash!' and 'Bharat Mata ki jai!'

While waiting for the applause to die and the audience to settle down, Peerbhoy got busy with his hands. He had recently introduced a new product that was selling extremely well, called the Patriotic Paan. Instead of folding betel leaves into their usual triangles, he made little rectangular trays of each leaf. Then he filled them with tobacco, chunam, and other ingredients, arranging the colours in three horizontal bands: saffron, white and green. A little round seed at the centre completed the representation of the Tricolour.

'Now, my fellow-countrymen,' continued Peerbhoy, 'let us remember' – he paused to stick a cheroot in his mouth – 'this is not the end, nor is it the beginning of the end. But it is the end of the beginning.' Those who got the joke broke into applause again: Too good, *yaar*, they said. But many had never heard of the cigar-smoking fat man, and were left in the dark.

Gustad looked at his watch and reluctantly tore himself away from the group. Ever since the blackout had begun, Dilnavaz had got into the habit of fretting, despite his repeated explanations that traffic was slower than usual because of the darkened streets.

*

Tehmul was on his hands and knees in the compound, running his fingers frantically over the pebble-studded brown earth. 'Gustad-GustadGustad. DarkdarkGustaddark. Odarkdarkdark.'

'What's wrong, Tehmul?'

'LostGustad. Lostlostindark.' He continued rooting in the dirt, distraught, mumbling to himself. Gustad clicked on his pocket torch.

Tehmul was enchanted by the beam. A radiant smile spread over his face and dislodged his agitation. Still kneeling, he reached an inquiring finger towards the source of luminescence and gently touched the lens. 'GustadbrightbrightshinyGustad. GustadGustad-lightsobright.' The rays played upon his beaming face, upon the innocent joy he displayed for the rusty old torch's meagre light. Sadness and affection filled Gustad's heart. In this pose, with his blissful smile, he thought, Tehmul's picture would fit right in among the others upon the black wall.

With the help of the torch Tehmul soon spotted what he was looking for: the little beaded bracelet from the doll's wrist. 'Found-foundfound. FoundGustadfound.' He was exuberant with gratitude. 'ThankyoufoundGustad. Thankyouveryveryverymuch.'

Gustad switched off the torch. 'Lightgone,' said Tehmul sadly. 'Lightgonedarkdarkdark.' Gustad patted his shoulder and speeded him on his slow, tedious climb up the stairs.

iv

After the euphoria of flags, banners, and victory parades had passed; after the crowds' last cheers for the Jawans and the Prime Minister had faded; after the enemy's unconditional surrender had

309

wiped out rankling memories of ignominious defeat at Chinese hands nine years ago, and 1965's embarrassing stalemate with the death in Tashkent of Shastri, the big little man; after the billboards and hoardings were divested of wartime exhortations; after the blackout was lifted and cities returned to light which, after long darkness, seemed like Republic Day illuminations: after all this, Gustad still did not remove the paper from his windows.

Darius and he dismantled their air-raid shelter and pushed the four-poster back to its original position. The phials of iodine and mercurochrome were replaced in the sideboard along with the gauze bandages. The empty biscuit tin went back to the kitchen. The light bulbs were allowed to shed their cardpaper cones. But the windows and ventilators were left untouched.

Dilnavaz was patient for one more day, then asked, 'What about the black paper? Or are you waiting for another war?'

'Why the big rush? I'll do it when I have some time.' Gustad went outside, and saw that the pavement artist had finished building his little lean-to at the far end of the wall. Inside were a few clothes, his sleeping mat, the Petromax, and painting supplies. His old crayon boxes were also there, for though the artist had come to regard these with fond condescension, relics of a time outgrown, he did not have the heart to throw them away.

He was trying now to maintain some semblance of order amidst the stacks of offerings. No sooner did one set of devotees depart than others arrived, and never empty-handed. He saw Gustad watching. He shook his head wearily, but it was obvious he was enjoying the hectic pace, the role of shrine custodian. His carefree peregrinations had definitely passed into the realm of memory. 'Victory in Bangladesh is making me work overtime.'

'Very good, very good,' said Gustad absently. Dilnavaz's gibe about the blackout paper was buzzing inside his head, worrying him like the flies and mosquitoes of old. By and by, however, the wall's fragrances wrapped their rich veils over him and made him forget.

For the next few days, newspapers continued to analyse the war. There were accounts of crucial battles, and moving stories of how Bangladeshis had cheered the arrival of the first Indian troops in Dacca. Gustad read whichever paper he could borrow in the canteen. And Dilnavaz, as she had been doing for the past few months since Mr Rabadi's bonfire, glanced over Miss Kutpitia's copy of the *Jam-E-Jamshed* each morning. Particularly the *pydust* notices. It would be inexcusable, she felt, if they were to miss the funeral of some relative, however distant.

*

The lunch-hour had ended, the canteen was empty except for the boy cleaning tables and Gustad reading the newspaper. He wanted to finish the last little bit. There was a detailed description of the surrender ceremony, with the text of the instrument of surrender included. Like everyone else, Gustad had begun to feel the glow of national pride. Every day, he read every page, column by column, which was fortunate, or he would have missed an item that appeared inside, in an obscure corner.

It was barely an inch of column space. And when he read it, the glow of national pride dropped from him like a wet raincoat. He did not turn the page after that.

The boy approached with his damp rag. '*Seth*, table please.'

Clutching the newspaper, Gustad raised his outstretched arms in the air mechanically, while the boy gave the table a quick wet swipe. The forearms thudded down. Gustad did not notice the boy watching curiously, or the dampness creeping through his sleeves.

He sat staring at the paragraph, reading it over and over, the small paragraph which stated that Mr J. Bilimoria, a former officer with RAW, had died of a heart attack while serving his four-year prison sentence in New Delhi.

He removed the page from the newspaper and folded it small to fit his pocket.

TWENTY-ONE

i

Dr Paymaster's dispensary, like everything else in the vicinity, was closed. Not even the House of Cages was open for business. The day of the *morcha* had arrived.

The people of the neighbourhood were ready for the march to the municipal ward office, to voice their protests against overflowing sewers, broken water-pipes, pot-holed pavements, rodent invasions, bribe-extracting public servants, uncollected hills of garbage, open manholes, shattered street lights – in short, against the general decay and corruption of cogs that turned the wheels of city life. Their petitions and letters of complaint had been ignored long enough. Now the officials would have to reck the rod of the *janata*.

All manner of vendors and tradespeople, who had nothing in common except a common enemy, were waiting to march. There were mechanics and shopkeepers, indefatigable restaurant waiters, swaggering tyre retreaders, hunch-shouldered radio repairers, bow-legged tailors, shifty transistors-for-vasectomies salesmen, cross-eyed chemists, sallow cinema ushers, hoarse-voiced lottery-ticket sellers, squat clothiers, accommodating women from the House of Cages. Hundreds and thousands gathered, eager to march, arm in arm and shoulder to shoulder, to alleviate the miseries of the neighbourhood.

Even Dr Paymaster and Peerbhoy Paanwalla enlisted. They had been reluctant at first, especially Dr Paymaster. He tried to temper the zeal and soothe the passions by attempting to explain the larger picture. He pointed out that municipal corruption was only a microcosmic manifestation of the greed, dishonesty, and moral turpitude that flourished at the country's centre. He described meticulously how, from the very top, whence all power flowed,

312

there also dripped the pus of putrefaction, infecting every stratum of society below.

But Dr Paymaster's friends and neighbours looked at him blankly, which led him to suspect that perhaps his vision of villainy and baseness in New Delhi was too abstract. He tried again: imagine, he said, that our beloved country is a patient with gangrene at an advanced stage. Dressing the wound or sprinkling rose-water over it to hide the stink of rotting tissue is useless. Fine words and promises will not cure the patient. The decaying part must be excised. You see, the municipal corruption is merely the bad smell, which will disappear as soon as the gangrenous government at the centre is removed.

True, they said, but we cannot hold our breath for ever, we have to do something about the stink. How long to wait for the amputation? We have to get on with our lives, our noses cannot remain permanently plugged. Once again their fervid exuberance bubbled forth, and Dr Paymaster and Peerbhoy relented, overpowered by the contagion of enthusiasm. Their friends, neighbours and customers convinced them of the valuable contribution they would make by leading the *morcha*. Their great ages, Dr Paymaster's revered occupation, Peerbhoy's chubby, swami-like demeanour, would all go a long way to bestow respectability upon the *morcha*.

Naturally, Dr Paymaster was to wear his white coat and stethoscope while carrying his black bag; thus, onlookers and the authorities could recognize at once how distinguished a profession was at the helm. Similarly, Peerbhoy would walk in nothing more and nothing less than his *paan*-selling attire: bare-chested, a low-slung loongi round his waist, so his august all-seeing navel, his venerable wrinkled dugs, and his massive forehead, furrowed with a thousand lines of wisdom, could inspire awe and esteem in bystanders.

The *morcha* directors, greatly impressed by Dr Paymaster's and Peerbhoy Paanwalla's examples, decreed that all participants should wear work clothes and display their work implements. The mechanics would don their hole-infested vests and grease-stained pants while carrying spanners, wrenches, ratchets, and tyre irons. Lottery-ticket vendors agreed to walk with their cardboard displays of lottery tickets slung from their necks; barbers would wield hair clippers, combs, and scissors; and so on.

In addition, four handcarts were loaded with huge barrels containing: oozing, slimy samples of sludge and filth from overflowing gutters; crumbling concrete, sand, and mortar from disintegrating pavements; examples of fetid, putrefying matter from the garbage hills; and stacks of mange-eaten rodent specimens, some dead, others barely alive. The barrels were to be emptied in the lobby of the municipal office building.

For several days, everyone had been busy making banners and placards. Slogans were rehearsed and the police informed of the *morcha*'s route, so necessary traffic arrangements could be made. The *morcha* would start near the House of Cages and take two hours to reach the municipal offices, where a *gherao* was to be conducted. All entrances and exits would be blocked by the marchers in the spirit of non-violence, and remain blocked until the neighbourhood's demands were met.

*

Dr Paymaster opened his black bag to empty it. After all, it was only a *morcha* prop, and would be lighter to carry. Then he gazed for a moment at the carefully arranged contents. Not once since starting out in practice had his bag been without its multitude of vials, syringes, scalpels, lancets, and the trusty sphygmomanometer. He changed his mind and let everything stay.

He clipped on his stethoscope, locked the door to the office, and, with his faithful old compounder by his side, stepped out. Like Don Quixote and Sancho Panza, he thought, wondering what follies and wisdoms were to be enacted this day, what new farces he was to witness with his tired old eyes.

The waiting crowd applauded as the two emerged. Too late now for regrets, thought Dr Paymaster. He acknowledged the cheers with a half-hearted wave. Peerbhoy, resplendent in his brightest and best loongi – maroon, with green and yellow vertical stripes – was already at the head of the column. Dr Paymaster took his place beside him. The compounder walked behind.

ii

After filling the water drums and buying milk, Dilnavaz opened Miss Kutpitia's *Jam-E-Jamshed* to the middle page and scanned the *pydust* section for death announcements. Her usual sense of anxiety gave way to relief as she came to the end of the list without encountering any familiar names.

Then she glanced at the Stop Press section on the first page, the little box that usually appeared blank; there was something in it. Puzzled, she read that the funeral of J. Bilimoria would be held this morning. There was no further information. With Miss Kutpitia's permission she borrowed the paper to show Gustad.

He was also puzzled: 'Who could have brought the body from Delhi?' Jimmy had no relatives that they knew about. Who had made the arrangements at the Tower of Silence?

They agreed it was probably someone else with the same name, and did not discuss it further, which relieved Gustad. What use was it to get emotional all over again? When he had brought the page home that day from office, it was all he could do to calm her and stop her crying.

'But what if it is our Jimmy?' said Dilnavaz after a while.

The uncertainty became oppressive. The only thing was to go to Doongerwadi, decided Gustad. 'If it is our Jimmy, and I miss the funeral, it would be unforgivable.' And if it was someone else, that would be all right too, there was no sin in attending a stranger's funeral.

So he set off to the Tower of Silence, thinking – second time in less than thirty days. And two friends gone. He looked up. Like old Cavasji, he felt like protesting, raging against the sky, but went his way in silence.

*

Later, after the prayers were over and he descended the hill, he was still wondering who had arranged and paid for the death ceremonies. He felt grateful to whoever it was; something had been put right; and now Jimmy was conveyed safely beyond the reach of his tormentors.

To think I almost did not come. Would have been no one in Jimmy's *bungalee*. To watch the fire, listen to his prayers. And to offer sandalwood, sprinkle *loban* in the *afargan*. Powder bursting into fragrant flames. Like shining from shook foil. Frankincense and myrrh, and sandalwood glowing red. Colour of the rising sun. And Jimmy's face through the thin white smoke. In Delhi he was . . . but strange how death. On the marble platform, looking again like our Khodadad Building Major. And the final walk up the hill.

315

So many for Dinshawji . . . the gravel path, a great ovation. But I alone for Jimmy. And the gravel spoke softly, like friends in a room.

By the time Gustad came down from the Tower, the *dustoorjis* were nowhere to be seen. He hoped the registration clerk at the office would know who had arranged the funeral.

*

The man at the desk was not pleased with Gustad's intrusion. Questions had become the bane of his life, and he looked up suspiciously, his nervous eyes darting around the room. As far as he was concerned, Jimmy Bilimoria's funeral was over and done with. He was tired of people coming to him, especially relatives of the deceased, with their strange requests.

The two women last week, for instance. So short, and slightly built, reminded him of little sparrows, the way they walked and moved their heads. But turned out to be tough as hawks. 'We forgot to remove a diamond ring from Grandmama's finger,' they said. 'Can you please shoo off the vultures for a few minutes? So we can go inside the Tower and get it back?'

What was he to say to such people? How to deal with two loose screws? He explained that before the *nassasalers* left the Tower they removed all clothing, every single article, as laid down in the Vendidad. So even if the ring was overlooked in the prayer *bungalee*, it would have been found in the Tower.

But the women told him to hurry before the priceless diamond ring wound up in a vulture's belly. Money was not the question, it was the sentimental value. 'We have no faith in the work of illiterate cretins like *nassasalers*,' they said, ignoring his reminders that laity were forbidden inside the Tower. Eventually, the clerk had to plead for help from the high priest who led the two away for further discussion, nodding his owl-wise head sagely in response to their arguments.

If this was the only problem besetting the clerk, he might have endured without turning embittered and suspicious. But, of late, luxury high-rises proliferating around Doongerwadi's green acres had blighted his life.

'Your vultures!' the tenants complained. 'Control your vultures! Throwing rubbish on our balconies!' They claimed that the sated birds, flying out from the Tower after gorging themselves, invariably snatched a final bite to savour later. And if the tidbits were lost in mid-flight, they landed on the exclusive balconies. This, said the indignant tenants, was absolutely intolerable, considering the sky-high prices they had been charged for their de luxe flats.

Of course, no one had proved conclusively that the morsels from the skies were human flesh. But before long, relatives of various deceased parties heard about the skyscraper scandal. They protested that they were not paying funeral fees to have their dear departed ones anatomized and strewn piecemeal on posh balconies. The bereaved insisted that the Punchayet do something about it. 'Train the vultures properly,' they said, 'or import more vultures, so all flesh can be consumed in the well. We don't want a surplus which can be carried off and lost in impure, profane places.'

Meanwhile, the debate was also raging between the reformists and the orthodox. These two camps had a history of battling lustily in newspaper columns, in letters to the editor, in community meetings – any forum where they were welcome. For a while they had engaged in rhetorical combat over the chemical analysis of *nirang*. Then there had been the vibration theory of Avesta prayers. When the vulture controversy erupted, the orthodox and reformists heartily joined the fray, delighted to sink their teeth into something after long inactivity.

The orthodox defence was the age-old wisdom that it was a pure method, defiling none of God's good creations: earth, water, air, and fire. Every scientist, local or foreign, who had taken the trouble to examine the procedure, using modern hygienic standards, sang its praises. But the reformists, who favoured cremation, insisted that the way of the ancients was unsuitable for the twentieth century. Such a ghoulish system, they said, ill became a community with a progressive reputation and a forward-thinking attitude.

The orthodox camp (or vulturists, as their opponents called them) countered that reformists had their own ax to grind in legitimizing cremation – they had relatives in foreign lands without access to Towers of Silence. Moreover, the controversy was a massive fraud cooked up by those who owned shares in crematoria, they charged: the chunks of meat were dropped on balconies from single-engined aeroplanes piloted by shady individuals on the reformist payroll.

Everyone (including a few orthodox backbenchers) agreed this was a bit far-fetched. Surely, they said, someone in the buildings would have seen or heard an aeroplane making a low run to deliver its payload. (Gliders were not even considered in the argument.)

But the vulturists produced written guarantees from world-famous ornithologists stating that vultures, as a species, were unable to fly after a heavy meal or if their talons and beaks were loaded. The beleaguered clerk greeted the experts' pronouncements with relief. Though not one given to controversy, he at once seized on the document to make photocopies for high-rise tenants who came to complain.

But none were satisfied. Aeroplanes were not involved, that much was certain. However, if the ornithologists were right, they demanded, could the clerk tell them the origins of the balcony meat? If not human, what was it supposed to be? Beef? Mutton? Were they to believe that *goaswallas* had suddenly become airborne, plying their trade in the skies, flying over the city with their butcher knives and cleavers? Were they riding their bicycles among the clouds, making deliveries through balconies instead of back doors?

The poor clerk no longer had any answers. He heard reproach and censure unceasingly in the speech of his fellow men, blame and reprimand even where none was intended.

To Gustad's simple question about Jimmy Bilimoria, he pounded the desk, his bloodshot eye blinking furiously: 'Tell? Tell what? You think this is the information bureau?'

Later, when he thought about it, Gustad was surprised he had not retaliated. Allowed a runt like that to speak to me thus. I grow old.

Taken aback, he wearily tried again. 'I just thought you might know who made the *pydust* arrangements.'

The clerk was encouraged. For the first time, he had successfully put a questioner (perhaps even a complainer) in his place. 'Who knows?' he said guardedly. 'The *behesti* was delivered, money order and death certificate with all proper attachments was delivered. Our chief *dustoorji* said, if there is a dead Parsi, our duty is to perform the funeral. We don't poke our noses anywhere else.'

'But what about the announcement in *Jam-E-Jamshed*?' persisted Gustad. Hopeless fellow, this. The clerk on duty that night, when I came for Dinshawji, was so helpful.

'*Pydust* announcements in *Jam-E-Jamshed* are always inserted by

318

the family of the deceased,' he answered stiffly. With his dignity
partially restored, he found it demeaning to have that paltry function attributed to him.

'This man had no family.'

'So?' Was he to be blamed for Mr Bilimoria's lack of family?
Anything was possible with the kind of crackpots he ran into these
days.

Gustad gave up. 'Thank you very much for helping,' he said, and
continued down the hill, his steps quickening with the slope.

Just within the entrance gate, a taxi was waiting in the shade of a
tree. Its meter was flagged to the side: out of service. The driver was
wearing dark glasses. And a moustache that was identical to
Jimmy's, thought Gustad. I know this man, he felt, as he got
nearer.

iii

Malcolm Saldanha studied the plans and drawings, checked a few
calculations, then skimmed through the rest of the file. The project
was to commence today under his supervision. He yawned twice in
quick succession. Bloody boring municipality. How he hated his
job, but was also grateful for it – steady income, thanks to Uncle's
influence. This bloody city, turning into a harsh, merciless place.
Regular salary was a powerful lure. No bloody security with piano
tuitions, no telling when students could vanish. Children these
days pampered with too much bloody freedom, discipline gone
completely from the face of the earth.

And the beautiful music was gradually disappearing too, as
surely as discipline. It was like watching the slow death of a loved
one. Thank God for the Time and Talents Club, thank God for the
Max Mueller Bhavan, for the British Council, for the GDR Cultural
Centre, for the USIS. Or the music would have died a long time
ago. But these were the last gasps – the golden age of Western
classical music in this city was definitely over. And that poor parent
yesterday, so embarrassed to say that his son wanted a bloody
Bullworker instead of piano lessons . . .

Malcolm sat up with a jolt. The word 'demolition' had caught his
eye, and clanged like a warning bell. So far the bloody file had
seemed fairly routine. Better concentrate. The story of a former
projects supervisor was well-known. Misunderstood his orders, the

319

wretched man. Demolished the wrong structure, and with it, his hopes of retiring with a pension.

So Malcolm stopped day-dreaming and started at the beginning. He read carefully, step by step, taking nothing for granted, jotting crucial features, making note of matters which could be easily overlooked when the workers were in full flush.

Then it was time to meet the crew at the depot, collect the equipment, and set off. Well, almost time. Five minutes to spare for a tea in the canteen. The musty smell of the rexine tablecloth rose to his nostrils. He lifted the saucer to his lips and blew to cool the tea. As the deflected steam condensed on his spectacles, the project's location surfaced from the morass of technical jargon in the file. The name of the building danced before his fogged lenses.

The address flitted familiarly through his head, coming close to but never touching the vital memory that would have made the connection. Khodadad Building, he repeated silently as he made his way to the depot. Khodadad Building.

The lorry set off. Malcolm's mind was soon occupied with planning details of a more immediate nature.

iv

As usual, Sohrab made certain of arriving during his father's office hours. Dilnavaz greeted him with joy and relief. She tore herself away for a moment to stir the rice and turn down the stove, then hastened back. She hugged him fervently, pressed her hands upon his cheeks, lamented he was losing weight for lack of proper nourishment. 'How long it has been! Won't you come back now? Haven't you tortured me enough?'

Sohrab shook his head and turned towards the window. What was the sense in repeating everything each time he came. He felt like saying that that was the reason why the time between his visits lengthened progressively.

'The house seems so empty. Do me one favour at least,' she said, touching his brow and brushing back his hair. 'Daddy will be home in a little while. Just talk to him nicely and then – '

'Home now?' Sohrab was perturbed at the prospect of coming face to face with his father. But he was also concerned about what could be wrong that kept him away from work.

Dilnavaz realized there was so much he did not know of, so

much about Dinshawji and Ghulam Mohammed and Jimmy that had happened in the weeks since Sohrab's last visit. She started at the beginning, and could see the shock on his face as she got to the end. 'Yes,' she said, 'we were all shocked.'

Repeating the details brought back the grief; she swallowed hard and continued, coating every word with loathing and bitterness. 'It's a shameless, wicked deed. A terrible, evil thing done by the government.' Her voice shook. 'Murderers! They took Major Uncle's life!' Her lips began to quiver as her mouth distorted, ready to cry, and it was all she could do to keep back the tears. 'But God is watching everything!'

'Where is Daddy gone now?'

She told him about the funeral announcement. 'We thought the same name was a coincidence. But how to say for sure? So Daddy went.' She looked at the clock. 'I have to go in a little while with Roshan's lunch. Her first school day, I did not want to give her dry lunch. But Daddy should be back soon. Just talk to him nicely. Please.'

Sohrab rubbed the nape of his neck, the way he did when he was unsure of something. 'It's no use. I spoilt all his dreams, he is not interested in me any more.'

'Don't talk like that!' she said sharply, then softened again. 'He is your father. He will always love you and want the best for you.'

'You know we will start fighting as usual.'

'No!' she said, shaking her head. 'Don't be stubborn.' She took his hand. 'So much has happened since you left. Daddy has changed. It will be different now.'

He continued to gaze out the window, refusing to meet her eyes. Proud and strong-willed, she thought. Another Gustad. 'Trust me. I did not ask you before. But now it is different.'

'OK,' he said, still not looking at her. 'If it makes you happy.'

v

As Gustad approached the taxi, he had no doubt. He recognized the man instantly; and then it struck him: he had arranged Jimmy's funeral!

Overwhelmed, Gustad still had to ask the question, to let him know he knew and was grateful. 'You . . .' he started, pointing behind at the Tower of Silence.

'Yes,' said Ghulam Mohammed.

'Thank you for . . . thank you, I – '

'Please.' Ghulam brushed aside the thanks, gesturing abruptly with his hands. 'All the prayers are over now?' His voice seemed to strain and choke.

Gustad nodded. He had seen many sides of the man: jovial, threatening, callous, cajoling, sarcastic. But never like this, never so emotional.

Ghulam raised his face, up towards the hill, up where the vultures were circling. Then he dropped his head and closed his eyes. Gustad waited. When he looked a few seconds later, Ghulam was weeping. Gustad averted his gaze and stood in silence.

Ghulam wiped his eyes with the back of his hand. He said, his voice steady now, 'Your Parsi priests don't allow outsiders like me to go inside.'

Gustad nodded guiltily. I feel Jimmy's loss too, he wanted to say, but I cannot cry. He offered his hand. Ghulam took it, then drew him forward to hug him, kissing both cheeks. 'Thank you for coming, Mr Noble,' he whispered, 'or Bili Boy would have been alone. Thank you very much.'

'Nonsense,' said Gustad. 'But why didn't you come and tell me? I would never have known if my wife hadn't seen the paper.'

'I had to take a chance. When I gave you the train ticket, I promised it was the last time I would bother you.'

'That was different. I would never refuse this.'

Ghulam took out his handkerchief and blew his nose, then put on his dark glasses and gestured at the taxi. 'I can drive you home. No charge.' He smiled.

'Thank you.' Gustad sat in the front with him. Ghulam made a U-turn and waited by the gate for a break in the traffic. 'So you are driving a taxi again after nine years?'

'Oh, that's normal when working in RAW. Sometimes bookseller, sometimes butcher; even gardener. Whatever is necessary to get the job done.'

Gustad heard and accepted the confession. 'But you are going to continue in RAW? After what they did to Jimmy? And they even tried to kill you, on your Lambretta.'

'You know about that? Of course, Bili Boy told you. Still, much safer for me to be inside RAW than outside.' He said softly, 'Bili Boy was a brother to me. When someone kills my brother, I get very upset. Someone will pay for it.' He nodded slowly. 'Yes, definitely. And by staying in RAW my chances are much better of collecting that payment.' His words were cold fingers tracing shivering lines down Gustad's spine. It was not empty talk.

'Timing is important, that's all. And there's no hurry. I may collect my payment tomorrow, or next year, or after ten years. From whoever is responsible. If it's the car manufacturer, he will have to pay. Lots of possibilities – his car might explode, for instance. He also likes to fly aeroplanes, so: bhoom, crash, the end. As I said, whatever is necessary to get the job done.'

Gustad responded by smiling weakly. Ghulam continued: 'And his Mummy herself has many enemies. Makes more and more every day, from Punjab to Tamil Nadu. Any one of them could do it. I am a patient man. Her life is as easy to snuff out as Bili Boy's, let me tell you. Like that,' and he snapped his fingers under Gustad's nose.

It frightened him to hear Ghulam Mohammed talk this way. He preferred to remember him in his moment of grief, he decided, as the taxi stopped under a policeman's outstretched arm. The intersection was blocked solidly by traffic, and the policeman was directing cars to alternate routes. 'It's OK,' said Gustad, 'not far from here. I can walk.' They shook hands. Gustad knew with certainty that they would never meet again.

The door slammed and the taxi drove away from the traffic jam. He stood watching till it turned the corner.

TWENTY-TWO

i

Malcolm Saldanha, aboard the first lorry to arrive at Khodadad Building, saw the painted wall and realized why the building name had sounded so familiar. Wondering which was Gustad's flat, he proceeded to display the court order repealing the landlord's injunction, gluing it over the municipal notice, in tatters now, that he had affixed to the pillar several months ago.

The pavement artist under his little lean-to observed the ominous presence of lorries and men and machines. When Malcolm broke the news to him, he crumpled. He gathered up his paints and brushes, boxes and belongings, and dropped them in the compound. There he sat, cross-legged, unable to summon up even a trace of the resources that had fuelled his wanderings in the old days.

Reluctantly, Malcolm gave orders for the workers to proceed. The flimsy lean-to was knocked out of the way. Theodolites and tripods and levels were set up to demarcate the requisite areas. It was discovered that the neem fell within the municipality's latest land acquisition, obstructing the project. Two men were dispatched to cut down the tree. More equipment was unloaded; the surveyors squinted through their instruments, pointing here and there; and Malcolm scouted around for an Irani restaurant that could supply tea for the team.

Meantime, the *morcha* entered the lane with banners and plac- ards. Slogans and cheers began drifting down over the din of city noises, then the marchers came into view, and crowds gathered to watch.

The *morcha* had almost been denied the opportunity to march with work implements, for the police sub-inspector in charge of crowd control classified these objects as potential weapons. But the *morcha* directors prevailed: Gandhiji, said Peerbhoy, used to appear in public meetings with his *charkha*, always spinning khadi. If policemen of the British Raj could permit that, why should a sub-inspector of Free India do otherwise? The tools of the *morcha* were no more weapons than was the Mahatma's *charkha*.

Thereupon, the column was allowed to proceed. One group chanted in unison: *'Nahi chalaygi! Nahi chalaygi!'* Will not do! Will not do! Another section responded, on the upbeat: 'Municipality *ki dadagiri nahi chalaygi!'* Municipality's bullying will not do!

The old staple of every demonstration: *gully gully may shor hai, Congress Party chor hai* – the cry goes up in every alley, Congress Party is a rogues' gallery – was also very much in evidence. But there were several originals as well. The Fernandes brothers, twins who ran a small tailoring shop and knew the rhetorical value of repetition, held identical posters: Give Us This Day Our Daily Water Supply. The mechanics, on a more melodramatic note, unfurled a long, wide banner: *Havaa-paani laingay, Ya toe yaheen maraingay*, an air-and-water variation on 'give me liberty or give me death'.

The cinema employees had procured an old hoarding advertising the film *Jis Deshme Ganga Bahti Hai*, and modified it to: *The Land Where the Ganga Flows – and the Gutter Overflows*. The hero's face was slightly altered: a clothes pin clung to his nose, pinching both nostrils shut. And the names of the actors, actresses, producer, director, screen-writer, music director were labelled over with names of municipal corporators and leading politicians.

'Nahi chalaygi! Nahi chalaygi!' rang out repeatedly, as the *morcha* approached Khodadad Building. Malcolm, his *mukaadam*, the labourers and surveyors, downed their tools and lined up at the curb. People leaned out of the office towers, customers and shop-keepers evacuated their shops, and the entire street suspended its business for the *morcha*.

The marchers drew abreast with the wall. A fresh vitality animated their slogans now. With a captive audience, their steps discovered a renewed bounce, their waving arms extra vigour.

Suddenly, one of the *morcha* directors signalled the column to a halt with three bongs on Peerbhoy's *paan*-vending brass tray. The tray had been selected over numerous other contenders: a hub-cap struck with a tyre iron, Dr Paymaster's silver desk bell, the local monkeyman's drum, the snake-charmer's piercing flute. All were rejected, for none could compare with the sonorous dignity of Peerbhoy's tray.

The shining reverberations of the three strokes soared in the air like birds of paradise, shimmering over the marchers' heads. 'Brothers and sisters!' the inspired *morcha* director called out. He raised his arms to appeal for silence, then repeated, *'Bhaiyo aur baheno.'* A hush settled over the marchers.

'You are asking: why have we stopped now, before reaching the municipality? And in answer I say to you: what better place than this sacred wall of miracles to pause and meditate upon our purpose? The wall of gods and goddesses. The wall of Hindu and Muslim, Sikh and Christian, Parsi and Buddhist! A holy wall, a wall suitable for worship and devotion, whatever your faith! So let us give thanks for past success! Let us ask blessings for future endeavours! Let us pray that when we reach our destination we will achieve our purpose! Let us pray that in the spirit of truth and non-violence we will defeat our enemies!'

The procession roared its approval, surging towards the wall. The municipal workers stood clear as queues formed before each portrait. At the painting of Zarathustra there was only one person: Dr Paymaster. Laxmi, the goddess of wealth, commanded the longest line. Genuflections, prostrations, head-bowings, hand-foldings, eye-closings, invocations, supplications, adorations, all followed fervently. Many concluded by leaving a coin or two.

A municipal worker said, to no one in particular, 'Save your money, *yaar*, the wall will soon be destroyed.'

Wall destroyed! The words percolated through the *morcha* and trickled through the crowds of bystanders. Wall destroyed?! Disbelief turned to indignation, then to outrage that surged through the congregation and swelled into a tidal wave, making the ground tremble as it galloped for the shore.

Impossible! said the wave with ten thousand mouths, raging and rumbling. The wall of gods and goddesses cannot be broken! We will see that not one finger is raised against the deities! We will protect them with our blood if need be!

The situation was fast deteriorating, and the *morcha* directors immediately summoned Malcolm. 'Is it true,' they asked him, 'that your men are to break down this wall and destroy the gods and goddesses?'

326

Malcolm had never learned to prevaricate. He nodded briefly. The *morcha* howled, the tempest raged and threatened – there was no misunderstanding, the satanic scheme had just been confirmed! But the *morcha* directors requested silence with a single mournful stroke of the brass gong.

'My friend,' said the chief director to Malcolm. 'What you are saying is foolish. It is foolish because it cannot be done. Here is a place of prayer and worship. Look for yourself. Neither man's wish nor government's orders can change that. Look at the pictures of Brahma, Vishnu, and Shiva. Look at Rama and Sita, Kali Mata, Laxmi, Jesus Christ, Gautama Buddha, Sai Baba. For every religion this place is sacred.'

The *morcha* cheered, the bystanders applauded, and the chief director gained momentum. 'See Nataraja and Saraswati, Guru Nanak and St Francis of Assisi, Zarathustra and Godavari Mata, and all the paintings of mosques and churches. How can you demolish such a holy place?' He spied the tiny silver crucifix on a chain around Malcolm's neck. 'You are a good man. Fall on your knees before this wall. Utter the Lord's Prayer, say a Hail Mary, confess your sins. Pray for a miracle if you like, but do not attempt to destroy the wall.'

'Really, I don't want to,' said Malcolm uncomfortably, finding his voice at last, and the people cheered. 'But,' he continued, as the cheers died, 'my men and I don't make the decisions. We just follow the orders of the bosses at the municipality.'

The municipality! That loathsome name again! The *morcha*, like a maddened monster sprawling in the road, seethed with renewed anger and hatred. They harass us in our neighbourhood without water supply! Without sewers! With gutters that stink! With bribes that empty our pockets and fill theirs! And now they want to destroy our sacred wall! '*Nahi chalaygi*! *Nahi chalaygi*! Municipality *ki dadagiri nahi chalaygi*!' the cry rang out, again and again, from every throat.

The loyal *mukaadam* felt he had to take Malcolm's side. He shouted over the clamour, 'We are also religious people! But we are poor, just like you! If we don't follow orders, we lose our jobs! Then how to feed our wives and children?'

The other labourers rallied round the *mukaadam*. 'That's right! You have jobs for us if the municipality kicks us out?'

Hydraulic Hema, tall and powerful, wearing her best and tightest garments, stepped forward from the House of Cages delegation. She snatched a tread-cutting tool from one of the tyre retreaders and brandished it before her. In her sandpaper voice she addressed Malcolm, the *mukaadam* and his men. 'You see that painting? Yellamma, Goddess of Prostitutes?'

Malcolm and his *mukaadam* nodded, gulping nervously.

She swung the tool, describing a circle in the air below the mens' bellies. The sun glinted on the short, nasty blade. 'You spoil that picture, you break any part of this wall, and I promise you, I will make *hijdaas* out of you all,' she said, once again lunging bloodthirstily with the tread-cutter.

The men lurched backwards, involuntarily covering the fronts of their striped shorts and dhotis. They were too embarrassed to retaliate. Silence, golden as the sound of Peerbhoy's brass tray, hovered over them for a few brief seconds.

ii

Easing the black velvet prayer cap away from his forehead, Gustad hurried homeward after Ghulam's taxi disappeared in the traffic. He was anxious to change out of his *dugli* and leave for the bank. But why all these big crowds and strict police *bundobust*, he wondered. And the street noisy as a festival day, like Ganesh Chaturthi or Gokul Asthami, packed from pavement to pavement.

He reached the gate of Khodadad Building in time to see Hydraulic Hema flourish the razor-sharp instrument. Malcolm spotted him: 'Gustad! Gustad!' he waved, then his voice was drowned by the uproar following the grisly threat, as the offended workers reached for crowbars and pickaxes. The policemen shuffled their feet and gripped their lathis, making a show of alertness. The sub-inspector, taking no chances, asked his jeep driver to radio the police station for urgent reinforcements.

Gustad craned impatiently – what was Malcolm doing in the middle of a rowdy *morcha*? One moment he saw him, the next he had disappeared. But he did not want to venture through the thick of it in search of him. Later, when things calmed.

Then Gustad spotted the woebegone pavement artist behind the gate; Tehmul was there, too, eagerly watching the unfolding drama. 'GustadGustadGustad. Bigbigbigmachine. Bhumbhum-

bhum.   BigbigloudloudmachinebigshoutingbigGustad.'   He   was
unable to stand still, weaving, waving his arms wildly, swaying
with delight and excitement. What with the colourful *morcha*, the
labourers and their intriguing equipment, the policemen and their
lathis, Tehmul was utterly exhilarated. Now, on top of all that, his
beloved Gustad had arrived. 'GustadGustadGustad. Somuchso-
muchsomuchfun.'

'Yes, very nice,' said Gustad. 'And very smart of you to stay
inside the compound. Well done.' He patted his back, relieved that
Tehmul had not wandered out into the maelstrom. No telling what
might happen, given the present mood of the crowd, if the dressed-
for-business prostitutes fanned his urges. What were the women
doing here anyway?

The pavement artist, awaiting his turn to speak, said despon-
dently, 'Please, sir, they are telling me I have to give up my wall.'
Gustad had gathered this from the new notice on the pillar, the
cement-mixers, and the waiting lorries. For the briefest of moments
he felt the impending loss cut deeply, through memory and time;
the collapse of the wall would wreck the past and the future.
Helpless amid the noise and turmoil, he searched for words with
which to console the artist. Then suddenly, he caught a glimpse of
Dr Paymaster. In the middle of the mob? First Malcolm; and now
the doctor? He went out after him, into the sea of angry faces.

Tehmul promptly followed. 'No, Tehmul. Be good now. Very
dangerous, stay inside only.' Crestfallen but obedient, Tehmul
returned to the compound.

Upon Gustad's fourth bellow, Dr Paymaster turned around. It
took some strenuous wading to close the distance. 'What a powerful *morcha* we have produced!' said the doctor, pumping Gustad's
hand vigorously. His initial regrets and misgivings had converted
to conviction and confidence – he would have been willing now to
tilt at windmills: 'Seeing is believing! The greatest *morcha* in the
history of our city!'

Gustad had never seen him in such genuine high spirits. All his
spontaneous emotions, bottled up for God knows how long (like
those green, dusty flasks of potions and pharmaceuticals at the rear
of his dispensary) were suddenly popping their corks.

'Almost the whole of our neighbourhood is here!' the doctor
boasted, like a rebel general who has succeeded in turning the army

against the tyrant. 'Onward we march! To the municipality! We will show them who is boss. We, the people!'

Gustad managed to steer him gradually to the pavement, away from the over-excited throngs, as Dr Paymaster explained what had led to the confrontation between the *morcha* and the construction workers. 'But that was not part of our programme. That was what might be called an act of God.' He chuckled: 'Or an act of artistry. Which comes to the same thing.' He waved and set off, anxious to rejoin his comrades in arms.

Gustad returned to the gate, where the *morcha* had attracted neighbours from the building. Inspector Bamji, Mr Rabadi with Dimple, Mrs Pastakia, and Miss Kutpitia were debating excitedly, trying to predict the outcome. Police reinforcements had not yet arrived. Gustad wanted no part in their speculations, but at a suitable moment he asked the Inspector, 'Soli, you think it would help if you try to persuade these people? Using your police seniority?'

Inspector Bamji laughed, shaking his head. 'Bossie, one thing I learned from working with these Maratha buggers is to freely say: *umcha* section *nai*. Without a guilty conscience.' Sohrab emerged from the flat and walked towards the group. He fleetingly met his father's eyes, then turned away.

Gustad was surprised to see him. After seven months he looks upon his father's face. Does he have the courage to . . .

'Bossie, are you listening or no?' The Inspector tugged at Gustad's sleeve. 'To answer your question, I never interfere when off duty. Enough *maader chod* headaches I have on duty.' Then he remembered the women's presence and playfully covered his lips with his fingers, as though to stuff the mother-offending word back into his mouth. 'Sorry ladies,' he said, smiling suavely, not repentant in the least. 'Bad habit I have, speaking mc-bc all the time.'

Miss Kutpitia sternly looked askance. Mrs Pastakia giggled her forgiveness. And a sheepish simper covered Mr Rabadi's face; not used to foul language, he tried hard to pretend he was.

Tehmul watched their expressions, listening intently to every word. After a minute passed in silence and Bamji's lapse was forgotten, he grinned at everyone and repeated gleefully: '*Maaderchodmaaderchodmaaderchodmaaderchod*.' He would have kept going had Mrs Pastakia not turned a horrified face to Bamji.

The Inspector cut him off with a wallop to his head. 'Scrambled Egg! Shut your bloody mouth!'

Tehmul retreated, nursing the spot. Gustad transformed his contempt for Bamji into a veiled barb. 'Poor fellow, he has no brains. Only repeats what others say.'

Thick-skinned as ever, Bamji replied, 'This will teach him repetition is bad for his health.'

Gustad was groping for words to cut deeply but courteously, when Malcolm Saldanha materialized on the pavement. Gustad hurried out: 'Where did you go? I saw you for one second, then you vanished.'

'Had to find a telephone,' said Malcolm. 'To let the office know what is happening.'

'What office?'

'Municipality. You see, I am in charge of this bloody project.'

So this was Malcolm's fate. My college friend, who used to summon the notes like magic. From the realm between wakefulness and sleep. For Chopin's nocturnes. Those evenings, so long, long ago. Now supervising pickaxes and churning concrete. 'And what did the office say?'

'That the municipality cannot back down before a mob, the work of the city must go on. Bloody idiots don't know how dangerous this is.'

'You better stay in the compound, much safer.'

'Oh, I will be all right,' said Malcolm. 'See you later.' Before Gustad could dissuade him, he slipped back into the crowds and headed for the lorries.

Old Cavasji, from his second-floor vantage, silently saw him go. Then he turned his face to the sky, his half-blind eyes unmindful of the sun's glare: 'No other place You could find? Here only all the trouble, always? The darkness, the flood, the fire, the fight? Why not Tata Palace? Why not Governor's mansion?' Inspector Bamji and the others looked up in amusement, but Cavasji's further reprimands were drowned by bloodcurdling screams from the road. The verbal assaults, genealogic insults, theological challenges being exchanged between the *morcha* and the workers had abruptly given way to savage fighting.

'O God,' said Gustad softly. He was thinking of Malcolm and Dr Paymaster.

'Net practice is over,' said Inspector Bamji. 'Now the test match begins.'

iii

The construction workers were outnumbered, but, with their pickaxes and crowbars, were formidably armed. Some of the *morcha* crowd's work implements also converted readily to close-combat weapons. Others scoured the roadside for projectiles: stones, bricks, broken bottles, whatever they could lay their hands on, while those near the four carts resorted to the contents of the barrels. The police leaned on their lathis, awaiting reinforcements.

Tehmul watched spellbound. As the missiles began to fly, his heartbeat quickened. His head swivelled from side to side, not wanting to miss a thing, and he edged closer to the gate.

'Tehmul!' warned Gustad.

Tehmul waved excitedly and moved back one step, his fists clenched. 'GustadGustad. LooklooklookbigrocksGustadbig. Flyingflyingflying.'

'Yes, I know,' said Gustad sternly. 'That's why you must stay inside.'

'InsideinsideIknowGustadIknow. YesyesyesyesGustad.' He moved his hands through the air in swooping, darting motions, an out-of-control Bharat Natyam dancer. 'Wheewheewheewhee.'

But outside was too much of an enticement. He shuffled forward again, and before Gustad realized it, was on the pavement where the view of flying objects was much better. Tehmul trembled with excitement. What fun. What an immense game of catch-catch. With a thousand players. Even better than the children playing in the compound. Naughty children, teasing him. Throwing the ball his way, laughing, watching him stumble and fall.

He clapped his hands with glee as a rock landed by the gate. What fun it would be to catch one. With his own hands. What fun. Just like the children catching the tennis ball. So much, so much fun.

He swung off towards the road, positioning himself for the next delivery. Gustad turned and saw him then: 'Tehmul! Come back!' Tehmul grinned and waved reassuringly. He was determined to get one of these things that zoomed by so hypnotically.

'Tehmuuuul!' yelled Gustad.

A brick sailed towards Tehmul, and he was deaf to the world. Entranced by airborne things, things that could soar and swoop and dive, agile things made to glide or dart or arch through the air, nimble things that could flit and float on soft feathers or gossamer wings: enchanted as always by all such things, Tehmul hobbled to catch the brick. And, as always, his twisted body let him down.

The brick caught him on the forehead, and Gustad heard the crack. Tehmul dropped without a sound, his figure folding gracefully. The dance was over.

For a moment Gustad stood paralysed. Then 'Tehmul!' he howled, and charged out the gate. A rock glanced off his back but he barely felt it. He bent to grab the unconscious frame under the arms. His prayer cap slid off and fell to the ground as he dragged Tehmul into the compound.

'A doctor! Quickly!' he shouted to Inspector Bamji and the women, before remembering: 'Dr Paymaster! Hurry, Sohrab – in the *morcha*!' As Sohrab ran, he heard his father call after him, 'Be careful, but!'

'Ambulance is definitely needed,' said Inspector Bamji, and Miss Kutpitia went to use her telephone. Blood gushed wildly from Tehmul's forehead. Gustad tried to staunch the flow with his large white handkerchief. Precious minutes ticked by, and he looked around in desperate anger. What was keeping that bloody doctor? He and his godforsaken *morcha*. The handkerchief was soaked through; Bamji gave him his. Gustad could feel, through the cloth, that the bone had staved in.

Sohrab returned with Dr Paymaster who was panting and sweating greatly, all his recent fiery enthusiasm doused. Born so very late in life, it had also died early, drowned in the sea of violent humanity raging outside the black wall. And it had taken something else with it: the professional veneer of wry humour and cynicism. Stripped bare, his pain was exposed for all to see.

He shook his head in despair. 'O God! What is the meaning of this? Poor fellow, poor fellow! Terrible!' With great difficulty he got down on his knees. He took a large wad of cotton wool out of his black bag and asked Gustad to press it over the forehead, while he administered an injection. 'Too much blood loss. Too much,' he muttered. It was disconcerting for the others to watch his distress. A doctor was supposed to reassure, and put things right, not be troubled by blood and suffering, like mere mortals. What kind of medical man was this?

While Dr Paymaster was bandaging the forehead, Tehmul's eyes fluttered open. He whispered, 'Gustad. Thank you, Gustad.' A smile passed over Tehmul's face, and his eyes closed.

The doctor continued with the bandage. Gustad waited anxiously, looking from Tehmul's face to the doctor's, searching for some sign of encouragement. 'We have called the ambulance,' he blurted, to break the silence.

'Good, good,' murmured Dr Paymaster absently, and completed the dressing. He felt for a pulse, then fumbled urgently with his stethoscope. 'Quick, open the shirt!' A second injection was prepared while Gustad tore at Tehmul's clothes, exposing his chest for the long needle. The doctor finished and flung aside the syringe to check the blood-pressure again.

He pulled off the stethoscope and dropped it in the bag. His head shook slowly, answering the question Gustad was about to ask.

'But hospital?'

'No use now.'

Gustad turned away and went to the black wall. He gazed out upon the road, at the vicious brawls being fought by people who seemed to have gone mad. Dr Paymaster returned his things to the bag. He made a half-hearted attempt to struggle to his feet, then held out a hand to Sohrab who leaned back and helped him up. The doctor dusted his pants. 'I will give the death certificate, of course,' he said, laying his hand on Gustad's shoulder. 'There will be no need to –'

'Yes, yes, thank you.' Behind Gustad, the others were already making plans for Tehmul. He found it intolerably offensive. Couldn't they wait a little?

Miss Kutpitia said, 'Maybe I should go and cancel the ambulance, phone the Tower of Silence instead.'

Inspector Bamji's advice was to let the ambulance come: 'Lots of injuries outside, it will be needed.' What about Tehmul, though, for the hour or so that the hearse would take to collect the body?

'It does not look right, the *ruvaan* lying like this near the gate,' said Miss Kutpitia. People were watching from the windows of the tall office buildings on either side. Come for the riot, some of their attention was now focussed on the compound. 'We must do something,' insisted Miss Kutpitia. But the idea of carrying the heavy body two floors up to Tehmul's flat was daunting. To make matters worse, his brother was still out of town.

'Maybe the best thing to do is just move him a little. To the tree, under the shade,' said Mrs Pastakia. 'And I can bring a white sheet to cover till the hearse comes.'

'Good idea,' said Bamji, 'sun is very hot. The Tower of Silence might take a long time, with this *tamaasha* outside.'

The tree was only about fifty yards away, a more welcome proposition than climbing two flights. Dr Paymaster also nodded his assent. Then Bamji glanced at Gustad to see if he would help. But his broad impassive back offered no indication, and Bamji was reluctant to ask. He looked at Mr Rabadi instead: 'OK, bossie, can you take the feet?'

Mr Rabadi blushed with self-importance. For once, the entire building would see him do something other than walk his dog. He held out Dimple's leash for Mrs Pastakia.

The Inspector and Mr Rabadi rolled up their sleeves slowly, queasily preparing for the task. But before they could lift the body, Gustad turned. He crouched beside Tehmul. The others exchanged looks: now what?

Without a word, Gustad slipped one arm under Tehmul's shoulders and the other under his knees. With a single mighty effort he rose to his feet, cradling the still-warm body. The bandaged head lolled limply over his forearm, and he crooked his elbow to support it properly.

'Wait! Bossie, wait!' said Inspector Bamji. 'He is very heavy, we will help, don't – '

Gustad ignored him and began walking down the compound, away from them all, towards the stairway to Tehmul's flat. They looked in silence now, too ashamed to follow. Sohrab gazed after his father with fear and admiration.

People watched from their windows as Gustad strode under their eyes without faltering, as though he and Tehmul were all alone, as if the dead weight of the grown man in his arms was nought but a child's. Some of the neighbours covered their heads and folded their hands together when the *ruvaan* passed by.

Without a trace of his limp, without a fumble, Gustad walked the length of the compound, past the flats near the gate, past the compound's solitary tree and his own flat, past Inspector Bamji's Landmaster, till he reached the end. When he gained the entrance to the stairs he stopped and turned around to look, once, at the group at the other end. Then he continued.

On the stairs, the weight in his arms made his feet come down heavily at every step. The sweat poured freely off his face, splashing on Tehmul's blood-soaked shirt. At the landing he could sense that people were watching through their spyholes.

The door to Tehmul's flat was closed. Locked? He still had the key. But the neighbour's door opened; she scurried out and tried Tehmul's door; it was unlocked. She ran back inside, her courage exhausted, preferring to observe the other way. Gustad heard the click of her spyhole cover reopening. He entered sideways, taking care that Tehmul's head did not knock against the frame. He kicked the door shut behind him and went inside to the bedroom.

Tehmul's dangling feet brushed aside the faded organdie curtain. The brass rings tinkled. The naked doll lay across the bed. He rested Tehmul on the edge of the mattress and freed one hand to nudge the doll aside. The warmth was slowly leaving the body, he realized, as he buttoned up the shirt, straightened the legs, and folded the arms together. He unlaced Tehmul's shoes and pulled them off, then the socks. Two rupee notes, folded very small, fell out. He put them under the pillow and covered Tehmul with the sheet.

The doll's clothes were on the chair, just as he had seen them the night of the air raid. Leaning over Tehmul, he picked up the doll and began clothing it in its wedding ensemble. The painted plaster felt as cold as Tehmul. When the doll was dressed he slipped it under the sheet, beside Tehmul. He moved the chair nearer the bed and raised a hand to adjust his prayer cap, but his fingers touched hair instead of black velvet. Then he remembered: the cap had fallen off in the road. He looked around the room for something to cover his head. Nothing, except Tehmul's pyjamas hanging on the bedrail. It was either that or his bloodied handkerchief. He picked up the pyjama top.

With covered head he sat, placing his right hand upon Tehmul's head. Tehmul's hair felt stiff under his fingers, matted where the blood had dried. He closed his eyes and began to pray softly. He recited the Yatha Ahu Varyo, five times, and Ashem Vahoo, three times, his bloodstained hand resting light as a leaf on Tehmul's head. Flies buzzed around the room, drawn by the smell, but they did not distract him. He kept his eyes closed and started a second cycle of prayer. Tears began to well in his closed eyes. His voice was soft and steady, and his hand steady and light upon Tehmul's head, as the tears ran down his cheeks. He started another cycle, and yet another, and he could not stop the tears.

Five times Yathu Ahu Varyo, and three times Ashem Vahoo. Over and over. Five and three, recited repeatedly, with his right hand covering Tehmul's head. Yatha Ahu Varyo and Ashem Vahoo, and the salt water of his eyes, as much for himself as for Tehmul. As much for Tehmul as for Jimmy. And for Dinshawji, for Pappa and Mamma, for Grandpa and Grandma, all who had had to wait for so long . . .

How long he sat there, repeating Yatha Ahu Varyo and Ashem Vahoo, he could not say. Then he felt there was someone in the room. He did not turn around. He had not heard the curtain rings tinkle, the faded organdie was hanging still as death, filtering the harsh verandah sunlight. He asked gruffly, 'Who is there?'

There was no answer. Again he asked, 'Who?'

'Daddy . . . Sohrab.'

Gustad turned around. He saw his son standing in the doorway, and each held the other's eyes. Still he sat, gazing upon his son, and Sohrab waited motionless in the doorway, till at last Gustad got to his feet slowly. Then he went up and put his arms around him. 'Yes,' said Gustad, running his bloodstained fingers once through Sohrab's hair. 'Yes,' he said, 'yes,' and hugged him tightly once more.

iv

A stench still hung in the air around the work area cordoned off by police, where the *morcha*'s barrel of sewer sludge and slime had been overturned. Malcolm sputtered and quavered, unable to find the words. His hands shook like crippled bird wings. 'You won't believe it! Crazy! Bloody crazy, I am saying. Absolute madness!'

Gustad put a hand on his shoulder. 'You want to come inside? Drink tea or something?'

'Just imagine it! Bloody thing hits me in the face! Big, furry, smelly thing! Imagine it! Rotting stinking rats, right in my face!

337

Aagh! Chhee! Thoo!' Malcolm clutched his head as though it was going to explode. 'What if I catch plague or something?'

He refused Gustad's offer to wash up. 'I at once opened a hydrant. And I've already promised a candle for Mount Mary. Some of those bloody bandicoots were still alive!' He shuddered again. 'I am also going to my doctor.'

But first he had to await replacements for the injured workers. 'Bastard police, taking their own sweet time. I bet you anything it was a bloody municipal plot. These crooks all work hand in hand.'

'I believe you,' said Gustad. 'Nothing is beyond the government. Ordinary people like us are helpless against them.'

The workers had started chiselling out the mortar between the stone slabs. Malcolm hurried to supervise, shouting instructions. 'O baba, *arya ghay!* Carefully, *arya, arya!*' The labourers set up a vigorous chant, full of muscle and vitality: 'Ahiyo-tato! Tahi-to-tato! Ahiyo-tato! Tahi-to-tato!' A truck of gravel and sand was being unloaded. The unmistakable crunching rose over other noises and reached Gustad's ears. Crunching, grating, rasping, as men with shovels trampled through the gravel. The sound made Gustad freeze for a moment.

Presently, the first huge block of black stone, the one with the Trimurti, was levered off with crowbars and sent crashing to the ground. As the dust settled, the pavement artist awoke from his trance of despair. He rose and went to Gustad. 'I am very grateful to you for providing me with the wall's hospitality. Now it is time to go.'

'Go? But where? Have you made any plan?'

'Where does not matter, sir.' The tumbling Trimurti had restored all his philosophical buoyancy. 'In a world where roadside latrines become temples and shrines, and temples and shrines become dust and ruin, does it matter where?' He began putting his things together. 'Sir, one request. Is it OK if I take some twigs from your tree? I like to control the creation, preservation and destruction of my dental health.'

'Take as many as you want.' The artist broke off seven small branches and put them in his satchel. 'Good luck,' said Gustad, shaking his hand.

'Luck is the spit of gods and goddesses,' the artist replied, and slipped out through the gate, padding softly in his bare feet.

Gustad noticed the large box of oil paints and brushes leaning against the pillar. 'Wait, you are forgetting your things.'

The pavement artist about-faced. He smiled and shook his head, walking backwards for a moment. 'I have taken everything I need for my journey.' He patted his satchel. 'My box of crayons is in here.' Then he bent by the kerb to pick something up. 'I think this is yours.' He tossed it towards the gate.

'Thank you,' said Gustad, catching his trampled prayer cap. The black velvet pile was crushed, coated with mud, and he did not put it on again.

The artist quickly disappeared from sight. It was well past noon, and the air was rank with the smell of diesel fumes. A shrunken shadow of the solitary tree crouched to one side. Two men were working on its trunk with a crosscut saw.

Gustad left the sun-flooded compound and entered the flat. Waiting for his eyes to adjust to the darkness, he slapped the prayer cap against his leg; a little dry mud flaked off. He dropped the cap on his desk, fetched a chair, and closed the front door.

Much of the noise from the road was shut out, save the persistent crunch of gravel. He stood upon the chair and pulled at the paper covering the ventilators. As the first sheet tore away, a frightened moth flew out and circled the room.